THE SPEAR OF TYRANNY

THE SPEAR OF TYRANNY

GRANT R. JEFFREY AND ANGELA HUNT

WORD PUBLISHING

NASHVILLE

A Thomas Nelson Company

Library of Congress Cataloging-in-Publication Data

Jeffrey, Grant R.
    The spear of tyranny / Grant Jeffrey and Angela Hunt.
    p. cm.
    ISBN 0-8499-4238-1 (tp)
    1. Second Advent—Fiction. I. Hunt, Angela Elwell,
  1957– II. Title.
    PS3560.E436 S74 2000
    813'54—dc21   00-043432
                                               CIP

Printed in the United States of America

0 1 2 3 4 5 6 PHX 9 8 7 6 5 4 3 2 1

AUTHORS' NOTE

LIKE ITS PREDECESSOR, *BY DAWN'S EARLY LIGHT*, THIS is a work of fiction based upon certain historical, present, and future facts. Isaac and Sarah Ben-David, Baram Cohen, Thomas Parker, and Adrian Romulus have been created from imagination. Their function is to represent people who will live through situations and circumstances similar to those detailed in these pages.

This novel depicts future events, predicted in biblical prophecy, as they *could* unfold. The archeology described, as well as the information about the Copper Scroll, is historical. The Spear of Longinus exists and currently resides in Vienna's Hofburg Imperial Palace.

Because novels should be fixed in a time and place, this story mentions certain plausible dates. We would not, however, want a reader to assume that we are *predicting* the timing of any prophetic events. Scripture makes it clear that no man knows the hour of the Lord's return for his church and other future events will unfold after that momentous occasion.

It is our prayer that you will take this story to heart and

walk in hope as the day of Christ's coming approaches. Each day that passes is one less to wait.

Maranatha! The Lord returns!

The Spear of Longinus
Located at The Hofburg Treasure House,
Vienna, Austria

Adolph Hitler Examining the Spear of Longinus with the Imperial treasures on the night Germany conquered Austria, March 11, 1938.

The scene of the German Fuhrer standing there before the ancient weapon must be regarded as the most critical moment of the twentieth century until the Americans claimed the Spear in Nuremburg in 1945.

HISTORIAN TREVOR RAVENSCROFT,
The Spear of Destiny, New York: G.P. Putnam's Sons, 1973

PROLOGUE

The Treasure House, Imperial Palace, Vienna

THE MUSEUM CURATOR PAUSED BEFORE THE DISPLAY. His hand trembled slightly as he gestured toward the velvet-lined case. "And here, of course, we have the famous Spear of Longinus, also known as the Maurice Lance. There is a legend associated with the spear; perhaps you are familiar—"

Adrian Romulus interrupted with an uplifted hand. "I know it well."

The curator fell silent and backed away as Romulus planted himself directly before the ancient artifact that had held Adolf Hitler spellbound. That German dictator referred to the spear as his "talisman of power." Owning it became an obsession for him, driving him nearly to the point of madness.

The crude weapon was certainly not much to look at. Safe within its protective glass case, the iron spearhead rested on a red velvet pillow. A wide base with metal flanges supported the long, tapered point. A hammer-headed nail lay within a central depression in the flat blade, secured by thin metal wire. Some pious soul had embossed a pair of golden crosses on the lowest portion of the base.

According to legend, the nail came from the cross of Christ. And some believed that this spearhead, black with age and infamy, was the blade that pierced the side of Jesus of Nazareth, drawing forth blood and water in a gruesome flow. Rumor held that whoever claimed this spear would rule the world.

Romulus reached out and pressed his hand to the cold glass. Like lines from a forgotten poem, Hitler's notation about the spear rose upon a tide of memory:

> I knew with immediacy that this was an important moment in my life and yet I could not divine why an outwardly Christian symbol should make such an impression upon me. . . . I felt as though I myself had held it in my hands in some earlier century of history—that I myself had once claimed it as my talisman of power and held the destiny of the world in my hands. Yet how could this be possible? What sort of madness was this that was invading my mind and creating such turmoil in my breast?

What, indeed, had aroused Hitler as he stood in this spot? The weapon was just one of thousands of historical *objets d'art* in this museum and one of hundreds of spearheads allegedly used at the Crucifixion.

Romulus stared at the black spearhead as if he could glimpse a picture of the future forming on its dark surface. Could the legend be true? Hitler had believed it, and so had

Napoleon. Even Gen. George Patton had gazed at this object in wonder when he pulled it from the secret vault in Nuremberg where Hitler had stashed his treasures . . .

Romulus shivered as an icy draft swirled from the domed ceiling above him. Strange, how the glass beneath his palm no longer felt cold, as if it had been warmed by his touch. The room, however, was chilly, kept cool and dry by an air-conditioning system meant to guard valuable imperial treasures of the ancient Hapsburg dynasty.

Stepping closer, he pressed his other hand to the glass, then lifted his head as the truth jolted him. The glass had *warmed* as he stood here, as if the spear had basked in his regard.

He stood silently, barely daring to breathe, as an odd warmth settled over him, a moist and darkly textured sensation like a breath from the supernatural realm. The sounds and scents of the museum faded into obscurity, while upon its bed of faded velvet the iron spearhead began to glow.

Romulus felt the breath of a supernatural being brush his cheek, stirring the air and lifting the hair upon his forehead.

Hitler was not mad.

A mocking voice, deep and resonant, whispered in Romulus's ear.

He knew the secret to world domination; he recognized the truth when he saw it. This is the talisman of power, the key to total victory. All who possess it shall control others, but woe to him from whom it is taken.

An incorporeal veil lifted from Romulus's eyes, exposing the swarm of transparent beings that flitted around the glass case. Bright and liquid, they flowed in a dimension Romulus accepted without understanding. Some of them, he knew instinctively, stood guard; others swirled around the display case in a frenzy of adoration and reverence.

The master had chosen this object. He had imbued it with power, and these immortal guardians had been placed here to safeguard it . . . until a man was found worthy to claim the spear and all it promised.

He would be the man. Romulus knew and accepted the call even as the deep voice of his spirit counselor confirmed it.

Romulus closed his eyes as the bright vision dimmed. When he lifted his lids again, the veil had dropped back into place. He was not surprised to see the curator regarding him with a curious expression. How long had he been staring at the spear? One minute, or ten? It didn't matter. When the time was right, he would claim the spear, by force if necessary. And with it firmly in his grasp, he would control the world's destiny and accomplish the task Hitler had failed to complete.

It was only a matter of time.

ONE

CAREFULLY MANEUVERING BETWEEN HIS EAGER DOG, her leash, and the front door, Isaac Ben-David stepped out onto his porch and shivered in the heavy morning air. The sky over Jerusalem wore a yellowish-purple tint, almost bruised-looking, and the birds that customarily warbled throughout the morning were silent. Even Lily, who usually pulled at the leash in mindless exuberance, stood in an uncertain stance at the porch's edge, her nostrils quivering as she parsed the atmosphere.

A sense of unease crept into Isaac's mood like a shadow. Obeying instincts forged through years of military training, he commanded the retriever to sit, then stepped forward and glanced quickly left and right, evaluating the activity on the street. Unlike some districts, the German Colony of Jerusalem was not known for boisterous crowds, religious fervor, or teenage hijinks. Elderly couples occupied the houses on both sides of the Ben-Davids, and a young family with two school-age children had recently rented the house across the tree-lined street.

The blinds in the young couple's house were still closed

against the morning light, and that was how it should be. The children would not head off to school for another hour. The older folks to Isaac's left and right were probably up and active, but he had never known them to be noisy.

He caught his breath and listened. The muffled chatter of the television news bled through the window; a car with bad brakes squealed at the stop sign half a block away. No other sound reached his ears. A Sabbath stillness reigned in this most secular of neighborhoods, with nothing but mechanical inventions to disturb it. Isaac could find no reason for the dog's hesitation or his own sense of foreboding.

Shoving his wariness aside, Isaac lifted the collar of his coat and stepped out onto the narrow walkway, assuring the golden retriever that nothing was amiss. The dog fell into step beside him, her whiskers quivering with the ghost of a growl.

From the house next door, Mrs. Arnan hobbled out onto her front porch, rocking slowly from side to side in the manner of the very old. She saw Isaac and lifted a gloved hand, to which he responded with a wave of his own. Why did she wear gloves? The idle question pricked his brain. October in Jerusalem was cool, not cold, but the chill probably affected the elderly more than the young.

Mrs. Arnan had walked no farther than the edge of her porch when Isaac and Lily reached her gate. He paused and lowered his hand, offering to open the gate for her, but she waved him away with a grimace. "Go along there, young man," she called. "Don't wait on an old woman. You've a wife and baby to tend to."

Isaac's polite smile froze as a flash of wild grief ripped through him. Yes, he had a wife. And a neighbor whose memory had seriously begun to slip.

Looking away, he thrust his hands into his coat pockets and lowered his head, focusing on the dog and her curiosity about every fence post and tuft of grass. He chided himself for the resentment that had risen in him after the old woman's remark, though she had unwittingly unearthed a sorrow he could not lay to rest . . .

Traffic had picked up by the time Isaac reached the corner newsstand. Ehud, the vendor, offered a smile along with Isaac's customary cup of coffee and newspaper. "A good morning to you, Isaac Ben-David," he said, snapping a plastic cover on the foam coffee cup. "And may you find more good news in your day than you'll find in today's *Jerusalem Post*."

"That shouldn't be too difficult." Isaac pulled money from his pocket and placed it on the counter, then took the paper without looking at the headlines. As he tucked the folded paper beneath his arm, Lily leaped upward, planting both paws on the edge of Ehud's booth.

"Ah, my beautiful Lily, I have not forgotten you." Ehud ducked down for a moment, disappearing beneath the newspaper-laden counter, then reappeared with a large dog biscuit. "My golden girl has *such* beautiful manners."

As Lily gently took the treat from the vendor's hand, Isaac felt the corner of his mouth lift in a wry smile. Though war and devastation had wracked the city beyond his street, this one ritual had remained nearly constant for four years. Lily and Ehud had been exchanging morning compliments for as long as Isaac and Sarah had been married.

"Lily says thank you very much," Isaac murmured as the retriever dropped to devour her snack. "She also says you are the kindest vendor in Israel."

Ehud smiled, his gold front tooth gleaming in the misty air. "I would never doubt the word of a beautiful lady." He tilted his head and looked pointedly at something beyond Isaac. "Here comes your neighbor. Every morning, the same thing: two bagels with lox and one *Jerusalem Post*." He leaned closer. "When her husband is not along, she also buys one copy of the *Prattler*. Mrs. Arnan likes her gossip."

Isaac grunted agreeably as he sipped his coffee. He didn't need to look to know that Mrs. Arnan was rocking her way up the sidewalk, her stout form enveloped in a dark woolen coat, her hands gloved, a white scarf wrapped around her head. She might smile and greet him, having forgotten that they had just spoken, but if she mentioned his family again . . .

He was about to thank the newspaper vendor and retreat when he saw Ehud's eyes widen in alarm. "By all that's holy—"

Isaac turned. Mrs. Arnan still stood on the sidewalk, but she was no longer moving toward them. From out of the bruised sky a crow had descended to attack the elderly woman. Mrs. Arnan lifted her hands and was striking blindly at the approaching assailant, but the huge bird would not be dissuaded. As the crow's black wings pounded the air, Mrs. Arnan's high, thin squeal shattered the dense stillness of the morning.

For an instant, Isaac's mind went blank with shock, then he rushed forward, oblivious to everything but the bizarre bird and the panicked woman. The crow's sharp beak pecked at Mrs. Arnan's exposed forehead, peppering her pale skin with red wounds. A trickle of blood began to flow from the woman's brow, and her mechanical movements ineffectively batted against an enemy she could not see through her tightly closed eyelids.

Isaac ran toward her, bellowing as he waved his arms. He hoped the commotion would frighten the animal, but the crow did not abandon his target. Upon reaching his neighbor, Isaac lifted his hands and caught hold of the bird's glossy body. He felt the rush of wind, a featherweight structure of skeleton and feathers, then a substantial amount of pain as the crow jabbed at the tender flap between his thumb and index finger.

In an instinct far more primitive than his survival training, Isaac slammed the bird toward the sidewalk. He had forgotten about the leash and the dog still attached to his wrist, but Lily, born and bred to the hunt, saw the malignant crow as prey. As Lily leaped forward and sank her teeth into the bird's neck, Isaac heard the snap and crackle of cartilage.

With the bird hanging lifeless in her jaws, the retriever looked up, expecting congratulations. A few feet away, Mrs. Arnan collapsed on the sidewalk.

Isaac took a moment to catch his breath, then knelt to tend the trembling woman. As he sank to her side, he saw that her wounds were superficial—cuts on the forehead and scalp and probably beneath the knitted wool of her scarf and gloves—and the creature had not harmed her eyes.

Isaac helped Mrs. Arnan sit up, then slipped an arm around her and urged her to stand. "Come, you must sit in our friend Ehud's booth while we call your husband." He cast the stunned vendor a pointed look as he led the woman toward the newspaper stall. "You will be fine, Mrs. Arnan. A strange accident, to be sure, but you are not much hurt."

"What happened here?"

A new voice reached his ears. Isaac looked toward the sound and saw that a small crowd had materialized on the corner; one car had even stopped in the middle of the inter-section. A red-faced man in a suit stood next to the car, his face contorted into a human question mark. "I looked up and saw the creature fighting with you and that woman—"

"It was only a crow." Isaac glanced down at Lily, who had lowered the bird to Ehud's feet as if she were presenting her favorite newspaper vendor with a trophy. "Just an ordi-nary crow."

"Pretty freaky, if you ask me." A teenage girl dressed completely in black stood outside the newspaper stall and puffed on a cigarette. "Like that Hitchcock movie. What if *all* the birds start to attack us?"

"This bird was probably sick." Ehud scuffed the feath-ered creature with the toe of his shoe, then bent down and grasped a leathery foot. "We'd better wrap it in newspaper and save it for the authorities. They might want to make sure it didn't have a disease that could infect the others."

The crowd slowly dispersed, returning to their homes and businesses. As Isaac settled Mrs. Arnan in the folding chair inside Ehud's small booth, he wondered if the man's hypothe-sis was true. Rabies could cause dogs and cats and raccoons to act strangely—but could birds contract rabies? And if they could contract an infectious disease like rabies, had Lily been exposed?

As Ehud wrapped the dead bird in a newspaper, Isaac made a mental note to call the vet when he returned home.

"For the authorities," Ehud said, placing a strip of tape over the wrapped newsprint, "if they come to call."

"You should probably contact them," Isaac said. "After

you call Mr. Arnan. I'll be sure to knock on his door, just in case you can't reach him by phone."

"Thank you," the vendor replied. His round face had gone pale, and, despite the chill, beads of perspiration shone at his temples. "And thank you for helping this woman. You dared to risk a kindness, and kindness is a rare thing these days."

"Indeed it is." Isaac found his newspaper and tucked it under his arm again. After whistling softly to Lily, he picked up his cup of now-cold coffee. "Indeed it is."

Ehud's words echoed in Isaac's brain as he and Lily made the walk back home. The newspaper vendor was right—life for the average man had drastically changed in the last few months, and Israel had not been the only nation shaken to its core. Since the dawning of the new millennium, the entire world had suffered cataclysms unlike any others in history.

The experts could not agree which events launched the current troubles with crime and unrest, but no one could dispute that Israel had nearly experienced complete catastrophe during the war they now called Gogol's Invasion. Not long after the turn of the century, Russia had allied with Israel's Arab enemies. The ensuing invasion threatened to decimate the tiny nation until a monstrous earthquake rattled the Middle East on the morning of December 21. Like a thundering attack launched by the Holy One himself, the earthquake threw Israel's approaching enemies into confusion. Biological and nuclear weapons intended for Israel's destruction fell instead upon the Arab and Russian armies, including Vladimir Gogol's elite troops. By the end of the day, Gogol was dead, the enemy was vanquished, and Israel's rabbis were proclaiming that the Master of the Universe had provided Israel's miraculous deliverance.

Isaac himself had been caught up in the religious fervor. He and his men had fought to repel the Russians, and Isaac had risked his life to single-handedly drive a Katyusha rocket launcher toward a column of advancing enemy troops. When the enemy fell, he danced in the street with his fellow soldiers, knowing that his father-in-law the rabbi would rejoice to know that his secular son-in-law had finally embraced the idea of God.

His dancing stopped, however, when he received the urgent message from HQ and learned of his son's death. Eighteen-month-old Binyamin Ben-David, his son and Sarah's, had been mortally wounded in his crib when the earthquake toppled a bookcase in the child's bedroom. A rugby trophy, one of Isaac's college mementos, struck the child and fractured his skull.

Sarah had not been home, of course. As a member of Israel's Shin Bet security service, she had been out doing her part to save the nation. Unaware of the danger, the baby-sitter cowered in a closet for hours, assuming that Binyamin slept. When the doctors were finally able to care for the child, they told Sarah they wouldn't have been able to save him even if confusion had not reigned at the hospitals. The boy suffered a tragic accident, nothing more.

Later that week, when he and Sarah buried their little son, Isaac watched the crowds of religious celebrants with clearer, wiser eyes. If God saved Israel with an earthquake, God was a murderer of innocent children. For the first time he understood the Talmud's saying, "A childless person is counted as dead." The feeling of death went far beyond the knowledge that his name would perish with him—something in his heart died with Binyamin, too.

As he struggled with his son's death and his wife's silent grief, Isaac thought he faced the worst life could offer, but the earthquake that toppled Gogol seemed to have shifted the entire world from its accustomed axis. The earth had literally shifted in several major cities, including Tokyo, Athens, Rome, Sydney, San Francisco, and Mexico City.

While those urban areas dug themselves out of earthquake rubble, New York, Atlanta, Washington, D.C., and Los Angeles dealt with a different kind of devastation. In the reigning confusion at the end of Gogol's Invasion, the Russians had activated an automated defense system that fired nuclear missiles at several targeted American cities. In the succeeding months, the proud, confident Americans seemed to close ranks around their wounded nation, all but vacating the world stage. Within the last few months, Israel's greatest ally had become one of her bitterest enemies. Though Isaac doubted that the United States would ever take military action against Israel, their lack of support made it abundantly clear that most Americans believed their present troubles sprang solely from the Jewish nation.

Because the world had known earthquakes and war before, Isaac knew life would have resumed its normal course eventually. But nine months after Gogol's Invasion, the world reeled from an unprecedented and unexpected upheaval known as the Disruption. Depending upon what newspaper you read, either millions of people disappeared from the face of the earth in an instant or they died in the anarchy that arose immediately after the war.

Isaac didn't know what to believe. He had seen reports

ranging from tabloid newspapers to classified IDF documents stating that millions of people—the vast majority from North America, China, and Africa—disappeared without a trace, but recent intelligence bulletins from the European Union headquarters implied that most eyewitness accounts of vanishings were nothing but fabrications. One of the European Union's computer analysts told a senior Israeli intelligence officer that a computer search on the names of five hundred missing people in the Netherlands proved that such people had never existed. The names were false identities in which certain properties and assets were unlawfully held in an effort to manipulate the rules of taxation.

Though several thousand tourists and a few hundred citizens apparently vanished on that Sunday in September, Israel had not been terribly affected by the Disruption. Most of Jerusalem was too busy preparing for Rosh Hashanah to notice that a few hundred tourists left the city without bothering to check out of their hotels. Isaac read one interesting editorial from a rabbi who wondered about the significance of the Disruption occurring just before the Feast of Trumpets, but none of the other religious leaders seemed to care if a few Christians chose to vacate an already-overcrowded earth. A few reporters hinted that the event might have been "the Rapture," an event ranting evangelicals had foretold for generations, but since several thousand self-professed Christians and church officials remained in Jerusalem after the Disruption, this argument seemed a moot point.

Speaking for the powerful and relatively unscathed European Union, Adrian Romulus appeared on international television and assured the world that life would continue as usual. "The Disruption," he told a global audience on a satellite network, "is a minor complication compared to the death and destruction still surrounding Israel and the disaster-struck nations. Mankind needs to focus on the task at hand and work for the future. We must not let the shenanigans of a few tax evaders distract us from the reconstruction process."

To aid with the task of rebuilding, Romulus proposed that the entire world unite in a single network of nations, a "universal movement" to combine resources and effort to work for the common goal of peace so "the world will never experience the horrors of war again." Since the United Nations building in New York had been destroyed and the United States seemed unwilling to put forth the effort to reestablish a global confederation, Romulus suggested that his European confederation lead "until the time that every surviving nation can be represented on the Universal Council."

As his image beamed into every home on the planet with a television, he outlined his plans for the future: "We will make plans to link the world by computer network, so that every man, woman, and child will have access to information, the most valuable commodity of the future. Through our Universal Movement, we will make certain that food, clean water, and medical supplies are available to all. And through our Universal Force, formerly known as the European Union Army, we will guarantee the peace and halt those who would continue to advocate unrest and violence. We want peace for our children. You may be certain we will obtain it."

Lily strained at the leash as if catching the scents of home, and Isaac felt the memories leave him as the roofline of their tiny bungalow came into view. He wanted to go inside and share the bizarre events of the morning with Sarah, but he had promised to visit Mr. Arnan.

He whistled to the dog and opened the Arnans' gate. It was probably good that he had this little task to complete, for Sarah might not be in a listening mood . . .

As Isaac turned onto his neighbor's walkway, his gaze fell upon the small stone wall bordering his own property. Since Binyamin's death, a wall seemed to have risen in his marriage, and he could do nothing to breach it when death, disaster, and disruption stalked the earth.

†

Tucked away in the ultra-Orthodox community of Mea She'arim, Rabbi Baram Cohen stood in his small office at the Ateret Kohanim Yeshiva and fastened his tefillin to his left arm, then his forehead. With the small boxes, each of which contained portions of the Hebrew Scriptures, firmly in place, he lifted his fringed prayer shawl over his head and prepared to say the *Adon Olam,* the poem to open the *Shacharis,* or morning prayers.

A year ago he had led a classroom of boys in these prayers . . . but that was before Gogol's Invasion. That classroom had been damaged in the attack, and the students dispersed to other yeshivas within the Orthodox quarter. Baram regretted the closing of the old yeshiva, but the cloud of tragedy bore a silver lining—according to the most recent reports, thousands of new students had been welcomed into the Orthodox community's schools. Many indifferent secular Israelis had seen evidence of HaShem's hand in Gogol's destruction, and many of those who had formerly spurned the Master of the Universe now sought to enroll their children in religious education.

Even the secular Zionists had begun to realize that the

Holy One watched over Israel. Soon they would understand that he intended to dwell among his people.

Baram closed his eyes and began to sway back and forth in the ancient practice known as shuckling as the words of the psalm floated in his consciousness: *All my limbs will say, "HaShem, who is like you?"*

His body obeyed the command to pray, but his rebellious thoughts kept drifting toward earthly concerns. Oh, how sweet would be the day when the Zionists realized that even they had been used by the Almighty! Those who established and governed the State of Israel were generally nonreligious and often antireligious men who cared more for nationalism than for the things of God. They believed Jews could bring about their own salvation through political and military means. But they would soon discover that HaShem had used them to serve his own purposes.

Baram would live in the land of Israel no matter who controlled the government. Living in the Promised Land was a *mitzvah*, a holy commandment, and he could never be happy living elsewhere.

"Master of the World who was King before any form was created," he prayed, lifting his eyes to the water-stained ceiling. "At the time when he made all through his will, then his name was called 'King.' And after all is gone, he, the Awesome One, will reign alone. And he was, and he is, and he will be in splendor."

A cold wind hooted outside the window, rattling the glass. Baram ignored the sound and closed his eyes, concentrating on his prayers.

"And he is One, and there is no second, to compare to him or be his equal. Without beginning, without end, to him is the power and rulership. And he is my God and my living Redeemer, and the Rock of my fate in times of distress."

Israel's recent trials had tested the faith of many, but Baram's faith remained strong. The great sages had predicted trials and struggles during the *Ikvot Meshicha*, the dire time just before the Messiah's appearance. The trials had begun slowly, like a woman enduring the early pangs of an impending birth. Children began to forsake the way of their parents, youths insulted their elders, and insolent pride infected young and old alike. The travail escalated with the invasion of Vladimir Gogol and his Arab associates, and though Israel had been spared at the eleventh hour, Baram felt the situation would grow worse before the Messiah defeated Israel's enemies once and for all.

Though the country now dwelt in relative safety, evil still stirred in the land. A malevolent presence hovered over the earth, stifling the rains and stunting crops. Even the animals seemed to sense the foreboding atmosphere. Evil stalked the land in the forms of pestilence and peril, and though many of his fellow rabbis assured their congregations that all was well, Baram knew it was not.

"He is my banner and he is a refuge for me, my portion on the day I cry out, in his hand I entrust my spirit, when I sleep and when I wake. And my soul shall remain with my body, HaShem is with me and I am not afraid," he murmured.

He would not be afraid, no matter what happened. The time was drawing near, and he was doing his part to usher in the *mashiach*, the Messiah. Like all Orthodox Jews, three times every day he prayed for the elements required to bring the mashiach: the ingathering of the exiles, the restoration of the religious courts of justice, an end to the wicked and heretics, a reward to the righteous, the rebuilding of war-torn Jerusalem, the restoration of the line of King David, and the reinstatement of the Temple service. Three times a day he prayed, "May it be thy will that the Temple be speedily rebuilt in our own time."

Two

Outside the Knesset, Adrian Romulus sat in an armored limousine. The driver put the car in park and cut the engine, then tapped his fingers on the steering wheel as a pop song played on the radio. Six security guards, all from Romulus's Universal Force, piled out of escort vehicles and stood outside the black limo, their eyes alert behind their dark glasses.

Though Romulus sat in the backseat of the vehicle with his eyes closed, he saw *everything*. He had been meditating throughout the half-hour drive, and now his spirit floated above his physical surroundings. With spirit eyes he could clearly see the Knesset, even the men waiting within the squat, modern building. They were waiting for him—some eagerly, others with a fair amount of trepidation. But by the time he left today, his name would be upon every man's lips, his praise upon their tongues.

He lowered his gaze and addressed himself to the guide who accompanied him on the journey. "What shall I say, Nadim, if they ask for more information about the Disruption? They are certain to be curious."

The golden light surrounding his spirit counselor fluctuated softly. "If you feel it necessary, give them the truth," he said, his red lips parting in a dazzling display of straight, white teeth. "But the Disruption was a supernatural event, and one must have faith to accept supernatural things."

Romulus tilted his head, acceding the point. "Many of these men are Jewish rabbis. They are accustomed to dealing with matters of faith."

Nadim gave him a bright-eyed glance, full of shrewdness. "Then explain to them why the master of all authored the Disruption. Like removing a blemish from a painting of perfect purity, he instantly eliminated all those who would hinder the Universal Movement of Faith. You are working with a fresh canvas, Adrian. Every individual remaining on the earth is capable of uniting with us. Only those with irreparably hardened hearts were obliterated."

A smile tugged at Romulus's lips. "The master of all is wise. But still, the task is great."

Nadim's dark eyes shimmered with light from the rising sun. "You are capable, Adrian. And you are beloved. The master has formed and fashioned you for this hour. To you have been given the keys of the world's kingdoms, and soon, if you serve him well, you will be given the keys to life and death."

Romulus felt a warm glow flow through him as he bowed his head in an expression of gratitude. The whistling wind seemed to permeate every particle of his flesh.

"They are coming for you now." The glory of Nadim's presence began to dim. "Return to your place. The master will empower you to convince the stiff-necked children of Israel that you are the one who can lead them into the future."

"I will do it." Romulus looked up as his spirit descended through the shimmering morning air. "Do not worry. They are not called children without reason."

THREE

ENTERING HIS HOUSE, ISAAC UNSNAPPED THE DOG'S leash, then dropped the newspaper on the kitchen table and followed the dog to her water bowl in the corner of the kitchen. He filled a pitcher with water from the tap, and accidentally splashed half of it on the tiled floor when he looked toward the bedroom. The television morning news still rumbled from the doorway, but there was no sign of Sarah.

Isaac wiped up the spilled water, tossed the damp towel in the kitchen sink, and went in to wake his wife. As he suspected, Sarah was still asleep, a petite mound beneath the comforter.

He sat on the edge of the bed and nudged the mound with his elbow. "Time to get up, Wife."

The comforter rocked slightly. A hand appeared at the upper edge, then fell limply back to the mattress.

"Come now, get up." Isaac nudged her again as his gaze moved toward the television screen. Sarah had never been an early or eager riser. A night owl by habit and temperament, she enjoyed working late hours and dreaded morning. The only time she had ever sprung out of bed with any energy was when the baby cried . . .

Isaac forced his thoughts back to the television broadcast. A news reporter stood on the street in front of the Knesset, where a group of men in dark trench coats stood around a black limo. Isaac knew without being told that the men were security personnel—their erect posture, dark glasses, and watchful expressions gave them away.

" . . . is meeting with the prime minister and several religious leaders," the reporter was saying. "This is Romulus's first trip to Israel since Gogol's Invasion. He has expressed nothing but admiration for how Israel has recovered from the war, and yesterday expressed particular admiration for the nation's cleanup efforts."

Isaac exhaled softly. The Israeli military had done little *but* clean up after the war. Eighty-four percent of the enemy army had perished while attacking Israel's borders. The sheer number of bloated corpses, many of whom had perished from biological and chemical weapons, posed a dire threat to public health. The prime minister authorized the Israeli Defense Force to create mass graves—a practical solution that reminded Isaac far too much of the huge trenches in which the Nazis buried Jewish dead in the Holocaust. From January through July, every Israeli citizen was called upon to aid in the search for bodies strewn in the fields and mountains surrounding Israel. Civilians were not permitted to touch the possibly contaminated bodies, so whenever they found even a single bone, they were required to mark the site with a red flag and wait for IDF personnel to remove the remains. On one visit to the Jezreel Valley, Isaac saw a field transformed into a sea of fluttering red flags.

The news report broke for a commercial, reminding Isaac of the time. "Come, Sarah." He nudged her again, more forcefully this time. "We'll be late if you don't get up. Don't forget, Adrian Romulus is in Jerusalem."

"I know." The flat words were muffled through the blanket. Sarah sat up, the comforter falling away from her, and gazed at Isaac with bleary eyes. "I was up until two working on security details."

"Care to fill me in?"

"Can't. It's classified." With that, she rolled out of bed and stumbled to the shower. Watching her, Isaac noted a heaviness in her step that had not been there twelve months before. Even at her most exhausted with the demands of work and motherhood, Sarah had never worn the look of weary resignation that had recently imprinted itself upon her lovely face.

Sighing, Isaac left the bedroom and returned to the kitchen, where Lily was munching noisily upon her breakfast kibble. The dog glanced up at Isaac for a moment, then returned to her bowl, eager to clean it. Isaac suspected she wanted Sarah to think he'd forgotten to feed her. On more than one occasion Lily's canine conniving had netted her two breakfasts.

Isaac sat down and skimmed the paper, finding nothing that particularly interested him. The front page featured a short story on Romulus's arrival in Jerusalem. Isaac read that the prime minister seemed intent on making the European leader feel welcome. With the United States damaged, Russia decimated, and Israel and her Arab neighbors recovering from the devastation of war, the European Union had emerged from Gogol's Invasion as the planet's most powerful and economically healthy federation. And Adrian Romulus, as the acting president of the European Union and its Council of Ministers, had sworn to use his newfound influence for the cause of peace.

For the first several months after Gogol's Invasion, Isaac had been too engrossed in Israel's problems to pay much attention to international affairs, but a friend who worked as a Mossad agent assured him that Adrian Romulus had never been guilty of anti-Semitic actions or utterances. He seemed to be a true friend of Israel.

Lily swept the inside of her bowl with her nose, assuring herself that no bits of kibble remained, then she walked to Isaac's side and gently rested her head on his thigh. Isaac lowered the newspaper and gave the dog a reproachful glance. "You've had enough, my little glutton. Now go lie down. Better yet, go tell Mom—Sarah—to hurry."

The dog huffed softly, as if she couldn't believe she'd been rebuffed, then turned and trotted toward the bedroom, her nails clicking rhythmically on the tile. Isaac made a mental note to trim her nails the next time he found her snoring at the foot of the bed.

After finding nothing of interest in the paper, he listened for sounds of Sarah's progress and heard the roar of her hair dryer. She'd be at least another fifteen minutes.

He glanced at his watch and bit down hard on his lower lip, then turned on the countertop television in the kitchen. Nothing to do but kill time. He picked up his cup of coffee and set it in the microwave, then punched on the power. While the coffee heated, he pulled a bag of bagels from the refrigerator. Leaning against the counter, he folded one arm across his chest as he ate a cold bagel and stared at the television screen. The news reporter had disappeared, replaced by a shot of the Knesset pressroom. The blue-and-white flag of Israel hung on the wall behind the lectern, and a host of reporters fidgeted in the rows of chairs before the dais. An unfamiliar reporter provided insignificant chatter in a voice-over, then the sound stilled as the Israeli prime minister, Avraham Har-Zion, entered the room and stood behind the microphone.

"Citizens of Israel and friends of the world," Har-Zion began, gripping the sides of the lectern, "it is with great pleasure that I announce the arrival of the honorable Adrian Romulus, president of the European Union Council of Ministers. He has come from far away with important news of great significance to the State of Israel."

Without another word, the prime minister stepped back. Isaac swallowed and stared at the screen. Har-Zion never relinquished attention easily, and Isaac could not recall an instance when the prime minister had allowed another politician to share the spotlight at a press conference.

Adrian Romulus, a tall, charismatic, and elegantly groomed European, moved into the space Har-Zion had vacated. He did not cling to the lectern, but clasped his hands at his waist in a confident gesture and sent a smile winging across the room. "Citizens of the world," he began, his baritone voice resonating throughout the room and over the airwaves, "it is with the greatest of pleasure that I approach you to announce a monumental achievement in the annals of human history. At the stroke of midnight last night, Prime Minister Har-Zion and Amir Ben Kalil Riyad, acting president of the Arab League, mutually pledged themselves and their nations to a seven-year treaty of peace."

A wave of polite applause swept across the room. Isaac

lifted a brow, wryly considering that a peace treaty now seemed like too little too late. The Arabs had been nearly obliterated in Gogol's Invasion, so common sense virtually demanded that they accept Israel's terms of peace.

Still, old hatreds and resentments died hard. And to the Arab mind, revenge was a dish best served cold. Seven years would be the minimum length of time they'd require to regroup and restrengthen.

He took another bite of the bagel and chewed it slowly. This peace treaty, though welcome, was certainly no surprise. So why did the prime minister look like a child about to burst from happiness?

Romulus waited until the applause died away, then he turned slightly and rested one arm upon the lectern. "For my part," he continued, "I and the military strength of the Universal Force do hereby confirm and guarantee Israel's security and peace. In return, Israel has agreed to respect the sanctity and significance of the Dome of the Rock and the Al Aqsa Mosque located on the Temple Mount."

A murmur rose from the crowd. As the victors in a war they did not initiate, Israel had every right to take possession of the Muslim holy sites. Indeed, for weeks the newspapers and politicians had been urging the government to oust the last of the Muslims from the Temple Mount.

Romulus seemed to train in on the camera; his face filled the television screen. "Last night, before I went to sleep, I read the words of the prophet Micah, who wrote that 'many nations will come and say, "Come, let us go up to the mountain of the Lord, to the Temple of the God of Israel." . . . All the nations will beat their swords into plowshares and their spears into pruning hooks. All wars will stop. . . . Everyone will live quietly in their own homes in peace and prosperity, for there will be nothing to fear.'"

Romulus paused, letting the silence stretch. "We have reached Micah's time of peace," Romulus finally went on, the camera focusing on his dark eyes. "The globe is uniting into one movement, with one government and one network. As one people, we shall all share in the prevailing peace. And so we all rejoice that the Jews have extended mercy and peace toward the Arabs with whom they share this holy land. In return for their act of respect and compassion, the Arabs have agreed to let the Jews of Israel build the Temple upon the Temple Mount without damaging the beautiful Dome of the Rock. The foundation for the third Temple, the Universal Temple of the New Millennium, will be established within the month."

For an instant Romulus's announcement hung in an astonished silence, then pandemonium broke loose in the staid atmosphere of the pressroom. Within thirty seconds, Isaac heard the sounds of shouting and firecrackers on the street. Israel had waited nearly two thousand years to rebuild her Temple, and now the miracle had come—

"I can't believe it."

Isaac turned to see Sarah standing beside him, her gaze focused on the tiny screen of the black-and-white television. "I never dreamed," she whispered, her dark eyes growing wet, "that we would live to see the Temple in Jerusalem."

Isaac turned back to the television, where the camera revealed a horde of reporters crowding around Adrian Romulus. Several of the media personnel were unashamedly weeping, their faces shining with the silvery tracks of tears.

"Your father will be beside himself," he remarked. When

Sarah didn't answer, he turned to see her staring at the television, a frown puckering the skin between her brows.

†

Sarah stared at the screen, seeing little but the image of Adrian Romulus. His photograph, plus those of his closest associates, had appeared on her desk last week, along with complete dossiers on each individual. The Israeli government had alerted her group that the European Union president and his entourage planned to visit Israel, and her job included learning anything and everything about Romulus that might pertain to national security. While Mossad gathered intelligence *outside* the nation, her division, Shin Bet, gathered information on people entering Israel.

Now she understood the significance of her supervisor's request. Romulus had entered the country with only a small entourage, surprising for a man of such importance. She had reviewed and memorized crucial details about Romulus; his chief adviser, Elijah Reis; a personal servant, a Frenchman named Charles Renoir; and half a dozen Universal Force security officers, most of whom had been hired in Paris. Aside from the French butler's fondness for several mistresses, nothing in any of the dossiers aroused her suspicion—and that fact alone drew her attention. Everyone had some sort of secret, but either the Mossad had found nothing interesting in Romulus's record or someone at a higher level had offered him a measure of privacy and protection . . .

She leaned against the refrigerator as the telecast continued. The pandemonium in the pressroom stilled and faded to silence when Romulus held up his hand and gestured toward a rabbi standing at the back of the dais. Sarah recognized him immediately: Baram Cohen, one of the leaders of the *haredim,* or ultra-Orthodox. An air of isolation clung to his tall figure, and his black hat, long black coat, and long white beard only accented his aloofness. She would have recognized him even if she didn't have a file on him in her desk drawer—Cohen was one of the leading spokesmen for the *haredim,* and one of the *Kohanim,* the descendants of Aaron and the priestly line.

The television camera played over the rabbi for a moment, then focused on a gleaming model of a Temple complex as an aide wheeled it into the pressroom. The assembled crowd, instead of cheering, seemed to falter in a silence that was the holding of a hundred breaths. Sarah realized that *she* had caught her breath. Could this Temple really rise from the ancient Temple Mount, or would some tragedy strike and put an end to the fledgling miracle in process? Ever since the conclusion of Gogol's Invasion, several rabbis had predicted that the Messiah would soon return because the Holy One had stepped in to deliver the lives of his people, but she had seen no sign of a miracle . . . until now.

An audible murmur of approval rose from the assembled group as the camera returned to Romulus.

"At the request of your prime minister and the joint Arab leadership," Romulus said, giving the camera a sincere smile, "my Universal staff and I will maintain a careful watch upon the building of the Temple to guarantee that the Arab holy sites are not harmed. The Universal Network will provide an international peacekeeping force to oversee Israeli construction and assist in negotiations, but we anticipate no major problems."

He paused and turned toward the prime minister. "I know that your people have been waiting to rebuild the

Temple for years, so all the preparatory plans are complete. It is with great joy, then, that I fully anticipate celebrating its dedication with you in less than twelve months."

Again, pandemonium erupted. The reporters cheered and shouted and pressed closer, but Romulus backed away from the lectern, his hands uplifted, a look of understanding indulgence upon his face.

Sarah turned to find her husband watching her. "You don't seem very excited," Isaac said. "I would think that you—"

"I'm curious . . . and a little surprised, that's all." She lifted one shoulder in a shrug as she opened the refrigerator. "I am thrilled about the Temple, of course. The project will do wonders for national unity and morale. But this Romulus—I'm a little baffled about why he's here." She pulled a bottle of orange juice from the shelf. "And why he's so interested in Israel."

Isaac moved closer, edging himself into her peripheral vision. "Perhaps he's one of those romantics who believe Israel is the center of the world."

"The last of those fools died off a long time ago." She took pains to keep her voice light as she picked up a glass and poured the juice. She could feel his eyes searching her face, probing—and she wasn't ready to endure the intensity of his stare.

"We're going to be late if we don't hurry." She took a moment to drain the small glass, then put the bottle back into the refrigerator, carefully avoiding Isaac's gaze. She moved toward the bedroom and called to him over her shoulder: "I'll be ready in a moment."

FOUR

THE BLINKING RED LIGHT ATOP THE CAMERA DIED AS the director yelled, "We're out." As security guards herded the reporters through an exit door, Romulus said farewell to the prime minister, then extended his hand to Baram Cohen, the aged rabbi whose gaze remained fastened upon the shining model of the Temple.

"Don't stare too long, my friend," Romulus said, "or the glory of God will blind you. Isn't that what happened to one of the Patriarchs?"

A flush rose to the rabbi's cheekbones as he turned and offered Romulus a stern smile. "You are thinking of Moses, but he was not blinded. His face merely reflected the glory of HaShem, blessed be his name."

"Well, then." Romulus crossed his arms, a little disconcerted by the rabbi's steady gaze. "I'm sure you would know more about such things than I. I am still confusing the legends of Medusa and Noah's ark."

The rabbi nodded, but his eyes had emptied—he had shifted the focus of his gaze to some interior field of vision Romulus could not see. Cohen's voice hardened slightly as he answered, "The miracles of our God are more than legend."

Romulus felt a sudden chill in his belly, as if he had just swallowed a chunk of ice. He had been troubled by these odd premonitions before, and on each occasion he had brushed up against a foe with real spiritual authority. This antiquated rabbi had power—but from where did it come?

Romulus shifted his weight and leaned away from the old man. "I would never want to cause offense, Rabbi."

Cohen's pupils focused and trained in on Romulus again, and the corners of his mouth lifted in a barely perceptible smile. "Thank you for your help with our Temple, Mr. Romulus. The Jewish people have been waiting a very long time for this day."

Romulus felt the hair at the back of his neck rise with premonition, but he ignored the sensation and fixed the rabbi in a direct gaze. "Ah, but a better day is coming. One year from today, my friend, we shall walk into that Temple together. And on that day we shall truly rejoice."

†

Isaac dropped Sarah at the nondescript office complex where her division of Shin Bet pretended not to exist, then he nosed the car back into traffic for the drive to the synagogue. Automatically, he minded the traffic signals and watched for pedestrians, but his thoughts circled around the sights and sounds of the morning.

Everyone knew the peace treaty was a *fait accompli*. The Arabs were in no position to make war, and a seven-year treaty would provide a breathing space for Arabs and Jews alike. The Jews would be able to establish their Temple on the Temple Mount without fear of interruption, and the Arabs could lick their wounds and let their surviving sons grow to maturity in peace. And even though the Arabs had histori-cally and histrionically called for Israel's expulsion from Palestine, the Jews did not wish to annihilate their Arab neighbors. After all, both nations were descended from Abraham, and the Jews themselves had suffered under the ruthless lash of genocide. They were not murderers. Every Jew who had grown up studying Talmud learned early on that "by three things is the world preserved: by truth, by judgment, and by peace."

Romulus was a peacemaker, no doubt. He had earned a reputation for establishing peace in the war-torn hot spots within the European Union; he had offered hands of peace to the world. Now he was offering the military strength of his Universal Force to ensure the peace as the Jews fulfilled the dreams of a thousand lifetimes and rebuilt the Temple.

Peace was all Isaac had ever wanted. As a boy he had lain on the sandy beach at Tel Aviv and stared at the endless canopy of blue sky, seeking that same quality of serene still-ness in his own life. Even while angry men shot at each other in the occupied territories, the sky was always tranquil, always pleasant, always far above the fray. As a young man, he had chosen one of Rabbi Hillel's maxims as his personal guideline: "Be of the disciples of Aaron, loving peace and pur-suing peace."

He loved harmony. He craved quiet. Why, then, was peace so hard to find?

A mocking voice inside his brain provided the answers: He could not find peace because his heart had broken when a ter-rorist bomb exploded aboard a Jerusalem bus and killed his mother. He could not rest because his soul had been torn asun-der when his only son died in an earthquake some attributed to the forces of war. With a broken heart and a shredded soul, he could not love his wife as he once had, nor could he adore the God who had always seemed more image than entity . . .

Now he wanted peace, and he would do anything to attain it.

He pulled into the synagogue's parking lot and sat for a moment, listening to the ticking of the engine block as it cooled. Though he considered himself a secular Jew, something in the traditions of his ancestors drew him to this place every morning. Though Sarah didn't understand his reasons, for over nine months he had been driving to this synagogue to say the Kaddish for his son. Jewish tradition demanded an entire year of mourning for a loved one whose soul had gone to *gehinnom* for purification, but to say the mourner's prayer for a full twelve months would imply that the deceased had been particularly wicked. Though Isaac did not believe his son's soul resided in a mythical purgatory, the act of saying the traditional prayer brought a semblance of peace to his soul.

Upon entering the synagogue, he saw that on this morning there were more covered heads than usual swaying in the silent rhythms of prayer. Isaac pulled a prayer shawl from a rack by the door, draped it around his neck, and remembered that long ago he used to know the proper blessing to be said when donning the *tallit*.

He knelt at the front of the synagogue and began to sway. "*Yitgadal ve-Yitkadash Shmei Rabbah*," he began, speaking the Aramaic words with more urgency than usual. "Magnified and sanctified be his great name throughout the world which he has created according to his will."

A firstborn son was typically known as a *kaddishl*, the one who would one day say the Kaddish for a parent. With no son and no kaddishl, Isaac had no one to carry on his name or fulfill his dreams. Even if Sarah one day warmed to the idea of another baby, he would not bring another child into a world where even the birds of the air seemed bent on violence and destruction.

Few of Isaac's fellow IDF officers understood what drove him to perform this ritual for his son. Most of them had no concept of the prayer's meaning and would have been surprised to learn that the Kaddish never once mentions death. Isaac, however, knew the meaning of the words and repeated them dutifully, lifting the paean to the cruel God whose ways were beyond human understanding.

As he prayed, an odd feeling rose within him, an unfamiliar sensation that seized him by the guts and yanked for his attention. Why was he wasting his time in traditional rituals that only comforted *his* soul? Thousands of Israelis had lost loved ones during the recent strife, and millions more had suffered in the generations of struggle before Gogol's Invasion. Why couldn't he offer his help to one who seemed to be appointed leader for the future? Adrian Romulus, strong and diplomatic, had promised to bring peace to the nations of the world. Why not help Romulus bring it to Israel and the Middle East?

Isaac felt as if his brain had become a lightning rod of ideas. He was a professional diplomat, serving in the liaison office of the Israeli Defense Force. Romulus would need a liaison officer to handle his dealings with the Temple, the Arabs, and the prime minister's office . . . The position would be a natural fit for an officer in the liaison division.

Isaac stumbled over the words of his prayer, then refocused his concentration, knowing that he would not return to say the Kaddish again. He would always grieve for his son, but the time had come to cease this symbolic mourning. He could not expect peace to come to him through prayer alone; often peace had to be sought on the wings of unity. After all, even the Talmud said, "Do not form yourselves into sections, but be all of you one band."

†

Isaac parked in a dusty lot near the archeological site at the southern wall of the ancient Temple Mount, then got out of the car. A security guard lifted a hand as he approached, then the man's tanned face split into a swarthy smile. "Major Ben-David! Your father will be happy to see you."

"I hope so." Isaac slipped his hands into his pockets and searched through the milling crowd of workers for a sign of his father's thin physique. "Where is he, Samuel?"

"He and the American are in the Western Wall tunnels. You can go down, if you like, but I'd take a flashlight."

The guard pulled a light from the tool belt at his waist, gave it to Isaac, then slapped him on the shoulder. "It is good to see you, my friend."

"Thanks, Samuel. I only hope my father will feel the same way."

"Of course he will. He understands that you are busy."

Isaac nodded, unwilling to explain that it wasn't his schedule that kept him from visiting his father's work. He hadn't visited the archeological site in months because any conversation with his father eventually veered toward Sarah and Binyamin, or, worse yet, the topic of other children. Though his father was a secular Jew, Ephraim Ben-David was staunchly traditional, and he considered childlessness almost as great a crime as reckless city planning.

Isaac didn't want to talk about his wife, he couldn't talk about his dead son, and he couldn't bear to think about other children. But now, for the first time in months, he felt a glimmer of hope for the future. Peace beckoned like a bright beam of sunshine peering over the ragged edge of a torn horizon.

"Which tunnel, Samuel?" He snapped the flashlight on.

"Tunnel A, two hundred yards down the main tunnel. He and the American have been down since six, so he will be ready for a break."

Isaac moved carefully into the main tunnel, smiling a greeting to several workers he recognized. Tunnel A appeared at his left hand, and he ducked as he entered the unlit narrow side tunnel that led in an easterly direction deep beneath the Temple Mount. The opening was barely two feet wide, so he turned sideways and crept into the darkness, allowing the beam of the flashlight to swing from right to left, revealing the path one step at a time. He'd grown up in tunnels like this one, having spent many of his summers and nearly every weekend underground. His father had dreamed that one day Dr. Ephraim Ben-David and his son, Isaac, would be as famous as archaeologist Eliezer Sukenik and his son, Yigael Yadin, but fate intervened in the form of a lovely Israeli girl. Once Isaac met Sarah, nothing could induce him to leave daylight for hours at a time to burrow underground. He had followed her into the military and never looked back.

Isaac found his father and another man in a small lantern-lit chamber. A grid marked the floor, and the two men were kneeling beside one square, carefully brushing dirt and dust from the surface of the soil.

"Father?"

Ephraim Ben-David lifted his head without looking in Isaac's direction, then squinted at his companion. "Did you say something?"

A slow smile spread over the other man's long face. He rested one hand on his thigh as he nodded toward Isaac. "We have a guest."

Isaac grinned as his father turned and looked at him through dusty wire-rimmed glasses. For a moment his eyes widened, then he laughed and pushed himself up from the ground. "Isaac! Whatever brings you down here?"

"Do I need a reason to visit you?" Isaac hugged his father, then stepped back and made a face. "You haven't been sleeping, Father. There are circles under your eyes."

"The rigors of age, Son, not sleeplessness." He gestured to the tall, thin man who had risen as well. "Have you met this American?"

Isaac shook his head. "I don't believe I've had the pleasure."

"Thomas Parker." The blond American swiped his heavy bangs out of his eyes, then took Isaac's hand in a strong grip. "Nice to meet you at last. Your father speaks of you often."

Isaac grimaced as his father slapped him on the back. "I say only good things, of course. You're a good son, even if I couldn't interest you in archeology as a career." He shifted his gaze to the American. "Isaac served his compulsory time in the IDF and rose through the ranks so rapidly I haven't been able to shake him loose."

Parker nodded, his eyes sweeping over Isaac's uniform. "That's all right. We need military men, especially in this day and age."

Isaac wondered what the man meant by that remark, but his father distracted him by pointing toward the grid on the floor. "Thomas came aboard this project to help with this tricky excavation. He has experience with this sort of thing."

"I think I've read about you." Isaac searched his memory, then snapped a finger in Parker's direction. "Didn't you work with Hanan Eshel at the Qumran dig? There were several caves—"

"Four of them, to be precise, and none worth digging," Thomas answered, grinning. "We were hoping for scrolls, but we found nothing but a few coins." He shrugged. "But it was an interesting experience. Every day in Israel is interesting."

Turning to his father, Isaac gestured toward the exit tunnel. "Could I talk you into a glass of water? Samuel tells me you've been down here a long time. It might be time for a breath of fresh air."

He stiffened as his father's eyes narrowed in the expression that always meant he was trying to read his son's mind. "Indeed. We will go up for fresh air, and you will tell me what brings you out here, my son."

Isaac stepped back, allowing his father to precede him through the narrow passageway, then soon found himself blinking in the harsh light of the sun. Thomas Parker led the way to a striped canopy, and beneath it Isaac found a cooler, several chairs, and baskets of fruit. While the American poured water into a paper cup, Isaac and his father settled into folding chairs.

"So," his father said in a low growl that was both powerful and gentle, "what brings you down here? You did not come to inquire about my bleary eyes."

"No." Isaac admitted the truth with a small smile. "I came because I was thinking of applying for a new position within the liaison department. It hasn't been offered, but I could probably request it."

"What is this position?"

"The liaison officer coordinating relations between the IDF and the Universal Force—specifically, I'd be working with Adrian Romulus."

A faint line appeared between his father's brows. "The one they call the peacemaker?"

Isaac smiled in relief. "You've heard of him. I was afraid you'd been so buried out here—"

"Of course I've heard of him. One of the workers told me all about his appearance on television this morning." He paused to scratch his ear, then gave Isaac a quizzical glance. "He really has plans for the Temple?"

"Apparently." Isaac paused, studying his father's face. "What do you think? He seems to be an honorable man, and the position would be a most challenging one. Romulus seems knowledgeable, but he is certain to appreciate some-one who can help him deal with the complexities of negotiating with the Israeli government, the Arabs, and the religious leaders—"

"I think you should do whatever you want to do. Decide what you want out of life, Isaac—and work until you get it."

Isaac's heart sank with swift disappointment. His father had never been shy about offering his opinion before, so why wouldn't he give a clear answer now?

"I don't know what I want, Father—but what I'm looking for isn't something you can put your hands on. I have a home, a wife, and a good job, but—"

His father lifted his gaze then, and in his eyes Isaac saw the unspoken accusation: *You ought to stop grieving and have more children.*

Isaac ignored his father's pointed look. "I want the world to be at peace, Father." He leaned forward and clasped his hands, allowing his heart to show on his face. "Now is the time, and perhaps this is the place to begin. Our land has run red with blood for generations, and now, while we are healing, I believe we can find a way to establish a permanent peace. The rabbis have long foretold that peace will come when the Temple rises again, and this Romulus seems willing to satisfy every faction in Jerusalem and the Middle East. To that end . . . I think I might be able to help him."

His father studied Isaac's face with considerable absorption. "What do you know about this Romulus?"

Isaac shrugged. "I know he is European. He lives in Paris. He often works out of Brussels, where the European Union is headquartered. He is known as a cultured, intelligent, and charismatic man. He did not support Gogol's Invasion and has generously offered to play the role of mediator between our people and the Arabs. From what I saw on television this morning, I'd say he has managed to overrule our prime minister's considerable ego—and that would require great skill and diplomacy."

His father's brows flickered. "Do you not find it odd that a man could be so . . . perfect? Is there nothing in his character that alarms you?"

Isaac frowned. "Should there be?"

"If the man is human," his father spoke slowly, as if carefully considering each word, "he will have faults, flaws, and secrets. If you seek this job, Son, be sure to keep your eyes open. Do not let yourself be disillusioned, but do not let yourself be overcome by charm and charisma, either."

Isaac straightened and lifted his chin. "You do not need to worry about me. I'm a grown man, and I know the ways of the world. I only want to make things right."

So we will not lose any more children like Binyamin. So we will not mourn the loss of women like my mother.

His father nodded slowly. "Go carefully, then, my son. You are a good man. I know you will choose the right way."

"Thank you, Father." Isaac stood, clasped his father's hand for a moment, then waved farewell to Thomas Parker, who had absently munched on an apple during the entire conversation.

"I hope you have a productive day," Isaac said. "Maybe you'll find something really exciting."

"Finding one of the lost Temple treasures would be nice," Thomas said, his lips twisting in a cynical smile. "If you believe they ever existed."

"If you do find them," Isaac quipped, "better keep quiet about your discovery for a while, or the rabbis will confiscate them for use in the third Temple."

After returning to his car, Isaac tapped the steering wheel in decision, then turned the car toward the Allenby Bridge and his office. He would write up a request for transfer immediately and route it to his superior's office. With luck and timing, he might find himself working with Romulus by the end of the month.

FIVE

SARAH SLIPPED OUT OF HER SMALL OFFICE AND WALKED toward the staff lounge, her coffee mug in hand. A chorus of voices swelled out of the doorway, and as she entered the room she wasn't surprised to discover that her fellow agents were discussing the recent press conference. "The Temple, in our generation," one woman said, her eyes wide. "My grandparents often spoke of it, but I never thought it would happen in our lifetime."

"It was only a matter of time." The deep baritone voice of Danny Melman, deputy director of the Non-Arab Affairs Shin Bet unit, cut through the conversation. He stood, as always, as though an invisible circle had been drawn around him, a circle few were bold enough to enter. "We've been expecting this ever since the Orthodox rabbis decided that our national problems stemmed from our failure to rebuild the Temple," he said, leaning against the wall with a grim look on his lined face. "They've been working toward this day since the capture of the Temple Mount in '67—and who can forget that brouhaha with the red heifer?"

Sarah looked away and smothered a smile. In May 1997,

a red heifer had been born at Kfar Hassidim, a small religious kibbutz near Haifa. According to the Torah, the ashes of a sacrificed red heifer had to be mixed with hyssop, cedar wood, scarlet, and water. The resulting mixture would be sprinkled on people to purify them from defiling contact with a bone, grave, or other person or vessel that had touched the dead. Because no pure red heifers had been seen in Israel for generations, many Orthodox Jews declared that the calf was a portent from God signaling that the time had come to begin preparations for the third Temple. When several of the Temple extremists began to talk of blowing up the Muslim Dome of the Rock in order to clear the Temple Mount, the Shin Bet went on full alert. Not until the cow developed white hairs that spoiled its purity were Sarah and her coworkers able to relax.

"They're still trying to find a pure red heifer," offered Yitzhak Peres, a man with a talent for stating the obvious. Under a thin, carefully clipped mustache, his lips curled into a smile. "Some American has been bringing red heifers to Israel for years now, but he says he's doing it to improve the quality of Israeli beef."

Sarah moved to the coffeepot. "Searching for a cow is not nearly as crazy as those women who have given their babies to the priesthood," she said, glancing at Melman over her shoulder. "I have the names of over twenty women who have given birth in religious compounds that observe *halacha*."

Under Jewish law, priestly lineage passed from father to son. Finding descendants of Aaron, the first high priest of Israel, had not proved difficult, for DNA evidence provided confirmation. But anyone who had come into contact with

the dead—or even the ground that might contain the dead—
would be ceremonially impure according to the Torah. The
state of uncleanness was known as *tumat hamet*, and since
the ashes of the red heifer had been lost at the time of the
destruction of the second Temple, everyone in Israel lived in
a state of tumat hamet—a major problem for those interested
in rebuilding the Temple.

The ashes of a red heifer could not be used to purify the
ground and the people unless an undefiled priest sprinkled the
ashes. A pure priest had to be one who was not only
descended from Aaron, but who had never touched the dead
or been under the same roof as the dead. Obviously, such a
priest could not have been born in a hospital.

To solve the problem and prepare for the eventuality of
the Temple's reconstruction, a number of ultra-Orthodox
rabbis had established an elevated compound where babies
whose fathers were kohanim—descendants from Aaron and
the priestly class—would be born and raised. The children
would remain in the compound, free from tumat hamet, until
a red heifer was found. Then they would prepare the mixture
that would purify the Jewish people and enable them to step
onto the Temple Mount and enter areas that to date had been
halachically off limits.

Turning to face the others, Sarah lowered her voice as she
stirred her coffee. "I couldn't imagine surrendering my child
for such a cause. They say the first child was born in '98.
There have been several others since."

Clearing his throat, Melman pulled himself off the wall.
Sarah tossed her spoon into a basket, knowing she should
change the subject. Religious talk always seemed to disturb
the deputy director. He was a secular Jew, a proud citizen of

Israel, and he did not like to be reminded of the religious activists who routinely brought media attention to the country. But everyone in Shin Bet knew the background of the Temple fanatics.

Religious zealots had always been eager to rebuild the Temple, and the red heifer was but one detail on their list of preparations for the project. Detailed blueprints for the third Temple, carefully derived from the Bible, Josephus, and the Middot commentary, had existed for years. Beginning in 1987, a group of rabbinical researchers, designers, and craftsmen busied themselves creating what they called a "Temple in waiting." Their efforts resulted in the production of seventy-five ritually qualified vessels and hundreds of priestly garments for Temple service, including the eight-layered woven robe, golden crown, and breastplate worn by the high priest, the special blue-purple dye for the priestly *tsitsit*, or fringes of the prayer shawl, and the eleven sacrificial incense spices. And while the Temple Institute's visitors' center prominently displayed a replica of the ark of the covenant, spokesmen for the Institute insisted that the ark would not be replicated. The original, they insisted, would be revealed at the appropriate moment and placed in the rebuilt Temple.

"Sarah." The deputy director's gaze turned toward her. "I need to see you in my office as soon as possible."

Sarah nodded and reached for a napkin, allowing the director to slip out of the room before her. When Melman had gone, Peres stepped closer and waggled a brow at her. "What's up, Sarah? Something we should know about?"

"Probably nothing you should know about," she answered lightly, wrapping a napkin around her coffee mug. She paused by the sink and glanced at the fragrant liquid. She

usually drank two cups of coffee in a morning, but judging by
the serious look in Melman's eye, today that second cup
might not be a good idea.

Peres backed off, grinning, then Sarah left the lounge area
and walked the short distance to the director's office. Melman
was seated at his desk, with several files stacked in front of
him. Sarah recognized the violet stripe that marked them as
classified material.

Melman wasted no time on common courtesies. "Did you
go through the dossiers I sent you yesterday?"

She nodded as she lowered herself into the chair before
his desk.

"What did you think? What sort of operation would you
assign to Romulus and his entourage?"

Sarah lifted a brow. Since the Europeans were already in
the country, it was a safe bet that a Shin Bet team was already
tracking their movements. Probably someone from the Tel
Aviv subsection of the non-Arab department. "Excuse me,
but I don't understand. Aren't they already under surveillance?"

"Only for the short term. We've got orders to put them
under permanent watch as long as even a single member of
Romulus's force remains within our borders."

She digested this information. From what she'd heard this
morning, Romulus intended to station members of his
Universal Force on the Temple Mount as long as the Temple
was under construction. That meant the director was talking
long-term surveillance and possibly even penetration—

"Were you given a time line for this operation?"

"It will be an open-ended action. This is classified, but
Romulus has told the prime minister that he intends to main-

tain an office here, ostensibly to support the new peace-keeping force. The prime minister has agreed that such an action is . . . . prudent."

Sarah inhaled swiftly, then blew out her cheeks. Israel had remained fiercely independent since the state's founding in 1948—she could never recall a previous government throwing open the doors to what sounded suspiciously like foreign occupation.

She set her mug on the edge of Melman's desk and leaned toward him, lowering her voice to a conspiratorial whisper. "How worried are the powers that be? Surely we won't require a high-level team for a man who's made himself a reputation for peacekeeping."

A familiar softness settled around Melman's mouth, the way he looked just before he smiled. "We trust no one, Sarah, you know that. I wouldn't trust Romulus if he were a card-carrying messiah."

Sarah leaned back, relieved by Melman's business-as-usual attitude, but she winced inwardly at the blasphemous statement. The daughter of a Reform rabbi could not shed years of religious training even if she no longer observed a religious way of life.

She picked up her mug and took a slow sip, then looked at Melman over the rim of her coffee cup. They'd worked together for nearly eight years, and this conversation was proof of his trust in her. "I'll put together a long-term team. We'll tap phone lines, install cameras, and insert an agent into their organization. And if one of his people wants to defect, we could arrange an exfiltration." She made a face. "It shouldn't be too difficult. After all, Romulus's people will be here while he's in Europe."

A smile gathered up the corners of Melman's stubborn mouth. "I knew I could count on you."

†

As Isaac's superior officer, Col. Meir Barak, droned on about the need for improved security throughout the Old City and along the walls of the Temple Mount, Isaac looked out the high reinforced window and studied the shape of a cloud moving slowly across the sky. The lecture was old material, rehashed and repackaged to suit the new situation on the Temple Mount. Isaac had heard the same speech for the past five years, but back then the emphasis had been on improving security at military bases in the occupied territories and along Israel's borders.

He had been part of the IDF Liaison Unit for nearly five years. His branch, stationed at the Allenby Bridge, was a comparatively small force dedicated to liaison with the Jordanian Liaison Unit and the United Nations Truce Supervision Organization. His duties consisted of protocol, diplomatic dinners, and altogether too much pencil pushing. He had thought of himself as a professional peacekeeper for years, but not until this morning had he believed worldwide peace might actually be possible. To think that the Temple might actually be built—and that the Arabs would not only allow the project, but bless it—staggered his imagination.

The colonel called for questions—there were none—then dismissed the meeting with a curt nod. As his fellow officers scraped their chairs and hurried to leave the stuffy room, Isaac stood and walked to the colonel's side.

"May I have a word with you, sir?"

Colonel Barak gave him the barest glance, then jerked his head toward the clock on the wall. "Only a moment, Major. I'm due in Tel Aviv for a lunch appointment."

Isaac stood in what he hoped was a relaxed, yet respectful pose as he framed his question. "Sir, I was most impressed by the press conference this morning."

The colonel placed a pipe in his mouth and proceeded to light it. "Quite a spectacle." He puffed on the pipe for a moment, then hooked it in the corner of his mouth and tilted his head. "What do you need, Major?"

Isaac felt a flush of nervousness. "I was thinking of Adrian Romulus, sir. Has anyone from the IDF been assigned to him as a liaison officer? If not, I'd like to apply for the position."

Barak puffed on his pipe, his eyes narrowing as they seemed to search Isaac's countenance for signs of personal ambition or religious mania. "Why you, Major? And why Romulus?"

"I was impressed with him, sir. The man seems truly committed to peace, and I'd like to see how he manages it. And if we were going to appoint an official liaison as a matter of course—"

The colonel interrupted with a brusque nod, then took his pipe from his lips and pointed in Isaac's direction. "I'll send your request up the line. A good position for a bright young man, I should think. And your communication skills are exemplary. Yes, I'll send your request along with my recommendation. You should hear from HQ before too long."

Isaac smiled. "Thank you, sir. I appreciate your help."

Barak grinned, his sudden smile temporarily erasing the stern lines of his face. "I'm not promising anything, Major. A position in Paris? I'm guessing there will be a dozen applications for that slot on the chief of the general staff's desk before noon."

Isaac lifted his chin. "All the same, sir. I'd like to try for it. It's . . . personal with me."

The colonel's smile faded, but his eyes held Isaac for a long moment before he nodded. "All right, Major. Best of luck to you. I'll see what I can do."

†

That night, in between bites of the roasted lamb Sarah had picked up at the grocery, Isaac told her that he had spoken to his commanding officer about serving as a liaison officer for Romulus's Universal Force.

For a moment astonishment struck her speechless. Isaac had never expressed discontent with his job or dissatisfaction in his present position, so what in the world had possessed him to do such a thing?

She looked up to study his face and saw the bright gleam of idealism in his eyes. That same bright gleam had filled his eyes and his heart when they first met; in fact, his bright-eyed optimism was one of the qualities that attracted her. But then they married and had a child who died, and the light in Isaac's eyes dimmed.

Now the light was back, and she could not understand what had put it there.

"Why?" The word slipped from her lips.

Isaac shrugged and concentrated on cutting his meat. "There are new undercurrents in the country, Sarah. Haven't you felt them? Though the earth itself seems to be restless and

ill at ease, there are men who still believe in peace. Adrian
Romulus has ensured peace for Israel, and the rabbis want to
restore the glory of the Temple. I believe peace is at hand. Not
everyone will warm to the idea of global unity, of course, but
we have to unite to find peace, and we have to do it soon. The
earth cannot continue in these dangerous crosscurrents much
longer."

Sarah stared at her husband as if she'd never seen him
before. Isaac Ben-David had always been a bit of a philoso-
pher. From his archeologist father he had inherited a love of
tradition, knowledge, and philosophy; from his mother's
untimely death he had been infected with a blood-borne grief
that sent his spirit crashing with every report of a terrorist
attack or random act of violence. He had remained in the IDF
long after completing his time of compulsory service because
he loved serving his country. He had risen in rank and authority because he was an odd pairing of traits—a visionary content to work behind the scenes.

He had never, however, volunteered to place himself in
the spotlight . . . or in the center of one of her investigations.
Sarah closed her eyes. Isaac didn't know, of course, that she'd
been assigned to surveil Romulus and infiltrate the man's
organization. Nor *could* he know; she never discussed her
classified missions, even with family members.

She drew a breath, torn between speaking honestly and
saying too much. "Did you talk to your father about this?"

"Yes, I did. He said I should do whatever I want to do."
Isaac looked at her, his expression guarded. "He warned me
to be wary, but he need not have bothered. I am not easily
swayed by power. I really believe Romulus is a man who can
change the world."

Sarah drew a deep breath. If Isaac had made a point of speaking to his father, he had already made his decision. He used to ask her opinion about things . . . but hadn't in a long time.

She looked down and idly dragged her fork through the chickpeas on her plate. "They say," she said, "that one man who worked closely with Adrian Romulus is now locked in a Belgian psychiatric institution. He's quite insane, I hear."

Isaac smiled, and from the shallowness of that smile she knew he hadn't noticed the change in the tone of her voice. "That's unfortunate. But mental illness can strike anyone, anywhere. I can't fault a man if one of his aides loses his grip on reality."

Sarah stopped stirring her food. Isaac used to heed her subtle cautions, but that warning had flown right over his head. "They also say," her voice flattened, "that the body of one of Romulus's most trusted associates was found in a frozen wasteland in Canada. He'd been killed by a suitcase bomb rigged to explode upon radio command. According to rumor, the bomb could only have been triggered by one of two people . . . one of them being Romulus himself."

That one hit home. Isaac blinked, his handsome features hardening in a stare of disapproval. "Are you saying that Adrian Romulus personally executed one of his own men?"

She shrugged. "The evidence is worth considering."

"But you can't prove it."

"I can't prove there's no God, either, but I believe it's true. And it makes a difference in the way I live my life. You won't catch me muttering purposeless prayers in a synagogue."

He didn't answer, but stared at her, his eyes hot with resentment. She knew she had raked a raw nerve. More than once she had chided him for his daily excursions to say the Kaddish, and some part of her knew her words wounded him. But she could not, *would* not, condone his foolish participation in a sentimental routine that did nothing to change the fact that they had lost their son forever.

"Several intelligence sources also suggest," she pushed ahead, "that Romulus may have been a silent conspirator in Gogol's Invasion. It is rumored that he encouraged the Arabs to attack Israel, that he actually *encouraged* Gogol to launch the nuclear missiles that struck the United States. They say that he—"

"Good grief, Sarah, stop playing games. I've heard the same rumors, and that's all they are. Just rumors."

Her lips puckered with annoyance. "Some of the reports come from Mossad."

"Well, Mossad isn't doing us much good these days, is it? And neither is Shin Bet."

Sarah dropped her fork as her mood veered sharply to anger. Ever since the assassination of Prime Minister Yitzhak Rabin in 1995, the Shin Bet, known to most Israelis as *Shabak*, had taken heat for failures both real and imagined. No one ever knew about the organization's successes, for those almost always remained classified, but whenever a plan failed or security lapsed, Shin Bet endured a storm of bad publicity. Isaac, however, worked in the very public Israeli Defense Forces, which operated in full view of friends and foes. He understood Shabak's need for security, but sometimes Sarah wondered if he didn't resent her for knowing more than she was allowed to share. She *knew* he resented her for not being home when the earthquake struck.

She drew a long, quivering breath, mastering the rage that

shook her. So that's how it would be. If by some odd chance Isaac was appointed to the liaison position, his work wouldn't hinder her team . . . in fact, he just might prove to be a valuable tool. She wouldn't need to plant an agent in Romulus's organization if her own husband worked closely with the man. She could use him. With or without his knowledge, he might well prove to be the most valuable asset Israeli intelligence had ever utilized.

She lifted her gaze to find him studying her.

"I hope you get the position," she said, standing. Without another word, she lifted her plate and took it into the kitchen.

†

After dinner, while Isaac sat in the courtyard with a cup of coffee, Sarah went into the bedroom, closed the door, and dialed her supervisor's cell phone number. Director Melman answered on the first ring.

"It's Sarah," she whispered, sinking to the edge of the bed. "I've had an interesting development on my end. My husband wants to work for Romulus. He's applying for the position of liaison officer with Romulus and the Universal Force."

Melman did not answer for a long moment, then he asked, "If we arrange it—will the situation be difficult for you?"

She wound the telephone cord around her fist. "I don't think so. In fact, Isaac might be useful. Of course, we can't know if Romulus will approve him. He's bound to discover that I work for Shabak—"

"We'll try to keep that quiet. I'll do what I can to make it happen from this end—if you're sure it's what you really want."

Sarah hesitated, knowing that Melman was giving her time to think like a wife instead of an intelligence agent. She had never manipulated her husband before, never hurt his pride by calling on her connections to advance or restrain him. She and Isaac had never allowed their careers to penetrate the marriage, but very little of that marriage seemed to remain . . .

"It's what I want," she whispered, her voice husky. "Romulus's people might reject him, and if that happens, so be it. But we may never have another opportunity like this."

"You're right." A note of satisfaction echoed in Melman's voice. "We should have an answer by the end of the week."

Six

Gen. Adam Archer, commander of Romulus's Universal Force, scowled as an aide dropped two folders on his polished desk. It was five o'clock on a Friday afternoon, and he was ready to sample the famed nightlife of Paris. "What's this?"

Gregor Rahn, the youthful, clear-eyed German officer who served as Archer's chief assistant, licked his lower lip. "Two files from President Romulus, sir. A report on a prospective Israeli liaison officer, and the latest on the two troublemakers we encountered in Jerusalem."

Archer picked up the first folder and opened it. To the inside cover someone had stapled a head-and-shoulders photograph of a striking Israeli officer in full dress uniform. The man had dark eyes and curly brown hair, and though Archer knew a photograph could be misleading, the set of the man's chin suggested a stubborn streak.

"Isaac Ben-David," he muttered, glancing at the biographical information on the following page. "A career officer with the IDF Liaison. A decorated soldier who has served his country with honor and courage, particularly during Gogol's Invasion . . ."

"You'll notice, sir" the aide leaned forward—"that the man's wife works for the Shin Bet. Though this is the man recommended by the IDF, I suggest we reject his application."

Archer rubbed a finger hard over his lip, quelling a sudden urge to laugh. "Why not hire a man whose wife is a spy? As we control him, we control the information his wife and Shin Bet receive." He handed the file back to his eager and naïve assistant. "We will always encounter spies, Gregor, they are as inescapable as death. Never forget the old adage: Keep your friends close, and your enemies closer."

"I'll see to it, then." Gregor inclined his sleek head, then accepted Ben-David's file. A look of discomfort crossed his face as he cut a quick glance to the remaining folder. "There, ah, remains the other matter—"

"Yes." Archer picked up the folder and opened it, then stared at photographs of the two religious fanatics who had made Jerusalem almost intolerable for Adrian Romulus. The photos featured two men, both of whom appeared to be in their late fifties. Long burlap robes covered their gaunt bodies, while leather sandals shod their feet. Both men wore unkempt beards and carried walking sticks. After the historic press conference in Jerusalem, they had stood outside the Knesset and shouted that Adrian Romulus was the spawn of Satan and the beast of John's Revelation.

Archer had been tempted to walk over and put a bullet into each of them, but Adrian had forbidden him. "Ignore the lunatics," he had said, climbing into his limo, "we'll get them, General, but we'll do it properly. Find out all you can first."

Archer had put a team of crack intelligence operators on the case, but those fools would have been more successful at unraveling the mystery of Amelia Earhart than discovering the background of the two Israeli troublemakers. According to the Israeli government, the two men had never been born, never held jobs, and never served in the IDF. They had no known family names. Their fingerprints were not on file with the Shin Bet or the police. They were religious madmen, to be sure, but neither the liberal Christian movements nor the right-wing haredim would claim them. They called themselves Elijah and Moses, and no one, not even Mossad, had been able to find any record of them before they began to bedevil Romulus.

Archer stared at the report in disgust. "Where were they today, Gregor?"

The aide blushed. "They demonstrated outside the sealed Eastern Gate. They arrived at sunrise and spent the day shouting that the Messiah would soon come and open the gate to usher in his kingdom."

Archer ran his hand over the stubble on his head. "They say anything else?"

Gregor cleared his throat. "Um—'Repent while there is yet time,' and 'God has not finished with the earth.'"

Archer forced himself to chuckle. "A pity they can't even be original. Well, leave them alone this weekend. Next week, however, we will have our troops remove them. Romulus is addressing the national Parliament Monday morning, and he's likely to lose his temper if he sees them anywhere near the building."

"Yes sir." Gregor jerked his head downward and clicked his heels, an affected gesture that Archer disliked intensely. He was, however, in Europe, where style and substance were too often confused . . .

Archer slid the folder toward his aide. "And Gregor?"

"Sir?"

"Assign a permanent surveillance team to Moses and Elijah. I want them quietly watched, twenty-four seven, for the next two weeks. I want to know where they eat, where they sleep, who they talk to—and who listens to them. Offer a reward for anyone who can provide the history of these men. They didn't just materialize out of thin air."

"I will do it immediately."

Gregor picked up the folder, snapped his head and heels again, then spun and whirled out of the room. Archer watched him go, then shook his head slowly and pulled a pouch of tobacco from his desk drawer.

Living in Europe had its advantages. Working with Romulus, de facto leader of the remaining world, had even greater benefits.

Life could be sweet when you held the reins of power.

SEVEN

SARAH SAT SILENTLY, LISTENING TO THE TICKING OF THE schoolhouse clock on the wall.

The Shabbat afternoon was quiet, but bright, with the sun jabbing brilliant fingers of light into the courtyard off the Ben-Davids' living room. Sarah and Isaac sat together at a small table, silently sharing a platter of cold chicken sandwiches. Even though she no longer cared to strictly observe the Sabbath, something in Sarah had grown accustomed to quiet Saturdays and cold lunches. She had also grown accustomed to a quiet house and a cold husband.

The telephone rang, startling her with its bright sound. Isaac gave her a polite smile, dabbed at his mouth with a napkin, then stepped into the living room to answer the phone.

He was back within two minutes. "That was Colonel Barak," he said simply, dropping his napkin onto his lap again. "I've been assigned the position of military liaison for Adrian Romulus and the Universal Force. I am to leave for a briefing in Paris within the hour."

Though she had strongly suspected that his appointment would come through, Sarah remembered to play the part of a surprised wife. She nodded wordlessly, fingering her napkin. Isaac continued eating, but his eyes were wide and as blank as windowpanes, as though the soul they had mirrored had long since flown away. Though he tried to behave as if nothing unusual had happened, his sandwich disappeared in three quick gulps.

"Where will you be staying?" she asked.

His dark brow slanted in a frown. "I'm not sure. But I'll make sure you have the contact information. I won't be out of reach . . . if an emergency should arise."

She pressed her lips together and looked down at her hands. He said nothing about missing her, nothing about coming back, nothing . . . *personal*.

Isaac sipped from his drink, then stood and paused a moment to pat Lily's head. After murmuring some sweet foolishness to the dog, he moved toward the bedroom.

A thousand questions raced through Sarah's mind about where he was going and whom he would meet and what they would ask of him, but those were the questions of an intelligence agent, not the queries of a loving wife.

She waited until he came out, in full uniform and with a small suitcase in his hand, before she asked the one question she could. "How long will you be away?"

"I have no idea."

He kissed her then, lightly and on the cheek, then went out the front door.

Sarah sat silently, alone with the ticking schoolhouse clock.

Eight

Isaac had once worked with a group of American operatives who spoke of inviting "Mr. Murphy" along on every mission—a reference to Murphy's Law, and that if something can go wrong, it probably will. Shortly after taking off from Jerusalem, Isaac became convinced that the invisible Mr. Murphy was riding shotgun on his military aircraft. Somewhere in the midst of the Mediterranean, the pilot announced that he had to turn back on account of shifting cargo in the hold. The unscheduled return was annoying, but upon returning to base Isaac discovered that the pilot's Labrador—who shouldn't have been allowed aboard the jet—had somehow escaped his kennel. The frantic canine had cut himself by scratching on an electrical panel and had tripped an alarm, and the entire cargo hold and nearly everything in it, including Isaac's small suitcase, was smeared with blood and dog drool.

Irritated beyond words, Isaac wiped his suitcase clean, strode to the ticket counter, and arranged to take a commercial flight to Paris. Because of his last-minute booking, how-

ever, he found himself sandwiched between a talkative grand-
mother and a sullen teenager with black lips and dark circles
above and below her eyes. He finally pulled the book he'd
just purchased from his briefcase and pretended to read *How
to Survive in France on Forty Fabulous Phrases*.

Rain was pelting the runway when he finally disembarked
in Paris. Isaac fought his way to a pay phone and called his
contact number. A man with a nasal voice answered the
phone, then told Isaac that Monsieur Romulus could not see
him that night. He should find a room in the city and call
again on Sunday. Romulus would be pleased to send a car to
pick him up the next morning.

"Any suggestions about where I might find a room?"
Isaac asked, feeling suddenly inept.

"One moment, please." The smarmy voice fell silent, then
returned to fill Isaac's ear with an adenoidal drone. "We suggest the Fleurs de Soleil," the man said. "It is a bed-and-
breakfast, the perfect place for an extended stay." He gave the
address, which Isaac frantically jotted on the back of his air-
line ticket folder.

A little stunned by the phrase *extended stay,* he hung up
and stared at the address. What, exactly, did Romulus have in
mind for him, and why would he need to find accommodations for a lengthy stay?

Half an hour later, he found himself inside a small but
functional room with the luxury of its own toilet and shower.
The hostess, a charming Frenchwoman who spoke little
English and no Hebrew, had stared at Isaac in confusion until
he mentioned Romulus's name. At that point, Isaac had been
ushered into the best room available. After five minutes of

searching, however, he discovered that the only telephone in the house was located downstairs in a public hallway.

He fell into bed without calling home.

†

Though it was but early October, nearly all the leaves had fallen from the trees on the outskirts of Romulus's Paris estate. On Sunday morning, Isaac sat silently in the backseat of a limousine and stared out at bare trees lifting black, bony arms toward a somber gray sky. He had not seen a ray of sunlight since arriving at the Paris airport.

The skeletal forest ended in a long stretch of driveway leading to a stately chateau. A meadow that might have once been green bordered the massive house, and a small flock of sheep huddled beneath a stand of trees a few yards away. At the sound of the limo's approach, they scrambled off, black legs working awkwardly beneath shaggy bodies.

"Nice place," Isaac remarked casually, raising his voice so the driver would hear.

"It used to be," the driver replied, his accent heavy. "There is a vineyard here, but nothing is growing now. With no rain, things are brown and—how do you say it?—withered. If ze rain does not come soon . . ." He shrugged, leaving Isaac to fill in the blanks.

"Things are dry everywhere," Isaac remarked, staring out the window. "We haven't had rain—"

"Since ze Disruption." The driver looked up in the rearview mirror and caught Isaac's gaze. "No one will admit it, but I know 'tis true. Everything has gone bad since they left."

"Since *who* left?"

The man shrugged. "Ze godly ones. Ze honest Christians."

Isaac wanted to hear more, but they had pulled into the circular driveway in front of the chateau. As the car stopped, two guards, clad in the blue-and-red uniforms of the Universal Force, stepped forward. One opened the car door while the other waited, a wandlike metal detector in his hand.

Isaac stepped outside the car and lifted his arms as the guard waved the metal detector over his clothing. When they were satisfied that he did not carry a weapon, the guard who had opened the door saluted sharply. "Welcome, Major Ben-David. You are expected. I am to usher you immediately into the reception hall. President Romulus is in a meeting, so you are to take a seat in the back of the room and wait."

Isaac nodded his thanks, then followed the man through a marble foyer and into a high-ceilinged chamber luxuriously crowded with antiques. A circle of chairs ringed the room, each occupied by a man dressed in a dark suit, the uniform of a European politician. Adrian Romulus sat in the circle, but next to the commanding fireplace, the focal point of the room.

Isaac's escort pointed to an empty chair near the double doors. He slipped into the seat, grateful for a few moments to acclimate himself before meeting with Romulus.

As the men debated, sometimes in French, sometimes in English, Isaac studied his surroundings. The walls of the room glittered with gilded ornaments and frames as shadows played flickering games around the high frescoed ceiling. Heavy Persian carpets lay scattered over the stone floor while the warmth of the fire provided a pleasing contrast to the gray day visible between the panels of velvet draperies. Isaac inhaled deeply. The décor was too ostentatious to suit his taste, but the scents of burning wood and furniture polish reminded him of home.

Isaac sank back against the gilt chair's upholstery, grateful that his entrance appeared to have gone unnoticed except by a handful of soberly dressed men in dark glasses who stood along the wall—security guards, undoubtedly, for most of them stood within a dozen steps of Romulus, though they blended into the shadows in an attempt to be inconspicuous. While the gentlemen in the chairs relaxed, these guys remained vigilant, their heads moving slowly from left to right as they surveyed every movement.

The object of their attention sat with his head turned toward a tall gentleman clad in a dark suit accented by a bright red tie. Isaac blinked as he realized that the man speaking was François Ibert, the French president. He addressed the group in French and spoke so rapidly that the content of his remarks escaped Isaac completely, but Romulus seemed to have no trouble following his guest's comments.

Isaac settled his attention upon his host. Adrian Romulus appeared younger in person than he did on television. Before leaving Jerusalem, Isaac had picked up a background brief which listed Romulus's age as fifty-two, but he could have easily passed for forty. His body was long and slender, his hands well shaped, his clothing classic. His handsome face was unlined but for laugh lines that radiated from the corners of his eyes, and a pair of parenthesis around his mouth gave him a look of firm resolve. He wore his thick hair in a contemporary style, short on the sides and top, longer at the nape of his neck. One stubborn lock tended to drape across his forehead.

Sarah would probably find him attractive. According to the brief Isaac had read, Romulus was often seen in the company of beautiful women, but had never married or expressed any desire to do so. Investigators who hoped to uncover sexual secrets and unsavory activities had tailed him for months without finding anything with which he might be coerced.

The French president stood and abruptly switched to English. "And so, my dear President Romulus," he said, bowing slightly, "it is with my whole heart that I pledge our service to you. As but one voice in the European Union, France stands behind you in this time of crisis. Because the EU is the single remaining world superpower, we must exercise strength and wisdom in this time of trial. We are willing to support you entirely. Whatever you say must be done, we will do."

A smattering of polite applause greeted this announcement. Romulus bowed his head in a gesture of humility, then stood and reached out to take the French president's hand. The applause strengthened, and as he joined in, Isaac looked around the room and recognized at least half a dozen European leaders. Apparently this was a meeting of European heads of state, perhaps a time for Romulus to reinforce loyalties and strengthen his support base before carrying the Universal Movement to the entire world.

Romulus released the Frenchman's hand and smiled as Ibert sat down. "You understand, then," Romulus said, looking around the circle, "that we must encourage the other nations to adopt our identity chip. We cannot effectively manage the global economy, world health, and the exchange of international currency unless we are all united through a common system. The Millennium Chip, introduced many months ago in Europe and the United States, has proved to be effective. Those countries that lie outside our jurisdiction must be persuaded to join us. We have the chips available— we lack only the manpower and legal supervisory authority to insure that every citizen of earth is correctly identified and recorded. Only then can we guarantee the rights of every human being on the planet."

Michael Moriarty, the British prime minister, stood and bowed his head toward Romulus. "With half the planet in a state of upheaval, someone must provide world leadership," he said simply. "You, Adrian, are that leader. You can count on us to supply manpower, technology, whatever the job requires. We urge you to move into the Middle East, the broken West, and the Far East. Do what must be done, and we will support you. We pledge our efforts to aid in your cause."

More applause filled the room. Isaac lifted his gaze from the circle of men and examined those who did not sit in the chairs, but stood around the room at various defensive positions. Directly behind Romulus's chair stood a balding, stocky man Isaac recognized as Gen. Adam Archer, the American who had gone to work for Romulus shortly before the turn of the century. Isaac had heard rumors, none of them confirmed, that Archer had been the mastermind behind the White House assassination attempt that resulted in the death of the former American president's wife. Archer now served Romulus exclusively as head of his military and security forces.

The man at Romulus's right hand seemed familiar, but Isaac had to search his memory to match a name to the swarthy face. Elijah Reis—a rather shadowy man who had risen to power with Romulus in the last decade of the twentieth century. Born of German Jews who survived the Holocaust and immigrated to Israel, Reis was a *Sabra*, a

native-born Israeli, but he had not lived in Israel since affili-
ating himself with Romulus. He, too, worked solely for
Romulus, and Isaac recalled that the brief he'd read stated
that the two men usually traveled together. Unlike Romulus,
however, Reis had often displayed a fondness for beautiful
women.

Isaac flinched slightly when the object of his study spoke.
"There is one other thing," Reis said, his cultured voice fill-
ing the room. "Many citizens of Asia and Africa are clinging
to outmoded customs and ideals. They are refusing to relin-
quish their right to total privacy." The grooves beside his
mouth deepened into a knowing smile. "As if the rights of the
individual could outweigh the rights of the majority during a
time of crisis. In any case, we have instituted a new program,
one that will define and reward any individual willing to join
our global community. We are encouraging all who receive
the identification chip, or who have already received it, to
also sign a statement of cooperation with the Universal
Movement."

"It is a good plan," Romulus added, his countenance
shining like gold in the flickering light. "But we know we will
encounter resistance. Every great idea is resisted in the beginning, for ignorant people cannot help but challenge what they
do not understand."

The room swelled with silence for a long moment, then
the air vibrated softly with the whispers of men who nodded
and smiled at one another. Romulus had won them over.

Another man lifted his hand, requesting permission to
speak, and Romulus granted it with a stately gesture. The
man, a stocky fellow with a belly that overrode his belt, stood
to address his fellow councilors. "Begging President

Romulus's permission, we must settle this issue of water rights," he said, his gaze swinging rapidly around the circle. "My country is dying of thirst. We have always had enough water, for we have been blessed with freshwater lakes, but the demand placed upon us by other members of the international network is tapping our patience and our supply. We are providing water for France, Spain, and part of Germany, and we must find a suitable compromise on this issue before my own countrymen lose their spring crops."

"Gentlemen, I leave you to work this out among yourselves." Romulus stood and smiled, his face radiant with an aura of power and authority. "I must attend to other matters. I give you good day."

With that, Romulus turned and exited the room through a door cleverly concealed in the ornate paneling. Isaac noticed that Archer and Elijah Reis followed immediately, then the portly ambassador turned again to his colleagues. "Please, gentlemen, I need your cooperation. My province must be released from the water agreements, at least until the spring rains come . . ."

Isaac felt a discreet tug on his sleeve, then turned to see a security guard just behind his chair. "The president will see you now," the man whispered.

Isaac rose and followed the guard, leaving the Europeans to wrestle with their water problems.

†

He had expected to be presented to Romulus in a formal situation, but the guard led him to a small study furnished with a desk and a pair of chairs before a fireplace. Isaac stood awkwardly in the tiny space, watching the fire's shadows dance on the spines of myriad books lining the walls. What was he supposed to do next? He didn't have long to consider the question, for in a moment, Romulus entered, his face flushed with pleasure.

"Major Ben-David," he said warmly, advancing with his hand outstretched. "It is indeed a pleasure to make your acquaintance. I've heard many good things about you."

Isaac felt his cheeks burn. He had not expected such a robust welcome—Romulus's manner was a pleasant surprise.

"Thank you, sir." He shook the European's hand. "I appreciate the personal welcome. I hope you did not leave an important meeting on my account."

Romulus made a face. "Bah! Water rights! I am heartily sick of the discussion. We have known drought before, and the earth has always survived. They quibble like children over nothing of consequence."

Releasing Isaac's hand, Romulus gestured toward the chairs. "Will you join me for a moment? I won't detain you for too long; I am sure you would like some time to settle in and explore Paris. But I did want you to know how very glad I am that you have joined our team."

"I am happy to be here," Isaac murmured, surprised by the man's reference to a *team*. Military liaisons were usually regarded as necessary evils, yet Romulus had welcomed him as a friend. Why was this man so different?

He sat down as Romulus did, then rested his hands on the arms of the wing chair as Romulus crossed one leg over the other and steadily held Isaac's gaze. "You might have noticed, Major Ben-David, that Israel and Jerusalem hold a very special place in my heart. Do you know why?"

Rattled by the direct question and the forthright manner in which Romulus presented it, Isaac felt himself flushing again. The politicians he knew rarely came directly to the point.

He stared at the carpet and tried to corral his runaway thoughts. He had memorized the background report on Romulus, yet from it he couldn't find a single clue to indicate why the man might be particularly interested in Israel. Romulus had been educated in Rome, he had served in the Italian government during the early years of his career, then advanced to a position of leadership within the European Union. The man did not claim to be either a Christian, Jew, or Muslim, so he had no reason to consider Jerusalem a sacred city. He had established himself as a friend of Israel, but he had also supported various other ethnic groups. So why on earth would he *particularly* care about Israel?

"I'm sorry, sir." Isaac lifted his gaze. "I could guess, of course, but something tells me you'd prefer that I be direct. So you'll have to tell me."

Romulus's rich laughter warmed the room. "I love it. I suppose I still possess a few secrets, after all." He leaned forward and gave Isaac a confidential smile. "I was born only five miles south of Jerusalem, Isaac Ben-David. In a little town, now Palestinian, called Bethlehem. We don't generally publicize that bit of information—it might lead to unwanted conjecture about whether my loyalties lie with the Jews or with the Arabs. But the truth remains—I am a child of Jerusalem, bred and born in the Holy Land. And that is why Israel holds a special place in my heart."

Isaac smiled to cover his surprise. "I had no idea."

"Of course you didn't." Romulus paused to pull a package of cigarettes from an inner coat pocket, then tapped one from the wrapper. "In medieval times, Jerusalem was thought to be the center of the world and in many ways, it truly is. The splendid City of David, the settlement on a hill, must shine again for the world to see. Why not reestablish Jerusalem as the center of the world's culture and worship? From her unblemished walls the rest of the world can draw inspiration and hope. They will see how the city whose gutters have literally flowed with blood through the ages can now shine with glory. They will witness the wonders we shall work in Jerusalem, the City of Peace, and the people of this planet will begin to rebuild their own shattered dreams. And, working together, we shall establish a peace unlike anything the world has ever known."

A flicker of a smile rose at the edges of his mouth as he lit his cigarette. "Did you know that Jerusalem's original name, Salem, means peace? It is appropriate that we begin our work in your city, Major. And it is appropriate that you serve as our liaison in this vital effort."

As he felt his reserve thaw, Isaac folded his hands and dared to speak freely. "I've heard that, of course. And if there was ever a time when peace can be accomplished, I believe that time is now. The Arabs are tired of fighting, and our people are ready to get on with their lives. We have spent ten months cleaning up the dead. Our people are ready to put death behind them and live."

Romulus looked at him with misty, wistful eyes. "I'm glad you agree with me, Major—may I call you Isaac? There is no need for formalities when we are alone . . . and I suspect we may be talking together often." He looked away, his eyes gleaming black in the firelight. "I am grateful you have come to work with us, Isaac Ben-David. I know about your mother. I know that after her death, your father poured himself into his work, neglecting the son he ought to have loved more than anything on earth. I know about your Sarah, and I know about the tragic loss of Binyamin, your son." His brow wrinkled, and something moved in his eyes as he turned to meet Isaac's gaze. "I know that you have longed for peace, and that longing has brought you to us. And so I welcome you, Isaac. And I promise to do everything possible to make certain you find the peace you are seeking. I know you can find it here . . . with me."

Isaac felt his breath being suddenly whipped away. He ought to have known that Romulus would have good intelligence, but how could he know so much about Isaac's personal life? For a moment, he felt as though Romulus had lifted the curtain shielding Isaac's wounded soul and looked at the heart within.

"I . . ." Isaac faltered, unable to find the words. He was here for the IDF, for Israel, but it was hard to remain aloof from Romulus's piercing eyes. "I will do my best to fulfill my mission here," he finally said. "If you have need of anything, you have but to ask for my help."

"I know I can count on you." Romulus drew deeply on his cigarette, then exhaled twin streamers through his nostrils. "We shall do great things in Israel, you and I. Together we shall pave the way to peace, and when we are done, every voice in the Middle East will rejoice and say that the City of Peace is once more the center of the world."

Romulus put his cigarette in an ashtray to smolder, then rested his elbows on the arms of the chair and brought his hands together, fingertip to fingertip. "Our first task shall be the implementation of the international identity chip. The Europeans and Americans have successfully used it for months, and the Middle East and Africa must be enrolled in the program as well. Israel, particularly, must implement the identification program and become assimilated into the Universal

Network. We simply cannot secure a sensitive area like the Temple Mount without the proper identification of each individual involved in the work. You understand this, of course."

Fascinated by Romulus's dark eyes, Isaac nodded.

"I'll need you to present our case to the prime minister. I have spoken to him already; he understands the need for a technological approach to security. He was concerned, however, about reluctance among military personnel and the religious leaders."

He paused, letting the silence stretch, and Isaac hurried to fill it. "The Israeli military is one of the most technologically sophisticated armies in the world. Our people understand the need for surveillance technology. I don't think you'll have any problem with the military. On the other hand, the religious leadership—" His mouth curved in a mirthless smile. "Well, problems are a natural consequence of dealing with those people. Some of the more extreme Orthodox sects have steadfastly refused to even acknowledge the government of Israel as legitimate representatives of the Jewish people. They are waiting for the Messiah to rule the country."

With a slow, secret smile, Romulus nodded. "May their wait soon be over." He lowered his forehead until it touched his uplifted fingertips, then closed his eyes. Isaac watched, perplexed, until Elijah Reis stepped into the room. With a soundless gesture, he beckoned to Isaac, calling him away.

†

When the Israeli had gone, Romulus opened his eyes, then pressed a button on the pager in his pocket. Within seconds, Adam Archer appeared at his side.

"Set up coverage on Ben-David's house in Jerusalem—and the Paris bed-and-breakfast," Romulus said, returning his gaze to the fireplace. "I want to know everything about the man."

Archer sat in the chair Ben-David had just vacated. The flickering firelight revealed the crimson spider webs of broken capillaries that netted his jowls. "So this man suits you?"

"He's reachable." Romulus gave the general a cynical smile. "He's not totally on board, but I didn't expect instant allegiance. Naturally, his first loyalties will lie with his people . . . until *we* become his people. Then he should suit our purposes nicely."

Romulus turned from the distressing sight of the general's florid face and stared into the fire. How lovely the flames, how warm the color! Almost as bright as Ben-David's cheeks when he heard Romulus speak of the secret things on his heart.

He lifted a finger as another idea occurred to him. "Write the IDF headquarters and congratulate them on sending such a well-qualified officer. Ask that Ben-David's assignment be extended indefinitely."

"I'll see to it."

"And make certain that we receive the information from his home as soon as possible. Nadim has shown me a great deal, but I want to know more. I want to know everything."

"Right away, sir."

Archer stood and moved out of the room. Romulus closed his eyes, allowing himself to slip into the mental image of the elevator that lifted him away from his study, away from his chateau, away from the barren and thirsty landscape. When he had entered the realm of light, Nadim came to him.

His face was like a patch of sun-hardened earth, seamed with deep-cut lines—a tangle of violent passions and irregular habits, but his eyes glittered with mischief and inspiration. "You met Isaac Ben-David?"

It was not a question, for Nadim saw everything that transpired in Romulus's home.

"I did. The information you provided was . . . most effective."

"He was impressed, then."

"*Astounded* would be a better word. I have a feeling he will serve us well."

Nadim showed his dazzling teeth in an expression that was not a smile. "We shall see, Adrian. Very soon, we shall know for certain."

NINE

As the knot of rowdy youths moved down the narrow aisle of the bus, Sarah drew her shopping bag closer to her chest and tried to act invisible. The boys had boarded a full five minutes before and had been taking their time finding seats, preferring to harass other passengers as they made their way toward the back of the vehicle. The driver, who should have refused to pull out as long as they remained standing, steadfastly refused to look in his mirror, though he had to hear the commotion caused by the obnoxious teens.

In her peripheral vision, she saw one of them pause in the aisle next to her. "Hey, pretty lady." Sarah kept her gaze turned toward the window, ignoring the boy who leaned into the empty seat at her left. His adolescent voice filled with intensity. "What's in the bag, pretty woman?"

"Something smells good." Another boy moved into the seat directly behind her. She studied his reflection in the window as he leaned over her shoulder. "What is that delicious smell? Is that your dinner? No, it's too sweet. It must be you."

"If I were you," Sarah said, keeping her gaze upon the reflection in the glass, "I'd back away and go find a seat."

"Oh, the lady's a tough one." The boy at her left sat down and edged closer while his friends crowed in delight. "Come on, baby, show me what you're holding there. Show me so we can get to know each other a little better."

Drawing a slow and steady breath, Sarah turned and met the boy's gaze. Part of her brain registered surprise—he couldn't have been more than fourteen, fifteen at the most. He wasn't old enough to even qualify for a driver's license.

"Young man," she said, spacing her words evenly as she looked him directly in the eye, "I suggest that you move away and take your friends with you. There are empty seats at the back of the bus."

"Oh, baby!" His boyish face crumpled in pretended hurt. "Why would you want to break my heart?" He clasped his hands upon his chest for an instant, then leaned toward her, his lips only inches from her ear. "Come on, baby, I know you're dying to go to the back of the bus with me."

"Really?" Slowly, carefully, she eased her free hand into the space between the shopping bag and her jacket. While continuing to hold the boy's gaze, she found the smooth handle of her Beretta 92F pistol, then pulled it from the shoulder holster she wore beneath her coat.

"Young man." She deliberately lowered her voice until he leaned closer. "So far you've been nothing but obnoxious and crude. If you touch me, however, or say one more word, I will be forced to take action." She nudged the gun forward and lightly grazed the front of the boy's shirt. "So unless you want to find out just how annoyed I have to be to use this, I suggest you back off. Quietly walk away, and take your friends along for the ride."

The boy's eyes widened slightly, his mouth opened, then

he pulled away. For an instant he stared at her, anger and fear warring in his eyes, then he jerked himself upright and sauntered down the aisle toward the rear of the bus.

Sarah put the Beretta back into the dark space between her bag and her chest, then stiffened as the bus pulled over for the next stop. If the troublemakers were going to make a move, they might act now . . . but the gang poured off the bus, leaving a stream of curses in their wake.

As the bus pulled away, Sarah looked down and saw the leader flick an obscene gesture in her direction. Lifting her chin, she eyed him with cold defiance. Punks like that understood nothing else.

Ten minutes later, bone tired and hungry, she stepped off the bus and crossed the sidewalk to her own front door. The neighborhood seemed quiet and sleepy, but she knew her older neighbors were afraid to venture out in the late afternoon. Each day the papers were filled with reports of a growing epidemic of vandalism and gang activity in what used to be quiet neighborhoods, and most older people tended to do their shopping in the morning, when schools were in session and young people were properly incarcerated.

She glanced toward the garage where the car sat, unused. She hated driving in the city and had come to depend upon Isaac's easygoing attitude behind the wheel. Since he had gone, she had taken to riding the bus. Incidents like the one she'd just experienced were trivial compared to what could happen to a woman alone on a deserted stretch of road.

Though she and Isaac had drifted apart in the last few months, she felt his absence keenly. He had been gone for little more than a week, but the passing of these silent days reminded her of how empty the house could be with no husband and no child . . .

She shifted the shopping bag to her left arm and fumbled for her keys in her purse, then unlocked the front door. And froze.

Her neat, tidy home had been violated. An overturned vase lay on the tile beside the door; stuffing from the sofa littered the living room carpet like bits of misplaced clouds. The drawers of her antique secretary had been overturned and emptied on the floor, and shards of blue glass from her favorite goblets sparkled in the light from the dining room lamp . . .

She dropped her shopping bag and withdrew her pistol. Holding the weapon in both hands, she swept the room in an arc and peered around the corner, straining to hear any sound that might indicate that the intruder remained in the house.

She heard nothing but the rapid pulse of her pounding heart.

Sarah crossed to the kitchen and knocked the phone from its stand. With one hand curled around the Beretta, she dialed Shin Bet headquarters, then set the receiver on her shoulder.

Melman was still in his office. "Director," she began, dismayed to hear a tremor in her voice, "my home has been invaded."

A harsh sound rose from his throat. "Are you all right?"

"I'm fine."

"Don't go prowling around; wait right where you are. Are you armed?"

"Yes."

"We'll send a team right over. When they give the all-clear, call the police."

"All right."

She replaced the phone in its cradle, then stepped back to the wall and gulped a deep breath. Why wasn't Isaac around when she needed him? If he hadn't gone to Paris, he would be with her now. He would have driven her to work, so she would have avoided that unpleasant confrontation with the boys on the bus. And if someone had been watching the house, they would have known that a man lived inside. But no, Isaac wanted to be in Paris. He wanted to chase dreams of peace while she remained home alone . . .

Convinced that neither the living room nor the dining room concealed an intruder, she slipped behind the bar separating the kitchen from the dining area. The kitchen had been ransacked, but no one hid behind the bar or the refrigerator. Stepping carefully over her broken china, she slid along the hallway toward the master bedroom, then methodically checked the closet and under the bed. She saw no one, but did see that her jewelry box had been emptied on the bed. Right away she noticed that her two most valuable pieces, a gold necklace and bracelet, were missing. Both had been gifts from Isaac and, aside from her wedding band, were the most precious items in the bedroom.

As her heart beat in a staccato rhythm, Sarah moved toward the closed door that led to Binyamin's room. Her grasping fingers touched the cold metal of the knob, then flung the door open. She thrust the pistol muzzle into the open space.

Her heart had been numb; now it broke. The intruder had violated this room, too, slicing the mattress on Binyamin's crib and decapitating his favorite teddy bear. With apparently fiendish glee, the person or persons unknown had gutted several other stuffed animals and flung the stuffing everywhere. Lumps of white fiberfill vibrated on the marble windowsill, stirred by the slow breath of an overhead ceiling fan.

Sarah dropped her heavy arms on the railing of her baby's bed as tears welled in her eyes. What sort of monster could take delight in destroying a *baby's* room? No one would hide treasures in a child's room—the treasure was the *child*. And her treasure had been stolen months ago . . .

Sadness pooled in her heart, a deep despondency akin to nausea. She gulped a few frantic breaths, then pushed herself upright and dashed the tears from her eyes. She would weep later. She would think later. Right now she had a job to finish.

After a check of the bathroom and the spare bedroom, she tucked her pistol back into its holster. The intruders had gone, probably some time ago. And the spare bedroom, which she and Isaac used as an office, appeared to be the least-disturbed room in the house. A few drawers stood open, one file had been riffled and emptied onto the floor, but apparently the burglars had realized that the couple kept nothing of monetary value in the desk.

She walked to the computer and stared at the keyboard. Had the perpetrators left fingerprints behind? Had they tried to access her computer files?

She heard the distant slam of a car door, then the crunch of boots upon glass. As a gruff voice called her name she stepped into the hall, her hands lifted.

"I'm all right, and the place is empty," she said, walking forward. The Shin Bet had sent an entire squad dressed in protective gear. Deputy Director Melman stood at the front of the pack.

"It looks like a simple burglary," she said, gesturing to the wreckage in the front room. "And they didn't find much. Isaac and I never keep cash in the house. There's a little television missing from the kitchen, and some jewelry from my bedroom . . ."

She looked up and saw a thought working in Melman's eyes. "Your computer?" he asked.

"It's still here, and it looks perfectly normal," she said. "But I didn't turn it on. You might want to dust the keyboard for fingerprints first."

"All your files were encrypted?"

She gave him a sour smile. "Everything except my personal financial records. My case files are encrypted, but if they got to my computer, they are probably accessing my bank account right now."

Melman gave her a smile of pure relief. "That's OK; you can alert the bank. And you're all right? You're sure?"

"I'm fine," she said, but suddenly her knees seemed to turn to water. She thrust out an arm to steady herself, and Melman caught her.

"It happens to the best of us," he said, smiling as he led her to the sofa. "First you run on adrenaline, but when that evaporates, you're left as limp as a noodle."

"Lovely." She pressed a hand to her forehead, realizing that a dull throb had begun to pound behind her right temple.

Melman cleared a space on the sofa for her, then gently pressed her down. "Did you call the police?"

"Not yet."

"We'll file the report. And I'll have one of our techs look at your computer. Maybe they didn't get that far."

He stared at her for a long moment, then reached up to pluck a strand of fiberfill from her hair. "You look beat. Hungry?"

She nodded, then shook her head. "I don't know. I think

so, but I'm not sure I can eat anything. I brought things for dinner, but I can't seem to remember where I dropped my shopping bag."

"Let me get you something. While we're out, I'll have a security team dust this place for prints. You come with me and try to forget about it, and we'll make this all go away."

Sarah swallowed hard, then nodded slowly. She wanted nothing more than to make the world go away, and if she left now she wouldn't have to face the sight of Binyamin's desecrated room.

Tomorrow, she'd close the door and concentrate on cleaning the rest of the house.

†

In a hidden basement room of Romulus's country chateau, Adam Archer bent over a sheaf of green-lined computer paper, his forehead wrinkled in thought. As someone flushed a toilet upstairs, the water pipes above Archer's head began to sing, momentarily covering the soft sounds of copiers, computers, and printers that blended together in a technological chorus.

"Are the files encrypted?" Archer asked the computer technician who sat before the mainframe.

"*Oui*, monsieur. All except the personal bank account records you have in your hand."

"I'm not interested in the bank accounts of military people. I already know what I'll find—a mortgage and not nearly enough income to recompense people who lay their lives on the line every day for the sake of national security."

The Frenchman ran his hands over the clattering keyboard. "I can break the code . . . but it will take time for me to find the proper keys. And there is no guarantee we will find anything interesting."

"What do you mean, keys?"

The man tugged on his ear. "Most computer encryption relies on a two-key cipher—two long numbers, one known to the sender, one to the receiver. What one key encodes, the other key decodes. This is a symmetric key cipher, and I will most likely be able to find it in these computer files. It is merely a matter of time. But I shall have to search through a record of every keystroke for a series of digits and test them—"

"I want you to break that code." Archer thrust the financial records of Sarah and Isaac Ben-David away and stared at the computer screen. "We must have access to the computers at the Shin Bet station, and it's a safe bet Sarah Ben-David has an access key on her home computer. Can you get me that key?"

The Frenchman made a face. "Oui, monsieur. I can do anything, given enough time. It is merely a matter of breaking these codes, then finding the repetitive keystrokes entered before a file is opened. The Israelis undoubtedly have fire walls to prevent hacking, but with the proper key, anything can be unlocked." He frowned. "Unless, of course, the Israelis are using double ciphers. That will be more difficult."

Archer drew a deep breath and crossed his arms. "Explain."

"For maximum security, each outgoing message might be encrypted twice—first with the sender's private key, then with the receiver's public key. When the message arrives, the receiver must decode the message twice, first using his own private key, then the sender's private key. These double ciphers are extremely confidential. If this woman has hidden her key in such a file, we will be unable to read it, even if we have the public keys of the sender and receiver. The only way to crack a two-key cipher is to guess all possible key combinations, and, well . . ." He shrugged. "I would have to set a computer to the task. Trying all possible forty-bit keys would take hours, or possibly days, but governments and banks routinely use 128-bit keys. It could take the fastest computer on earth *years* to unlock such a code."

"Just do it." Archer rapped on the desk with his knuckles, then backed against the wall and crossed his arms, watching the little man work. The Frenchman was supposed to be a computer genius, one of the best in the world, and it had cost Romulus a small fortune to install him in this hidden fortress of advanced computer technology. But what good was this expensive genius if he could not break into an Israeli housewife's home computer?

"Send word to me the moment you are successful," he said, turning to leave. "Romulus is very concerned about the Israeli operation, and I want no surprises. If the Shin Bet plans to put any roadblocks in our path, I want to know about those plans as soon as possible."

The little computer gremlin did not answer, but merely tugged on his earlobe and stared at the flashing screen.

TEN

SARAH STEPPED FROM THE BUS ONTO JAFFA ROAD AND wavered for a moment in the blinding sun. Her father's small apartment complex, which had been built on a hillside, rose before her like an ivory wedding cake. A pair of children played on the flat roof of the first apartment, and the sound of their laughter cascaded down toward her, reminding her of days long ago.

She was no longer a child, but when her father called, she answered. He was of the old school and she of the new, but she could not shake the age-old tradition of respect for parents.

She moved up the walkway, stepping aside to let an elderly lady pass. The woman didn't speak or even look up in gratitude, but lumbered ahead, her purse tucked tightly beneath her arm. Sarah shook her head and walked on by, understanding the woman's fear. Crime had escalated to alarming proportions in the past few months, and few elderly people felt safe venturing onto the streets even in daylight hours. If she did not have a gun resting in the holster beneath her jacket, Sarah might not have felt safe, either.

She wandered across a strip of grass bordering the apartment complex, then entered a shaded alcove before a bright red door. Even without the brass nameplate that read Rabbi Aaron Lerner, the mezuzah on the doorpost notified one and all that a religious Jew dwelt therein. There were many mezuzahs in this quarter, almost as many as one would find in the Mea She'arim, the quarter inhabited by the ultra-Orthodox. Her father considered himself to be modern Orthodox and often found himself torn between the values of the black-hatted haredim who clung to ancient traditions and the practicalities of the secular Jews who controlled the government and business.

She tugged on her skirt, then took a moment to run her hand through her hair. She could not appear before her father looking unhappy or sloppy—he would know in a moment that something was wrong, and what would she say? He knew, of course, that Isaac had been in Paris for three weeks. He knew about the break-in and that she had changed all the locks in the house. But he did not know about her nightmares or the late hours she'd been keeping at work. She had taken great pains to ensure that he would not know that she and Isaac had become as distant as strangers long before he left for Paris.

She pasted on a smile and knocked on the door. Her father answered almost immediately, then greeted her with an embrace. "My Sarah," he said, his dark eyes sweeping over her form as he pulled away. "You look tired. Are you working too hard?"

"No harder than usual, Papa." She rose on tiptoe to plant a kiss on his cheek, then moved inside. An elderly man sat at the large table occupying most of the living room space, and she recognized him as one of the elder members of her father's congregation. As always, several thick books lay on the table. She knew without looking that the men had been searching through Torah studies and thick commentaries.

"Sarah, you remember Yusef Levison?"

"I do." She smiled at the elderly man and inclined her head as a sign of respect. He lifted his hand in an absent gesture, then gently touched the edges of his white beard.

Sarah turned to her father. "You seem to be working hard."

"No harder than usual," he parroted, his tone light. He pulled out a chair for her, then paused behind it, as formally as if he were an old friend instead of her father. "Can I get you a cup of tea?"

"No, Papa, please sit down. I don't need anything." She waited until he took his chair, then she gently asked the question that had bothered her all morning. "I am curious, though, about why you needed to see me."

He leaned back and gave her a troubled smile. "I need to know something, and I hope you won't mind giving your father and Yusef Levison an honest answer. I don't want the story Shabak gives the public, Sarah. I want the honest truth, as much as you are able to tell us."

Tiny warning bells rang in her brain, but she fixed her father in a steady gaze. "Go on."

"It's about the Universal Network's identification chip." He paused and ran his hand over the open text on the table before him. "The haredim won't take the chip, you know. A few may be persuaded to accept an encoded identification card, but they would never agree to accept a chip implanted beneath the skin. Most of the people in my synagogue will also refuse."

Sarah tilted her head, a little surprised. Her thoroughly modern father, a leader among the Orthodox movement, had walked a dangerous tightrope to combine the nationalistic values of Zionism with the tenets of Orthodoxy. He kept a kosher kitchen, prayed three times a day, and always wore a *kippa*, or skullcap. Israeli tour guides were fond of telling tourists that the larger the kippa, the more Orthodox the wearer. Her father's kippa was not of the small knitted variety worn by men for whom religion was only a token exercise, nor did he wear the large black skullcap and black hats of the ultra-Orthodox. In all things he sought the middle road, so she had been certain that a tiny computer chip wouldn't violate his sense of ethics.

"For what possible reason would they refuse?" she asked, searching her brain. At times like this, she wished she had paid more attention to her Torah studies.

"Let me show you." Yusef Levison held up his arm, then tugged on his black sleeve. As he turned the flesh of his arm in her direction, she saw the inked numbers . . . and understood the reason for his reticence. He had been but a small boy when the Allies liberated the death camp at Auschwitz, but the scars still remained.

"With all due respect, Mr. Levison," she began, choosing her words carefully, "this is not a Holocaust. The captives in concentration camps had no choice but to accept those tattoos, but—"

Her father interrupted. "They were forced to accept those identifying marks, true. And yes, the Holocaust might have something to do with the resistance I sense among our people. But the real reason for our objection is rooted much deeper in history. Our sages have always looked upon marking or cutting the skin as an abomination. According to Maimonides, marking was the custom of the Gentiles who inscribed themselves for the worship of false gods. He implied that anyone who takes a mark is a slave enlisted for idol worship."

Sarah gave her father a look of utter disbelief. "Father, you're talking about an ancient culture," she said, a reproving tone in her voice. "No one is worshiping idols today. And the Americans and Europeans have used the identification chip for years."

"But now Adrian Romulus is taking it a step further," her father insisted. "He is insisting that our people follow the rest of the world like sheep."

"He's not insisting. It's voluntary."

"If he is not insisting now, he soon will be. History assures us that he will. Look at our past and consider the tyrants who have persecuted us. One after the other, they prove that the hunger for absolute power is insatiable."

Sarah bit back the argumentative words that rose to her tongue. She must be patient. The people of her father's and Yusef Levison's generation would never forget the Holocaust. They tended to regard every strong international leader as Hitler incarnate.

"Father," she began, speaking slowly, "the Jews of the Holocaust had no choice. But no one is forcing our people to take this identification chip. It is only a convenience."

"Look around you, girl!" Yusef Levison's thin hand slapped the table. "We cannot buy groceries at Sorek's market without the Universal Chip. Sorek is trying to win favor with the authorities, and no one without the identification chip is welcome to do business there. We cannot cash checks at the bank without the chip. If we cannot handle money without the chip now, how long will it be before we cannot buy and spend without it?"

Out of respect for her elder, Sarah remained silent, but she had to admit the old man had a point. The government directly deposited her paycheck into her bank account, and she paid for groceries with a debit card, so she had not stopped to consider that people like Yusef Levison still dealt with coin and paper currency. Many of the older people of her father's congregation still clung to the familiar shekel, yet within a few months the banks would not honor them without an implanted Universal Network identification chip. And it was only natural that merchants had begun to identify themselves with the Universal Network, for that organization offered exceptional incentives to businesses that joined.

"Well," she finally said, spreading her hands. "I do not know what to say. I respect your opinions, Mr. Levison, but I see no danger in the identification chip. What harm can an invisible microchip possibly do?"

"Sarah," her father's voice was faintly reproving, "you are thinking of physical harm. Consider for a moment that *spiritual* harm may be inflicted by such a mark. Those who take the identification chip must also sign a statement of cooperation, no? And we are to be loyal to God first and foremost. Besides, the prohibition against the cutting of the flesh did not originate with the sages, it came from the Almighty himself, blessed be he. In Leviticus 21:5, HaShem told our fathers, 'They shall not shave their heads, neither shall they shave off the corners of their beards, nor make any cuttings in their flesh.'"

Sarah stared at her father, not knowing how to respond. She had never been able to debate Torah with him, for in his eyes common sense could not refute anything God had commanded.

With a long, exhausted sigh, she pressed her hand to the table. "What would you have me do, Father?"

He leaned toward her, covering her hand with his own. "Do not take the identification chip, Daughter. No matter what happens, do not let Isaac take it, either. My soul trembles to think of how easily this system could fall into the hands of a future Hitler."

She closed her eyes, resigning herself to the foolish promise, then looked at her father and nodded gravely. "Thank you for your concern. I promise—no identification chip."

There was a short silence and her words seemed to hang there as if for inspection, then her father and Yusef Levison smiled in approval.

"*Al-hámdu li-llá*," murmured the old man.

"Thanks be to God," her father echoed, his eyes soft with concern. "Thank you, my Sarah."

†

A week later, Sarah stepped back from the bureau and studied her face in the mirror. How pale her skin looked! Her eyes were too dark in her face, and, despite her careful makeup application, dark pockets lay beneath her eyes. Would Isaac notice? Would he guess that she had not been sleeping well?

She ran a brush through her hair, then reached for her lipstick and swiped another stroke across her lips. The color seemed to help, so she gave the mirror a practice smile, then backed away again, a little surprised by her own behavior. She was behaving like a sixteen-year-old on her first date with a new boyfriend, not a thirty-year-old who'd been married over four years. Even though an entire month had passed since she'd seen Isaac, in the early years of their marriage work separated them for longer periods. When they came together again, it always seemed as if no time at all had passed . . .

So why were her hands trembling?

It wasn't like they hadn't spoken since he left for Paris. Isaac called at least twice a week and asked about the neighbors and her work. Then, after she assured him that all was well, he spoke in guarded tones about Romulus and the progress of the Universal Network. She knew the information he shared was public knowledge and freely available on the Internet, but he seemed to take pleasure in telling her about the Universal Network's success in Africa, Mexico, and South America. The European Union Army had been completely reoutfitted as the Universal Force, he told her, and in a spirit of ecumenicalism, the World Council of Churches had recently changed its name to the Universal Faith Movement, with Adrian Romulus named as its titular head. In an effort to purge the world of old-fashioned intolerance and what Romulus called "religious apartheid," this religious movement had united all faiths into one belief system. Religious Jews, however, had been exempted according to terms in the recent peace accord.

The United States had joined the Universal Network, Isaac told Sarah, and Canada had followed almost immediately. China remained a problem, as did several African countries, but Romulus was working on the problem of compliance . . .

As she listened to Isaac share details that revealed not one shred of new information, Sarah wryly thought that

Shabak had mishandled a golden opportunity when they arranged to have her husband appointed to this liaison position. They had hoped that his loyalty to his wife might be useful in gleaning useful details about Romulus's intentions for Israel, but they hadn't known that Isaac's spousal loyalty had faded months ago.

After sharing the obvious, Isaac always dutifully inquired about her health and her work. She gave him obvious facts, too. Lily was well, the Arnans were fine, the weather was turning cool, and the tourists were out in force.

She did not mention the break-in. She didn't want to worry him, and she didn't want him to come galloping home when his presence wouldn't change a single aspect of the situation. The intruder had not returned, and, if the truth were known, Sarah reasoned that she was as well equipped to handle an intruder as Isaac. She carried a gun and knew how to use it, and she was nobody's fool.

That's why she couldn't explain her anxiety about this dinner. In an effort to keep the situation calm and pleasant, she had invited Isaac's father to dinner as well, on the pretext of giving him a chance to visit with his long-absent son. The men would talk archeology at dinner, and their banter would cover the awkward silences that routinely fell between Sarah and Isaac these days.

She went to the kitchen and peeked at the roast lamb in the oven, then swiped at the counter with a wet cloth. Her father would frown at her nonkosher kitchen, but he had never tried to balance a busy military career with the demands of marriage and . . . *motherhood.*

The word ambushed her consciousness before she could prepare, but she pressed her lips together and slammed the palm of her hand against the refrigerator, beating back the attack with a barrage of pain against her own flesh. As she pulled away, she turned her thoughts toward the fresh agony and refused to consider the old.

Motherhood no longer mattered. Her days of nurturing and tenderness had passed away with Binyamin. She felt no maternal urges now; she felt little other than a dogged determination to do her job and do it well. All she wanted was to earn respect from her peers and do her part to help guide Israel into a new and strangely different era.

She flinched as the front door buzzer set Lily to barking. Of course Isaac would have to use the buzzer—she'd changed all the locks. He was probably standing on the porch with his suitcase, wondering if the cab had dropped him at the wrong house.

She hurried forward, smoothing her stinging palm on her slacks, then opened the front door. Her careful smile cracked in relief when she saw Danny Melman standing on the porch.

"Director Melman?"

He flashed a smile, then waved a folder before her startled eyes. "I hate to bother you, Sarah, but I thought you ought to have this information. It came over the wires about ten minutes ago."

"You were at the office on Shabbat?" She cringed inwardly when surprise echoed in her voice.

The tip of Melman's nose went pink, but she couldn't tell if he was embarrassed because he'd been working on a religious holiday or because he had nothing better to do than go to the office on his day off. "I had some important work to do," he told her, still looking somewhat abashed. "And I like working on Saturday. It's quiet."

"I'm sorry—I didn't mean anything by the comment."

Sarah wavered, not certain whether she should just take the file or invite him in, but he settled the question for her. "As long as I was coming over here, I thought I'd take a look to make sure your locks are tight," he added. "I still shudder when I think about what might have happened if you had surprised the intruders who broke into your house."

How could she refuse that kind of gallantry? "That's very kind." She stepped aside and welcomed him with a smile as she held Lily's collar. Melman was a tall man and seemed suddenly taller when he filled the small space that served as her foyer. His brow lifted when he spied her dining room table set for three.

He looked at her, his eyes direct and questioning. "I'm sorry. Are you expecting guests?"

"Isaac's coming home." Her words came out hoarse, forced through a constricted throat. "I expect him and his father any time now."

"Then I'll just have a quick look at the locks and be on my way." With the efficient air of a law enforcement officer, Melman walked through the kitchen, inspected the back door's deadbolt, then moved into the living room. Driven by curiosity and a desperate need for attention, Lily followed him.

He paused by the sliding doors that opened to the courtyard. "These doors are a disaster waiting to happen, you know," he said, jiggling the sliders on their track. "Any determined thief could take these things down in a flash."

"I'm hoping no one will be that determined." Sarah leaned against the wall and smiled. "Since they found nothing of value here last time, I'm hoping all the street punks know I'm broke. I don't think they'll be back."

Melman grunted, then turned to face her. "I'll be honest—there's another reason for my visit. I've noticed that
lately you seem . . . a little distracted. Are you really all right?
If the break-in is bothering you, I could arrange to have a
guard posted outside—"

Sarah lifted her hand and managed a laugh. "There's no
need for anything so drastic. Break-ins are common these
days, so I don't expect special treatment. And I can take care
of myself."

"Then"—his gaze dropped like a stone—"is something
else troubling you?"

Sarah closed her eyes. She would love to confide in someone safe, but she wasn't sure the deputy director was an
appropriate choice. Yet she had no women friends outside the
office, she refused to burden her friends *within* the office, and
she couldn't tell her father without breaking his heart. No one
in her life would want to know about the cold wasteland her
marriage had become.

"There is something," she began, staring at her hands,
"but it's personal, and I'm trying to come to terms with it."
She drew a deep breath and forbade her voice to tremble. "I
just need a little time . . . and something to keep me busy. I
get lonely if I sit around and think too much."

"I understand loneliness."

"You do?" She caught his gaze for a moment, then broke
eye contact, her gaze drifting off to safer territory. Danny
Melman seemed the epitome of confident competence, and he
was all she had ever wanted in a boss. Could he be all she
needed in a friend?

He coughed slightly and extended the file. "Well, this is
what I wanted to give you—the computer guru's report. No

files on your hard drive were tampered with, but the registry log did record a start-up at 10:43 A.M. that day. I'm assuming you were at work by that time."

Sarah opened the file and stared at the report, her mind working. "Yes, I'm always at work by nine. So if they turned the computer on at 10:43—"

"The log says the machine shut down at 10:48. So apparently they booted the machine up, took a quick look around, and decided you didn't have anything worth taking."

Looking up, Sarah saw something moving behind his eyes. "What aren't you telling me?"

Melman shifted his weight, obviously uncomfortable. "Well, if we're talking someone more sophisticated than street thugs, there are things they could do even in so short a time. In five minutes they could download the entire contents of your hard drive if they wanted to. So, just in case, the computer guys are going to install a new fire wall on our proxy server. They're thinking that all the damage in your home could have been intended to distract us and cover up their primary target—your computer."

Sarah's thoughts raced. "Why would anyone want to access *my* computer? If they wanted access to Shin Bet, there are a thousand easier targets."

"But only one Shin Bet agent is closely associated with the Universal Force." Melman leaned back against the wall and folded his arms, a watchful fixity in his face. "Don't forget about your husband's new position. *He* may have been the target. They may have wanted to pull his files off the machine. We just don't know."

Sarah turned the thought over in her mind. Isaac? His work in Paris seemed miles away, but Melman had made a good point. The invasion had occurred after he left for Paris, so someone might have hoped to steal his files, his passwords, or even his e-mails to his wife . . . if he had been thoughtful enough to send any.

Sarah dismissed that chafing thought and looked up at her boss. "I encrypt everything that has to do with my work," she said, thinking hard. "So if they did copy my hard drive, they won't be able to break the code."

"Never say never." Smiling, Melman straightened and came toward her, then lifted his hand and trailed his fingers along her cheek. "Nothing's impossible anymore, Sarah. Never forget that."

She stiffened at his touch. He never touched her in the office, never came this close. She stood without moving, locked in a paralysis of disbelief while his gaze traveled over her face and searched her eyes.

The front door buzzed again. Lily sprang toward the foyer, her tail wagging.

With a sigh of gratitude, Sarah looked away. "That must be Isaac or his father."

"Say no more. I'll be going."

He spoke gently, as if assuring her that he did not want to cause trouble or put her in an awkward situation, yet she heard no trace of uncertainty in his voice. Danny Melman excelled and succeeded in everything he did, and with that one touch, Sarah intuited that he intended to succeed with her, too. He was an expert at reading people, and he had read her like a book. He knew her marriage was dead, and he knew her husband hadn't been home in over a month . . .

She lowered her eyes as she moved toward the door, praying that Isaac wouldn't notice the blush that burned her cheeks. But it wasn't Isaac—Ephraim Ben-David and another man Sarah had never met stood on the porch in an awkward silence. Director Melman stood behind Sarah as she made hurried introductions, then Ephraim introduced his companion as Dr. Thomas Parker, an archeologist from America.

"A pleasure to meet you," Melman said, stepping through the doorway. "*Aleichem shalom* to you both."

As Melman moved down the sidewalk to his car, her father-in-law turned to her. "A friend, Sarah?"

"My boss," she answered. She tapped the folder in her hand. "He had to bring me an important report."

"Ah," Ephraim said, moving into the house, "that explains it."

But it didn't. With crystal clarity, Sarah realized that Melman didn't have to bring the report. He had come to her home, on his own and on his day off, to check on her welfare . . . and to tell her, however subtly, that her marriage was so obviously dead that he felt at liberty to advance.

Something clenched in her stomach. As Ephraim and the American struggled to move past Lily's enthusiastic greeting, Sarah turned toward the door to hide the look of pain that surely filled her eyes.

"Sarah," Ephraim called, his voice seeming to come from miles away. "I hope an extra guest will not inconvenience you. You are such a gracious hostess, and Thomas and Isaac have met before—"

She forced an answer through her thick throat. "It's no trouble. I'll just set another place." Leaving the dog to entertain her guests, she hurried toward the kitchen, grateful to have something to do with her hands.

ELEVEN

ISAAC SLIPPED HIS KEY INTO THE LOCK AND TURNED, BUT the mechanism did not give. Perplexed, he dropped his suitcase and pulled the key from the door, then noticed that the shiny brass lock did not match the dull color of the key in his hand.

A new lock. Why?

He pressed the buzzer, and in a moment heard the muffled sound of a male voice. Stiffening in surprise, he glanced around to be certain he had approached the right house, then the door opened.

Isaac gaped at his father.

"My son!" Careful not to spill the drink in his hand, Ephraim Ben-David held out one arm in greeting. "Welcome home!"

Isaac stepped into his father's embrace, patted him quickly, then picked up his suitcase and moved inside the foyer. The house seemed smaller than he remembered, but after the spacious rooms of Romulus's chateau, he suspected anything would seem small and cramped.

Lily stood at his feet, her front paws clicking the wooden

floor in a tap dance of canine delight. Isaac stooped to rub her silky ears. "Has Sarah, um—"

"Sarah's in the kitchen, polishing up a leg of lamb or something. Whatever it is, it smells heavenly, and we are so hungry we were about to start without you."

We? Isaac shoved his suitcase into a corner and peered into the living room. A tall, familiar man sat on the sofa, and he stood as Isaac approached. Lost for a moment as he mentally shifted between Paris and Israel, Isaac searched his memory for the man's name and came up with it just as the fellow thrust out his hand. "Thomas Parker. It's good to see you again, Major."

"Call me Isaac. And the pleasure's mine."

Isaac felt his mouth twist in bitter amusement as he looked from Thomas to his father. He had been looking forward to time alone with Sarah, but obviously someone had made other plans. "So, Father," he said, gesturing to the sofa so the men would sit, "what's the occasion? I would imagine that nothing short of a miracle could tear you away from that dig."

"Sarah insisted." His father paused to sip at his wine glass. "She wanted to throw a little surprise dinner for you. A nice idea, if you ask me."

Isaac smiled. "Very nice."

"She's a lovely girl," Thomas Parker offered, crossing his long legs. "And so bright! Your father tells me she works for the Shin Bet."

"That's right." Isaac glanced over his shoulder toward the kitchen, where he heard the creak and slam of cupboards. "And if you gentlemen would excuse me, I'd like to say hello to her."

His father lifted his glass toward the kitchen. "A good idea, go. A man should speak to his wife before entertaining his guests."

Isaac stepped from the living room back into the foyer, then paused and glanced back. Was that a new rug by the sliding door? Or had she hung new curtains? Either something in the room was decidedly different, or he had been gone entirely too long . . .

Creeping into the kitchen, he saw Sarah at the sink with a roasting pan in her hands. As running water covered the sound of his approach, he drew near and slipped his hands around her waist, drawing her close. "It's good to be home," he whispered, leaning down to let his lips brush her ear.

A smile flickered over her lips as she lifted her head. "Hello, Husband." She lifted her suds-covered hands out of the water. "Forgive me for not greeting you properly, but I'm in a rush to get dinner on the table."

"All right." Awkwardly, he kissed her cheek, then released her and moved to the other side of the kitchen. Waiting to gauge her mood, he leaned against the counter and crossed his arms.

"So," she said, rinsing her hands, "how was your flight home?"

"Fine, nothing unusual."

"And the weather in Paris?"

"Cold, but normal for this time of year, they say. But I spent last week in Brussels. That's why I wasn't able to call you."

She shrugged as if she hadn't noticed. "Busy?"

"Very busy. Romulus wanted me to see how well the Universal Network works in the European capital. There the

system works like a dream—all banking, government pro-
grams, educational institutions, and social welfare systems
are all monitored by the identification chip."

In the midst of reaching for a dishtowel, Sarah froze suddenly. "Do the Europeans all have the microchip?"

Isaac frowned. "The Universal Chip?"

She took the dishtowel and slowly turned to face him,
keeping her eyes downcast. "Is that what they're calling it?"

"Of course." Isaac shifted his weight. "It's really no big
deal. Europe has been using the identification chip for nearly
two years. Most people consider it a great convenience to be
associated with the Universal Movement—even an honor."

For the first time since his return, Sarah looked directly
into his eyes. "You're kidding."

"Why would I?"

Her eyes took on a distant look, and he knew her attention had just left him. Her thoughts were now centered on
some project or piece of intelligence that had crossed her desk
in the last few weeks . . .

He stepped forward and caught her waist again, pulling
her to him, face to face. "Sarah," he whispered, staring into
her eyes to forcibly draw her from wherever she had gone, "I
was hoping we would have this night together, alone. I have
meetings in the morning and have to return to Paris tomorrow afternoon."

The wariness in her eyes froze into a darkness as cold as
the bottom of a well, though her lips stayed curved in a calm
smile. "Oh?"

For the first time he noticed the hollows beneath her eyes,
dark, bruised-looking circles. She hadn't been sleeping.

"I'm sorry you have to go so soon," she said, looking

away as she moved out of his grasp, "but that's not my fault, is it?"

He faltered in the sudden silence and stepped back when she passed and lightly pressed a hand to his chest. "Now go and entertain your father while I get dinner on the table. I know he wants to talk to you."

Stunned by the coolness with which he'd been rejected, Isaac returned to the living room and his guests.

†

Sarah kept a watchful eye on her guests' plates and refilled them until each man assured her he could eat no more. She said little during dinner, but played the part of hostess, preferring to hide her anxiety and hurt under a concealing apron of domesticity. Her disguise must have worked, for while the men ate and talked Isaac firmly avoided her gaze, preferring to expend his attention upon his father and their American guest.

The dinner conversation was pleasant enough. Isaac politely asked about the Temple construction (about which, Sarah suspected, he knew far more than his father) and listened patiently as Ephraim extolled the wonder of seeing the third Temple rise from the northwest corner of the Temple Mount as the Universal Force guards stood watch. Fortunately, the construction was proceeding without interference from the Muslims.

Even prior to Gogol's Invasion, Ephraim reported, archeologists and Hebrew University physicists had conducted months of research to compute the Temple's proper location, using angles of line-of-sight measurements between the

Mount of Olives and the eastern court of the Temple where the Great Altar once stood. This work confirmed that the bedrock identifiable within a small cupola located 330 feet from the Dome of the Rock had been the foundation stone within the Holy of Holies. When workers removed the surface flagstones that had been put in place centuries before, they had gazed in awe at the huge foundation stones of the previous Temple.

"Interestingly enough," Thomas Parker said, lifting his glass, "the site fulfills several Old Testament Scriptures that predict the Messiah's return. There's a verse in Ezekiel that makes it clear the Messiah will enter the Temple Mount and then go directly into the rebuilt Temple by way of the sealed Eastern or Golden Gate, which he will somehow open."

Ephraim rolled his eyes. "Listen to the Gentile expert! Like a child with bucket on the beach, he has been digging for treasure in the Bible. He's about to drive me crazy with his notions."

Sarah took advantage of the humorous moment to enter the conversation. "The Messiah," she said, smiling at the American, "will not be a miracle worker, Mr. Parker. You may be applying a Christian connotation to the Messiah, but we are not expecting a son of God to come and open the Eastern Gate. That wall has been sealed for generations."

The archeologist shot her a lopsided smile. "If he's not the Son of God, why follow him?"

Not wanting to embark upon an often-combustible topic, Sarah looked at her plate, so Parker looked to Isaac for an answer.

"Don't look at me." Isaac threw up his hands. "*She's* the rabbi's daughter."

"You'll have to give me the answer then." Parker set his glass on the table and smiled at Sarah with warm spontaneity. "Please. I'm really curious. I find this project fascinating."

Resigned to the inevitable, Sarah drew a deep breath. "The Messiah, or *mashiach,* will not be our savior in the sense that you probably understand the word. He will be a great political leader descended from King David. He will be well versed in Jewish law and observant of its commandments. He will be charismatic and able to inspire others to follow him. He will be a great military leader, and he will win battles for Israel. He will be a great judge who will make righteous decisions." She frowned and looked across the table at her father-in-law. "Have I forgotten anything?"

"Just one thing." Ephraim smiled at his younger associate. "He will be a human being, not a god."

"So why," Thomas asked, looking at Sarah, "are you so sure that Jesus of Nazareth *wasn't* the Messiah? After all, there are dozens of churches in Jerusalem alone, and they're all convinced—"

"Jesus," Ephraim interrupted, his voice flat, "did not fulfill the mission of the mashiach as it is described in the Torah. According to the Scriptures, the mashiach must bring about the political and spiritual redemption of the Jewish people by bringing the nation back to Israel and restoring Jerusalem. Jesus didn't. The mashiach will establish a government in Israel that will be the center of all world government, both for Jews and Gentiles. Jesus didn't do that. The mashiach will restore the religious court system and establish Jewish law as the law of the land. Jesus didn't do that, either. The mashiach will rebuild the Temple and reestablish Temple worship."

Parker chuckled with a dry and cynical sound. "From

what you've just told me, Adrian Romulus might well be the messiah. After all, there would be no Temple today without him, right?"

Sarah turned to her husband as a small strangled sound escaped Isaac's throat. His face twisted in a small grimace of pain, as though someone had suddenly struck him across the face.

"Perhaps," Sarah said, looking from her husband to her father-in-law, "we shouldn't discuss this. I wouldn't want to offend Mr. Parker if he considers himself a Christian."

"I never said I was a Christian," Parker countered. "But I've been reading the Bible lately, and I find all the stories and prophecies absolutely mesmerizing. I'm just trying to under-stand more."

Ephraim's mouth twisted in a wry grimace. "Tell her why, Parker. Tell her the real reason you're so curious."

Parker's smile deepened into laughter. "It's no secret. I'm looking for the ancient Temple treasure."

Sarah glanced at Isaac, but his eyes were distant and un-focused, his thoughts apparently a million miles away. As always, he had left her alone to handle things.

She turned to her guests and lifted a brow. "I'll admit it— I'm lost. What ancient Temple treasure are you talking about?"

"The treasure of the Copper Scroll," Ephraim said, pulling an after-dinner cigar from his pocket. "It is pure myth, and my friend Parker knows I speak the truth."

"I most certainly do not." The American's eyes blazed with the fire of enthusiasm, brighter than the light from the dinner candles. "I believe the treasure exists and that we shall soon find it. The time is right, can't you feel it? I believe"—he hesitated and gripped the edge of the table—"I believe in God just enough to feel that this is what he wants. For years, mankind has ignored him, but now you are rebuilding his Temple. So he will surely want the Temple treasures to be discovered."

Ephraim gave his colleague a smile that was ten percent patronization and ninety percent challenge. "Believing in God 'just enough' is a dangerous thing, my friend. He is not someone to be trifled with."

Thomas Parker shook his head, but kept grinning. "I don't know how to explain it. I just have this feeling. The Temple treasures are out there, the Copper Scroll holds the key, and"—he paused for dramatic effect—"I believe I will find them."

Ephraim snorted with the half-choked mirth of a man who seldom laughs, while Isaac pressed his lips together. Something had brought him back to the conversation, and Sarah knew the impulse to explode in laughter was just below the surface of his calm. Amusement sparkled in his eyes like diamonds.

"You have big dreams, my friend," Isaac remarked, reaching for his glass.

"Is my dream any bigger than that of a third Temple?" Parker countered. "For years, no one could imagine a Temple coexisting on the Temple Mount with an Arab mosque. Before that, no one could imagine that tiny Israel could defeat a Russian-Arab coalition." He pounded the table. "Shoot, years ago no one could even imagine the Berlin Wall coming down. These are exciting times, my friends, and the word *impossible* is best left to our unenlightened forefathers. Nothing is impossible for us now!"

Sarah smiled at her guest. "Tell me about this Copper

Scroll. You forget, I didn't grow up in a household of archeologists."

While Isaac and Ephraim grumbled good-naturedly, the
American leaned closer to Sarah. "In 1952, the Copper Scroll
was discovered among the caves near the Dead Sea. After they
were painstakingly unwrapped and deciphered, archeologists
discovered that the Copper Scroll contained a list—an inven-
tory—of golden treasures . . . along with the descriptions of
the spots where they were hidden."

"And, of course," Sarah offered, "no one alive today can
identify exactly where those hiding places are."

"Unfortunately, you are correct." Thomas's countenance
fell. "The towns and villages referred to in the list have disappeared without a trace. One chest, for instance, filled with
treasure and sixty talents of silver, is listed as being hidden
under the entrance of the upper pit at Mount Gerizim. But
even Mount Gerizim, a location that would appear to be
unmistakable and unmovable, cannot be definitely identified.
The commonly accepted Mount Gerizim was a holy place for
the Samaritans, and it's highly unlikely that the Jews would
hide part of their Temple treasure there. There was another
Mount Gerizim near Jericho, so that's a possibility. But even
if we found the correct Mount Gerizim, how on earth am I
supposed to find one pit on a hilltop dotted with *dozens* of
pits and cisterns?"

"If the treasure is hidden as far away as Mount Gerizim,"
Isaac interjected, "why do you think the Temple reconstruction will help you find it?"

The American did not hesitate. "Because the greater part
of the Copper Scroll's treasure was deposited in and around
Jerusalem. Modern Jerusalem sits upon a vast network of

ancient underground tunnels and chambers, many of them constructed in biblical times, and hundreds of them within the walled city have been sealed off from exploration until recently." His blue eyes gleamed as he explained, "For instance, one notation tells us there is a pitcher containing a scroll buried at three cubits in the northern entrance of the platform of the Double Gate."

"I know that gate." Ephraim stroked his beard. "The high priest and his party went through that gate to the Mount of Olives to sacrifice and burn the red heifer. It is logical, I suppose, to assume that a sacred pitcher might be stored in a cavity beneath that gate, but you will never find it. A Muslim cemetery blocks the approach."

"Nothing is impossible anymore." The American grinned. "All in all, there are two dozen potential treasure locations situated within the Temple area. And in the new spirit of cooperation between the Jews and Muslims, I hope to find all the treasures of the Copper Scroll."

"Fascinating," Sarah murmured.

Isaac pushed his plate away. "Now that dinner is done, can Sarah bring anyone coffee from the kitchen?" He did not look at her, but at their guests. "Coffee, Father? Mr. Parker?"

"That would be nice," Ephraim added.

Sarah nodded abruptly and went into the kitchen, sealing her lips as she went. Isaac had come home for only a few hours, paused to tell her he was unhappy because she had wanted to surprise him, and now he was treating her like a housekeeper. Fine. She would act like a housekeeper, then, and let him spend his entire time at home with the men.

Isaac was in the midst of a story when she returned with a tray loaded with four steaming cups of coffee.

"And so," he said, barely glancing at her when she set the tray on the table next to him, "the legend states that whoever possesses the spear will control the world. A fairly insane assumption, of course, but Hitler believed and took pains to capture and secure the spear. Napoleon also believed and demanded the spear after the Battle of Austerlitz. He never received it, however, because secret operatives smuggled it out of Nuremberg and hid it in Vienna just to keep it out of his hands. They didn't want anything—mystical or not—to fuel his tyrannical ambition."

Sarah offered coffee to Ephraim and Thomas Parker. "I assume we're no longer talking about the Copper Scroll."

"Quite right." Her father-in-law smiled at her. "Isaac says Adrian Romulus sent him to inquire about the Spear of Longinus, an ancient relic presently on display at the Hapsburg Treasure House in Vienna. It's an obscure weapon with an incredible legend attached to it."

Thomas Parker gave Sarah a sympathetic smile. "I'd never heard the story, either. European history is not my forte."

"It's a simple story, really." Ephraim pushed his glasses up the bridge of his nose, then folded his hands on the table. "They say the spear, also called the Maurice Lance, is the blade used to pierce the side of Jesus of Nazareth at his crucifixion. The spear was passed from monarch to monarch through the ages, eventually ending up with King Otto, a German who gained an amazing victory over the Mongolian armies whose infamous mounted archers devastated Europe. The next recorded mention of the relic was in the ceremony when Otto knelt in Rome before Pope John XII to be established as holy Roman emperor. In that rite, the pope touched Otto on the shoulder with the spear."

"It is mentioned several times in the history of pre-Christian Rome," Isaac added, looking at Parker. "They say that Mauritius, commander of the Theban Legion, held the spear within his grasp as he was beheaded for refusing to worship the pagan gods of Rome. The entire Theban Legion, all Christian, stood under penalty of death for refusing to worship the emperor's pagan gods. As a devout Christian, Mauritius knelt before the ranks of his men to offer himself in their place. Inspired by his example, however, his men threw down their weapons and knelt to bare their necks for slaughter. The emperor Maximian, fool that he was, massacred the entire legion as an offering to his gods."

"And as you might expect," Ephraim added, smiling at Sarah, "this act so impressed the pagans of Rome that it was only a matter of time before the entire kingdom converted to Christianity."

"Amazing." Sarah shook her head. "I've never heard of this spear."

"I hadn't either, until Romulus asked me to prepare a report on it," Isaac said, directly meeting Sarah's gaze for the first time since dinner had begun. "But there's more. You're probably familiar with the story about Constantine the Great's victory at the Battle of the Milvian Bridge. According to legend, the night before, he dreamed that Christ told him to put the symbol of Christ, presumably a cross, on his soldiers' shields. He did and consequently won the battle." Isaac leaned forward with one arm upon the table. "What is *not* often reported is that Constantine carried the Spear of Longinus into that battle. He also held the spear at the first church council, the Council of Nicaea. He also reportedly carried the spear as he staked out the boundaries of Constantinople, the city he founded."

"Surely those events were nothing but coincidence," Parker said. "Constantine believed the legend, and his faith gave him confidence. It's just like my relationship with the Scriptures. I don't believe there's any real burning-bush kind of power there, but the accuracy of the archeological record has given me a great deal of confidence in the Bible as a historical document. I believe in it enough to stake my career upon it."

As Isaac rubbed his hand across his face, Sarah heard the faint rasp of his evening stubble. "I don't know what kind of power the spear wields, but I find it interesting that so many military men believed in it," he said. "According to history, Theodosius tamed the Goths with the spear, and Alaric the Bold claimed the spear after he sacked Rome in the fifth century. With the spear, Aetius and Visigoth Theodoric rallied Gaul to vanquish the barbarians at Troyes and turned back Attila the Hun. Justinian lifted the spear as a symbol of his authority when he exiled Greek scholars from his realm—a foolish mistake, perhaps, but his action did change the world. The Frankish general Karl Martel used the spear to lead his army to a miraculous victory over the Arabs at Poitiers, and Charlemagne founded his entire dynasty upon his confidence in the spear. In his forty-five-year-reign, he launched forty-four successful military campaigns. His attachment to the spear went far beyond mere belief—he insisted on sleeping with it within reach. When he accidentally dropped it while returning from his final victorious campaign, his subjects considered it an omen of tragedy and death . . . and time proved them right."

"Time can prove almost anyone right," Ephraim said, lifting a brow at his son. "Charlemagne had to die eventually."

Isaac shook his head. "There's more to it than mere circumstance, I think. Altogether, forty-five emperors between the coronation of Charlemagne and the fall of the old German empire possessed the spear. After that, the spear passed through the hands of five Saxon rulers, then the powerful Hohenstaufen emperors of Swabia. Frederick II prized the spear above all his possessions and made it the focal point of his life. From that point, the spear became part of the imperial regalia and was housed in an Austrian museum until Hitler became enamored of the legend and took possession of the spear. At a little past two on the afternoon of April 30, 1945, American forces led by Gen. George Patton discovered the spear in a locked vault within a secret underground bunker. At three-thirty on that same day, Adolf Hitler, who had just lost the spear and the war, committed suicide."

Intense interest glowed in Thomas Parker's eyes. "Where is the spear now?"

Isaac's mouth curved in a one-sided smile. "Back in Vienna's Imperial Palace . . . where I hope it will stay. The world has endured enough tumult and war."

"You are right, Son, of course," Ephraim said, nodding, "but we are not done with trouble. A resistance movement is growing in Jerusalem, and I've heard reports of similar opposition in other Israeli cities. Many Jews distrust your Adrian Romulus. They will not take his ID chip, nor do they wish to worship in his Temple." He shifted his gaze to Parker, the only Gentile at the table. "Rashi, one of our great medieval sages, insisted that the Temple must descend directly from heaven when the Messiah comes. On the other hand, other sages say God's command to build the Temple is irrevocable."

Sarah picked up her coffee cup and smiled at the American. "Do not be surprised, Mr. Parker. We Israelis have a difficult time agreeing on most things. A recent newspaper poll indicated that though most of us think it is time to rebuild, many thousands still believe we should wait for the Messiah."

"This resistance"—Isaac's brows puckered with thought—"how pronounced is it? Romulus needs to know."

"You know the old saying—get two Jews together and you will have three differing opinions," Sarah quipped, bringing her cup to her lips. "I don't think the resistance is serious, but it won't go away. My father himself is strongly against the Universal Chip. He says no Orthodox Jew will allow himself to be cut in such a way." She looked at her husband as she sipped her coffee, then lowered her cup. "Their resistance to the Temple is not important, is it? Won't Romulus understand that in Israel, extremist politics are nothing unusual?"

Isaac frowned and stared at the table. "It may not matter . . . yet. But Romulus may begin to think of resistance as a sign of disloyalty to the Universal Network. I know he's troubled about reports of those two men—"

"The ones who call themselves Moses and Elijah?" Ephraim interrupted.

Isaac nodded. "The same. They seem to foment rebellion wherever they go, and Romulus is afraid the resistance will increase if they are not silenced. If the world does not learn to pull together, we shall pull apart. The Universal Movement cannot work unless every country, every government, every individual is united in purpose and spirit."

He looked at Sarah then, and even though they had been separated for weeks, she knew what he was thinking—that Shabak would know all about the troublesome prophets and might be persuaded to help Romulus contain their rabble-rousing. She lowered her gaze to her coffee cup. He couldn't ask her for help without asking her to divulge classified information. And at the beginning of their marriage, they had agreed that work-related secrets were off-limits for discussion.

Perhaps, she thought, cradling the cup against her palm, if they had not established so many limits then, they would not be dealing with so many now.

†

As Sarah cleared the table, Isaac walked his father and Thomas Parker to the door.

"Thank you for a delightful evening," Parker said, stepping onto the front porch as he pulled a cigar from his shirt pocket. "I can't remember when I've enjoyed such a stimulating discussion." He glanced over Isaac's shoulder toward the kitchen. "And be sure to thank your wife again for me. She's a lovely woman . . . and quite perceptive. A rare treasure."

Night had fallen while they ate. The air over Jerusalem had cleared, and the stars blazed like diamonds in a sky as cold as airless space.

Isaac's father stepped onto the porch, too, then turned and placed his hand on Isaac's shoulder. "My son knows how blessed he is . . . and if he doesn't, I'd like to remind him." Isaac smiled in puzzlement as his father gestured toward the darkened street. "Parker, would you mind waiting in the car? I'd like a private word with my son."

Parker grinned and flashed Isaac an *uh-oh* look, then thrust his hands in his pockets and slouched away, whistling in the dark. Isaac waited until the lanky archeologist had been engulfed by the night, then turned to his father. "Something wrong?"

"Perhaps." Lines of concentration deepened along his father's brows. "I am worried about you, Isaac. I know you are away from home for long periods of time . . . How has this affected your marriage? Are you and Sarah as close as you ought to be?"

Isaac crossed his arms. "Sarah and I are accustomed to the demands of our work. This assignment has been inconvenient, but no worse than others. Sarah stays busy. Sometimes I doubt she even misses me."

"I am not speaking to her now—I am speaking to you. Tonight I watched you. You scarcely glanced in her direction. I could sense tension in the air."

Isaac's voice went hoarse with frustration. "We had a bit of a disagreement in the kitchen. It's nothing. It will pass."

His father did not answer immediately, but his eyes filled with infinite distress. Finally he said, "I know about marriage; your mother and I were not perfect. But we made a pact—we never went to bed angry with one another."

"Well, Father," Isaac struggled to lighten his voice, "if you will leave and give me some time with my wife, perhaps I can emulate your example."

"I'm not finished." His father's sparkling brown eyes sank into nets of wrinkles as he forced a smile. "You were very young, only two, so I doubt you remember when your mother lost the baby that would have been your brother."

Isaac's body stiffened in shock. "A baby?"

Ephraim stroked his beard. "Yes. A stillborn child. Your mother enjoyed a healthy pregnancy, and everything seemed fine. We went to the hospital together, and then the baby was born with the cord wrapped around his neck. An act of God, they said. A tragic accident, they said. But it broke our hearts."

"I never knew," Isaac said after a long pause. "I don't remember."

His father shook his head. "We didn't want to burden you with the story. But for a month or two after the baby's birth, your mother and I went through a difficult time. Deep inside, I wanted to blame someone for the accident—the doctor, the nurses, even your mother. She wanted to blame someone, too, but mine was the only name on her list. Finally we realized that tragedy had tremendous power—it would either tear us apart or bind us together. We made the choice, a conscious choice, to cleave to one another."

Like blood out of a wound, silence welled from the darkness and covered the porch, but Isaac heard the unspoken lesson clearly: *You and Sarah must come together, or you will be torn apart.*

"Sarah and I are doing fine, Father." He tried to smile, but the corners of his mouth only wobbled uncertainly.

His father opened his mouth, then hesitated, closing his eyes. "Perhaps I shouldn't say anything . . . but if it were me, I would want to know."

Isaac's heart tightened in sudden anxiety. "Know what?"

His father's eyes opened. "When Parker and I arrived, a man was here. Sarah introduced him, but I sensed that she was uncomfortable doing so."

"Who?" Isaac forced out the word.

"His name was Danny Melman."

Isaac slumped in relief. "That's Sarah's boss, the deputy director. Sarah has worked with him for years."

His father's left brow rose. "In all those years, I have never heard about a deputy director coming to your house."

The thought froze in Isaac's brain. Neither had he. In fact, Melman had no reason to come to the house unless . . .

"Take heed, my son." Ephraim's hand fell upon Isaac's arm. "Love your wife and do whatever it takes to win her back. Do not let her slip away through neglect."

And then, without another word, Isaac's father turned and disappeared into the night.

TWELVE

FOR ISAAC, THE FOLLOWING MONTHS PASSED IN A flurry of activity. He spent far more time in Paris than at home and began to think of his French landlady at the Fleurs de Soleil as sort of a maiden aunt. The wheels came off his suitcase; his attaché developed that rough, worn look common on well-used leather. And his wife grew more distant.

Sarah was pleasant enough when he came home, of course, but he'd never known her to be inhospitable to anyone. She always greeted him with a brief hug and a kiss on the cheek, and together they would sip coffee and exchange safe pleasantries that touched neither her job nor his. He asked about her father and his; she asked about Paris and the appeal of French cooking. When fireworks launched from a naval destroyer in the Mediterranean Sea lit the night sky over a celebrating Tel Aviv on December 21, Isaac watched from his hotel room and realized that a full year had passed since Gogol's Invasion.

A full year. So much had happened in the past twelve months, not all of it good. Israel had celebrated a miraculous victory over her enemies, and she had seen her Temple begin to rise from the holy mount. But she had also suffered severe drought and famine as well as internal strife. The two prophets continued to spread their message of judgment and repentance throughout Israel, and from the latest reports, Isaac feared their influence was spreading.

Springtime, with its festivals of Purim, Pesach, and Shavuot, came and went. The heavy winter rains that usually soaked the Holy City did not come, however, and the usual variety of colorful Jerusalem flowers failed to bloom in April and May. The *hamsin*, a wind from the Sahara Desert, turned its hot breath upon the city and often sent the temperatures soaring to over one hundred degrees Fahrenheit. Human bodies could not cope, and cases of colds and flu filled the hospitals and physicians' offices.

For Isaac, the days fell like leaves from an oak tree, one after the other, virtually indistinguishable. He usually awoke in a nondescript hotel room, then dressed and joined Romulus for a press conference in some international city, then rode to the airport where a jet whisked him and Romulus's entourage to the next stop on the itinerary.

Though Romulus's position as president of the Universal Movement seemed completely secure, he behaved as though he were campaigning for global office, crisscrossing the globe to make speeches, deliver humanitarian aid, and pose for the hungry lenses of television reporters and newspaper photographers. Isaac found himself invited to accompany Romulus on more occasions than he would have believed possible at the outset of his appointment. Apparently Romulus trusted him and often requested that Isaac stand in the background when the cameras began to flash. Isaac obliged, of course, and suspected that his presence might be calculated to win over the still-stubborn element of Israelis who refused to report for their identification chips.

When it came to compliance with the standards required by the Universal Network, Israel lagged far behind the rest of the world. All Temple workers, Israelis and foreigners, had received identification chips, but Romulus worried incessantly that some unidentified saboteur or terrorist might infiltrate the construction area. And work on the Temple, Romulus explained, deserved the highest priority. Why couldn't every citizen of Israel understand that the chip was necessary for security reasons?

On a warm afternoon in June, just after they had disembarked at the Brussels airport, Romulus stopped before a television suspended from the ceiling in the airport gate area. As CNN reported live from Bethlehem, the television camera panned a demolished building licked by angry orange flames. An expression of hurt and bewilderment crossed Romulus's face as he watched, and something in the expression caught Isaac by surprise. He had seen many emotions cross Romulus's face, but never before had he seen the man looking in the least bit bewildered.

"No," Romulus groaned. He brought his hand to his neck as he stared at the screen. "Bethlehem! For what possible reason could the resistance want to bomb that city?"

Straining to hear over the noise of the airport, Isaac moved closer to the television. The newscaster was explaining that a truck loaded with explosives had detonated in the heart of the city only half an hour before, killing five children on a playground and sending at least thirty other people to the hospital.

The camera cut to a woman sitting behind a news desk,

her face as expressionless as a mask. "Officials are pointing fingers of accusation at the two demonstrators known as Moses and Elijah," the newscaster said. "They walked the streets of this quiet neighborhood several days last week, calling citizens to repent of their sin and turn to God. Though it has been confirmed that the two protestors were not in Bethlehem at the time of the explosion, it is believed they might have urged others to instigate acts of terror." The newscaster, a pretty brunette, stopped and shook her head slightly. "In this age of peace and universal unity it is hard to believe that old-fashioned intolerance and hate have not yet been eradicated."

"Those two will have to go."

Isaac looked up, not certain that he had heard Romulus correctly. The president had spoken in an odd, inflectionless voice, and the customary pleasant expression was missing from the curve of his mouth and the depths of his eyes.

Isaac lifted a brow. "I beg your pardon, sir?"

Romulus turned away as if he had not heard, then sauntered toward the moving walkway with long strides. As Isaac had suspected, a horde of reporters waited on the curb outside the building. When they spied Romulus, they ran forward, cameras and microphones ready.

"Mr. President! Mr. Romulus!"

Romulus stopped as the horde swarmed nearer. Isaac stepped back, allowing Romulus's security guards to form a protective phalanx around him, but then Isaac insinuated himself into the mob, wanting to listen.

Romulus nodded toward the first reporter. "You have a question?"

"Yes sir. What did you think when you heard that

Bethlehem had been bombed? Will this act of violence stall your efforts for peace in the Middle East?"

Romulus lifted his head as his brows drew together in an agonized expression. "I was devastated by the news, gentlemen, completely overwhelmed. Not many people know this, but I was born in that small city. My heart, even now, aches to think of that quiet little town in flames. You may be sure we will do all we can to find out who is responsible for this tragedy."

"How will you find the perpetrators?"

Romulus paused, tucked his hands behind his back, and glanced around as if he could find the resisters in the crowd. "As you know, citizens, we have encouraged the use of personal identification chips for every member of the human race." He gave the group a bleak, tight-lipped smile as the cameras flashed. "I'm afraid we may now have to *require* the Universal Chip as a means of ferreting out those who insist upon resisting the common good and our common goals. Everyone who is a law-abiding peace seeker will want to have this microchip, while those who are opposed to peace will fall outside the law. I must meet with my cabinet and speak with other national leaders, but I fully expect that we shall implement this plan within sixty days."

Romulus's faint smile held a touch of sadness. "All who are not for me shall be against me," he said, his voice ringing over the asphalt walkway. "A world divided against itself cannot stand. We must have peace . . . and have it we shall. I had hoped to eradicate the cancer of violence through peaceful means, but if we must take the scalpel to those who insist upon destruction, we shall not hesitate. We will cut them out from among us so that all men may live in peace."

Isaac squared his shoulders as Romulus held up his hand and moved away, drawing his entourage and the reporters after him. The action the president had just proposed seemed harsh in the light of all his talk about peace, but the man was right. The day of reckoning couldn't be postponed forever.

†

One month later, at 10:10 on a Monday morning in July, Isaac slipped into the chateau's conference room and quietly took a seat in a row of chairs behind the men who sat around the table. Romulus had called a meeting of his top advisers in order to prepare for his upcoming trip to Israel for the Temple dedication ceremony, and Isaac had been specifically asked to attend.

Charles, Romulus's butler, approached with a cup of coffee on a tray. Isaac accepted it, then peered around the butler standing at his side, determined not to miss another word of this important meeting. He had already made the mistake of coming late—he'd had problems finding a taxi at the bed-and-breakfast—but it would be a greater faux pas to miss some important detail and make an embarrassing blunder.

Romulus sat in the center of the long side of the table, flanked by his security chief, General Archer, and his minister of finance, a Frenchman Isaac had not yet had an occasion to meet. Elijah Reis stood at the head of the table, and he presently had the floor. Every eye but Romulus's was fixed upon him, and Isaac felt a sudden chill when he realized that Romulus was staring at *him*.

He looked at the European president, inclined his head slightly in apology for his tardiness, and sighed in relief when

Romulus nodded in return. After the exchange of that silent greeting, Romulus returned his attention to Elijah Reis.

"The highlight of the Temple dedication ceremony," Reis was saying, "will be the procession and placement of the ark of the covenant. The ark is the single most important article used in Temple worship, and its reinstatement will be tremendously significant to both religious and secular Jews. The ark was originally created during the first year of Israel's wandering in the wilderness, and, according to Jewish legend, God himself dictated the details for its construction. It is rumored to contain three objects: the rod used by Aaron, Israel's first high priest; a bowl of manna, the supposedly heaven-sent bread the Jews ate while wandering in the wilderness; and the two stone tablets on which Moses wrote the Ten Commandments. The ancient Jews believed so strongly in the power of the ark that the children of Israel carried it into battle in order to defeat their enemies."

"Talk about rallying around a national symbol," Archer said, looking around the table. "We know how inspiring the sight of a mere flag can be on a battlefield. This ark must have held those primitive people in complete thrall."

A smile crawled to Reis's lips and curved itself like a snake. "The ark was reported to have supernatural power," he said, crossing his arms over his chest. "Jewish Scripture records the story of a man who was instantly struck dead simply for reaching out to steady the ark when it nearly tipped over in transport." A flash of humor crossed Reis's face. "*He* believed it had power, and that belief ultimately killed him. But all the Jews felt the ark was holy. They believed the glory of their God, called the *Shekinah*, dwelt above the golden lid, also called the mercy seat."

"If it was such an important military talisman," Archer asked, "why did they hide it away in the Temple?"

Reis lifted one bony shoulder in a halfhearted shrug. "They say they hid it away because God commanded them to do so. Solomon built the first Temple and had the ark placed in the Most Holy Place. They organized a lavish ceremony, which won't be terribly different from the dedication we will attend next month. But by the time of the Temple, for reasons unknown, nothing remained inside the ark except the two tablets of stone. The ark rested in the Temple until the final years of King Solomon's reign. After that time, the Jewish Scriptures fall strangely silent about the artifact's fate. All we know for certain is that none of the Temple preparation organizations even attempted to reconstruct the ark. All of them sincerely believed it would be revealed and restored to its rightful place."

"As it will be." Romulus smiled and glanced around the room. "And we, my friends, have been invited to participate in the great ceremonial event to be held next month on the Temple Mount. My heart rejoices to know that we will be among those celebrating the Temple of the City of Peace."

A frown crossed Archer's wide forehead. "But where has the ark been all these centuries?"

Annoyance struggled with humor on Reis's face as he cast a pointed look at Isaac. "The Israelis won't tell us, but we know the ark has been either hidden in a secret chamber beneath the Temple Mount or locked in an IDF hangar, where it was taken shortly after the collapse of a Communist regime in the early 1990s."

"You're talking about Ethiopia?" The minister of finance laughed. "How did a Jewish artifact find its way there?"

Reis's mouth spread into a thin-lipped smile. "It's a long story, but I'll try to condense it. Apparently, the Ethiopian queen known in Scripture as the Queen of Sheba visited Solomon in Jerusalem. Jewish Scripture says that Solomon gave her everything she desired, and eventually she returned to her own land. According to the Ethiopians, the one thing she desired most was a son . . . which Solomon was completely happy to provide."

"She bore Solomon's son?" The words slipped from Isaac's lips. The story was new to him.

Reis's mouth quirked with humor. "Yes. According to legend, the boy, known in the Ethiopian royal chronicles as Prince Menelik I, grew up in the Jerusalem palace and was educated by the Temple priests. He became a strong believer in the Jewish God. At nineteen, however, he returned to Ethiopia, taking with him a large number of Jews and the ark of the covenant. His father, you see, had succumbed to the habit of marrying pagan women and consequently became derelict in his duties toward the true God. So the priests commissioned a *replica* of the ark and switched the real relic with the fake before the prince's departure. Menelik took the ark back to Ethiopia, kept it concealed and guarded, and there he and his descendants reigned until Emperor Haile Selassie's mysterious death in 1975. The ark remained in Ethiopia until the brutal civil war that finally ended in 1991. As Israel launched Operation Solomon to transport tens of thousands of Ethiopian Jews out of that war-torn land, Israeli agents and Ethiopian generals began to negotiate for the ark's return to Israel. Some of our intel sources claim that the Israelis artfully arranged a ransom— several million in cash. The Communists accepted, the exchange was made, and the ark of the covenant has been awaiting the third Temple ever since."

Reis directed his dark gaze toward Isaac. "I'm told that the money given to the corrupt Communist officials turned out to be counterfeit American dollars, while the *real* money donated for the ark's return was distributed to the rebels who had just reclaimed their capital. At least that's what my sources tell me. The Israelis won't confirm anything."

Isaac merely smiled. He had heard nothing about either the whereabouts of the ark or negotiations with Ethiopian Communists, but he'd been working in a liaison unit. Though such things did not fall in his area of expertise, he would never have admitted his ignorance.

"So what, exactly," General Archer said, tapping the end of his pen on the polished tabletop, "is the significance of the ark now? The Israelis can't be planning to carry it into battle. Is it wise for us to allow them to use it at all? It if becomes a symbol of Israeli independence, the resistance may try to use it against us."

Reis's mouth took on an unpleasant twist. "A very good question, General, and well worth our consideration. According to my sources, most Jews see the ark as a historic relic, but some in the Orthodox community may see the ark's restoration as a step toward instituting the kingdom of God on earth. One rabbi told me about a detailed prophecy concerning Gogol's Invasion—which, he believes, was foretold by the prophet Ezekiel. One verse in that passage reads, 'I will set my glory among the nations,' and the term 'my glory' almost always refers to the Shekinah cloud that reportedly surrounded the ark of the covenant. The Orthodox element, therefore, may see the restoration of the ark as a fulfillment of this Scripture in Ezekiel. But what does that mean in practical terms? Almost nothing."

Archer frowned, his eyes level under drawn brows. "That's it? They won't see it as a call to arms?"

"Of course not." Reis's expression held a note of mockery. "The Israelis are in a mood for peace, not war. They have had their fill of suffering and strife."

Romulus glanced toward Isaac as if searching for confirmation. Though Isaac's mind whirled with thoughts and facts he had never before considered, he nodded.

His mind drifted back to a dinner months before, when Sarah had told the American archeologist about everything the Jews were searching for in a messiah. As cold, clear reality swept over Isaac in a terrible wave, it suddenly occurred to him that, intentionally or not, Adrian Romulus was preparing to give his people exactly what they wanted—a rebuilt Jerusalem, a Temple, and peace in the land.

A quotation from the prophet Micah rose from the dusty memories of Isaac's years in yeshiva school: "But you, Bethlehem Ephrathah, being small among the clans of Judah, out of you one will come forth to me that is to be ruler in Israel; whose goings forth are from of old, from everlasting."

Romulus had been born in Bethlehem.

Isaac's mind bulged with the question he did not dare ask aloud: Could Adrian Romulus be the long-awaited Messiah?

THIRTEEN

SITTING IN THE LECTURE HALL AT SHIN BET headquarters, Sarah looked over her notes and memorized the details of her disguise. She and every other available Shabak agent would be mingling in the crowd tomorrow, watching for subversive activity or suspected terrorists amid the celebrants who had come to observe Rosh Hashanah and celebrate the Temple dedication. The untrained eye would not notice the myriad security measures—the Temple authorities had insisted that there be no sign of armed guards, metal detectors, or bulletproof shields. They did agree to allow the guards of the Universal Force to stand at the gates leading to the Temple Mount, realizing that since the UF forces had been stationed at those posts for months, they had more or less become acceptable to the citizens of Jerusalem.

Security would be tight and undetectable. State-of-the-art weapon detectors had been concealed in resin pillars situated throughout the outer courtyard just beyond the entrance gates. These cutting-edge devices measured distortions in the natural electromagnetic waves generated by the human body and transmitted a silent warning when those distortions sig-

naled a hidden weapon. The security patrols who would hear
the warning through specially made earpieces were members
of Shin Bet, Sayeret Mat'Kal, Sayeret Tzanhanim, Ya'Ma'M,
and the secretive Mista'Aravim. These security personnel,
wearing Kevlar sheaths beneath street clothes, would mingle
among Israeli citizens. Though the security officers would be
armed with nothing but their wits and the confidence that
came from knowing they were the world's best warriors,
Sarah did not think they would fail to apprehend any individual with mischief on the mind. In simulation after simulation, not a single armed individual had been able to venture
more than five feet beyond the gate armed with an explosive,
a blade, or any type of gun.

The undetectable security measures would make the real
difference, but to reinforce the public's perception of security,
no one would be able to enter the Temple Mount area without sliding his or her hand beneath a scanner that registered
the logistics of the individual's personal identification chip.
As each visitor stood at the insertion point, his or her image
flashed upon a small screen, along with such vital statistics as
name, age, and address.

The religious Jews had railed against this requirement,
but many of them had relented as the date for the Temple
dedication drew near. Only the most Orthodox had vowed
never to set foot upon the holy mountain if it meant violating
God's prohibition against cutting the flesh. Sarah was not surprised to learn that her father had allied himself with this
group.

Sarah had received her identification chip only a week
before. She often found herself scratching at it—not because
it itched, but because it bothered her conscience. She had

promised her father that she wouldn't take the chip, but she found herself with no other option when it became clear that no one could enter the Temple Mount without it. Finally she submitted and offered her hand to the officer at the Universal Force security station. Her father wouldn't be able to actually *see* the chip, she told herself, and though he would probably figure out that she had broken her word, he would just have to realize that she was neither a child nor a religious Jew. The old ones could cling to their outdated ideas, but she had a job that required functioning in the twenty-first century. When Director Melman playfully teased her about her reluctance to take the chip, she had left his office without another word.

She was thirty-one years old, the captain of a Shin Bet squad, and unafraid to live on her own. Why, then, was she helpless to cast off her father's shadow? Sitting at her desk, she shook her head slightly, then refocused her attention on the diagram in her hand.

Melman stood in front of the classroom, going over last-minute details for his team. Each member of Shin Bet would wear an earpiece and carry a radio. The team captains would stand at various points in the court and around the Temple, and from there they would direct their team's activity. The only other object team members were allowed to carry was a pair of plastic handcuffs, to be used only if necessary.

Sarah lifted her gaze to the map of the Temple on the projector screen. A full-scale model occupied the table in front of Melman, but it was easier to follow his instructions by studying the map.

Like its predecessors, the rectangular third Temple lay between the subterranean Western Gate and the sealed Eastern Gate. An expansive Court of the Gentiles surrounded the

Temple structure, and this huge outer court contained the Dome of the Rock, the Dome of the Chain, and the Al Aqsa Mosque. A low wall separated the Jewish Temple worship area in the northern half of the Temple Mount from the Muslim areas in the south. Throughout the construction, the Israelis had been careful not to offend their Arab neighbors by desecrating sacred Muslim sites.

Though Sarah and her team had been practicing in a mock theater designed to replicate the environment of the Temple Mount, last week they had been permitted to tour the completed Temple. Though their mock Temple was a masterful copy, when Sarah stared up at the great blocks of white limestone, she thought nothing in the world could compare to the real thing.

The amazing edifice seemed to glow in the desert sun. Entering from the east, through the Beautiful Gate, Sarah crossed the Court of the Gentiles and stepped into the large inner court actually inside the Temple walls. Several storage rooms had been built into the corners of this area, and the Temple guide explained that these provided meeting rooms for the priests and secure storage areas for the golden vessels used in Temple worship.

After proceeding through the inner court, Sarah and her security team stood on the threshold of the next court and studied the layout of the Court of the Israelites, also called the Court of the Priests. This area, open only to those descended from the priestly tribe of Levi, featured a brass altar for sacrifice, ten brass lavers, and a brass "sea." The sea, regulated by state-of-the art plumbing, kept a flow of fresh, purified water flowing into the court. Soft recessed lighting filled the room with light, even though there were no exposed windows.

From where she stood at the entrance to the Court of the Priests, Sarah could see the House of God rising like a gleaming beacon before her. It stood upon the highest ground in the enclosure and was divided into two compartments—the sanctuary, or Holy Place, and the Holy of Holies. One entered the sanctuary through a great doorway closed by golden doors—82 feet high and 24 feet wide—exactly like those of Herod's Temple. Though Sarah would never be permitted to look inside the sanctuary, she had seen pictures that revealed an amazingly beautiful room with cedar walls overlaid with gold. In it stood a golden altar for incense, ten tables for showbread, and ten golden candlesticks. A veil of fine linen colored in blue, purple, and scarlet separated the Holy Place from the Holy of Holies.

At present, there were no objects inside the Holy of Holies. However, two colossal cherubim were embroidered into the huge veil curtain with gold threads. Each fifteen-foot-tall cherub had outstretched seven-and-a-half-foot wings. With the tip of one wing, each angel touched a sidewall, and with the other wing it reached to the center of the room and touched the corresponding wing of its companion. The cherubim's wings stretched across the veil guarding the Holy of Holies and faced the sanctuary.

Tomorrow, the ark of the covenant would finally reside behind the veil of the Holy of Holies.

The Temple had risen in an amazingly short time, due, of course, to the extensive preparations that had begun years before, when the new Temple consisted of nothing but prayers and fervent hopes. It gleamed now from the Temple Mount like a shining jewel, a testimony to all those who had pledged their prayers, their hopes, and their fortunes to see it become a reality. Though the Temple had been modeled on the plans contained in Scripture, the new structure boasted of electricity, lights, and modern plumbing, all discreetly installed according to the demands of halacha, the religious law.

The search for qualified personnel to serve in the Temple had been aided by the discovery that descendants of Aaron carried a unique aberration of the Y chromosome. Members of the Levite tribe, who had been forbidden throughout history to change their surname, enthusiastically enrolled in Temple service. The first group of ceremonial priests had been trained and purified, and a young member of the Kohanim, a boy of thirteen, had been secretly born and raised in a special complex that preserved his state of ritual purity. And eighteen months earlier, with the aid of American ranchers, the first of several pure red heifers had been born, allowing the purification of all priests who would enter the sanctified area to perform the holy tasks. The sacrifice of the red heifer had produced the waters of purification that were required to cleanse the temple area.

"Any questions?" Melman's gruff voice brought Sarah back to her surroundings. She glanced around at her teammates and saw that they all seemed clear-eyed and alert, ready for the morning to come. This operation would be the biggest challenge of their careers—and possibly the most significant.

"Dismissed," Melman said.

The meeting broke up with the scraping of chairs and the quiet slap of closing notebooks. As most of the others headed toward the doors at the back of the room, Sarah lingered at her desk, her gaze on the white model, her thoughts a million miles away. She had thought her father would be happy to see the Temple standing on Mount Zion, but something had moved in his eyes when she last spoke to him. The only explanation she received when she asked about his thoughts was an enigmatic comment: "The time of Jacob's trouble is fast approaching."

She'd gone home and looked in her Bible, but the only reference she could find to Jacob's trouble was a verse in Jeremiah that read, "Alas! For that day is great, so that none is like it: it is even the time of Jacob's trouble, but he shall be saved out of it."

"I don't think I've ever seen such a pensive look on your face."

The director's voice again snapped Sarah out of her reverie. She gave him a quick smile, then folded her hands on the desk. "It's nothing. I was just thinking about something my father said."

"Shall we discuss it over dinner?" As Melman extended an arm toward the doorway, Sarah glanced back and frowned. She must have been more lost in thought than she realized, for she and Melman were the only two remaining in the room. He probably thought she had been waiting for him—a message she didn't intend to send. Over the months of Isaac's absence, the director had kept himself at a thoughtful distance, patiently waiting for some sign . . . which she might have inadvertently just given him.

"Thank you, but I don't know if dinner is such a good idea." She looked down at her notes. "I think I'll go home and study the plan for tomorrow again. I want to be as familiar with the layout as possible."

"You already know the area inside and out. Maybe it's time to give your brain a rest and think about something else."

Touched by his concern, Sarah gave him a smile. In the past few months, she had spent increasing amounts of time alone, and the idea of dinner with an intelligent and considerate man *did* appeal to her. Isaac seemed to be in constant motion these days, traveling to and from Paris, Jerusalem, Tel Aviv, and Brussels. She could count on one hand how many times in the past year they had slept in the same bed . . .

Melman looked down at her, an easy smile playing at the corners of his mouth. An odd, faintly eager look flashed in his eyes as he straddled the chair in front of her desk and sat down to face her. "How are you, Sarah? How are you *really?*"

She gave him a smile that felt false. "I'm fine. Really. I like being busy, and the job's kept me very busy these last few months."

"Do you hear from Isaac often?"

"The job keeps Isaac busy, too." She tossed her head. "Sometimes I think he lives on a jet. Romulus has been sending him all over Europe to settle one issue or another." She frowned. "Tomorrow's ceremony, you know, is a high priority for Romulus and his people."

"That's why we're paying special attention. You know what the intel said—and we *will* keep things under control. If you're worried, well, you shouldn't be."

She closed her eyes, well aware of the warnings they had received. According to their informants in the religious community, a growing number of Jews had become convinced that Adrian Romulus was the Messiah. They had heard and confirmed that he had been born in Bethlehem, they knew he had no peer as a political and military leader, and they themselves had witnessed his role as peacemaker. He had initiated the building of the Temple, they said, and he had encouraged the rebuilding of war-torn Jerusalem. Lately certain rabbis had even hinted that Romulus was the guiding force behind Gogol's defeat.

Sarah pressed both hands over her eyes as they burned with weariness. "I think I ought to go home and get some rest. After all, it will soon be Shabbat, and I am a rabbi's daughter." She removed her hands and smiled. "Some habits die hard."

"But you've got to eat." A spark of some indefinable emotion lit Melman's eyes, and Sarah wavered at the sight of it. It would be so easy to go with him. The dinner would be perfectly innocent, two coworkers who had decided to share a meal. If she were a man, or he a woman, she'd accept his invitation without hesitation.

But he *was* a man, and she a *married* woman. And even though she had managed to shrug off many of the guilt-spawning constrictions of her father's religion, something in her warned that dinner with Melman would not be wise.

"I'll think I'll pass, but thank you." She looked up, trying to soften her refusal with a smile. "I appreciate the invitation, I really do, but . . . not tonight."

He paused, his eyes searching hers, then he nodded slowly. "I understand, Sarah. But when you feel the time is right, I trust you'll let me know?"

Sarah looked down and cleared her throat, pretending not to be affected by the flicker of interest in his intense eyes. How long had it been since Isaac looked at her that way?

She gathered her notes and stood. "I need to go."

By some miracle, she found the door before the temptation to accept overtook her.

FOURTEEN

ISAAC WALKED STIFFLY BEHIND THE MORE SENIOR members of Romulus's entourage, trying to keep his mind on his duty even as he searched the crowd for a glimpse of his wife. In his last communication with HQ at Tel Aviv, he had confirmed that undercover Shin Bet agents would be working the Temple dedication, so in every woman's face he hoped for some sign of Sarah.

But he would never find her among the estimated eighty thousand people who had jammed the Temple Mount. The third Temple's dedication ceremony had blossomed into the event of the decade, far eclipsing the extravagant millennial parties that had marked the turn of the century. Israeli citizens and supporters of Israel from across the globe had flown to Jerusalem to celebrate this special day, and not even the Olympics could rival the event in terms of international appeal. Because the dedication had been set for Rosh Hashanah, the first day of the Jewish civil year, most of the attendees wore white, the traditional color for the holiday.

As he waited in a VIP line to advance through the gates leading to the Temple Mount, Isaac looked around and silently congratulated the Israeli security agencies on a job well done. Aside from the occasional uniformed policeman mingling in the Jerusalem crowds, he saw no signs of overt security. Yet he knew no other event had been so closely monitored. Dignitaries and leaders of nations from across the globe had come to Jerusalem today; Egyptians, Africans, and Americans waited in the same lines and hoped for a glimpse of what would surely become a wonder of the modern world. Barbra Streisand and Larry King had taken rooms in Romulus's hotel, and last night Isaac had stepped out to fill his ice bucket and found England's Prince William accepting a Diet Coke from his bodyguard in the hallway.

If he had worked on the preparations in Jerusalem, he might have been more aware of the logistics involved, but now, as he stood in line and prepared to pass his hand and ID chip beneath the security scanner, Isaac moved woodenly, feeling as though he was passing through a surreal landscape.

After a half-hour wait in the VIP line, he reached the checkpoint and pulled his battered Universal Force ID card from his wallet. Because he often traveled in parts of the world where the Universal Chip technology had not yet been fully implemented, he had not yet had his own Universal Chip implanted. The microchip-encoded card had served him well in remote portions of Africa and China, so he'd been in no hurry to visit a Universal Force security station.

His plastic card slipped beneath the scanner, and instantly, his official photograph, ID number, and address flashed upon the notebook-sized screen in the young UF guard's hands. Isaac stared at the address and felt his mouth twist when he read the address—Jerusalem. It had been months since he slept in his Jerusalem residence.

He removed the card and prepared to follow the others, but the guard stopped him. "I'm sorry, Major," the young man said, reading Isaac's rank from his uniform. "But no one is allowed to sit in the VIP section without the Universal Chip implanted in their hand. No exceptions allowed."

Isaac pulled out his wallet and began to shuffle through other identification cards. "I have a diplomatic pass that includes a holographic photograph. I have a security pass to enter the Universal Movement headquarters building in Brussels—"

"Those won't do, sir. I have strict orders: Absolutely no one enters the VIP area without an implanted chip."

To his annoyance, Isaac felt himself flush. "This is ridiculous—I am in nearly constant contact with President Romulus and so am obviously no threat. Call your superior, please. Call Col. Meir Barak, my CO. Call the prime minister's office, if you like—they will confirm who I am."

"What's this about?"

Isaac felt his flush deepen when he turned and saw Romulus standing beside him.

"I'm sorry, Mr. President, sir." Twin stains of scarlet appeared on the guard's cheeks, but he did not back down. "My orders are not to allow anyone in without an implanted Universal Chip. The order is for your own protection."

A shadow of annoyance crossed Romulus's face, then he gave Isaac a wintry smile. "My friend, the Major," he drawled with distinct mockery, "has been very busy. And I'm afraid I am at fault for not giving him the time to receive his Universal Chip. Surely you understand." His voice dropped to a low, melodic tone as he smiled, and something in the young man's features began to melt.

"So I'm sure you can see why you need to let Major Ben-David pass," Romulus said, lifting a brow. "Don't you agree?"

"I agree," the young man echoed. His eyes had gone curiously flat. "I see why I need to let Major Ben-David pass."

Romulus stepped aside and waved Isaac through the checkpoint with a curling gesture. "Thank you, young man." His hand fell on the guard's shoulder. "You shall go far in the Universal Movement."

As Romulus walked away with long strides, Isaac hurried to catch up. "I am truly sorry," he said, helpless to halt his embarrassment. "I haven't had time to get my chip, and the ID card has been sufficient in every other situation—"

Romulus stopped him with an uplifted hand. "You do not need to explain anything to me, Major. I understand far more than you think I do." His gaze lifted toward the VIP section. "Ah—there's General Archer and the prime minister. Shall we join them? I believe we're to be part of a procession or something."

Intensely humiliated, Isaac followed Romulus into the noisy stands.

†

An hour later, well into the program surrounding the official Temple dedication, Isaac couldn't help wondering what Solomon would have thought if he were alive to see how modern Jews celebrated their religious heritage. A *kittel*-clad children's choir sang before roving video cameras as their images appeared on screens scattered around the Temple Mount and positioned at strategic locations within the Old City. A marching band paraded around the Court of the

Gentiles playing traditional Hebrew music while fireworks lit the night sky with pyrotechnic delights.

Political speeches followed the more secular entertainments. The prime minister spoke at length and ended his speech in tears. Representatives from Jordan, Egypt, and Saudi Arabia brought golden gifts to be used in Temple service. The American president read an enigmatic poem by Maya Angelou. One-hundred-year-old Frieda Gertz, one of the oldest Holocaust survivors, spoke of unity and survival and the urgent need for peace. Then Elijah Reis stood and read a congratulatory message from Adrian Romulus.

Isaac blinked in surprise when Romulus himself did not stand to speak, but apparently he was content to allow his assistant to claim the spotlight. Isaac found the gesture oddly touching. Romulus had been the driving force behind the rebuilding of the Temple, but at this shining hour he was willing to remain out of the spotlight. Such humility was rare, especially in politics.

When the secular speeches had concluded, the newly installed Kohanim priests, dressed in white linen robes constructed by a unique six-ply linen thread, walked slowly around the Temple proper, each of them lifting their hands in the split-fingered salute used to symbolize the open windows of heaven through which God poured his blessings. Isaac rubbed his hand over his face as they lifted their hands toward the crowd. The gesture was symbolic, but every time he saw it he couldn't help but think of the old Star Trek episodes where Mr. Spock had raised his hand in the Vulcan gesture for "live long and prosper." Someone from that show—perhaps even Leonard Nimoy himself—must have lifted the symbol from the Rosh Hashanah ceremony.

After the priests' procession came the musicians, several of whom carried *shofarim,* the curved rams' horns tradition-ally blown upon the Feast of Trumpets. As the drums pounded a pulse-quickening rhythm, the musicians blew the horns traditionally said to awaken sinners and confuse Satan.

The youthful high priest walked at the end of the proces-sion. Like the other priests, he wore a white linen robe, but there the similarities ended. In addition to the linen robe, the high priest wore a square breastplate made of gold, set with four rows of precious stones, three per row, each inscribed with the name of one of the twelve tribes. Beneath the breast-plate, he wore the ephod, an embroidered vestment worn like a sandwich board over the front and back and clasped at the shoulder by onyx stones. Beneath the ephod, he wore a sleeveless cloak of deep, majestic blue and fringed with alter-nating pomegranates and golden bells. Around his waist he wore the high priest's *avnet* belt, dyed with the blue dye known as *tchelet.* The unique dye, which came from a sea snail once thought extinct, had recently been obtained from divers who discovered that the snail had not been obliterated after all.

Isaac narrowed his eyes to trap a sudden rush of tears as the young man came closer. Upon the high priest's head rested a crown of pure gold, the *tsitz zahav tahor.* Blue tchelet thread attached the crown to a linen turban, and a gold plate hung from the front by a blue ribbon. Though he could not see the engraving upon the plate, Isaac knew what it said: *Holiness to the Lord.*

Immediately after the high priest passed and took his seat in the special section reserved for the Kohanim, the prime minister of Israel stood and walked to the podium in the Court of the Gentiles.

"Citizens of Israel and the world," he said, scanning the crowd before focusing on the television camera before him, "it is with great joy that we welcome you to the dedication of the third Temple of Israel."

A great roar arose, vibrating the aluminum footrest beneath the soles of Isaac's shoes. The crowd around him rose in unison and merged into a sea of swaying bodies in white. Glancing down the row of seats, Isaac was surprised to see that even Romulus, Reis, and Archer had stood and lifted their hands in exultation. When the spontaneous moment of celebration had passed, the prime minister took his seat, and Rabbi Avidan Joseph, one of the most outspoken leaders of the Temple movement, walked to the podium and placed his hands upon the lectern.

"Clap your hands, all you nations!" Joseph's voice rumbled through the speakers as his eyes peered out from beneath his prayer shawl. "Shout to God with the voice of triumph! For Yahweh Most High is awesome. He is a great King over all the earth. He subdues nations under us, and peoples under our feet. He chooses our inheritance for us, the glory of Jacob whom he loved."

For a moment, Isaac wondered why Baram Cohen wasn't leading the ceremony, then common sense supplied the answer. Though Rabbi Cohen had been the first to hear of Romulus's plans to instigate the rebuilding of the Temple, he was probably among those who had refused to accept the Universal Chip. Avidan Joseph, on the other hand, was an eminent leader and more liberal in his opinions.

As the shofarim blared, Isaac recognized the Scripture

passage as one he'd heard a hundred times in his youth. Joseph was reading Psalm 47, traditionally recited seven times during the Rosh Hashanah service.

Rabbi Joseph continued when the shofarim fell silent,

"God has gone up with a shout,
Yaweh with the sound of a trumpet.
Sing praises to God, sing praises;
sing praises to our King, sing praises.
For God is the King of all the earth.
Sing praises with understanding.
God reigns over the nations.
God sits on his holy throne.
The princes of the peoples are gathered together,
    the people of the God of Abraham.
For the shields of the earth belong to God.
He is greatly exalted!"

The crowd erupted in an ecstatic, ripping mayhem of noise that made the very air vibrate. Isaac marveled at it and felt his breath catch in his throat as he heard his own heart pounding. Was this religious or nationalistic fervor? Perhaps it was enthusiasm resulting from pure and simple relief. As a people, they had come far and surmounted terrible obstacles, but today they had rebuilt what the ages had seemed intent upon destroying.

Rabbi Joseph waited until the sound faded before he continued. "When Ezra the priest brought the Law before an assembly like this one," he said, his dark gaze sparkling on the screens where the video cameras captured his image, "the people wept because during their exile they had not kept the

Law of God. Many of them had completely forgotten the Lord their God. Many of you may feel like weeping today because you have forgotten that Rosh Hashanah is the beginning of *Yomin Noroim*, the Days of Awe. These coming days are concerned with the life of the individual, with religious feelings and inner probings. Unlike other nations, we do not greet the New Year with noisemakers and party hats, though our hearts are overflowing with gratitude for the Temple. Instead we turn our thoughts toward God; we bend our hearts in serious contemplation and contrition. But we feel awe, not terror. We realize that God is understanding, merciful, and loving."

As Rabbi Joseph stepped back to take his seat, a single shofar blower stood and lifted the ram's horn. A thousand flashbulbs sparked the night as he sounded the ancient notes of the *tekiah*, a long, clear note, then the *teruah*, nine very short notes, and finally the *shevarim*, three short notes. And as Isaac stood there, momentarily lost in wonder, he was overcome with the feeling that he was a link in an unbroken chain of Jews who had stood beneath a night sky and the sound of the shofar. The melodious sound seemed to stretch from antiquity into the depths of his soul. From far away, a voice from the distant past whispered, *The shields of the earth belong to God; he is greatly exalted.*

For a moment Isaac forgot where and what he was. Thoughts of Sarah, Romulus, and his task vanished as his mind filled with thoughts of the God of Abraham, Isaac, and Jacob, the Holy One whose glory had once filled a Temple very much like this one.

And then he saw it. The ark of the covenant, carried on staves by eight of the Kohanim, appeared on the video screens. The priests, all dressed in spotless white linen, were outside the Temple Mount, walking in the center of a security escort. The cameras picked up the tracks of tears on the faces of men and women and children as the ark passed, leaving a trail of reverence and awe in its wake.

The silent air around Isaac vibrated, the quiet filled with wonder. Isaac glanced at Romulus and Reis, who sat farther down the row, and saw that neither man watched the video screen. Both men had their gazes fixed on the open doorway of the sanctuary, through which the ark would eventually pass. Isaac studied the sanctuary for a moment, wondering if they had spied something amiss, but nothing about the structure seemed unusual.

Then the Kohanim procession moved inside the Temple Mount, eliciting spontaneous sounds of prayer and blessing from the people they passed. Riding high upon the shoulders of the priests, the two cherubim atop the golden artifact seemed to float through the crowd before it disappeared into the Court of the Priests. Isaac knew the Kohanim would pass through the Court of the Priests, enter the sanctuary, and then place the ark on the foundation stone in the Holy of Holies.

Like all the others, he waited breathlessly for a long moment, then felt his skin tingle when a cloud of white smoke billowed out of the sanctuary doorway. "Look! The glory has returned!" a man behind him cried. The cry was caught and repeated, and soon the entire crowd was shouting praise to the God whose glory had filled the Temple.

At that moment Romulus looked at Reis, and the peripheral movement caught Isaac's attention. The president gave his chief assistant a cynical look filled with derision, and Isaac suddenly wondered if what appeared to be a miracle was only a cheap theatrical trick. Could the Kohanim have arranged such a thing? He doubted it. But one of the more liberal rab-bis might have been willing to rig something, believing that a man-made miracle might be excusable if it stimulated faith among those who were stubbornly secular.

He leaned forward and caught General Archer's gaze. His brow lifted the question as he silently mouthed the word: *Smoke?*

Archer's round face creased in an indulgent, patronizing smile.

Rabbi Joseph stepped onto the podium again, and Isaac noted that he gripped the lectern with trembling hands. "Know this, O Israel!" he said, his voice ringing over the sound system. "The Holy One, blessed be his name, is not limited to dwelling in the Temple; he still lives in heaven! Not even all of heaven can contain him!"

The crowd roared again, and the rabbi held up a hand for silence. "I pray," he said, his voice quieter, "that our nation will remain true to HaShem, may his name be forever praised, and that the Holy One will forgive us when we sin. I pray he will not let us be totally destroyed by the wars brought on by our own sinfulness."

The murmurs of approval ceased, and Isaac felt jarred by the abrupt change in mood of the audience. Though this crowd was eager to celebrate, they didn't want to hear about sin and war and judgment. They had been primed for peace and victory and success.

"I pray, too," Rabbi Joseph pushed onward, "for the for-eigners who so graciously aided us in the rebuilding of our Temple. I pray that the Master of the Universe will extend grace to any foreigner who expresses faith in him."

As the crowd around the Temple Mount watched live and

by closed-circuit television, Rabbi Avidan Joseph fell to his knees, then lifted both hands and gripped the edges of the prayer shawl over his head. "*Barukh atah HaShem, Eloheynu, melekh ha-olam,*" he prayed. "May your eyes be open to the supplication of your servant and to the supplication of your people Israel, to listen to them whenever they cry to you. For you did separate them from among all the peoples of the earth, to be your inheritance, as you spoke by Moses your servant, when you brought our fathers out of Egypt, Lord Yahweh."

When he had concluded his prayer, the aged rabbi stood and spread his hands toward heaven. In a voice that set the microphones to squealing, he shouted, "Praise be to the Lord, who has given rest to his people Israel, just as he promised! And may these words of mine, which I have prayed before the Lord, be near to the Lord our God day and night, that he may uphold the cause of his servant and the cause of his people Israel according to each day's need, so that all the peoples of the earth may know that the Lord is God and there is no other!"

Restored to a supportive mood, the crowd cheered again, the roar rising and cresting in a tidal wave of sound. While Isaac applauded with the more subdued spectators in the VIP section, the priests of Israel led several cattle and sheep out from their holding pens and reinstituted the ancient practice of sacrifice unto the Lord.

As Isaac watched, fascinated, Elijah Reis reached out to tug on his sleeve. "Quite gory, this," he shouted, striving to be heard above the crowd. "Is it really necessary?"

"I suppose so," Isaac shouted back, wondering if any rock concert had ever equaled this level of sound.

"We're going to dinner." Reis jerked his thumb toward Romulus, who was watching the sacrifice with an odd look of amusement. "Will you join us?"

"If you don't mind," Isaac said, leaning closer to reach Reis's ear, "I'd like to take some time to visit my wife."

Reis nodded in understanding, then nudged Romulus. On cue, the president and his entourage stood and began to file out of the row in which they'd been seated.

"Look! It's President Romulus!" a woman behind them shouted.

Isaac automatically reached for the weapon he hadn't been allowed to carry, but Romulus did not appear to be alarmed by the woman's enthusiasm. He waved to the throng behind him, eliciting cheers and applause as he made his way through the bleachers. Soon the crowd inside the courtyard had picked up a chant: *Rom-u-lus! Rom-u-lus!*

"Adrian Romulus!" A young man wearing black trousers, a white shirt, and a generous kippa—the uniform of the haredim—stumbled through the crowd and fell to his knees at Romulus's feet. "We ought to be honoring you, sir! *You* made this possible! *You* are the leader who restored our Temple and vanquished our enemies!"

"Thank you, son," Romulus said, gently lifting the young man to his feet as flashbulbs lit the scene with flashes of white light. "Rejoice in this hour, but leave me to my other work. My time is not yet come."

And then, like a European prince bidding adieu to his subjects, Adrian Romulus waved and moved toward the exit while the mob chanted his praise.

FIFTEEN

ISAAC ARRIVED AT THE HOUSE LONG BEFORE SARAH DID. He wasn't surprised, given the traffic and the security issues surrounding the Temple dedication, so he used his still-shiny key to let himself in, then sat in the front room, watching television. Scenes from the glorious Temple event formed a collage of images and sounds that flashed across his consciousness until he fell asleep.

The sound of a key in the lock roused him from a shallow doze. Isaac sat up and scrubbed his hands through his hair, trying to throw off the lingering wisps of sleep. He hadn't seen Sarah in over two months, and he didn't want to appear bleary-eyed and drowsy when they met again . . .

The sound of a woman's soft laughter and a man's baritone growl brought him instantly awake. He recognized the female voice as Sarah's, but who was the man?

A rectangle of light flooded the foyer as the door opened. A man stepped into the house, his hand upon the key in the knob, and Sarah followed. As she fumbled for the light switch and flipped it on, Isaac realized he could either make his presence known or remain silent and witness something he wasn't prepared to face.

"Sarah?" He was dismayed to hear an edge of desperation in his voice.

Surprise blossomed on Sarah's face as she peered into the shadows. The gloom had suited his mood, so only the flickering gray light of the television lit the front room. "Husband? Is that you?"

Standing, Isaac moved forward and recognized Danny Melman, Sarah's supervisor. The man his father had warned him about. Had his father been right? Were Sarah and Melman more than coworkers?

Isaac slipped his hands into his trouser pockets and stepped into the light. "I was hoping to catch you before I had to leave again," he said, wishing he could think of something more profound. He had a thousand things he wanted to ask her, but he couldn't say any of those things with Melman standing there.

Sarah's lips twitched with amusement. "So why were you sitting here in the dark?"

Isaac gave Melman a brief, distracted glance and tried to smile. "The dark was . . . peaceful."

"Well, Sarah, I'll be on my way," Melman said, avoiding Isaac's gaze. "I'll see you tomorrow at the debriefing. Rest well."

"Thank you, Danny."

Since when had their friendship risen to the level of first-name familiarity? Isaac said nothing as Sarah closed the door and slipped out of her coat. She wore a long skirt and a long-sleeved blouse covered by a vest, and he knew she probably wore Kevlar beneath it. He shouldn't confront her with his suspicions in the aftermath of what had to be one of the most stress-filled days of her life, but when else could he speak to her?

"So," he heard himself saying, "does Danny Melman now have a key to our house? You didn't even give *me* a key to the new lock until I asked for it."

Sarah threw him a reproachful look as she unbuttoned her vest. "He doesn't have a key. He was being a gentleman and unlocked the door for me. In case you haven't noticed, I'm exhausted."

Isaac accepted this news in silence, then stepped back to let her pass. "So," he continued, following her toward the bedroom, "does he often give you a ride home? I thought you preferred to take the bus."

"I haven't taken the bus in months, Isaac." Moving to her bureau, she unfastened the remainder of the buttons, then tossed her vest onto the bed. In one swift movement she unbuttoned the blue cotton blouse, pulled it off, and tossed it onto the bed, too. Isaac watched, but Sarah halted as if she had just realized that she was undressing in front of a stranger.

Clad in a formfitting bulletproof bodysuit that extended from her neck past the waistband of her full skirt, she crossed her arms over her middle and turned to face him. "Any other questions I can answer for you?"

Isaac pressed his lips together. A thousand questions bubbled beneath the surface of his consciousness. Did she still love him? Did they still have a marriage? Was any part of their relationship worth saving, or had he lost her completely?

He lowered his gaze. He might be swatting at monsters that didn't exist. Trouble was, he hadn't been around long enough to know how things stood between him and Sarah. They needed time together, time to share their thoughts and fears, time to heal the wounds that had been festering for long months.

As he opened his mouth to whisper her name, the cell phone at his belt chirped softly. Sarah's gaze immediately dropped to it.

"Your master calls," she said. As Isaac unsnapped the phone, she turned and moved into the bathroom, closing the door behind her.

Isaac unsnapped the phone and pressed the receive key, then listened to the brief message from one of Romulus's aides. The president and his party had finished dinner, the aide explained, and the jet would depart Jerusalem in an hour. Romulus wanted to discuss a proposal for the Israeli prime minister en route to Paris, so he had arranged for a car to fetch Isaac. The vehicle was on its way and would arrive momentarily.

Isaac pressed the off key, then moved toward the bathroom door and tested the doorknob. Locked. Closing his eyes, he gently rapped on the door with one knuckle.

"Sarah," he called, hoping she could hear over the soft sound of running water, "I have to go. But I'll be back. And I love you."

If she heard, she gave no response.

†

Sarah hesitated, one hand beneath the running faucet, as Isaac murmured his farewell. She waited until she heard the slam of the door, then she cut off the water and pulled her robe from the hook behind the door. Wrapping the robe around her, she hurried to the front window and watched as Isaac stepped into a black sedan. The door closed; the sedan moved away.

Just like that, he had come and gone. Without warning, he had appeared in her house; without hesitation, he had left her alone when Romulus rang. And he suspected *her* of unfaithfulness! His suspicions about her and Director Melman had been evident in his eyes and in his words. How dare he suggest that she had been disloyal! She had struggled to maintain a marriage that had gone as cold as a corpse when she could have walked away at any time.

She stepped into the living room and sank into a chair, her mind thick with fatigue and clouded with memories. Why had he come back? To keep tabs on his worldly possessions or to ruminate about old times? And why had he behaved like a jealous husband? He knew Melman was only a coworker.

Running her hand through her hair, she mentally replayed the bedroom scene. Before leaving, he had said he loved her— at least that's what she thought he said. Did he really love her? How could he? Sometimes she felt as though they scarcely knew each other anymore.

She pressed her hand to her forehead as another thought rose in her brain. Any other modern woman would divorce him. But could she walk away from Isaac? Perhaps, if they'd been fighting or if he had been abusive, but she could never end their marriage on the basis of indifference. She'd have to get to know him again at some point and see if his association with Romulus and the Universal Movement had changed him. If his ambitions had grown too grand or this little house too cramped, perhaps he would want to end the marriage . . . if he could divorce her without damaging his pride.

Achy and exhausted, she brought her hand to her temple. What had happened to them? Her world used to revolve around Isaac. Her days began with his kisses and ended with his arms around her in the sanctuary of their bedroom. But he no longer needed her; he no longer wanted to come home. Moving in lofty circles of influence and position, he spent his days with prime ministers and presidents and kings and counselors . . .

He no longer needed her. He no longer wanted her. He had placed his future and his passion on the altar of world peace, and, perhaps unwittingly, he had placed her there, too. She was a sacrificial lamb, and she knew it.

Her heart had been dead these past months. Why, then, did it still ache?

Sixteen

29 months later

Peering out the window of the jet, Isaac decided that from 35,000 feet aloft, Europe looked more like a computer simulation than an actual landmass. He pulled the shade on the window and closed his eyes, feeling his attention drift away on a tide of weariness. In the nearly two and a half years since the Temple dedication, he had spent more time in the air than on the ground. He had traveled throughout Europe, Africa, and the United States, all the while seeking to portray Adrian Romulus as the great peacemaker who wanted only the best for the world and its people. As the world suffered under the blistering sun and relentless drought, Isaac urged starving people to be patient and wait for the rains that would surely come. Sometimes they believed him. Sometimes they did not.

He closed his eyes. He needed time to relax, to clear his mind, and to redirect his energies. Trouble was, every time he consciously turned his thoughts from Romulus, he tended to think of Sarah, whom he hadn't seen in over two years. They had not parted on good terms when he last saw her in Jerusalem, and in a series of curt phone calls they had decided upon a trial separation. He would live at the B&B in Paris; she would keep the house in Jerusalem. He waited now for word that she wanted to divorce him.

At the end of each day, he was a little surprised to discover that she hadn't.

"Major Ben-David." Opening his eyes with an effort, Isaac looked up to see Elijah Reis standing in the aisle. "Adrian would like to see you."

"Now?"

Reis's eyes flashed a warning as the stupid question slipped from Isaac's lips. "Now," Reis said.

Isaac gathered his remaining strength and stood, then pulled his coat from the overhead bin and slipped it on. Reis was already moving toward Romulus's private office at the back of the jet.

Reis paused outside the door and gestured toward it. "Go on in. Adrian is meditating, but he specifically asked to see you."

Isaac came to an abrupt halt in the aisle, his heart jumping in his chest. Romulus rarely met with him alone. He lifted a brow, telegraphing a silent question to Reis, who only smiled and jerked his thumb toward the door. "Go on in."

Isaac reached out and felt the cool metal handle under his palm. Clearing his throat to announce his arrival, he opened the door and stepped into the private cabin.

The office was surprisingly luxurious—compact, but with every comfort a traveling executive could wish. A desk occupied the flat back wall, while a long couch sprinkled with pillows filled the curving wall along the side of the plane. Another small door stood at the very back of the cabin, undoubtedly leading to a private rest room, and a pair of tufted leather chairs and an oak table occupied the center space.

Romulus sat in one of the chairs, his posture relaxed, his eyes closed. His arms rested upon leather armrests while his palms faced the ceiling and his fingers curled naturally upward. One leg was crossed over the other at the knee in the simple, confident posture of an American businessman.

At the metallic sound of the door latch, Romulus's heavily lashed eyes fluttered without opening, then a smile lifted his lips. "Welcome, Isaac Ben-David," he said, his words running together in a velvet sound. "Sit down. Make yourself . . . comfortable."

Isaac sat, feeling vaguely embarrassed and awkward. Romulus's eyes had not opened, so how could he know for certain that Isaac stood before him? Of course, he had sent Reis to fetch him, but Reis could have been the one coming through the door . . .

"You are wondering how much I can see in this meditative state." A secretive smile softened Romulus's lips. "I see everything in this room, Major, and in this entire aircraft. For I am seeing now with spirit eyes, and my spirit is not located in the physical body you see before you. I am hovering above you. If you believe in the mystical, you might call it an out-of-body experience."

Feeling foolish, Isaac looked up. He saw nothing above him but the soft glow of recessed lighting shining on the jet's vinyl ceiling.

"You should try meditation sometime," Romulus said, slurring words between his teeth. "It is quite . . . empowering."

The president's voice died away as his head dropped forward and his hands turned to clench the leather armrests in a spasmodic grip. For a moment Isaac tensed, afraid that something was physically wrong with the man, but before he could move Romulus lifted his head, his eyes alert and bright.

His smile flashed briefly, dazzling against his tanned skin. "You prefer to converse with me in the flesh, don't you, Isaac? I don't blame you—most people are uncomfortable with matters of the spirit. But I have found great strength in meditation. Focusing one's spiritual energy renews the body as well as the soul."

Romulus drew a deep breath, then linked his fingers and leaned forward. "In the last hour, I have spoken with my spiritual counselor, and he told me the time is right. Our meeting with the American Jewish leadership today was a precedent-setting event, but we are far from reaching our goals. The next step is a simple one, but terribly crucial—and I know you are the man I should trust to see it through."

The wings of shadowy foreboding brushed Isaac's spirit as he sat there, blank and shaken. "Me, sir?"

"Yes, you." Amusement flickered in Romulus's dark eyes. "I find a delicious irony in the task I will ask you to perform. Hitler took possession of the spear and tried unsuccessfully to unite the world by eradicating the Jews. So I will send a Jew to take the spear . . . and I will succeed where Hitler failed."

Isaac listened with a vague sense of unreality. He'd been around Romulus long enough to know that the man often spoke in riddles, but this one made no sense at all.

Romulus's mercurial black eyes deepened. "I have been in negotiation with the curators of the Hapsburg Treasure House. They agree, of course, that as president of the

Universal Network the Imperial Regalia is at my disposal, but what do I care for a crown and scepter? The treasure I want—the piece I must have—is the Spear of Longinus. I could send an armored car to fetch it tomorrow, but that would draw unwanted attention, as would my presence in Vienna. And so I am sending you, Isaac Ben-David. You will go to the Imperial Palace in Vienna, and you will quietly receive the Spear of Longinus in my name. And then you shall bring it to me in Paris."

Unnerved by the sudden change in agenda, Isaac looked up and blinked in bewilderment. "Sir, I work as the liaison between you and the State of Israel. I'm not sure I see how this task has anything to do with Israel's interests—"

Romulus smiled then, but it was the smile he used to freeze men's blood. "Is Israel part of the Universal Network?"

"Well, yes. Of course."

"Did Israel not send you to serve me?"

Isaac shrugged to hide his confusion. "They did."

"Then how can you hesitate to fulfill this request? To serve me is to serve Israel, for Israel and I are one. Jerusalem and I are one." Passion flickered in Romulus's eyes like heat lightning. "Do you remember the crowd at the Temple dedication? And did you hear those gathered in Times Square today? On both occasions, Isaac, my name was on every tongue. Jerusalem will soon be the capital of my new empire, and from Jerusalem I will send peace to cover the land like a blanket."

Isaac said nothing, but nodded soberly. "When am I to go on this errand?"

"Very soon, perhaps tomorrow." Romulus lifted his head then, like a cat scenting the breeze. "As soon as Nadim tells me the way is clear. He will prepare your path."

Isaac clenched his jaw, instinctively knowing that the subject of Romulus's spirit counselor was not open for discussion. Nearly everyone who moved in Romulus's inner circle had heard several references to the elusive Nadim, but never had anyone questioned his existence. Isaac wondered if this so-called guide might even be a manifestation of some sort of mental illness, but thus far Romulus had not made an impolitic move . . .

The president leaned back in his chair, a beatific smile creasing the fine wrinkles on his face. "You are wondering about Nadim."

Isaac blinked. Could the man read minds? "I am curious," he admitted.

Romulus seemed not to take offense. He smiled, his dark eyes creasing in an expression of admiration. "Nadim is not to be feared, Major. He is not evidence that I manifest multiple personalities, as some have suggested, nor is he a figment of my imagination. He is a spiritual being, as real as the air this jet floats upon, as real as the life that sparks in your blood. I am not a slave to him, of course, but he is wise, he knows things, and he recognizes . . . my unique gifts."

His expression stilled and grew serious. "We don't talk about Nadim in the media because most people's minds are too darkened to understand. But one day I will bring the light of clarification to everyone. All of mankind will recognize the true spiritual glory and light and power that have surrounded men and women for eons. And then, at last, we will truly be one with the gods. We will be at peace."

Romulus looked at Isaac with an intense but secret expression. "That's what you want, isn't it, Major? Peace in your nation, in your city, in your home."

Keenly aware of Romulus's scrutiny, Isaac nodded.

"Your home is particularly troubled." Romulus paused to run his finger along the arm of his leather chair. "You and your wife are practically strangers, and you have been estranged for months. Is this not true?"

Isaac drew himself up, swallowing to bring his heart down from his throat. How could Romulus know these things? Isaac had not spoken to anyone about his relationship with Sarah. He was too angry, too hurt, and too confused to even speak of his wife and yet . . .

Across the cabin, Romulus closed his eyes. A glow rose in his face, as though he contained a candle that had just been lit. Beneath his eyelids, Isaac could see the fluttering of his eyes, like the heartbeats of baby birds.

"You fear your wife no longer loves you," Romulus whispered, a faint bite in his smooth voice. "Nadim knows this. If you want to know the truth, you have to ask. Nadim will search the matter out and give you an answer."

Isaac stared wordlessly at Romulus, his heart pounding. Surely he had misunderstood something. Exhaustion had confused his thoughts. Because this was either a very bizarre dream or the most powerful man in the world had just offered to act as a psychic on Isaac's behalf.

He squeezed his fist and felt the muscles along his arm contract. He was awake, and Romulus sat in the chair, his eyes closed, his face perfectly blank, waiting. The man had offered to help, and Isaac had questions aplenty.

He opened his mouth, but the words would not come. Years of religious training clogged his throat; fortunetelling was an abomination; any and all occult practices were detestable. But though he had obeyed the Law throughout his childhood and youth, what had the Holy One done for him? HaShem had taken his child, left his marriage a cold and barren wasteland, and destroyed his personal peace . . .

"I want to know the truth." Isaac forced the words past his unwilling tongue, "Does my wife still love me, or does she want a divorce?"

Romulus's eyes twitched again beneath the thin covering of his lids, then he drew a ragged breath. "Your wife, Sarah," he said, in an aching, husky voice Isaac scarcely recognized, "is in love with . . . his name is Melman."

Isaac shook his head, disbelieving. This could all be a trick. Romulus had spies everywhere, every nation, even the allies of the Universal Network kept their intelligence agents busy. Sarah's association with Danny Melman could be a lucky guess.

"Tell me something I don't know," Isaac insisted, his voice hoarse. "Tell me something no one else would know. Tell me the truth."

Romulus's face twisted, then he said, "The last time you were home, many months ago, you stood in the bedroom with your wife." He paused and shuddered slightly, then continued in a voice that seemed to come from far away. "She began to undress, but stopped and stepped into the bathroom. She did not proceed because she did not want you to see . . . that she was expecting another child. But she miscarried that baby and swore you would never know what happened."

Cold sweat prickled on Isaac's jaws. Sarah, pregnant? Impossible. If she'd been pregnant and had a miscarriage, his father would have told him . . . unless Sarah did not want anyone to know.

He took a deep, quivering breath to quell the leaping

pulse beneath his ribs. Romulus opened his eyes slowly then, seeing Isaac's expression, reached out a hand in silent sympathy. "I'm so sorry," he said simply, dropping his hand in his lap. "I know this is hard to hear from anyone, but at least you heard it from a trusted friend."

"Please." Isaac closed his eyes. He did not want to talk about Sarah now. He didn't want to talk about anything.

Romulus leaned forward in his chair and rested his arms on his knees. "Renounce your old life, Isaac, and become one of us. Divorce your faithless wife and join me. Do you want a beautiful woman on your arm? I can arrange it. Do you want another child to carry on *your* name? I can arrange that. I can arrange anything on earth you require to be happy, if only you will join my cause, Isaac Ben-David. We are larger than Israel. We are the world."

Isaac drew a deep breath and felt a dozen different emotions collide. Every step in his life until this moment had carried him in the wrong direction. As a boy, he had given his devotion to a God who did not hear the desperate prayers of his people. As a young man, he had given his strength to a country that could not protect innocent citizens as they rode upon city buses. As a mature man, he had given his love to a woman who had not needed or wanted him for years.

Well, today Romulus had lifted the blinders from his eyes. Sarah had been playing him for a fool, living under his roof and using his name while living a secret life.

He would play the fool no longer.

Isaac looked up and met Romulus's steady gaze. "Tell me what you want me to do."

A look of dark satisfaction crept over the president's features, a look almost of gloating. "In order to establish and preserve global peace," Romulus said, as calmly as if they were discussing the weather, "we must eradicate all resistance. Charisma and pleasant words can only accomplish so much, Isaac, so we will need to add authority to our arsenal. To insure our power, I must possess the Spear of Longinus. You will go to Vienna and accept delivery of the spear, then bring the relic to the Paris chateau. There you will place the spear into my hands. It is most important"—Romulus paused for emphasis—"that you do not tell anyone in Tel Aviv about this task. It is a classified mission, known only to you, me, and Elijah Reis."

Isaac leaned back and considered the proposal. Though the spear could not have any real power, the legend surrounding it would enhance Romulus's authority. The obscure story would have to be widely disseminated, of course, but the Universal Movement's PR machine could spread a dozen variations of it around the globe within an hour. And the relic itself was nothing, just an ancient spearhead with a colorful history. Its purported powers came from the imaginations of men, not from the iron molecules that formed its composition.

He shifted his position as he mentally weighed the other side of the argument. His superiors at the IDF would probably not approve a mission that had nothing to do with Israeli security or diplomacy. But his mission at the Universal Network was to do his part to preserve world peace, and this mission did fit within the parameters of that goal. Finally, in the grand scheme of things, what the IDF did not know would not matter . . .

Isaac looked up. "I'll do it," he said. "As soon as you give the word, I'll go."

A faint smile hovered about Romulus's lips as he nodded.

SEVENTEEN

ISAAC SAT IN A PRIVATE COMPARTMENT ON THE TRAIN, relaxing to the easy rhythm of the wheels. After flying to Vienna, he had decided to return to Paris via rail for two reasons: First, the train was the least likely mode of transportation for a diplomatic attaché carrying a priceless relic; second, he needed quiet time alone to think about his wife.

The pickup in Vienna had gone as Isaac expected, with few problems. The curator at the museum had been expecting him and seemed quite relieved to have the spear removed from his custody. The curator personally escorted Isaac into his office, where he locked the door and then took a leather briefcase from a vault behind his desk. With trembling fingers, he unlocked the briefcase, then waved his hand over the contents.

Isaac leaned forward and frowned. He had expected the Spear of Longinus to be some glorious and shining weapon, but the triangular object lying on faded red velvet was black with age and wrapped with a gold sleeve and metallic thread. As a weapon, it appeared incredibly primitive. As a treasure, it appeared misnamed.

"That's it?" he asked the curator.

The man nodded so vigorously that Isaac feared his wire glasses would fall from his nose.

"All right, then."

With a sigh of resignation, the curator snapped the briefcase shut, then whirled the dials on the locking mechanism. "Finally," he said, producing a pair of handcuffs from a drawer, "there is this."

Isaac said nothing as the little man fastened the handcuffs first to the briefcase, then to his own wrist. He had transported classified documents before—less openly than this, but they had certainly been more crucial.

"You know, of course," the curator said, pausing as he gave Isaac the handcuff key, "about the legend of this relic."

"I've heard of it."

The thin line of the curator's worried mouth clamped tight for a moment, and his sinewy throat bobbed once as he swallowed. "I believe the story. The relic has been safe here, tucked away with so many other pieces of history. I shudder just to think of it going forth into the world again—"

Isaac gripped the handle of the attaché case with both hands. "Adrian Romulus is a man of peace. I assure you, sir, the spear is merely symbolic for him."

A tide of fear washed through the man's eyes. "I certainly hope so. The last time this thing left the museum, over sixty million people died before it was returned."

Not knowing how to answer, Isaac nodded to the curator, extended his free hand in courtesy, then picked up the briefcase and left the curator's office.

As he traversed the museum and moved toward the exit, he couldn't help noticing the gleaming crowns, swords, and scepters worn by other Germanic kings. Why hadn't

Romulus chosen one of those objects to symbolize his consolidation of power? They did not have legends attached, but the brains employed by the Universal Movement could certainly have invented a new one to suit the occasion. And backstopping a legend was a relatively simple matter—an agency merely had someone place forged documents in places where they would likely be stumbled upon by a reporter or researcher. Romulus could have invented a convincing legend for any of the more attractive relics and convinced the world that every word was true.

Odd, that he would so fervently desire this spearhead.

Isaac was fairly certain he spied at least one surveillance team as he left the museum—a man and a woman, following at wing and tail positions. As he paused to buy a newspaper from a vending machine, he saw the woman, about ten feet behind him, freeze on the sidewalk like a startled deer. The man across the street was more composed; he kept walking for about eight paces, then stopped to look in a window—an old and obvious trick that allowed an agent to watch his rabbit in the window reflection.

"Amateurs," Isaac muttered. He walked quickly through the lunchtime crowds, mingling as best he could, then ducked inside an alley. While mentally counting from one to fifteen—the longest time a tail might wait without panicking, he fished the handcuff key from his pocket and released the briefcase from his wrist, then pulled off his overcoat. After untaping a bright red shopping bag from the underside of his coat lining, he wadded up the garment and stuffed it behind a pile of cardboard boxes. He slid the briefcase into the shopping bag, then pulled a folded Chicago Bulls baseball cap from his trouser pocket and fitted it to his head.

"Fourteen, fifteen. Ready or not, here I come." Easing back into the flow of pedestrian traffic, he quickened his pace and caught a glance of himself in a store window. To any observer, he appeared to be a happy American tourist on a shopping spree. The shopping bag had come from a department store on the same block, and his step was far livelier and less encumbered without the heavy overcoat.

After crossing the street in a crowd, he stood on the corner and lifted his face toward a posted bus schedule. His gaze, however, followed the tails, both of whom were now working in an expanding circle, searching for the man in the black coat.

Isaac suppressed a smile, then stepped into the street and lifted his hand to hail a taxi. When a cab stopped, he slipped into the backseat with his shopping bag and told the driver to take him to the train station.

Now, riding in the smooth rhythm of the rails, Isaac wondered who had sent the surveillance team. They weren't Israelis—no Mossad agent would ever be as clumsy as those two. The Americans had sharply curtailed their overseas operations after the Disruption, so the surveillance could have come from any disgruntled nation affiliated with the Universal Network . . . or even Romulus himself.

Isaac tapped the shopping bag across his lap and felt the reassuring heft of the briefcase within. If he were Romulus, he would definitely have sent a surveillance team. The president had deliberately chosen a low-profile means of transporting an artifact he considered important, but he would never trust a single individual with such a crucial task.

Isaac made a mental note to speak to General Archer about the clumsy operatives. They were probably freelancers, people pulled from the ranks of the former East German Stasi. The man was old enough to have worked for the former Communist secret police. The woman could have been his wife.

"*Karte, bitte.*" The conductor knocked on Isaac's door, then stepped inside, his hand outstretched for the ticket.

"Certainly." Isaac pulled his train ticket from the shopping bag and handed it to the conductor, who searched it, then nodded in approval.

The conductor spoke in English. "Your identification, please."

Isaac held out his right arm as the conductor pulled his scanner from his pocket, then waved it over the back of Isaac's hand. The conductor's smile flattened. "This identification code is incomplete, sir. There is no UFM suffix."

"I'm an Israeli citizen," Isaac said, lowering his hand. "We are exempt from membership in the Universal Faith Movement, so the UFM code is not necessary."

The conductor frowned. "Not necessary, but certainly desirable, sir." Drizzling disapproval, he spun on his heel and left the compartment.

Isaac leaned his head on the train window and stared at the scenery rushing by. By now Sarah had certainly taken the identification chip, but had her father and the other resistant religious Jews? With the advent of the Universal Network's technology, they now had to find everyday life difficult. Most stores, even in Israel, required a Universal Chip even to purchase something as trivial as a pack of gum.

They would soon be two steps behind the rest of the world. Many of the Western nations had begun to require a UFM code within a citizen's identification chip. At this point, the UFM code served public relations purposes only—Romulus wanted the nations of the world to unite in peace, and what better way to do that than through a religious organization? The UFM code, which could be painlessly applied to any individual's Universal Chip through the skin, silently proclaimed an individual's membership in the Universal Faith Movement every time he or she moved through an ID checkpoint or a grocery store.

The Jews had been exempted from required membership in the Universal Faith movement, but more than a few forward-thinking rabbis had already contacted Romulus and expressed a desire to join. By exempting the Jews, they insisted, Romulus's organization was subtly encouraging anti-Semitism. If everyone in the world who longed for peace belonged to the Universal Faith Movement, what might a thinking person assume about a group of people who refused to join?

No matter what the rest of the world thought, Isaac knew Sarah's father would never join with any organization that had sprung from the World Council of Churches. Sarah would be more pragmatic about the issue, but she would not accept the UFM code without struggling through a severe bout of conscience . . .

Nausea followed that thought, rippling like a slippery snake through Isaac's abdomen. How could his Sarah be unfaithful? If Romulus had not exposed her falseness, Isaac would have never believed his wife capable of adultery and deceit. Perhaps she had already taken the UFM code. Perhaps he didn't know her at all.

Isaac pulled the shopping bag to his chest and crossed his arms over it, steeling himself to the long and lonely journey ahead. The burning bitterness in the pit of his gut wasn't going anywhere.

†

"Reis?" Isaac turned and pressed the cell phone closer to his ear, trying to avoid a pair of noisy women. "The objective was accomplished. I'm at the Paris train station."

"Romulus wants you to bring it immediately."

"I'm on my way. ETA thirty minutes."

"Very good."

Isaac punched the power off, then dropped the phone into his pocket. The train trip had been uneventful, with little to disturb his long thoughts. Now the sun was setting on the western horizon, and Romulus waited at the chateau.

A cabby pulled to the curb in front of Isaac, brakes squealing sharply. The little man inside bent down to catch Isaac's eye. "Taxi, monsieur?"

"No, merci." One of the first rules of intelligence work was *never accept the first cab that comes along.* Ignoring the cabby's curse of frustration, Isaac walked to the next cab in line and gave him the address of Romulus's chateau.

Half an hour later, with the sun securely tucked behind the trees, the cab pulled up outside the tall gates of Romulus's chateau. *"Cieux de merciful! Romulus habite ici, n'est ce pas?"* the driver exclaimed, slouching in his seat to catch a glimpse of the house through the iron bars.

"I'm not at liberty to say who lives here," Isaac answered, getting out with his precious parcel. He paid the driver with a fistful of euros, then walked to the security panel and waved his hand beneath the scanner.

"Bonsoir, Monsieur Ben-David," a mechanical female voice purred over the speaker. "You may proceed through the gate."

At that moment, the iron gate swung open. As Isaac walked through, he knew hidden electromagnetic devices were scanning his form for weapons or other contraband. As soon as he cleared the first checkpoint, the gates swung shut and locked.

"An escort will arrive for you momentarily." The pleasant voice poured from another speaker, this one hidden behind a tree. "A possible weapon has been detected in your luggage. Please remain where you are until further notified."

Isaac gripped the briefcase and said nothing as he waited. Overhead, the moon played peekaboo, hiding her face in the clouds one moment and shining down on him in the next. The great stars were little more than silvery points and the small ones were lost in the haze over Paris.

From somewhere in the distance, a sprinkler whirred water over the thirsty landscape. Apparently the international regulations of mandatory water rationing did not apply on Romulus's estate.

Finally a figure appeared, the round beam of a flashlight bouncing on the path ahead of him. Isaac expected to see the burly figure of one of the night security guards, but no less a personage than Elijah Reis himself came and stood before Isaac. He shone the flashlight beam directly into Isaac's face for a moment, then snapped the beam downward.

"Major Ben-David, you are awaited." A note of solemnity filled the man's voice.

Isaac gestured toward the house. "Is President Romulus—"

"He's in the great hall," Reis interrupted. "Come with

me, and you will see. Many have gathered here, and we have
been anxiously awaiting your return."

Isaac lifted a brow at this, but the darkness must have
hidden his expression, for Reis did not comment further. The
man said nothing for a long moment, then jerked the flashlight toward the briefcase in Isaac's hand.

"So that's it?"

"Yes."

"Did you have any trouble?"

"No. I spotted one surveillance team, but I lost them with
no trouble. And if anyone wanted to follow, I assumed they
would surveil the airport. That's why I took the train."

"Very clever." Reis spoke in a tone of surprised respect.
"Can you imagine who might have wanted to follow you?"

"The only person that comes to my mind is Romulus
himself," Isaac answered, his voice dry. "No one else would
care much about this ancient relic."

"Never underestimate the power of the opposition." Reis's
voice dissolved in a thready whisper. "If they understood its
significance, they would do anything to stop us. If Romulus
says the sky is blue, they would say it is green."

They walked in silence a moment more, the sound of their
shoes on the gravel walkway the only sound. Then Reis said,
"Did you hear about the two lunatics?"

"Moses and Elijah?" Surprised, Isaac cut a look to his
companion. The moon slipped from behind a cloud to cast a
silvery light upon the other man's face.

"Yes, though I cannot speak their names without feeling
disgust." Reis's mouth curled and rolled like he wanted to spit.
"To think that I should share a name with one of them—"

"What did they do?" Isaac interrupted, trying to keep his

companion centered on the topic. "More trouble in Jerusalem?"

"Worse. They came here yesterday. They stood outside the gates of this chateau and cursed Romulus's name. The locals were horrified, of course, and Adrian was terribly embarrassed. Worst of all, an unfortunate accident occurred in the midst of the trouble. Two of our security guards spilled gasoline on themselves, then one of the fools lit a cigarette. Both were severely burned. Neither survived, I'm afraid."

Reis's face went bleak with sorrow. "The president took the news very hard. I've never seen him so upset. He was disturbed, of course, because two of his employees died, and I've never seen him so angry. If the two troublemakers had not left the area by nightfall, I'm not sure what Romulus would have done."

Isaac shook his head in confusion. "Why couldn't the guards arrest them?"

"They tried. But that's when the fire broke out. They escaped in the confusion."

They had reached the front door. Reis opened it, then stood back and gestured for Isaac to precede him. "The honor belongs to you," he said. His small, bright eyes grew somewhat smaller and brighter, the pupils of them training in on Isaac like gun barrels. "Go straight into the hall and take the spear directly to Romulus. Everyone is waiting."

Nodding, Isaac passed through the doorway and crossed the tile floor.

EIGHTEEN

FEELING A BREATH OF CHANGE IN THE ATMOSPHERE, Romulus opened his eyes. The relic had finally arrived, borne by Isaac Ben-David, the son of a Jew and a descendant of David. Later, those who learned of this night would note the significance. Romulus straightened in his high-backed chair and stared at the double doors that would open momentarily.

"Look, he's awake. He sees!"

The whispers began as several of the men who sat facing him lifted their heads. The atmosphere in the hall was spiced with incense and the prayers of those who had found Romulus faithful and able. Dozens of candles served to illumine only the central portion of the great hall where Romulus sat in his ornately carved chair. A canopy of shadows covered the ceiling above, while flickering firelight decorated the walls and moved with every breath of wind through the clerestoried windows.

One of the double doors opened. Major Isaac Ben-David stood in the fissure, backlit by the bright light in the foyer. He stood motionless for a moment, as if to adjust his vision to the darkened surroundings, then his eyes sought and found Romulus upon his throne.

Yes, Isaac Ben-David. Seek me and find me. Come!

Drawn by the unspoken command, the Israeli stepped forward, bearing the briefcase in his hand. The two dozen men in the room caught their breath at the sight of it, and quiet shushings echoed through the chamber as Isaac approached.

Romulus leaned forward until he sat on the very edge of his chair, then held out his hand. "Isaac Ben-David," he said, his voice breaking like thunder over the silent chamber, "you have brought what my soul longs for."

"I have brought the spear." Ben-David stopped as if uncertain of his role in the drama, then he saw the small table to the right of the throne. Sensing its purpose, he set the briefcase upon it, then flipped the rotating locks with sure, swift movements. The locks clicked open, the audience gasped in appreciation of the moment, then Isaac Ben-David stepped forward with the open briefcase in his hand.

Romulus felt the sting of tears in his eyes as he stared at the spear. He had waited so long for this moment! He had felt the spear's lack before he even knew it existed. And now that he understood its power and possessed it, he would succeed where so many others had failed. He would harness the powers of the world's true master; he would lead the world to acknowledge the source of all worldly ambition. He would be victorious.

Romulus reached out and ran a questing fingertip over the rough iron. His fingers slipped between the velvet cushion and the blade, then gripped the chiseled edge that had pierced the body of the One who called himself Almighty.

Death and power, in one instrument. Eternal authority to gain.

"Elijah," he whispered into the darkness behind him.

"Here, Adrian."

"The shaft."

From out of the darkness, Elijah Reis stepped forward, a polished wooden pole in his grasp. Romulus took it with his free hand and held it aloft in the candlelight so that all might appreciate the full significance of the moment. A Jewish craftsman had hewn the shank from Israeli acacia wood. While he held the pole upright, Adrian slipped the spearhead into place, then wrapped his hand around the metal flanges, molding them to the tapering line of the wooden shaft.

The weapon was complete. As Reis melted back into the shadows, Isaac Ben-David stood motionless in the candlelight, his gaze fixed upon the talisman of power.

Romulus threw back his head as his breath caught in his lungs, then spilled out onto the gathering in a rush of words.

†

Isaac took an instinctive half-step back as Romulus began to speak. The words were foreign to his ear, sounds unlike any tongue he had ever heard, and suddenly they mixed and mingled with other tongues, other *voices*, that poured from the throat of a single man. Isaac stood rooted to the spot like a frightened child, as the men behind him began to weep, lift their hands, and sway to and fro like Orthodox Jews praying on the Day of Atonement.

It wasn't possible; somehow he must have been drugged, and now he witnessed the effects of a visual and auditory hallucinogen. For now Romulus was actually *glowing*, his head emitting an aura that alternated gold and silver in the flickering firelight. One voice from his throat spoke French, another German, another English, another that strange guttural tongue

Isaac had never heard. And over and over the voices Isaac could understand were repeating phrases about power and control and victory.

Was Romulus mad? Was *Isaac?*

Tearing his gaze from the bewildering sight of Romulus and the spear, he looked around and saw that the other men in the room were as amazed as he. But they were now kneeling in homage, in *worship*, of the one who held the spear. Wave after wave of shock slapped at Isaac, compounded by sights and scents and sounds until he was unable to bear the noise and confusion any longer. Leaving Romulus in a transport of ecstasy, Isaac resisted the urge to clap his hands over his ears and slipped through the worshipers.

When he reached the safety and relative normalcy of the tiled foyer, he stood in front of one of the tall mirrors and pressed his damp palms to the silvered surface. "You're not crazy," he told his reflection, noting that a trickle of perspiration crept down the flesh just before his ear.

"No, my friend, you are not."

Isaac snapped his mouth shut and turned. General Archer stood beside him, clad in his blue uniform with the top button of his dress coat undone. The gaping button was a touch of normalcy juxtaposed against a sea of madness.

"Excuse me, General." Isaac dropped his hand, then thrust his arms behind his back. "I suppose you think I've lost my mind, but I don't always go around talking to mirrors."

Archer's blue eyes warmed slightly, and the hint of a smile acknowledged the success of Isaac's mind reading. "I don't blame you, Major, for feeling confused. These other men, after all, are the upper echelon of the Universal Faith Movement. They have known him for years and have awaited this moment nearly as long as he. They understand the power of the spear—and you are just beginning to understand."

"I don't understand a thing."

Archer put his hand upon Isaac's shoulder. "You understand more than you think you do. And soon, very soon, you will understand all. But for now, I have been sent to tell you good night. You performed a heroic feat with admirable success, and the president himself will thank you later. He wanted me to send you to your hotel for a well-deserved rest. We've reserved the jet to return you to Jerusalem soon, but before you go, we want you to enjoy a bit of a vacation. See Paris. Take in a show at the theater. Indulge in the rewards of your excellent labor."

Isaac turned toward the door, which Archer opened with another smile. A limo, one of the finer ones from Romulus's garage, stood outside with the motor running and a chauffeur standing ready.

"There is one more thing," Archer said, lifting his brows. "It is a minor thing, purely ceremonial, really. But Romulus has mentioned that you really should have a UFM code included in your ID serial number."

Isaac said nothing, but blinked in stunned silence.

"I know the Jews were exempted by the terms of the peace accord, but so many things have happened since those days," Archer said, tilting his head as he looked at Isaac. "Times are rapidly changing. And it is not without precedent—you know we have heard from several Jewish groups who want to join us."

"I know," Isaac said slowly. "But there are so many others who will always have strong feelings about the matter. It's not a question of my loyalty, for Romulus surely knows I am willing to serve him however I can—"

The general put out a silencing hand. "The time for complete unity is upon us, Major. And the president knows that many of the Jews are reluctant to join the Universal Faith Movement on account of their religious beliefs. We, therefore, must show them that it is possible to be a Jew, an admirable citizen of Israel, and one who is loyal to the Universal Movement." His face creased in a sudden smile. "You have become a bit of a hero to your countrymen, Isaac. They know about your efforts to aid in the rebuilding of the Temple. They respect you. You must be their example."

Isaac felt a curious, tingling shock. "You are asking me to join the Universal Faith Movement . . . *publicly?*"

"Of course." Archer gave Isaac a thin smile utterly without humor. "We want you, in fact, to accept the UFM code on international television. We've arranged for a meeting with the prime minister, in which you will both have the code applied to your Universal Chips. And after your countrymen see that it is possible to be loyal to Israel and universality, they will renounce their old prohibitions and embrace the principles of unity and peace."

Isaac felt the corner of his mouth twist with exasperation. "If the prime minister was involved in this negotiation, why did I not know about it? I am supposed to be the liaison between Romulus and the prime minister's office."

"My dear young man," Archer said, patting him on the shoulder in a paternal fashion as he escorted him out, "you were away from us on a far more important mission. This notion came to me rather suddenly, and Romulus thought it a brilliant idea. So go to your hotel, get a good night's rest, and plan on returning to Jerusalem later this week. We'll be in touch later, once the details for the observance have been settled."

As he stepped down the marble stairs toward the car, Isaac felt the truth all at once, like an electric tingle in the pit of his stomach. Archer was lying. Isaac had only been away from Paris for two days, and such a sudden idea could certainly have waited forty-eight hours. But they didn't want him to speak to the prime minister's office about the UFM code, and they didn't want him in Jerusalem while they made plans for this televised ceremony.

If Archer was lying about something so trivial as this, nothing at Chez Romulus was as it seemed.

What else had they lied about?

†

At a small café two blocks from his Paris B&B, Isaac stood before a pay phone and dialed his home in Jerusalem. Sarah answered almost immediately. For the briefest instant Isaac wondered if she had leaped to answer a call from Danny Melman, but he shoved those thoughts aside to address a more pressing issue.

"Sarah?" Knowing the Israelis and Romulus's people probably monitored her phone line, he took pains to keep his voice light. "Hi. I was just wondering—is Uncle Laban coming to dinner tomorrow?"

He knew he'd caught her by surprise; still, the long hiss of the telephone line concerned him.

"Uncle Laban?" she finally said, a catch in her voice. "Why, yes. I expect him at ten. We're having dinner at the little bistro. The one nearest our house."

"I hope you have a good time." Isaac paused, listening to the silence. There were so many things he wanted to say, but this was not the time or place. "Sorry, but I have to go," he said. "I love you."

She didn't answer, but he thought he heard the sound of a muffled sob before he disconnected the call.

Every Shin Bet officer and IDF liaison learned lessons in basic intelligence tradecraft, and he and Sarah had just practiced a lesson from basic telephone evasion techniques. "Uncle Laban" was the nearest Israeli agent in Paris, probably someone in Mossad. She'd told Isaac that he would arrive at ten, which meant she'd send a contact to rendezvous with Isaac at either nine or eleven that night. And the bistro "nearest our house" meant whichever restaurant was closest to the Israeli embassy in Paris.

A light rain had begun to fall when Isaac stepped outside the café. He pulled the collar of his coat up to shield his throat, then thrust his hands into his pockets and hunched forward, walking into the night.

NINETEEN

AT THE SHABAK OFFICE IN JERUSALEM, DANNY MELMAN paced beside the conference table, his face contorted in frustration. "What did he say exactly, Sarah? We need every detail."

Irked by his cool, detached manner, Sarah glared up at her boss. "I've told you what he said. If you want a word-for-word rendition, pull out the tapes and listen for yourself. I know my phone is tapped."

Melman scrubbed his hand through his hair in frustration, then looked at the Mossad director seated in the briefing room with them. "You heard her. Ben-David needs an agent tonight, so something's up. He's never called for help before."

"I'll see to it." The Mossad director smiled a grim little grin as he stood and turned to edge past Melman. "We've been expecting something. Romulus's people have been in touch with the PM's office, and we think the major was left out of the loop—until tonight, apparently."

Sarah watched him go, then clasped her hands and looked up at Melman. "Do you think Isaac's really in trouble? I heard about what happened in Paris today—"

"We don't know what happened in Paris."

She laughed, a bitter note in her voice. "You mean we don't want to *accept* what happened in Paris. But I saw the entire thing. A French cameraman caught it on film, and CNN sent it out over the satellite. They aired it once before the Universal machine pulled the plug—"

"Hush." Melman glanced toward the open door. "You don't know that the tape was censored. They're now calling it a fabrication."

"A fabrication?" Sarah's lower lip trembled as she stared at her boss. "Does that make sense to you? I saw it, Danny, and what I saw was too bizarre to be a fabrication. Those two prophets were standing outside Romulus's gates when two of Romulus's security guards came down to arrest them. The security guys were at least fifteen feet away when they drew their weapons, and from the look of the video I saw, I'd say they got off at least one shot each. But then the one who calls himself Moses pointed at the guards and *whoosh!* Just like that, the man lit up like a human torch."

"The official story is that they had an accident," Melman said, his gray eyes darkening as he held her gaze. "The latest press release stated that the men spilled gasoline on their uniforms and ignited when one of them tried to light a cigarette. Or maybe what you saw was accurate, and a spark from the guy's discharging gun ignited their clothing. But what you're saying couldn't be true. It's not humanly possible."

"The laws of nature and physics don't seem to apply to those two." Sarah turned in her chair and raked her fingers into her hair, leaning her head on her hand. "I mean, think about it. They said they would block up the heavens because humanity would not repent, and now we're in the middle of the worst drought in history. They predicted famine, and half the world is starving today. They predicted pestilence, and Africa is now in the grip of bubonic plague, and AIDS, and that horrible new virus I can't even pronounce—"

Melman snorted softly and sat on the edge of the table. "It's all a matter of natural progression, don't you see? The drought brings the famine, and the famine brings the pestilence. Those men didn't cause any of this. They're just crazies, like the *majnoon* that invade Jerusalem every Easter. And I hope they stay in Paris—I'd rather they bother Adrian Romulus than come back here and bedevil us."

Unwillingly, Sarah's thoughts turned to the man on whose account she had called this late meeting. "Isaac is in Paris," she said slowly, running her hand through her hair. "And he needs our help, or he wouldn't have called us."

"And we're going to take care of him. He's one of ours." Melman stepped closer and took her hand, prying it from her tangled hair. "Don't worry, Sarah. Everything is going to be fine."

†

Adam Archer stood in the steady drizzle of a cold Paris street and watched as Isaac Ben-David entered Au Caveau Montpensier, a cozy English pub merely a stone's throw from the Israeli embassy. The man had been careful. If not for the unexpected call to his wife—one that consisted of cryptic language and ended with a surprise profession of love—they would not have expected Isaac to do anything but go back to the hotel and go to sleep. But instead, he had gone out into the rain, his head lowered in thought. The agents stationed outside the B&B had let him go and concentrated on the signal from the homing beacon hidden inside the pen Archer slipped into Ben-David's pocket as he ushered the Israeli out the door.

Ben-David hesitated outside the bar for a moment, then opened the door and entered. Archer jogged across the street and splashed through a puddle, then stood on the sidewalk outside the establishment and peered through a stained-glass window. Ben-David was sitting at the bar, the picture of a lonely military man.

Now another man approached. The other agent.

Archer grinned and crossed his arms, not caring that the drizzle had chilled him to the bone. Though he hadn't been in the room when Ben-David presented the spear to Romulus, he'd heard enough to know that the experience had fallen just a hair short of a circus sideshow. Reis had admitted as much and suspected that this born-and-bred Israeli might be thinking about jumping ship . . . or raising the curtain before Romulus was ready.

Archer stepped beneath the shadow of an awning and pulled a cigarette from his pocket. After taking a moment to light the tip, he inhaled deeply, then watched the smoke flow out into the chilly air. Nothing could surpass the satisfaction of a job well done. And his hunch had proved true.

After ten minutes, the second man leaned close to Ben-David, briefly placing his hand on his comrade's shoulder. Then he turned and moved toward the doorway. Archer flung his cigarette onto the sidewalk and left it to drown in the rain.

The agent walked quickly down Rue Montpensier, his head covered by a brimmed hat, his hands hidden within the pockets of a beige jacket. Archer lengthened his stride until he walked next to the man, then greeted him with a broad smile. "Hello! Haven't we met before?"

The agent blinked, then waved a hand. *"Pardon, mais je ne parle pas anglais."*

"I think you speak English just fine." Archer pulled the Heckler & Koch .45 from the holster beneath his coat and allowed his quarry a quick glimpse before shoving it into the man's rib cage. "We're going to step into this alley, and you're going to tell me everything you and Isaac Ben-David talked about."

The man pressed his lips together, but lifted his hands in a "don't shoot" pose and allowed Archer to escort him into the darkened alley. Archer pulled the man into a shadowed corner behind a trash receptacle, frisked him and pulled a gun from his shoulder holster, then stood him against the wall.

He shoved the man's gun deep into his coat pocket, then waved his own gun slightly, but kept it pointed toward the man's chest. At this close range, they'd be scraping rib chips out of the brick building if he fired. "Tell me about Major Ben-David."

Archer had to hand it to the Israelis; their agents didn't fluster easily. The man only held up his hands and lifted his shoulders in an impatient shrug. "I don't know who you are talking about."

"The man in the bar, you fool. I saw you talking to him."

"I never caught his name."

Archer gritted his teeth. "What did you talk about?"

The man only stared, wearing his face like a mask. "We talked about the weather."

"You lie!"

Stepping forward, Archer slammed the handgun across the man's right cheekbone. The fellow doubled over, then gripped his knees and panted heavily. "We talked," he repeated, glaring up at Archer, "about the weather."

"All right, let's say you did." Archer settled the gun again, aiming this time for the man's dark head. "Where were you going just now? Who else would be interested in the major's little weather report?"

"I was going home to my wife and children."

Archer hit the man again, on the same cheek. The skin separated, and even from where he stood, Archer could smell the metallic tang of blood.

His victim hunched further, perspiration beading upon his forehead. A muscle moved beneath the sheen of blood on his jaw, and he breathed through his nose with a faint whistling sound.

"You're not going to talk." Archer stated it as a matter of fact, not a question. The Israelis had always possessed remarkable resolve. They occasionally failed spectacularly, but their failures were rare, and they had more chutzpah than any intelligence agency in the world.

The man looked up, his eyes glittering like a paralyzed bird that sees the serpent approaching.

Archer pulled a Waterman pen from his pocket. "This idea," he held the pen before the wounded man's eyes, "came from the Soviets. There's a cyanide capsule in the barrel. One bite from you, one *hard* bite, and it'll all be over. Your agency will have a few questions, no doubt, but they'll know you made your own choice. If they find you splattered all over this wall, however, they'll always wonder how much you gave away before you died."

He paused, allowing his words to sink in. "So—do you want the pen or not?"

The Israeli's dark brows rose, graceful wings of scorn. But then he reached out and took the pen.

Ten minutes later, Archer slid into a booth in a French McDonald's and punched Romulus's direct number on his cell phone. "It's done," he said when Reis came on the encrypted line. "No one will know anything until the time is right."

"Well done, General." Satisfaction purred in Reis's voice, then abruptly vanished. "But what of the two renegades? They are creating chaos and confusion; I've just heard that they turned water into blood."

Shifting in his seat, Archer watched a young boy dip his French fry into a puddle of catsup. "I'm working on that."

"The president is losing patience."

"We'll get them." Archer wrapped his palm around his coffee cup, then took a sip and enjoyed the warmth of the hot beverage. "After all, I doubt they've included immortality in their bag of tricks."

TWENTY

ISAAC KNEW HE WAS BEING WATCHED. FOR AS LONG AS he'd been in Paris, he'd been certain that Romulus's security people kept tabs on his goings and comings, but he had not felt the pressure of constant surveillance until after his return from Vienna. He wanted to blame the heavy sensation of foreboding on paranoia, but common sense reminded him that in the international arena, paranoia could be a healthy instinct. As an agent friend had once reminded him, "Paranoid means you know a *little* of what's going on. There's usually a lot more under the surface."

Following Archer's instructions, he followed a quiet routine. He slept late in his bachelor's room at the bed-and-breakfast, went for leisurely walks through the neighborhood, and even took in an English production of *Jekyll and Hyde* at the Opera Bastille. Every nerve in his body screamed with the urgent need to warn Sarah and Colonel Barak about the latest disturbing development in Romulus's program, but he had already done his part. He was but one player among many, and the Mossad would handle the information. If Romulus meant to do something evil now that he possessed the spear,

Israel would be forearmed. Knowledge was power, and now they knew that he had a bent toward the occult and he truly seemed to believe in the spear as a talisman of supernatural power . . .

As Isaac watched the production of *Jekyll and Hyde,* he couldn't help wondering about the twin poles he had observed in Romulus. The man could be charming, easy-going, and pleasant. He laughed easily and charmed everyone from babies to old men with the ease of a practiced politician. Isaac had recently read that the name Adrian was a new favorite for both boys and girls born in the last three years. Even Romulus had made the top-ten list of baby names.

But he could not deny the man's dark side. When Isaac placed the spear in Romulus's hand, he felt something akin to evil emanating from the man's core. Polite society, of course, would find such a notion laughable. No one these days believed a man could be pure good or pure evil; every individual was a mix of good and bad. No man was completely Jekyll; no man was purely Hyde. Neither was Romulus.

On Friday evening, after nearly a full week of waiting, Madame Blanchette, the mistress of the B&B, summoned Isaac to the phone. General Archer's aide was on the line and curtly told Isaac that he needed to be at the airport at seven the next morning. "The general has arranged a meeting with Avraham Har-Zion for 1:00," he said, his voice clipped, "so you will have a little time before your meeting with the prime minister if you wish to visit your father. The jet will depart soon afterward to return you to Paris, where General Archer will expect a full report upon the situation in Jerusalem."

Isaac agreed to meet the jet, then hung up. He stood in the

little foyer for a long moment, knowing that he had come to a crossroads. In the name of international peace, he could follow Romulus's plan and join the Universal Faith Movement. Thousands of Jews would watch as he and the prime minister accepted the UFM code on their Universal Chips, then they would do likewise, pledging their lives and loyalty to Romulus and the Universal Faith Movement.

Or he could refuse. But what would happen if he did? The IDF or Mossad should have sent him a message by now. He had not withheld much from the agent in the bar, so they knew about the spear, about the televised interview, and about Romulus's belief that whoever held the spear would rule the world. And though he had not told the agent about the voices pouring from Romulus's throat during that eerie ceremony, he planned to tell anyone who would listen when he returned to Jerusalem. They would not be able to doubt his sanity when they saw the light of earnestness in his eyes.

All the anxieties that had been lapping at his subconscious suddenly crested and crashed. Why would Romulus, a self-proclaimed man of peace, choose to fixate upon an object of violence and war? Why had his eyes sparked when he took the ancient relic in his hands? And how would he explain the legion of voices and languages that poured out of his throat? The ancient Jewish sages would say such voices were the work of demons.

Isaac closed his eyes and shook his head. He did not believe in magic or amulets or folk tales. He did not believe in demons, either, especially since Jewish tradition described them as shadowless, thumbless creatures that haunted trees, ruins, and toilets.

Yet he could not deny that what he had witnessed in the

chateau came from a supernatural realm. His experience in the chateau's great hall lay beyond the domain of technology. Technological things he could understand; he'd been trained to expect and circumvent computer wizardry. But until recently he had dismissed the supernatural, decreeing that neither God nor Satan had any place in his life.

Now the supernatural had engulfed him. And he had never felt so frightened.

He needed help . . . from someone who understood such things. Sarah's father might be the man to ask for guidance; he really seemed to live according to his beliefs.

Isaac rapped his hand on the wall, grateful for an answer that seemed to have come from nowhere. Tomorrow he could use his free time in Jerusalem to visit Aaron Lerner.

That thought brought another in its wake, with a barb that struck the center of Isaac's heart. Strange, that Archer's aide had suggested that Isaac visit his father instead of his wife. Did he know about Sarah's infidelity? Had Romulus told his entire staff? If so, why?

An ugly swarm of thoughts he scarcely dared formulate came welling up as Isaac walked back to his room. Archer had undoubtedly lied to him about his contact with the prime minister's office. In an effort to win Isaac's loyalty, Romulus himself might lie. Romulus wanted Isaac to be an obedient puppet. He wanted a Jewish war hero to stand before a television camera and lift his hand in an oath of loyalty to the Universal Faith Movement . . . and what better way to convince a reluctant warrior than to cut him off from his Shin Bet wife and Orthodox father-in-law?

Reaching his room, Isaac walked to the closet and pulled out a dark coat, then slipped back down the staircase.

Madame Blanchette had already gone to bed; no one in the house would see him leave. And if a surveillance team lingered on the street, well, he'd give them a challenge unlike any they'd faced before.

He paused at the back door and plucked Madame Blanchette's bright pink rain hat from the pegboard above her gardening clogs. He stuck the hat on his head, turned up his collar, then pulled the hems of his pants up beneath the edge of his coat. Madame Blanchette was not exactly a petite creature, and she might be inclined to step down to the corner store for a bottle of milk for tomorrow's breakfast.

Darting into the shadows, Isaac hurried toward the store and its public phone . . . his link to Sarah.

†

Wearing pajamas, a heavy chenille robe, and socks, Sarah sat on the floor before the television in her front room. A stack of videotapes leaned against her left knee; a scrawled legal pad occupied the rug at her right. Behind her, Lily lay stretched out on the carpet, snoring in a steady rumbling sound.

The television screen displayed the bumpy video footage of a woman and her small children who were playing in a clearing adjacent to the Peace Forest, a spot near Kibbutz Ramat Rahel, a southern point of Jerusalem. The woman appeared to be about Sarah's age, and the children, a boy and a girl, were both younger than school age. Sarah stared at the little boy, her vision still gloomily colored with the memory of her own small son. Binyamin had hair just as dark as this boy's, but he had been quiet, not loud and boisterous like this little fellow . . .

Suddenly, without warning, a puma emerged from the darkness of the forest and leaped onto the mother. As the large cat crumpled the woman beneath its weight, the air filled with the screams of the children and the predator. For a sickening instant, Sarah saw one of the puma's claws rake the victim's face, then the screen went black. The husband had dropped the camera.

She glanced at the report that had accompanied the tape. The husband had been unable to frighten the animal away, and after ten terrifying minutes a policeman had appeared and shot the crazed animal. The woman had been taken to the hospital, but arrived DOA, a victim of extreme blood loss. The puma had severed the woman's jugular vein.

At least the children had been spared.

Sarah picked up the remote and pressed the off button. Melman had sent her home with more than a dozen video-taped incidents of bizarre animal attacks that had occurred in the last six months. For no apparent reason, three European circus elephants had trampled their handlers, a newly cap-tured African lion had nearly decapitated a zookeeper with one swipe of his claw, and a California jogging trail had reportedly been haunt-ed by a pair of mountain lions that killed nearly a dozen suburban athletes who refused to believe wild animals would attack with impunity in broad daylight. And domestic animals were not immune from whatever had infected creatures in the wild. Included among the videotapes was footage of a pet boa constrictor that had asphyxiated a two-year-old while the enraged father hacked at it in horror with a butcher knife.

What had happened to the world? Though civilized soci-ety had been on a downward slope from the beginning of time, since Gogol's Invasion it seemed as though creation and everything in it had begun to disobey even the laws of nature. Though the numbers had not been widely publicized, various governments had reported deaths by animal attack that totaled in the hundreds of thousands. In the last six months, the Israeli government alone had documented over 250 incidents of vicious, unprovoked animal attacks. Thirty children had died, including ten from a preschool class on a field trip to a dairy farm. While the children watched the milking operation from behind the safety of an iron gate, two cows broke through a restraining bar and began to trample the youngsters with what Sarah could only describe as mad vengeance.

The destruction did not end with animals. In certain spots of the globe, anarchy reigned as the poor rioted against the rich. The devastation of the earthquakes and nuclear attacks associated with Gogol's Invasion had effectively destroyed many governments, and in some provinces even Romulus's Universal Force could do almost nothing to stop criminal gangs' widespread reigns of terror. The lack of rain and resulting famine only exacerbated the problem—in many areas a single bag of groceries cost a full week's wages.

Disease had begun to stalk the earth in numbers unheard of since medieval times, when the Black Plague had wiped out entire cities. Without proper food and nutrition, children and the elderly fell prey to viruses that would not respond to modern antibiotics. The war-torn countries fared far worse than those that retained a degree of civilization, but even Israel had lost several thousand people to viral infections that had responded to chicken soup and decongestants in Sarah's youth.

The scientists, of course, had not hesitated to blame the

planet's condition on Vladimir Gogol. They insisted that the madman's biological and chemical attacks had upset the delicate balance of the environment. But in time, they promised, mankind and nature, working in harmony, would set things right.

Sarah took a deep breath and flexed her fingers, irritated as always by the smug, superior experts who continued to ignore the truth. The world's situation was not improving; it had worsened in the four years since Gogol's Invasion. Mankind would never rise above the calamities that men themselves had inflicted upon the planet. Situations never improved without intervention, and she could see no miracle on the horizon of this dark and forbidding planet.

Isaac's call earlier this week had been a sort of miracle, but he had kept the conversation focused on business except for that cryptic farewell just before hanging up. Melman assured her that Mossad had dispatched an agent to meet Isaac in Paris, but they had not given her any further information. Apparently, Isaac had not needed exfiltration; he was safe and Romulus still trusted him.

Why, then, could she not stop worrying about him?

She looked at the pile of videos on the floor, then laughed aloud. No wonder she had such difficulty finding peace. She had surrounded herself with turmoil and despair.

For the briefest moment, the picture of her father's face hung in her mind's eye—faint at first, then as vivid as a photograph emerging in a tray of developer. She had not seen him in over a month, when she visited his apartment to light the candles and enjoy a Shabbat meal with him.

"Sarah," he had said, placing the Talmud in her hand, "read what will happen in the last days, before the son of

David will come. In the first year it will not rain, and in the second year the arrows of famine will be let loose. In the third year famine will be severe, and men, women, and children will perish. In the fourth year there will be plenty and not plenty. In the fifth year there will be great abundance, and in the sixth year there will be voices from heaven. In the seventh year wars will occur, and at the conclusion of this seven-year period the son of David will come."

Lifting her head, Sarah blinked the images of the past away. People were always placing books in her hand. Just before leaving the office today, Danny Melman had given her a black notebook and said, "Read this tonight."

She read the typed label. "An Analysis of the Current Environmental Calamity in the Light of John's Revelation?"

Melman's eyes clung to hers, analyzing her reaction. "I'm not saying you have to agree with it—I just want feedback. We're supposed to consider every possible angle, right?"

The notebook sat beside her now. She lifted the thin volume and opened it, relieved to see that it contained no more than forty typed pages. Despite her reluctance to read material that had probably originated with a raving Christian lunatic, reading seemed infinitely preferable to watching bizarre animal attacks on video.

She thumbed past the first few pages and halted as an indented quote caught her eye:

> He required everyone—great and small, rich and poor, slave and free—to be given a mark on the right hand or on the forehead. And no one could buy or sell anything without that mark, which was either the name of the beast or the number representing his name.

Sarah paused, recalling her father's aversion to the Universal Chip. Had he read *this*?

She flipped backward a few pages and halted when another section grabbed her attention:

As I watched, the Lamb broke the first of the seven seals on the scroll. Then one of the four living beings called out with a voice that sounded like thunder, "Come!" I looked up and saw a white horse. Its rider carried a bow, and a crown was placed on his head. He rode out to win many battles and gain the victory.

When the Lamb broke the second seal, I heard the second living being say, "Come!" And another horse appeared, a red one. Its rider was given a mighty sword and the authority to remove peace from the earth. And there was war and slaughter everywhere.

When the Lamb broke the third seal, I heard the third living being say, "Come!" And I looked up and saw a black horse, and its rider was holding a pair of scales in his hand. And a voice from among the four living beings said, "A loaf of wheat bread or three loaves of barley for a day's pay. And don't waste the olive oil and wine."

And when the Lamb broke the fourth seal, I heard the fourth living being say, "Come!" And I looked up and saw a horse whose color was pale green like a corpse. And Death was the name of its rider, who was followed around by the Grave. They were given authority over one-fourth of the earth, to kill with the sword and famine and disease and wild animals.

The phrase *wild animals* stopped her cold. For a moment, she had thought she was reading about some past event, but never in recorded history could she recall so many deaths by animal attack. And though the history of the Jews recorded terrible sieges where the scarcity of food forced people to do unspeakable things, the warning about bread selling for a day's pay seemed as contemporary as her morning newspaper.

A tide of goose flesh rippled up her arms. Did this passage pertain to *this* day and age? The entire world had certainly experienced warfare and famine and disease and wild animals. Did more atrocities lie in the future?

Unable to stop herself, she kept reading:

And when the Lamb broke the fifth seal, I saw under the altar the souls of all who had been martyred for the word of God and for being faithful in their witness. They called loudly to the Lord and said, "O Sovereign Lord, holy and true, how long will it be before you judge the people who belong to this world for what they have done to us? When will you avenge our blood against these people?" Then a white robe was given to each of them. And they were told to rest a little longer until the full number of their brothers and sisters—their fellow servants of Jesus—had been martyred.

I watched as the Lamb broke the sixth seal, and there was a great earthquake. The sun became as dark as black cloth, and the moon became as red as blood. Then the stars of the sky fell to the earth like green figs falling from trees shaken by mighty winds. And the sky was rolled up like a scroll and taken away. And all of the mountains and all of the islands disappeared. Then the kings of the earth, the rulers, the generals, the wealthy people, the people with great power, and every slave and every free person—all hid themselves in the caves and among the rocks of the mountains. And they cried to the mountains and the rocks, "Fall on us

and hide us from the face of the one who sits on the throne
and from the wrath of the Lamb. For the great day of their
wrath has come, and who will be able to survive?"

Sarah felt her heart leap uncomfortably into the back of
her throat as the telephone rang.

TWENTY-ONE

GENERAL ADAM ARCHER STOOD OUTSIDE THE CLOSED
door that led to Romulus's private study. He waited a moment,
straining for sounds from behind the paneled door, but he
could hear nothing but the quickened beating of his own heart.
Half in anticipation, half in dread, he knocked.

The butler, Charles, opened the door and gave Archer one
of those looks that always made him feel like some species of
bug. The butler was a classic beta male, subservient to the
core, yet he always made Archer feel inferior.

"Yes?" The man sang the word, the latter note a bass
growl.

"The president sent for me."

Charles arched a brow in what looked like wry amusement. "Then enter. Please."

Archer strode past the butler, glad to be done with that
encounter. Romulus was sitting before the fire in a velvet-
covered wing chair. His feet—which seemed too small for a
man, really, and almost feminine—were propped upon a
richly upholstered footstool, while his hands were uplifted

and pressed together, fingertip to fingertip. He stared silently into the fire, but Archer could see thought working behind those dark eyes.

"Good evening, sir."

"Please, General." Romulus spoke in a polite tone, yet he did not lift his eyes from the flickering flames. "Have a seat and give me another moment."

Archer sank into the chair, idly wondering what had precipitated this summons. He had received the call at ten, and Romulus did not usually conduct business at this late hour. Whatever problem had spurred this meeting must have recently come to Romulus's attention.

Archer rested one elbow on the arm of his wing chair, then propped his head on his fist, turning toward the fireplace while he discreetly studied the profile of the man across from him. Romulus's classically handsome features seemed as composed as always, but Archer had begun to know the man well enough to see behind the facade. The eyes were the window to the soul, or so they said, and tonight insecurity and trouble shadowed Romulus's gaze.

A deep silence filled the room, broken only by the occasional snap of a log and the brush of oak branches against the windowpane. Archer waited, patiently biding his time, until finally Romulus spoke: "I'm concerned about Isaac Ben-David." He shifted his gaze from the fireplace to the general. "When he invested me with the spear, I saw doubt in his eyes, and we know he met with a Mossad agent later that night. I'm worried that he might desert our cause . . . and he has seen too much to leave us now."

Archer shook his head in disbelief. "He has done nothing this week out of the ordinary, and we've had him under nearly constant surveillance. He has not been able to sneeze without one of our agents taking note—"

"I saw the doubt in his very soul." A thin gleam of resentment entered Romulus's eyes. "At what should have been the greatest moment of his life, I glimpsed doubt and fear, not honor and humility. I am not easily fooled, General, and I know what I saw. Isaac Ben-David is not sure of us, and his confusion has grown over the last few days. I'm not certain he can be trusted."

Archer shrugged. "We could get someone else to meet with the prime minister."

"We've invested too much in the major. I have brought him this far, and the Israelis respect him. In addition to his personal recommendations, his father is a respected archeologist and his father-in-law a respected rabbi who will greatly influence the religious Jews." Romulus's gaze shifted back to the fire and thawed slightly. "I have caused a rift between Ben-David and his Shin Bet wife. Their marriage was dying; I made certain the ax would fall."

Archer pressed his fingertips to his lips, thinking. Romulus was not often unsure of himself, and Archer could see no clear reason why Ben-David should be considered dangerous. He had kept a low profile these last few days, and tomorrow he would only be in Jerusalem for a few hours. They certainly didn't have to worry about him briefing his comrades or masterminding a revolutionary plot . . .

Archer straightened himself. "Let me assure you, Mr. President, that Major Ben-David will prove worthy of your trust. Tomorrow he will travel with us, then he will perform for the cameras as planned. All Israel will see him join the Universal Faith Movement and accept the UFM code on his microchip. Afterward, we will immediately bring him back to Paris."

Romulus's eyes, alive with calculation, shifted to Archer. "And how can you be sure he will do as you say?"

"I could call upon his father." A reluctant grin tugged at Archer's mouth. "Surely Dr. Ben-David would like to be present when his son takes such an important oath. And as long as the good doctor stands by my side, the dutiful son cannot help but do as I ask."

When he spoke again, Romulus's voice was firm and final. "I am beginning to see your point, General. Set agents upon the major and monitor him every moment. And take the father into your custody until the ceremony has concluded." A thoughtful smile curved the president's mouth. "I know the time is not yet right, but I almost wish I was going to Jerusalem myself."

†

Sarah gasped when she recognized the voice on the phone. She opened her mouth to say Isaac's name, then caught her breath when he identified himself as "Uncle Laban."

"Uncle?" Her feeling of uneasiness suddenly turned into a deeper and much more immediate fear. Was he in such trouble that he had risked calling her twice? "To-to what do I owe this pleasure?" she stammered, gripping the phone more tightly. "We haven't heard from you in . . . too long."

"I've been . . . deceived," Isaac said slowly. His voice had the flat, tinny sound she had heard in the voices of fearful men. "I was led to think I would not be welcome in your home."

Sarah turned and leaned against the table. "Who would lead you to such a conclusion? You are always welcome here, Uncle. You are *family*."

She heard nothing, not even the whisper of a sound, then Isaac said, "I will come tomorrow. I will not have much time, so I would like to see as many family members as possible. Alert them now, if you please. I have so much to tell you all."

Sarah's thoughts raced. Whatever had put the note of urgency in Isaac's voice would not wait, or he would not have risked telephoning her. Though this Uncle Laban disguise would fool a live eavesdropper, more sophisticated technology would certainly reveal the voiceprint as Isaac's. He had risked this call because he knew neither the IDF nor the Universal Force would have time to do a trace and voiceprint analysis.

"By all means, come as soon as you can." Turning, she pulled a pen from the chipped mug by the phone and scrambled for a sheet of paper. "Do I need to prepare anything special?"

"I'd appreciate anything you can do." His voice was low and controlled, but she could hear an undertone of desolation in it. "I'm scheduled for a meeting tomorrow with my friend Avraham—I'm picking up a gift for the *shabtsitvainik;* there's to be quite a big production arranged for him. The meeting is scheduled for just after lunch." He paused. "Did you get all that?"

"Just a moment, please. I'm trying to take it all down."

Her brain worked as she jotted down the phrases. A bedrock of meaning lay somewhere beneath this sea of obfuscation, and Sarah strove to catch a glimpse of it. Avraham? The most likely Avraham to meet with Isaac would be the prime minister. *Big production* might refer to an important summit or some task Isaac was overseeing for Romulus—but if it was some unclassified mission, he wouldn't have called and he *definitely* wouldn't be speaking in riddles. She frowned at the word *shabtsitvainik*. Isaac had used the word as if he wanted to honor the man, but every Jew who spoke even a smattering of Yiddish knew that a *shabtsitvainik* was a false religious prophet or self-proclaimed Messiah. The word was always spoken scornfully, but Isaac had said he was picking up a gift for this person . . .

Who was the false religious leader? Not the prime minister, surely. It could only be Romulus or one of his associates, for Isaac wouldn't have used a Yiddish word to cloak his meaning from the Israelis. So—he was picking something up for Romulus, and in a big production—a press conference?

"I think I've got it all." Her voice, like her nerves, was in tatters. "Am I to assume that my father won't be happy about having this *shabtsitvainik* in the family?"

"You are brilliant as always, my Sarah." She heard approval and a note of relief in Isaac's voice. "The entire family will be upset, I'm afraid."

Disbelief struggled with yearning as she forced a reply: "I'll do what I can to smooth things over, Uncle."

"I knew I could count on you." He said these final words in a hoarse whisper, as though he had been too worried to utter them in a normal voice.

She brought her free hand to the phone, not ready to let him go. "Uncle?"

"Yes?"

"I want you to read something before you come."

Isaac managed a brittle laugh. "I don't exactly have much reading material with me."

"You'll have to seek this out. It's an old book by a man named John . . . and it's called the Revelation. Please read it as soon as you can. I think you'll find it fascinating. I do, though I don't understand everything I read."

Silence, as thick as wool, wrapped itself around her, binding them together for a long moment, then Isaac said: "Our American friend might be able to help. Try him, and I'll see you tomorrow."

She hung up quickly, not daring to say anything more. Her brilliant husband was a resourceful man. And though he may not love her as he once did, he had always respected her advice. If a copy of the Christian Bible existed within a mile of where he stood, he'd find a copy.

She stared at the phone for five minutes, replaying the conversation in her mind, then picked up her secure cell phone and dialed Danny Melman's number.

TWENTY-TWO

THE MEDITERRANEAN SPARKLED LIKE CRUSHED BLUE diamonds beneath the Universal Force jet, then disappeared beneath a cloud bank. Isaac waited until his traveling companions had settled into their seats before pulling the small French testament from his coat pocket. With no time to visit a bookstore, he had asked Madame Blanchette if he could borrow a copy of John's Revelation. Her brow wrinkled in puzzlement until she realized what he wanted. "*Oui, ce fait partie du Testament Nouveau,*" she said, pulling a small blue book from a drawer in her dining room hutch. "*Bonne chance. Je n'ai jamais pu le comprendre.*"

Isaac gave her a smile, then slipped the book into his pocket. "*Merci.* I may not be able to understand it, either, but I shall try."

Now, staring at the little book's table of contents, he felt a wave of relief. The New Testament had been printed in both English and French, so at least he wouldn't have to struggle through difficult material in a language he had yet to master.

Knowing that he had at least two hours to read, he slouched down in his seat and turned toward the window, silently sending the message that he wanted to be left alone on the flight. Sighing, he ran his finger down the page until he spied a listing for The Revelation of Jesus Christ to Saint John. The last entry, of course.

Flipping to the back of the book, he scanned the pages, looking for familiar words that might have meant something significant to Sarah. He couldn't imagine her reading a New Testament, either, so he knew she would not have urged him to read any part of a Christian Bible unless the information was crucial.

He ran his gaze over the page, staring at the words, waiting for one to leap up and scratch the mental itch that would not let him rest. And then he saw a simple phrase, "And no one could buy or sell anything without that mark, which was either the name of the beast or the number representing his name."

A mark or a number on the right hand or on the forehead . . . numbers. Just like the ones encoded into Isaac's Universal Chip.

He flipped through several other pages and saw the phrase again, this time in a different context: "Anyone who worships the beast and his statue or who accepts his mark on the forehead or the hand must drink the wine of God's wrath."

Isaac's stomach tightened into a knot as fear brushed the edge of his mind. What could this mean? He did not know what beast the writer referred to, and he knew nothing of a statue or a mark, only the microchip and the UFM code. Perhaps this had nothing to do with Romulus. Perhaps Sarah was imagining threats that didn't exist.

He skimmed down the paragraph and read another sentence: "The smoke of their torment rises forever and ever, and they will have no relief day or night, for they have worshiped the beast and his statue and have accepted the mark of his name."

He closed his eyes to clear the haunting words from his field of vision. If this was true, whoever took this mark—whatever it was—would face some pretty serious consequences.

A tremor of fear shot through him as a meaty hand fell upon his shoulder. "Dozing off there, Major?"

Isaac shoved the book into the narrow space between his leg and the seat as he turned to look up at General Archer. Though he had to be concerned about the day's events, the American's face seemed to be locked in neutral. Isaac had taken pains to conceal his reservations, but men like Archer had built-in antennae. Their lives depended upon it.

Raising his chin, Isaac assumed all the confidence he could muster. "I wasn't dozing—just thinking."

Archer cocked his head to one side, as far as his multiple chins would allow. "Must be a great pleasure for a man like you to go back to Jerusalem as a symbol for your people. Thousands will watch as you join the Universal Faith Movement today. I know they will be inspired by your example."

Isaac shrugged in mock humility. "I don't consider myself all that inspiring. But I am happy to do what I can."

"We are pleased you are so willing." Archer lifted his hand from Isaac's shoulder, then clasped his hands and stooped forward, pretending to look out the windows of the jet. "Beautiful view. A lovely day. What will you do in the free time we'll have before the meeting?"

Isaac sat very still, his eyes narrowing as he considered the question. The general's nonchalant attitude and the seemingly casual query were neither nonchalant nor casual, and Isaac knew his answer would be weighed and judged. If he was caught in a lie . . .

"I will go see my wife," he said, knowing that this answer might surprise the general. "Things have not been going so well between us . . . and I have some issues to discuss with her."

Archer nodded, apparently satisfied. "Divorce can be a messy situation. But you have friends in high places, Major. If you need anything, you have but to ask. Whatever you need will be provided."

"Thank you, General." Isaac waited until Archer moved away, then folded his arms and closed his eyes, pretending to sleep.

†

Sarah felt her heart rise to her throat when the doorbell buzzed. Her father lifted his head at the sound, and Thomas Parker and Ephraim Ben-David glanced at each other.

Melman spoke first. "Go," he said, jerking his head toward the door. "They'll be watching, so let him in quickly."

She hurried to the door and opened it, then stepped back as Isaac entered the room. Once the door closed, she clasped his hand. "Husband! I am glad you are home." She kissed him lightly on the cheek, then led him into the dining room where the others sat around the table.

Isaac's father was the first to rise. "It has been too long, Isaac." He drew his son into an embrace, then pulled away, tears shimmering in his eyes. "I fear for you, Son. Thomas and Sarah have been reading to me . . . about things I have never considered."

"I am eager to hear about it." Isaac embraced Sarah's father, then shook Thomas Parker's hand. He hesitated before Danny Melman, then forced a smile and addressed the group. "If you gentlemen will excuse me, I must speak to my wife before we talk of anything else."

Sarah felt a rich blush stain her cheeks as Isaac took her hand and led her through the narrow hallway, past Binyamin's closed door, to the privacy of their bedroom. Without speaking, he gestured for her to stand in the corner, then he began a systematic search of the walls, running his hands behind the mirror, along the bureau, over the molding of the closet door. And then, without a word, he pulled the Monet print from the wall, laid it face down on the bed, and silently pointed to the back.

Sarah stepped forward, transfixed. A small black rectangle, no thicker than a credit card, had been affixed to the back of the painting.

"That would never come from our people," she whispered, horrified.

Isaac ripped off the device and broke it in half, then stepped into the bathroom. She heard the clatter of plastic hitting the metal trash can, then he reappeared at her side.

"Camera," he said simply, rubbing his hands on his trousers as if he didn't know what else to do with them. "High-resolution digital images transmitted through wireless technology."

"But how did you know—?"

He shook his head, cutting her off. "I was given information that led me to believe someone in Romulus's organization had access to our bedroom."

Sarah winced. Though she usually undressed in her bathroom, she couldn't help but feel invaded. Someone had actually watched her most private moments, even while she slept . . .

"That's all finished now." Isaac sat on the edge of the bed, then reached out and took her hands in his. "Sarah, I can't go on like this." Misery was visible in his face—the sockets around his eyes seemed thin and brittle, his skin pale and moist. "Do you want to divorce me? Are you in love with someone else?"

She closed her eyes, astounded and ashamed by the direct question. No man should have to ask his wife such a thing, no matter how long they had been apart.

She drew a deep breath. "I do not want to divorce you, but I will not contest a divorce if you want one. And I have been faithful to you."

"Look at me when you say that."

She opened her eyes and saw a tortured man sitting before her. A muscle clenched along his jaw, and suffering carved merciless lines upon his face. And his eyes—those dear, beautiful eyes!—were filled with deep longing and unutterable agony.

"Isaac." She pulled her hands from his, then cradled his head. "You are my husband. I could love no one else. These distant years have been hard, but I have never stopped loving you. It's just that I stopped . . . knowing how to care for you. I could barely take care of myself, and by the time I had healed enough to reach out . . . you were gone."

"You . . ." He paused, and the look in his dark eyes pierced her soul. "You and Director Melman. They led me to believe that you and he—"

She brushed her fingers across his lips, cutting him off. "We are coworkers and friends, nothing more. He's here today because I asked him to help you." She pressed her hand to Isaac's jaw and brought his chin up as she looked into his eyes. "What did they tell you that could bring such pain?"

His square jaw tensed visibly, then relaxed. "Never mind what they told me," he said, looking up at her. "I trust you, Sarah."

"A roomful of people out there want you to trust them." Lowering her forehead to his, she raked her fingertips through his hair. "And you can trust me, Isaac Ben-David. I would risk everything for you."

And then, while the men outside waited to decide their futures, Sarah kissed her husband, with promise and anguish all mingled and the salt of her tears in their kiss.

TWENTY-THREE

As ISAAC RODE THE ELEVATOR TO THE PRIME MINISTER'S
office, he was again overcome by the sense, unanchored but
strong, that he stood at a crossroad in his life. Until today he
had been resilient and resolute, capable of acting alone, able
to reason and rationalize and refute anything that did not
consist of physical matter or verifiable properties. From his
father he had learned that physical evidence alone was trustworthy; from his job he had learned to observe and record
confirmable facts and hard evidence.

In the later years of his life, no one had ever encouraged
him to acknowledge the spiritual, yet in the past few hours he
had been convinced that the Bible, even the Christian New
Testament, could hold the keys to understanding the action he
was about to take. Thomas Parker, whose study of the Bible
had not yet resulted in physical treasure, shared that from the
Scripture he had lately received an entirely different kind of
wealth—understanding. Holding a battered Bible from his
hotel room, Thomas had sat at Isaac's dining room table and
shared Scriptures from Daniel, Zechariah, Paul's second letter
to the Thessalonians, and, of course, the Revelation.

"It is my belief," he had said, dropping the open Bible to the table, "that Adrian Romulus must be the one the Bible calls by many names, including 'the king of fierce features,' 'the prince who is to come,' and 'the willful king.' Most people simply know him as the Antichrist."

Isaac expected his father to turn away, but he said nothing. Even Rabbi Lerner remained silent, merely lifting a brow as the American spoke.

"Romulus is a false messiah, but many Jews will believe he is the mashiach," Parker went on, looking around the circle. "He negotiated the rebuilding of the Temple. He orchestrated the peace treaty with the Arabs. But though many Jews adore him now, the prophet Daniel wrote that after three and a half years, he will mightily offend the chosen people."

Sarah's father shook his head. "How could he offend our people? They consider him a hero."

"It's right here in Daniel." Parker tapped the page with his index finger. "The prophet wrote, 'He will make a treaty with the people for a period of one set of seven'—that's seven years—'but after half this time, he will put an end to the sacrifices and offerings. Then as a climax to all his terrible deeds, he will set up a sacrilegious object that causes desecration, until the end that has been decreed is poured out on this defiler.'"

Isaac ticked off the timeline in his head. Romulus had held international power since the Disruption well over three years ago.

"A sacrilegious object?" Ephraim's eyes gleamed with interest as he stared at Parker. Artifacts had always fascinated him. "Like what? A statue of a pig?"

"The prophet doesn't say what the object will be." Parker closed the Bible and bent to pick up the leather folio by his side.

"But I stumbled across something the other day as I visited an Arab friend who designs statuary. I'd gone to consult with him about one of the Temple treasures I hoped to find in the excavations beneath the Temple Mount. As I passed his workbench, I glanced down and saw a sketch of his latest project. He quickly hid the paper, but there was no denying what I saw."

Parker paused for effect, but Sarah urged him on. "Don't leave us hanging. What was it?"

"A larger-than-life statue of Adrian Romulus himself." Parker jerked his head in a decisive nod, sending his heavy sheaf of blond hair flopping into his eyes. "From what I saw, it's Romulus holding a spear in his right hand."

Though he had felt warm all day, Isaac felt suddenly warmer, and slick with a different kind of perspiration—the cool, sour sweat of fear.

"Impossible." Rabbi Lerner slammed the table with his clenched fist. "The Kohanim would never allow such a thing in the Temple! No graven image could even pass through the courtyard, and such an abomination must never—"

"If you think Romulus is powerful now, just wait a while." Isaac heard his own voice, as cool as the smoke off dry ice despite the hot fear that churned in his belly. "We have talked about the Spear of Longinus—well, Romulus now possesses it. I myself escorted it from Vienna to Paris, and I am convinced he believes that it is a talisman with which he can control the world through supernatural power." He shifted his gaze to Sarah. "As much as it pains me to admit it, I believe he is correct. There is more than human effort involved in this situation. I have seen and heard things that cannot be explained by the laws of nature."

Sarah gazed at him with chilling intentness for a long

moment, then her fine, silky brows rose a trifle. "Well," she said, glancing at the others around the table, "I suggest we get busy and do all we can to prevent the first order of business on Adrian Romulus's agenda. My husband must not be used as a pawn. We must prevent him from leading others astray by joining Romulus's false religious movement—"

"And yet we must protect him," Ephraim interrupted. "He can't simply walk away. Romulus will be watching Isaac's every move."

As one, every member at the table turned to Danny Melman, who had listened in silence. "I think," he had said, glancing at his watch, "that if we hurry, we can formulate a plan."

Now, as the elevator doors to the prime minister's office opened, Isaac stared past them in silence and fervently prayed Melman's plan would work.

†

General Archer drew in a hard breath as Major Ben-David and his wife walked into the room. Things had *not* gone according to plan, but if all went well here Romulus need never know. Archer had sent two men to tail Major Ben-David and another two to fetch Dr. Ephraim Ben-David to the prime minister's office, and only the first two had met with any degree of success. Dr. Ephraim Ben-David had not answered his door and none of the neighbors knew where he was, but the major had kept his word and gone to the house of his estranged wife. According to the agents, she had greeted him without an embrace of any kind, then allowed him into the house.

Closed window shades had prevented any further visual surveillance until the couple emerged two hours later. The agents had followed them across town to the prime minister's office. According to the phone records, the residence telephone had not been used all morning.

Archer rubbed his fingers on his trouser leg, a nervous habit he frequently indulged in situations where smoking was frowned upon. He thought it odd that the wife would accompany a soon-to-be ex-husband to such an important meeting, but the woman was a political agent. Perhaps she was thinking of her own career and wanted to be in the thick of the action.

He tilted his head and looked at her more carefully. He could see no lingering gleam of affection in those black-lashed eyes. Her brown eyes were sparking with emotion, though, her lips pressed tightly together.

Archer smiled. She probably wanted to claw Ben-David's eyes out.

Archer retreated to a corner of the room and leaned against a wall, content to watch the drama unfold.

†

Feeling more nervous than he ever had in his life, Isaac stood behind the television camera, idly staring at the tiny black-and-white screen through which the cameraman peered at the scene before him. The prime minister sat at his desk, his expression tight with strain, and General Archer stood behind the prime minister—out of camera range but close enough to exert mental pressure on the obviously uncomfortable Israeli leader. To the prime minister's left stood Elrad Altschul, a young rabbi in a black coat, black hat, and the long earlocks known to the Orthodox as *pe'ot*.

Isaac suppressed an expression of surprise. The little play they were to enact apparently had three acts: the first, in which the prime minister would express appreciation to Romulus for preserving the peace of Israel; the second, in which an Orthodox rabbi would accept a Universal Chip; and a third, in which an Israeli military hero would actually join the Universal Faith Movement.

Beside Archer, a young blonde nurse in a white uniform stood with a tray of instruments in her hand. Isaac knew they had considered using a doctor to implant the Universal Chip into the nervous-looking rabbi, but they finally chose to employ the most unthreatening administrator possible. The blonde certainly looked unintimidating—the corners of her mouth were tight with anxiety, and the instruments on her tray rattled with the trembling of her hands whenever the prime minister or General Archer looked her way.

The television news crew talked to one another through the headsets as the director, working from the mobile truck parked outside, called out settings for the lights and the boom microphone. Trying to ignore the confusion around him, Isaac stood with his hands folded and mentally rehearsed his role in the upcoming drama. Their plan had been formulated quickly, and Murphy's Law was certain to intrude . . . unless the God who had foreordained these things sought to look down with favor upon them.

The feeling of an unformed thought teased his brain as the television lights brightened the room. If what he read this morning was true, then the man Isaac Ben-David was an insignificant player in events that God had foretold thousands of years ago. If God could foresee and foretell events that would happen in the months and years to come, then Isaac had been arrogant to rebel against him. As an egotistical creature, he had gazed upon creation with unwilling eyes, refusing to see the Creator. He had discounted the written record, a miracle in itself, as mere oral tradition and man-made myth.

He had behaved like a spoiled child when he declared that a God who would take his son was unworthy of worship. The God he glimpsed this morning was omniscient and so powerful that humans must seem like mere ants to him . . .

Sarah, who had ostensibly slipped away to the ladies' lounge, came back into the room, flashed her badge at the guard by the door, then walked to Isaac's side. Discreetly, he dropped his hand and felt her palm slide into his. A gentle squeeze—the signal. The last-minute details had been arranged.

A balding man wearing a headset and glasses stepped into the center of the room and held up his hand, fingers spread. "Sixty seconds until introduction. We need quiet on the set!"

Isaac looked up and caught Archer staring at him. The general studied Isaac's face with an enigmatic gaze for a beat, then bent to say something to the tense nurse beside him.

Isaac felt Sarah squeeze his hand again. "It will work," she whispered, not looking at him. "If there is a God in heaven, this will work."

The bald man stepped forward again and held up his hand. "In five," he shouted, his carnival barker's voice sounding strangely out of place in the prime minister's plush office. "Four!" He continued the countdown with his fingers alone, flashing them before the camera in a stiff, practiced gesture.

Then a red light atop the camera began to glow, and the bald man wheeled and pointed at the prime minister.

"*Aleichem shalom*, citizens of Israel," the prime minister began, his eyes focused on the unblinking eye of the camera. A cold, congested expression settled on his face. "It is with great pleasure that I would like to introduce you to a man who has done great things for Israel, and a man who has my full and complete support. Would you please give your full attention to Adrian Romulus, president of the Universal Movement."

The bald man held up a warning hand, the prime minister remained erect, then the floor director's arm fell in a sharp gesture. "We're out," he called, flashing a quick smile around the room. "The video feed will play for ten minutes, then we'll need you, Rabbi. Will you take your position, please?"

With his hands clasped protectively in front of him, the rabbi crossed in front of the camera and sidestepped his way to an area behind the prime minister's desk.

Har-Zion, his face flushed, rolled back in his chair and cast Isaac an apologetic look. "Sorry to drag you back here to do this," he said, shooting Isaac a twisted smile. "But Romulus said you would be a great example for our people. I had to agree, of course."

"It's all right, sir."

As the prime minister stood and vacated the area, an aide stepped forward and wheeled Har-Zion's executive chair out of the way. The young rabbi glanced over at the young nurse, who managed a tremulous smile as she lowered her tray of instruments to the prime minister's desk. "I promise to make this as painless as possible," she said, her gaze fixed to the tray. "I've implanted hundreds of microchips, but never on television."

General Archer eased his bulk forward and clamped a

heavy hand on her shoulder. "Don't worry, young lady. I know you'll do an excellent job."

Isaac said nothing, but thrust his hands behind his back and shifted his attention to a television monitor on the floor. The video feed from Paris was rolling, and Romulus's image filled the screen. The volume had been turned low, but as the participants in the next phase of the telecast quietly adjusted to their positions, Isaac was able to hear Romulus's words.

"Within thirty days from today," Romulus was saying, a thin smile on his lips, "every citizen of Israel will be required to have the Universal Chip. We have not made this decision lightly or without great deliberation. We have been troubled of late by reports of sedition, destruction, and anarchy in provinces throughout the globe and in the streets of Jerusalem. Justice and fairness demand that we stop those who are disrupting the peace. By requiring a statement of cooperation, we can insure that the resistance movement will be snuffed out once and for all. Citizens who take the chip will have full access to all goods and services, including commercial shopping sites, Internet access, and employment. Any individual or group who refuses to submit to the greater good will be arrested and swiftly punished."

Romulus's image disappeared, replaced by footage of a male sniper on a rooftop shooting down at innocent women and children in a courtyard below. "This resister," Romulus continued in a voice-over, "was detained only two hours after this rampage when he tried to purchase food from a small shop in Belgium. The store owner's computer silently alerted the police, who captured the suspect within five minutes of his aborted shopping excursion."

Romulus's image shimmered back onto the screen. "Join

us, citizens of the globe, in uniting to rid the world of violence. In a moment, you are going to meet an upstanding citizen of your community, a rabbi of Israel, who understands
the potential for peace in this marvelous age. And after the
rabbi leads you by his example in taking the Universal Chip,
you will meet another man you know well—a man who has
demonstrated loyalty through bravery and sacrifice. You will
see this peacemaker, Maj. Isaac Ben-David, accept his regis-
tration number in the Universal Faith Movement. He is joining other citizens of the world who understand that matters
of the spirit matter more than matters of the flesh."

The camera zoomed in on Romulus's magnetic eyes.
"Won't you join the rabbi and the major? You can follow in
the footsteps of peace without worry. There is nothing to fear,
my friends, unless you deliberately choose to remain outside
the common good. So heed my warning. Those who are not
for us are against us and will pay the penalty."

The background music swelled from the monitor, then
the floor director stepped forward and pointed at General
Archer. The lights brightened as Archer stepped forward,
and the rabbi blinked under the lights as the general introduced him.

Standing at attention, Rabbi Altschul nodded stiffly into
the camera, then turned toward the nurse. She picked up the
small surgical injector that would implant the tiny microchip
beneath his skin, then paused for a moment. Her gaze fluttered to the ceiling for a moment as if she'd forgotten her next
line, then she smiled in relief. "Rabbi, will you take the stamp
on your hand or on your forehead?"

He thrust out his arm. "My right hand."

She took his hand, held it on her own, then pressed the

plunger on the device. The rabbi flinched slightly but did not speak.

She smiled brightly into the camera. "Did that hurt, Rabbi?"

"Not at all." Altschul flexed his hand and held it aloft for the camera to see.

General Archer stepped forward and mugged for the camera. "And now I'd like you to meet Maj. Isaac Ben-David of the IDF." He straightened, assuming a military posture, and Isaac automatically moved into position.

"Major," Archer said, adopting a light tone, "do you believe in God?"

"I do," Isaac answered truthfully.

"Do you believe that the path of peace with God holds the future for all mankind?"

Isaac nearly found himself smiling. "I do."

"Then do you swear to support the Universal Faith Movement, to attend to all its bylaws and precepts, and to conduct yourself as an upstanding citizen of the world, endeavoring to keep the unity in the bond of peace?"

"I do." Isaac accented his answer with a definitive nod. How ironic, that this moment had brought him to a firm conviction in the things of God . . .

Archer reached for the computer scanner and flashed it over Isaac's hand. There was a brief hum as the subdermal receptors picked up the wireless transmission of his UFM code, then the scanner flashed DATA TRANSFER COMPLETE.

"You see, citizens of Israel," Archer said, shutting off the scanner, "both of these processes are simple and painless. You will need your Universal Chip within thirty days. And if you wish to prove yourself a friend of peace, you can join the

Universal Faith Movement at the same time you receive your identification chip. It cannot be lost or washed away, so there is no danger of ever losing your link with the Universal Movement."

Isaac rubbed the flesh over his hand as the general showboated for the camera. In the last sixty seconds, he had either led millions of people astray or he and his friends had pulled off one of the most significant deceptions of his career.

Only time would tell what he had done.

†

In his Paris office, Adrian Romulus watched the Israeli telecast with a feeling of satisfaction. Isaac Ben-David and Rabbi Altschul were the perfect representatives, and they looked especially tall and striking alongside the petite nurse. Archer had appeared competent, and the prime minister, while not exactly enthusiastic, had performed his job as required.

Romulus frowned as the scene faded to a commercial for the *Unitas*, the Universal Movement newspaper. He had tried to convince Rabbi Baram Cohen to participate in the telecast, for that old man still commanded a great deal of respect among Israel's Orthodox Jews. But the old fool continued to dig in his stubborn heels . . .

Swearing softly, Romulus pressed the remote and silenced the television. He would have consigned all Jewish religious leaders to prison long before this, but the Orthodox rabbis wielded too much power in Jerusalem. Things were changing, however, and soon he would control them like his puppets in Rome. In thirty days, if they did not cooperate and follow his orders, he would have them arrested and set to work in prison camps. If they would not join the system, they would labor for it.

Justice in the new world order would be swift and efficient.

†

Sarah caught herself holding her breath as the television floor director yelled "cut" and the light atop the camera winked out. She caught Isaac's hand as he moved past, and together they left the prime minister's office, neither speaking as they walked past the security checkpoint and out into the bright daylight. Only after they were well clear of anyone who might want to eavesdrop did she lift her head to whisper: "I have a number to call for confirmation."

"Call it," Isaac replied.

Stopping beneath the shade of a sprawling tamarind tree, Sarah pulled the cell phone from her purse and dialed the number. When a curt voice answered, she asked, "Is Rebecca in?"

"She's out," came the reply, just before the line clicked and went dead.

Sarah disconnected the call and looked up at her husband, her lips trembling with the need to smile. "We did it," she whispered, barely daring to speak. "They managed to jam the signal. No one within one hundred miles of Jerusalem saw that broadcast."

Isaac gave her a smile that sent her pulses racing. "And your father?"

She held up the phone. "According to the response I just received, his message went out. While everyone in Europe watched your little drama, the citizens of Israel saw my father warning them not to take Romulus's Universal Chip."

The corner of Isaac's mouth drooped in a droll smile. "I take it he didn't quote Revelation in order to convince them."

She grinned. "I think he was planning to quote a passage in Zechariah about the worthless and false shepherd. And the Book of Zerubbabel refers to a *Romulus Armillus*, who will be the enemy of Israel in the last days. My father is a learned man; I'm sure he knew what prophecies would convince them."

For a moment they simply stood there, basking in each other's smiles, then Sarah reached out and tenderly ran a fingertip along Isaac's jaw. "So," she whispered, looking up at him, "what do we do now?"

"We meet with the others," he answered, slipping his arm around her shoulder. "And we celebrate."

TWENTY-FOUR

THE LITTLE GROUP OF CONSPIRATORS MET TO MAKE merry at a small bistro called Mamma Mia, a kosher Italian restaurant in the heart of Jerusalem. Over sparkling glasses and a huge platter of meatless spaghetti, they toasted their success.

"You know, don't you," Isaac's father said, meeting his son's gaze, "that today was only a temporary measure at best. We know Romulus has spies scattered throughout Jerusalem. Sooner or later—probably sooner—he will know we have tricked him."

"Romulus is nothing if not arrogant," Isaac countered, not ready to dull the keen edge of victory. "He will not believe that we could fool him on such short notice. He will not want to believe that I could be disloyal."

"But he will know," Rabbi Lerner said. "And he will not be pleased when he sees you again."

"That settles it, then. I'm not going back to Paris." With a flourish, Isaac pulled the pager from his belt, held it up for all to see, then dropped it into the crystal water pitcher in the center of their table.

Sarah gasped in horrified surprise, then laughed.

"I don't know if that was such a wise move," Danny Melman said, his eyes narrowing. "We could use you as an informant in Romulus's camp. It would almost be worth your going back to have a man on the inside—"

"Absolutely not." Sarah lifted her chin and met Melman's gaze straight on. "Isaac will not work for Romulus, not under any circumstances. It's too dangerous."

Melman shrugged. "Surely you don't believe everything we read this morning."

"Even if there is but a *slight* chance it is true," Sarah answered in a rush of words, "I would not risk my husband." Her tone softened as she glanced around the table. "I care for each of you and hope none of you will ever submit to his plans. Romulus is right—there *is* a resistance movement, but his own actions have given birth to it. He is evil and opposed to all that is holy. As the people of God, we must resist him."

"Hear, hear." Ephraim lifted his glass. "Well spoken, Daughter."

Smiling, Isaac lifted his glass and drank, too, but already his mind had begun to consider an urgent next step. Romulus's jet was scheduled to leave Jerusalem within the hour, and Archer would be waiting for him at the airport. When he did not arrive, Archer would initiate a search.

"Today went well," Isaac said, setting his glass back on the table, "but you know we are outcasts from this hour forward. I do not dare go home—they'll be looking for me before sundown. And thirty days from now, none of us who lack the Universal Chip will be able to operate freely in any modern city. Life as we have always known it will end."

A silence settled over the group as each person at the table considered the full implication of Isaac's words. Standing in the prime minister's office, Isaac had weighed the facts and made his decision, but now he saw a host of considerations play across his friends' faces. Who among them would choose to stand and resist Romulus?

"I suppose," he added softly, lowering his gaze to the table, "I will need a place to spend the night. Sarah is safe for a while, I think, because Romulus thinks we are estranged. But General Archer will be searching for me soon, if he isn't already."

Isaac's father nodded decisively. "A son should stay with his father in a time of crisis."

Danny Melman lifted his hand to the rim of his glass. "No, Dr. Ben-David. Your apartment is the first place they would look." Featherlike lines crinkled around his eyes as he shifted his gaze to Isaac. "You will call them and say you need to take a few personal days to work out a family problem. You will give them your father's phone number, so they will assume you are staying with him. And then you will stay with me. My apartment is the last place they would expect to find you."

Ephraim put out a hand in protest. "But if they think he is staying with me, why can't he? A son's place is—"

Isaac dropped his hand over his father's. "Thanks, Dad, but I don't think it's wise. They'd put us under surveillance, and neither of us would be able to move without Romulus knowing of it. As it is, they'll watch your house long enough to realize I'm not there, then they'll move on and search for me."

Melman nodded. "Believe me, Dr. Ben-David, it's better that your son lie low for a few days. He needs time to make plans for the future."

Though Melman was the last man on earth to whom Isaac wanted to be indebted, he knew the director was right.

†

Though he hated saying good-bye to Sarah in the restaurant, Isaac did not complain as he rode with Melman to the small apartment complex where the director lived. He gaped in astonishment, however, when the director unlocked the door and dropped the key into Isaac's hand.

"Sarah told me what you were led to believe," he said. Something that looked almost like bitterness entered Melman's face. "I won't lie to you—I would have given anything to make Sarah look at me the way she looks at you. But you're the one she loves, and you're her husband. So I will send her to you tonight."

Isaac clutched the key, surprised again by this unpredictable man. "Here?"

"Why not?" Melman shrugged. "If they truly believe she and I are having an affair, they won't be surprised to find me at your house. If they send someone to look for her, I'll say that she has gone out for groceries. They'll believe me." Slowly, he lifted his arm so that the shiny skin on the back of his hand caught the light from a street lamp. "I have the Universal Chip, you see, complete with the UFM code. I learned . . . too late."

A warning bell trilled in Isaac's brain. Could this man be trusted? With the addition of the latter code, he had become part of the Universal Faith Movement, ostensibly committed to follow Romulus into the future. But surely he would not have helped them today if he did not sympathize with their cause.

Melman must have read his thoughts, for he smiled without humor as he backed away. "It's a little late to question my motives, Major. If you trust me, wait here. I'll send your wife to you."

He turned and walked back to his car, whistling a tune from the radio. As he walked away, Isaac's brain filled in the other half of the equation: *If you don't trust me, run. You might evade capture . . . but you'll definitely miss out on a private night with the wife who needs assurance of your love.*

Without hesitation, Isaac crossed the threshold into Melman's apartment.

†

As the hands of the clock in Melman's bedroom blended into a single vertical line, Isaac listened to the midnight chimes and drew Sarah more closely to him. She had come, just as Melman predicted, and over the course of the evening they had talked, wept, and recommitted themselves to their marriage, finally giving themselves to each other with sweet abandon.

Now Sarah lay snuggled in his arms, her eyes closed, her breath soft upon his chest. Lily slumbered at the foot of the bed as she had in days gone by. Isaac knew he ought to sleep, but his heart and mind were too full to rest.

Odd, that he should find the object of his quest in Jerusalem. He had journeyed to Paris and beyond in search of peace, and tonight it had crept over him in the house of his supposed enemy and the arms of his estranged wife. The world he had grown up with was collapsing around him and his future had never seemed so bleak, yet at this moment Isaac felt completely serene.

This afternoon he had discovered that someone larger than Adrian Romulus controlled the world stage . . . and, believing that, Isaac knew he could rest.

Sarah moaned softly in her sleep, disturbed by a dream. Isaac threaded his fingers through her hair until she quieted under his touch, then he surrendered to sleep, wrapped in a blanket of exhaustion and peace.

†

"It occurs to me, Husband," Sarah told Isaac the next morning as they scrounged for dog food and breakfast in Danny Melman's kitchen, "that we have overlooked two people we really need to interview. They are mentioned in John's Revelation," she shot him a speculative glance, "and they've been under my nose for months. I've compiled huge files on these men, but until yesterday I couldn't see them for who they really are."

Isaac dropped the newspaper and gaped at her like a man faced with a hard problem in trigonometry. "Are you going to make me guess?"

She slid into the chair next to him and pulled a black binder from a stack of newspapers on the kitchen table. "The two prophets, Moses and Elijah. Look—they are mentioned here in Revelation, but not by name. John refers to them as the *witnesses*."

Ignoring Isaac's look of confusion, she opened the binder, ran her finger over a few columns, then nodded. "Here it is. Listen: '"And I will give power to my two witnesses, and they will be clothed in sackcloth and will prophesy during those 1,260 days." These two prophets are the two olive trees and the two lampstands that stand before the Lord of all the earth—'"

"Now *that*," Isaac jabbed his finger toward the notebook, "makes no sense. What does he mean by lampstands and olive trees?"

"I looked that up in one of my father's old commentaries." She pulled a leather-bound book from her large purse and set it on the table, then flipped to a page marked with a sticky tab. "According to this sage, the term *lampstand* refers to the fact that they are lights in a dark world."

Isaac grunted softly and rested his head on his folded arms. "That certainly fits. Go on, Sarah."

She tossed him a quick smile of appreciation, then began to read again. "'If anyone tries to harm them, fire flashes from the mouths of the prophets and consumes their enemies. This is how anyone who tries to harm them must die. They have power to shut the skies so that no rain will fall for as long as they prophesy. And they have the power to turn the rivers and oceans into blood, and to send every kind of plague upon the earth as often as they wish.'"

Isaac lifted his head as she paused for breath. "That fits as well. Two of Romulus's UF soldiers were immolated when they tried to shoot Moses and Elijah. And we've already heard about bloodied waters. And there's the worldwide drought and famine and plague . . ." His brow arched. "What else does the Revelation say about them?"

"This part isn't so good." She looked down at the page and couldn't help grimacing a little at the words she read: "'When they complete their testimony, the beast that comes up out of the bottomless pit will declare war against them. He will conquer them and kill them. And their bodies will lie in the main street of Jerusalem, the city which is called "Sodom" and "Egypt," the city where their Lord was crucified. And for three and a half days, all peoples, tribes, languages, and nations will come to stare at their bodies. No one will be allowed to bury them. All the people who belong to this world will give presents to each other to celebrate the death of the two prophets who had tormented them.'"

Shock flickered over Isaac's face. "They're going to *die?* Is that how God repays them?"

Sarah held up a warning finger. "Let me finish. 'But after three and a half days, the spirit of life from God entered them, and they stood up! And terror struck all who were staring at them. Then a loud voice shouted from heaven, "Come up here!" And they rose to heaven in a cloud as their enemies watched.'" She lowered the notebook and looked at her husband. "God will allow the beast to exercise power, but only temporarily. In the end, God will be victorious."

Isaac leaned back and rubbed the stubble on his chin. "You said they died in the city where their Lord was crucified." He looked at Sarah, and she saw reluctance in his eyes. "Was John talking about a great Jewish hero?"

Slowly, Sarah shook her head. "I'm 90 percent certain he was talking about Jesus of Nazareth. After all, that's whom the prophets are talking about. Jesus."

Isaac bit his lip, then idly picked up his fork and began to push the remnant of a scrambled egg around on his plate. "That's an idea I'll need time to accept. For so long I've been taught that he did not do anything the Messiah was supposed to do—"

"He'll do those things when he returns," Sarah whispered, understanding her husband's reluctance. "I don't understand all of it, either, but I do know this—the two prophets are speaking for God, and they are speaking about Jesus. That's why I'd like to find them and hear more of what they have to say."

Isaac's face twisted in a sudden expression of distaste. "Christians! Sarah, don't you realize these are the people who have persecuted Jews for centuries? Can we forget the Crusades, and the Inquisition, even the anti-Semitism of the twentieth century?"

"I'm trying not to judge God by those who exhibit hate," she said, spacing her words evenly. "I'm trying to be fair and open-minded. I just want to find the two prophets and hear what they have to say."

Isaac stared at her for a long moment, then he leaned forward and lowered his voice. "Do you know where they are?"

Sarah stirred sugar into her coffee. "They shouldn't be hard to find. Shabak has had them under surveillance for months. I can call HQ and get an update."

A half-smile crossed Isaac's face. "You'll call headquarters? And you think they'll tell you?"

"Why not?" She dropped her spoon. "I'm still an active agent. You're the fugitive, not me."

"You won't be an active agent for long. Romulus will put pressure on your office as soon as he realizes I'm AWOL."

"Then let's act quickly." She rose from the table, taking her coffee cup with her, and grabbed her cell phone.

The Shin Bet agent on duty took Sarah's request without comment, and within ten minutes Yitzhak Peres, a coworker from Sarah's unit, called her with the latest update on the two prophets. "After a trip to Egypt, they reentered Israel six days ago. They are staying with a rabbi who lives on Mendele Street."

Sarah jotted down the information, then slid the sheet of paper across the kitchen table to Isaac. "Anything else on them?" she asked.

"They're still being surveilled," Peres answered. "They spent most of yesterday walking the streets of Yemin Moshe, calling the people to repent. Our agents report that they're still on the move through that neighborhood this morning."

"Pretty fancy neighborhood for such a message," Sarah remarked.

Peres laughed. "Yeah. They aren't enlisting many converts, but who knows? After your father's broadcast yesterday, not many people are rushing to get their Universal Chips, either."

Sarah's smile broadened in approval as she looked at her husband. "Thanks for the update, Peres. I'll be in touch."

She disconnected the call, then slipped the phone into her purse. "Our targets are hanging out with the rich people today. They were last reported in the Yemin Moshe neighborhood."

Isaac stood and picked up his jacket. "I have always liked that area."

Sarah stood before him as he slipped into his coat. "I have always liked you," she whispered, then rose on tiptoe to give him a quick kiss.

They took a cab to Yemin Moshe and disembarked in front of Montefiore's Windmill, a well-known Jerusalem landmark. Sarah played a hunch that the two prophets might try to take advantage of the crowds that typically gathered to photograph the ancient mill, and within the hour her intuition proved right. As she and Isaac sat on a bench and watched the sun climb overhead, the two who called themselves Moses and Elijah approached the windmill without hesitation, their eyes seeming to train in on Sarah and Isaac as they drew near.

Sarah marveled at their appearance as they came forward. Though it was mid-September, the midday sun bore down upon the road, the heat making the air quiver and shimmy as it rose from the asphalt. The tourists who milled about wore cool cottons and linens, but these two men wore long brown robes of a coarse material that looked like burlap. Leather sandals covered their dark feet, and sweat dripped from their faces as they climbed the hill. The man with darker hair—Sarah didn't know whether he was Moses or Elijah—wore a pair of binoculars around his neck. Sarah wondered whether he used them to watch birds or people.

"Nice outfits," Isaac remarked under his breath. "Not even the haredim choose to be that uncomfortable."

Sarah ignored his comment and stood. The older prophet—or at least she supposed he was older because his beard had gone completely white—smiled and raised his head in a silent greeting.

"Shalom." She stepped closer. "My name is Sarah, and this is my husband, Isaac. If you have a moment, we'd like a word with you."

The younger man, whose face was just as lined as his companion's, but whose hair still carried streaks of reddish brown, gave her a slow smile that blossomed out of his beard like a rare flower. "Moses and I were expecting you, daughter of Israel. And we have time, for we must make the most of every opportunity for doing good in these evil days."

Sarah shot Isaac a quick glance, but he appeared to be momentarily speechless in surprise. After a moment, he gestured to a pair of benches in a small courtyard. "Shall we sit and talk there? Or would you rather go someplace more private?"

The older man, the one called Moses, began moving toward the benches. "This is the time to live in the light," he said, his words drifting over his shoulder toward them. "The night is coming soon, so let us enjoy the light while we can."

The night comes soon? A thrill of fear shot through her as she remembered the Scripture she had read that morning. The witnesses would only prophesy for 1,260 days, and she had known about them for well over three years. Did they believe that their own end was fast approaching?

To Sarah's surprise, Moses sat on one bench and Elijah chose the other, forcing her and Isaac to separate and sit next to each of the prophets.

When they had all taken a seat, Isaac addressed himself to Moses, somehow sensing that he was the elder and, therefore, the leader. "My friends," Isaac began slowly, feeling his way, "my wife and I have been searching the Scriptures. We have recently learned of one called the Antichrist, and we have reason to believe this man lives among us now."

"There have always been antichrists," Moses said, a livid hue overspreading the visible parts of his face. "The spirit of antichrist has always been in the world."

"But this one, this Romulus," Isaac continued, leaning forward, "is forcing people to accept an identification chip."

"That is not the mark of the beast—the fulfillment of his evil has not yet come." Elijah's long, narrow face furrowed with sadness. "On that day, all those who refuse his mark and his authority will be killed, and their spirits will cry out to God for vengeance."

Sarah breathed a silent sigh of relief. She had suffered nightmares in which Isaac was condemned to eternal torment because his Universal Chip contained the UFM code. But if this was not the mark of the beast, what was?

Elijah leaned forward, sweat beading in hundreds of tiny pearls on his skin as he stared at Sarah. "Do not worry about the future, daughter of Israel. Be faithful today. Remember what the Lord told us: 'If any of you wants to be my follower, you must put aside your selfish ambition, shoulder your cross, and follow me. If you try to keep your life for yourself, you will lose it. But if you give up your life for me, you will find true life.'"

Sarah looked down at her hands and felt a droplet of sweat trace the course of her spine. She had read more of Revelation than Isaac, and though there were many things she did not yet understand, she knew things he did not. The two witnesses would not be the only ones to suffer and die.

"Why would God allow this?" A tremor touched Isaac's lips, and Sarah knew he was thinking of far more than their present situation. "Why would an all-powerful God allow such pain and suffering and evil?"

Moses lifted his gaze to Isaac's face in an oddly keen, swift look. "Who are you, a mere man, to question God? Should the thing that was created say to the one who made it, 'Why have you made me like this?'" The prophet's eyes narrowed in a calculating expression. "The Lord says, 'My thoughts are completely different from yours, and my ways are far beyond anything you could imagine. For just as the heavens are higher than the earth, so are my ways higher than your ways and my thoughts higher than your thoughts.'"

Elijah looked at Sarah, his face displaying an uncanny awareness. "The rains and snow come down from the heavens and stay on the ground to water the earth. They cause the grain to grow, producing seed for the farmer and bread for the hungry. It is the same with God's Word. He sends it out, and it always produces fruit. It will accomplish all God wants it to, and it prospers everywhere he sends it. God will use every person—even Adrian Romulus—to demonstrate his glory. Do not doubt it."

Sarah looked at Isaac, who was staring blankly at the prophet with his mouth open. He was trying to use human logic to understand, she realized, and human understanding had nothing to do with the situation these men were describing.

"Have you a warning or a word of advice for us?" She reached out, daring to place her hand on Elijah's bony arm. "We have decided not to cooperate with Romulus and his Universal Faith Movement, and we know the days ahead will be dangerous."

Elijah pinched his lower lip with his teeth, then reached out to pat her hand. "I encourage God's holy people to endure persecution patiently. Remain firm to the end, obeying God's commands and trusting in Jesus."

"Jesus?" The word slipped from Isaac's lips.

Moses ignored Isaac, but fixed Sarah in his gaze. "Blessed are those who die in the Lord from now on. Yes, says the Spirit, they are blessed indeed, for they will rest from all their toils and trials; for their good deeds follow them!"

"What does Jesus have to do with it?" Isaac asked, turning to Moses with a petulant look on his face. "All my life I've been taught that he was nothing but a madman, if he even existed."

"My son," Moses answered, rising, "he is the Lamb, the Judge, the Beginning and the End. Blessed are those who put their trust in him."

Without another word, Elijah rose, too. The two prophets walked away, their odd appearance parting the tourists at the windmill as effortlessly as another Moses had parted the Red Sea.

"I'm beginning to see why Romulus hates them," Isaac remarked, watching them go. "They never once gave me a direct answer to my questions."

"Yes, husband," Sarah whispered, her vision blurring as her eyes filled with tears. "They did."

†

Isaac and Sarah planned to spend a second night at Melman's apartment, but Isaac knew they could not stay longer. If Romulus had begun to search for him—and Isaac was certain he had, though probably through clandestine channels—the Universal Force would have agents sitting outside Sarah's house. Soon they would report that Sarah Ben-David had not returned, then they would check phone records and discover an alarming lack of calls between Sarah and Melman.

Along the way, Isaac had taken steps to secure his safety. Soon after receiving the summoning page from Archer, he called the airport from a pay phone in a busy area of the city and told the general to return to Paris without him. Archer seemed to accept the story that Isaac needed to spend some personal time with his father and that telephone call probably bought them twenty-four hours.

But if Romulus's people had watched his father's house, they would know something was amiss. So he and Sarah would have to move on, and it would be best if they left Melman's apartment before sunrise. Though as a deputy director Melman had power within the Shin Bet, Romulus had an international security force at his disposal.

While Sarah fretted at Melman's computer, searching for outmoded airports and train stations through which they might be able to slip without having their identification chips scanned, Isaac sat with his elbows propped on Melman's desk, an open Bible spread before him. He had been reading for several hours, and very little of what he read made any sense at all.

In the last few days, the world had turned itself inside out. As a Jewish boy, he had grown up doubting whether Jesus of Nazareth even existed. Even if he had, and if the Christian Scriptures were reliable—a matter open to speculation—one thing was undeniably clear: Jesus did not do many of the things that the mashiach was supposed to do. He did not establish a world government in Israel. He did not bring about the political and spiritual redemption of the Jewish people. He did not establish Jewish law as the law of the land; in fact, on several occasions he seemed to flout it.

If pressed to pick a messiah from the ancient times, Isaac would have chosen Shimeon bar Kochba, who lived nearly a century after Jesus of Nazareth. Bar Kochba fought a war against the Roman Empire and took Jerusalem from the invaders. He resumed sacrifices at the Temple site and outlined plans to rebuild the Temple. He established a provisional government and even began to distribute coins bearing its name. If his plans had been successful, he would have undoubtedly been hailed as the mashiach. But the Roman Empire rose and crushed his revolt.

Isaac had long ignored the Christian Jesus, considering him less than nothing, but since this afternoon, the two prophets and the Revelation of John had confirmed that Jesus was *everything*. The truth and the life. The beginning and the end.

What in the world was that supposed to mean?

During their lunch after the telecast, Thomas Parker had suggested that Isaac read the book of Daniel in conjunction with his study of Revelation, but Isaac felt himself resisting that instruction. Judaism did not even consider Daniel a prophet! His writing included visions of the future, but God chose prophets to convey a message or teaching to his people. Daniel's book contained writings that had nothing to do with the people of his day; they were intended for future generations . . . people Isaac had always thought of as living in a distant century. And yet, here he sat, his hands pressed to his forehead, reading words from Daniel that sent a thin, cold blade of foreboding into his heart.

The king will do as he pleases, exalting himself and claiming to be greater than every god there is, even blaspheming the God of gods. He will succeed—until the time of wrath is completed. For what has been determined will surely take place. . . . His army will take over the Temple fortress, polluting the sanctuary, putting a stop to the daily sacrifices, and setting up the sacrilegious object that causes desecration. He will flatter those who have violated the covenant and win them over to his side. But the people who know their God will be strong and will resist him.

Was Romulus the king Daniel described? And was Daniel trustworthy? Thomas Parker certainly seemed to think so, and Sarah now accepted everything she read in the Bible at face value. She had spent most of the afternoon on the computer, pulling up Web pages that had been floating in cyberspace since before the Disruption. Piles of printed pages now littered the floor of Melman's small study, and nearly all of them carried dire warnings about a man who would rise after a bizarre global event called the Resurrection or Rapture. The Web sites predicted that this man would institute a one-world government, an international economy, and a global religion. This man would be the Antichrist, for he would be arrogant and crave power with ruthless ambition.

Isaac picked up one of the pages he'd been studying earlier and glumly compared its quotes to the Scripture he'd just read. They matched perfectly; someone had written about the very chapter he was trying to understand. According to the author of the Web page, all these signs pointed to the day when Satan himself would empower his human puppet on earth . . .

"It can't be," Isaac murmured, dropping the page.

Sarah looked up from the computer monitor. "Did you say something?"

"It wasn't important." Isaac closed the Bible, then leaned back in the chair and crossed his arms, trying to think. In twenty-nine days, anyone caught in Israel without the Universal Chip would be arrested and subject to imprisonment and execution. Leaving Israel would be next to impossible. Though many nations still operated old-fashioned airports without identity-chip scanners, Israeli airports were state-of-the-art. There'd be no leaving Jerusalem by air or train or bus. The highway checkpoints would be manned with Universal Force guards, too, if they weren't already. If he and Sarah tried to drive out, they'd be as helpless as doves caught in the coils of a snake.

Twenty-nine days. A man could do a lot in twenty-nine days. Write a book, plant a garden, plan an escape . . . or plot a murder.

If Romulus planned to rule the world through evil, why not rid the world of evil by killing Romulus? Isaac closed his eyes, mentally chewing on the thought. He was a soldier. He had taken life before in the defense of his country, and he could do it again. And even if he had somehow misunderstood the Scriptures, his memory of the night when Romulus took the spear was enough to convince him that the man intended to dominate the world through evil.

The thought of destroying Romulus gave Isaac a dark little pleasure. He'd have to resign his position with the Israeli Defense Force, of course. The IDF wouldn't understand, and they didn't approve of career liaison officers murdering the officials they'd been assigned to assist. But those in the IDF high command had already demonstrated blind weakness. In their effort to appease Romulus, they had done nothing to stop his requirement of the Universal Chip, so in twenty-nine days he would be unwelcome even among his Israeli comrades.

He'd have to distance himself from his friends and his father, and even from Sarah . . . unless she was willing to follow him into exile.

Opening his eyes, he looked over at her. With her gaze focused on the computer screen, a pencil clenched between her teeth, and a pair of Melman's reading glasses perched on the end of her nose, she seemed the most intelligent and beautiful woman he had ever seen. Love for her welled within his breast, temporarily cutting off his power of speech. Could he leave her? Would he have to?

If he did not make this attempt, both of their lives were already over. Sarah would rather commit hara-kiri than work for Romulus's puppet regime, so both of them would be outlaws in twenty-nine days. But if Isaac made the attempt and succeeded . . . life just might return to normal.

The thought gave him courage to continue his deliberation.

†

By mid-March, Isaac had a reasonably good idea of how he could approach Romulus. Security might be a challenge, but not an insurmountable one as long as Romulus believed that Isaac remained loyal to his cause. That assumption was risky, but as the deadline for the ID chip and UFM code approached, life itself was a risk.

Isaac could do nothing until Romulus returned to Jerusalem, but he knew that day would not be long in coming. Through news reports and quiet messages from friends who still worked within the system, Isaac learned that Romulus intended to open an affiliate branch of the Universal Faith Movement in Jerusalem. Though that news stunned Sarah's father and other religious leaders who believed Romulus would honor the peace treaty and exemption for religious Jews, Isaac wasn't at all surprised. The Scripture predicted such a move, and it also spoke of the statue that Thomas Parker had learned of in his friend's office. If Isaac understood Scripture correctly, more atrocities were yet to come, but Isaac would not speak of them to his loved ones. If all went according to his plan, he might be able to spare them from future horrors. Didn't Abraham save the righteous of Sodom and Gomorrah by his fervent prayer? If Abraham could persuade God to spare his loved ones, Isaac prayed that God would strengthen his arm to spare the nation.

Shortly after sundown on April 5, exactly one month after the Jerusalem telecast, the arrests began. People who had been brazen enough to refuse Romulus's order and naïve enough to remain in their homes were forcibly drawn out by armed militia and taken to desert prison camps surrounded by razor-wire fences. "For a period of twenty-four hours," a loudspeaker blared to all new arrivals, "President Romulus will grant mercy to all who will join the Universal Faith Movement. Those who accept the Universal Chip and the UFM code will be allowed to return to their homes. Those who refuse will be imprisoned and set to hard labor."

Most of those arrested in the first assault wave capitulated immediately, for they believed living with a Universal Chip was infinitely preferable to sweating in a desert labor camp. But when faced with the shining desert sun and the implacable faces of prison guards, most of the Orthodox Jews who had stubbornly refused to accept the ID chip clung just as tenaciously to their resistance.

From the Shin-Bet safe house where Melman had hidden them, Isaac and Sarah could hear the screams of agonized Israelis who watched as their loved ones were dragged away. Lily paced the room in consternation, confused by the screams and the dreadful ululations of mourning. Sarah worried about her father, who had abandoned his apartment, and Isaac wondered what would become of men like Rabbi Baram Cohen.

The morning newspaper said it all: Ten thousand arrested in Jerusalem, with an estimated 900,000 Israelis unaccounted for. Thousands had fled in the night, running like rats from a sinking ship.

"Where are they going?" Isaac murmured, shaking out the paper he had picked out of a trash bin. Sarah, who lay beside, stirred uneasily.

"Isaac?" she murmured, her voice husky with sleep.

He dropped his hand protectively to her head. "Right here, love."

The shadow of a smile flickered across her lips. "Did we make it through the night?"

Isaac stroked her hair. "We did."

She made a soft sound of agreement, then curled tighter into a ball, pulling the thin blanket over her shoulders. Isaac heard his stomach growl and reflexively tightened his abdomen, not wanting the noise to bother Sarah. Yesterday, they had shared a bunch of carrots, and the day before the only food they could find was a stale loaf of bread. As Romulus's deadline approached, Isaac had purposefully distanced himself from friends who had taken the ID chip, knowing that Romulus would not easily forgive the crime of hiding a fugitive. But now he and Sarah had no means of legally obtaining food. Though they had Universal Chips, by now their numbers had undoubtedly been entered into the Universal Criminal Registry. If they visited even a simple grocery store, the alarm would flash and alert every Universal Force patrol within a five-mile radius.

In time, when this initial manhunt had abated, he might dare to renew some trustworthy friendships. But right now, while Romulus sought desperately to cleanse the city of anyone who might oppose his increasing control, Isaac didn't want to put any of his loved ones at risk.

The sharp sound of a footstep upon gravel made him straighten. Leaving Sarah, he rose to his feet and walked in a crouch to a window that looked out onto a nearly deserted street. A man in a beige overcoat and hat stood there, a shopping bag in his hand. The man walked slowly forward, peering up and down the street, one hand holding the edge of his coat back as if he night need to reach for a weapon . . .

Isaac hurried toward the door as he recognized Danny Melman. He had come here today either to betray Isaac or to help him.

Trusting the man's love for Sarah, if nothing else, Isaac stepped out of the deserted apartment. Melman had moved farther down the block, in order to draw attention away from the safe house, and Isaac lengthened his stride to catch up with him. The sound of Isaac's footfalls made Melman turn abruptly, his hand ready to draw his weapon, and his expression relaxed only slightly when he recognized Isaac.

Stopping on the sidewalk, Isaac crossed his arms. "You wanted to see me?"

Melman held out the shopping bag, his face as blank as stone. "I knew you'd be needing some provisions."

Isaac stared at the bag with one eye halfway closed, as if it were a bomb that might explode.

"Go on, take it." A note of exasperation filled Melman's voice. "If I were going to turn you in, I'd have done it long before this."

"How do I know," Isaac said, deeply inhaling a delicious aroma that came from the bag, "that you don't want to remove me so you can have Sarah?"

"Because Sarah doesn't want me." Melman set the bag on the sidewalk and stepped back as if Isaac's reluctance bored him. "Despite what you may think, Major, not everyone who still works for the government is evil. Some of us are just trying to do our jobs."

Isaac bit his lower lip. "I'm not sure we should stay here any longer. Romulus has spies everywhere, and someone in Shabak may discover we are hiding here—"

"I was going to suggest that you move on today. But first, take these things—I want to help you and Sarah. If you'll let me, I will."

Isaac stepped forward and peered into the shopping bag. The tantalizing aroma came from a loaf of freshly baked wheat bread, accompanied by a generous slab of cheese, some packets of dried beef, and a half-dozen bottles of water.

Before lifting the bag, however, he looked up and caught Melman's eye. "Thanks. From me and Sarah."

Melman shrugged. "We're both military men, Isaac. You would do the same for me if the situation were reversed." He took another half-step back, talking as he moved. "Enjoy what I've brought, and be careful. The crackdown is scheduled to continue for several weeks, so you'll have to be cautious in everything you do."

Isaac glanced quickly left and right. The streets appeared to be empty, and nothing moved at any of the windows in the nearby buildings. He swallowed hard as he picked up the bag. "Aleichem shalom," he said, nodding.

"Peace be to you, too," Melman said, and Isaac read a world of meaning in his dark eyes before he moved away.

†

Sarah drew her shawl forward over her head, then retreated into the crowded alleys of the old city's marketplace. Due to the famine, few farmers were participating in the chaotic melee, but the changing fortunes of the city had resulted in a more interesting market. People without the Universal Chip and UFM code were trading jewels and rare collectibles for unregulated shekels with which they could buy bread. Those who had complied with Romulus's orders sold meager loaves of bread for a week's wages or bartered for gemstones and works of art. It was, Sarah decided, a more horrific picture of corruption than Orwell's spoiled pigs in *Animal Farm*.

She walked slowly, one hand holding her shawl halfway over her face in the way of modest Muslim women, the other prodding at what few fruits and shriveled vegetables were available. In the past two weeks, she had realized that the key for survival lay in the market. Many of the people here were outlaws like herself, and, like her, they cared nothing for Romulus or his rules and regulations. The vendors at this black market yearned simply to get rich—because people will part with anything when their stomachs demand to be fed. As transient salesmen, they lacked the proper equipment with which to check for identification chips and the UFM code, so they bargained and made deals without proper authentication. When the occasional Universal Force patrol motored through the marketplace, they simply covered their wagons with blankets and picked up their newspapers, pretending to while the day away with nothing to do.

After nearly an hour of searching, Sarah spied a clucking chicken in a rusting birdcage atop one cart. The hen appeared healthy and might even be persuaded to lay a few eggs before the situation grew dire enough for Isaac to wring its neck.

She approached the vendor and pointed to the bird. "How much for the chicken?"

The vendor, a walrus-mustached older man with dark sweat stains beneath his arms, squinted in her direction. "What do you have to trade, little lady?"

Sarah fumbled at her wrist, then held up Isaac's watch. Once upon a time it had come from Tiffany's; now she prayed it would tempt a man who would have been too intimidated to even walk into that jewelry store before the Disruption. "It's a very good watch," she said, draping it across the vendor's wide palm. "Waterproof and shock resistant. The battery is new. It can be set to give the correct time in three different time zones."

"I don't need three different time zones."

Though his words made her heart fall, still he held the watch. "I don't know if all these fancy gadgets are worth a chicken. What else do you have?"

Sarah felt a moment's blind panic. She had nothing else of value, nothing at all. She lowered her head and put out her hand, about to retrieve her watch and walk away, but a gravelly voice growled in her ear. "You young women," a woman said, her bony arm slipping around Sarah's waist. "You are not used to the ways of the marketplace. This, my dear, is a place that calls for chutzpah."

Sarah looked up to see Rachel Levison, an elderly woman

from her father's congregation. She had not seen Rachel in years, but by the gleam in the older woman's eye, Rachel knew she'd been recognized.

"How are you?" Sarah murmured, wondering how much she could say in this public place. Rachel's husband, Yusef, would never have taken the Universal Chip, so they had to be outlaws, too.

"We are well." Rachel turned slightly so the merchant could not read her lips. "If we are separated in the crowd, you and your Isaac must come to the tunnels under the Western Gate. There are many of us who meet in the secret caverns under the Temple Mount. It is a safe place."

Sarah nodded, then felt the pressure of the older woman's hand on hers. "Now, let me show you how to deal with this bully. You want the chicken?"

Speechless, Sarah nodded again.

"Then demand a rooster." The old woman crossed her bony arms and took a half-step back, smiling in encouragement. "Go ahead. Remember you are the daughter of Rabbi Lerner, and do not take no for an answer."

Sarah smothered a smile as she stepped up to the merchant's cart. In her work with Shin Bet she had learned how to interrogate suspected spies and prevaricate without wavering, but no one had ever taught her how to haggle with a junkman. How different could it be?

She waved her hand and caught the merchant's attention. "I'll be taking my Tiffany watch now," she said, extending her palm. "You say it is not worth a chicken?" She gave him a hostile glare. "Such a watch is worth a chicken *and* a rooster! You should be offering me something else to go with that scrawny bird."

"It's a good bird," he replied sharply.

"Does she lay eggs? My husband wants his scrambled egg in the morning."

"He'll have eggs if you take the chicken. And you didn't say the watch was from Tiffany's."

"But how do I *know* I'll have eggs?"

"How do I know this watch will run tomorrow?"

"How do we know *anything?* Only the Master of the Universe knows such things."

She threw the words at him like stones, then halted, her fist uplifted, as the merchant's granite face cracked into an unwilling smile. "OK, lady, you can have the chicken," he said, slipping the watch into his pocket. "Though I will take a loss for giving you this fine bird."

Sarah tossed a triumphant glance toward her tutor, then silently basked in the glow of her small victory as the bulky merchant turned to lift the cage from the top of his heaped wagon. Isaac would probably laugh when he saw what had taken her an entire morning to win, but if by some miracle the bird *did* lay an egg for breakfast—

"Sarah? Sarah Ben-David, is that you?"

The voice caught her by surprise. She turned to see a man with his hand uplifted, then recognized Yitzhak Peres, her coworker in the Jerusalem office. He stared at her across another vendor's piled wagon, then smiled when she turned to face him. Sarah was about to speak, then remembered. Yitzhak had been one of the first in her office to receive the ID chip and UFM code, and he was one of the few who outspokenly supported Romulus.

She pulled the edge of her shawl across her face and lowered her head as a trembling rose from within. Rachel

Levison immediately stepped to Sarah's left side and filled her peripheral vision. "Ignore him, child."

"Sarah!" Peres called. "I need to speak to you!"

Rachel lifted her head and croaked out a command to the merchant. "Will you hurry with the chicken? She doesn't have all morning."

The mustached merchant glanced over his shoulder, then hesitated, one hand on the birdcage. From the expression in his eyes, Sarah knew he understood that she was an outlaw, anxious and uncertain, and the arm of the law was about to reach for her.

"Sarah!" Battling the pedestrian traffic, Yitzhak came closer. Sarah stood her ground, torn between the desire to flee and the need for the chicken she had sacrificed to earn.

"Sarah!" Rachel whispered in her ear now. "Run, child. I'll get the bird."

As Sarah hesitated, Yitzhak's bony fingers closed around her upper right arm. She whirled to face him, but kept the shawl over her nose and mouth, allowing him only a glimpse of her eyes.

"I am sorry, sir," she murmured in Arabic, "but I do not know you."

"Cut the foolishness, Sarah, I know it's you. And we all know you've joined the resistance." He jerked his head toward Rachel. "This old woman—is she with you?"

"No!"

Ignoring Sarah's protest, Yitzhak tightened his grip and lifted his free hand. "Over here!" he yelled, waving to catch the attention of a Universal Force patrol in the distance. "I've found a pair of resisters!"

Sarah cast one last longing look at the chicken, then gave

Yitzhak a swift kick below the knee. Howling, he went down like a shot dog, and Sarah took Rachel's hand. "Hurry," she cried, tugging hard on the woman's arm. "We can lose them in this crowd."

Rachel took three steps, then cried out and fell. Sarah stared, horrified, and saw that Yitzhak had grabbed the woman's ankle and pulled her down to the ground.

"Go!" Rachel cried, looking up at Sarah with wide eyes. "Remember what I told you! Now go!"

Too frightened to think further, Sarah ran.

TWENTY-FIVE

IN A SECRET SUBTERRANEAN VAULT, SARAH AND ISAAC sat with a handful of other Jewish resistance members and quietly mourned Rachel Levison's loss. They had learned of her death only an hour before, when one of the small errand boys had witnessed the most recent transfer of prisoners. The boy, barely nine years old, stood in the circle of adults and described Rachel Levison perfectly. With tears in his eyes, he said that she had limped bravely to the prison truck, then collapsed to the ground, her hand clutching at her shoulder. "They said she was dead," the boy said, shifting his gaze from Isaac to Sarah. "A heart attack. She just lay there in the street, not moving."

"They said she was a criminal." Yusef Levison groaned and pulled on the tufts of white hair that grew from the sides of his head. "My Rachel, a criminal? They could not convince even this innocent child of such a thing! But now they have killed her, and she never did wrong to anyone."

Sarah watched silently as her father came forward to embrace the older man. "At least," her father said, placing his hands on Yusef's shoulders, "she will be among the martyrs.

We have read their story, Yusef. We know they are with Jesus and waiting for us in heaven."

Sarah pulled her shawl around her shoulders and sat down. Despite Isaac's attempt to encourage them, she could feel discouragement and defeat seeping through the chamber like a fog. So many of their friends were missing . . . as was Lily, who had slipped through the fence around the safe house garden and did not return. Sarah wanted to go back to their house to see if Lily had found her way home, but Isaac warned her it was too dangerous.

Isaac sat, too, as did most of the others. The underground chambers and tunnels, hewn out of stone so many generations ago, seemed to fill with preternatural silence. From one of the other chambers Sarah heard the ghostly chatter of a laptop keyboard, but stillness reigned in the small room where she and her friends had gathered.

Isaac pulled a battered Bible from an inside coat pocket. He had begun to carry it with him at all times, like the pistol he used to carry so long ago.

"I read something the other day," he said, his gaze moving around the room and resting for a moment on each face. "Jesus was talking, and Matthew recorded his words. The odd thing is that Jesus was talking about the last days—*these* last days. His words were so clearly applicable to what we're going through that I can't believe no one ever pointed them out to me."

No one spoke, but several people shifted their positions in order to look at Isaac as he opened the Bible. Sarah noticed that Ephraim Ben-David tilted his head to gain a better perspective of his son.

"Jesus' disciples had asked him for signs that would

reveal the end of the age," Isaac said, introducing the passage. "And Jesus replied that first they would hear of false christs, wars and rumors of wars, and earthquakes in various places. Then he said, '"Then you will be arrested, persecuted, and killed. You will be hated all over the world because of your allegiance to me. And many will turn away from me and betray and hate each other. And many false prophets will appear and will lead many people astray. Sin will be rampant everywhere, and the love of many will grow cold. But those who endure to the end will be saved. And the Good News about the Kingdom will be preached throughout the whole world, so that all nations will hear it; and then, finally, the end will come.

'"'The time will come when you will see what Daniel the prophet spoke about: the sacrilegious object that causes dese-cration standing in the Holy Place"—reader, pay attention! "Then those in Judea must flee to the hills. A person outside the house must not go inside to pack. A person in the field must not return even to get a coat. How terrible it will be for pregnant women and for mothers nursing their babies in those days. And pray that your flight will not be in winter or on the Sabbath. For that will be a time of greater horror than anything the world has ever seen or will ever see again. In fact, unless that time of calamity is shortened, the entire human race will be destroyed. But it will be shortened for the sake of God's chosen ones."'"

Sarah's mind, lulled by the even pitch of Isaac's voice, exploded into sharp awareness. *How terrible it will be for mothers nursing their babies . . .* Binyamin would have been older than a nursing baby, but she could not imagine dragging a child through the dangers she and Isaac had endured in the last few days. Providing for Lily was difficult enough; how could she have ever managed with a *child?*

She closed her eyes, knowing in her innermost heart that she would have done anything, including joining the Universal Faith Movement, to create a safe haven for her son. And as a result, she and Isaac and Binyamin would have followed Romulus into eternal damnation.

She swallowed the lump that had risen in her throat and looked again at her husband. God had been merciful to take Binyamin when he did. The baby had gone to heaven, where she and Isaac would be reunited with him. She could not see the hand of the Holy One in the tragedy before this moment, but she could clearly see it now.

Isaac paused and skimmed over several sections with his fingertip. "There's more here, about how no one knows exactly when the Lord will return to put an end to the suffering, but that's not what I wanted to show you—ah, here it is."

He lifted his Bible and held it in a stream of light coming from a high vent cut into the wall above. "'But when the Son of Man comes in his glory, and all the angels with him, then he will sit upon his glorious throne. All the nations will be gathered in his presence, and he will separate them as a shepherd separates the sheep from the goats. He will place the sheep at his right hand and the goats at his left. Then the King will say to those on the right, "Come, you who are blessed by my Father, inherit the Kingdom prepared for you from the foundation of the world. For I was hungry, and you fed me. I was thirsty, and you gave me a drink. I was a stranger, and you invited me into your home. I was naked, and you gave me clothing. I was sick, and you cared for me. I was in prison, and you visited me."

"'Then these righteous ones will reply, "Lord, when did we ever see you hungry and feed you? Or thirsty and give you something to drink? Or a stranger and show you hospitality? Or naked and give you clothing? When did we ever see you sick or in prison, and visit you?" And the King will tell them, "I assure you, when you did it to one of the least of these my brothers and sisters, you were doing it to me."'"

The keyboard clatter from the other room ceased, and Sarah smiled as two others joined the circle to listen.

"'Then the King will turn to those on the left and say, "Away with you, you cursed ones, into the eternal fire prepared for the Devil and his demons! For I was hungry, and you didn't feed me. I was thirsty, and you didn't give me anything to drink. I was a stranger, and you didn't invite me into your home. I was naked, and you gave me no clothing. I was sick and in prison, and you didn't visit me."'"

Isaac looked up and surveyed the room. Sarah saw confusion and wonder mingled with affection on several faces. They liked Isaac, they wanted to believe him, but they weren't certain what he wanted of them . . .

Isaac let the silence stretch, lifting his head only when the quiet was broken by the soft popping sounds of a little girl wearing flip-flops in the hall.

"The Christians," Isaac began, looking first at his father, "the believers, the born-agains, the Messianic Jews, whatever you want to call them—they were taken up in the Disruption. Romulus has said that only the people whose hearts were hardened beyond redemption were eliminated— well, in a way he was right. Those people belonged to Jesus, they were the bride of Christ, and so they were spared from the judgment we are now enduring. But we have been spared, too. Though we are suffering, this is nothing compared to the suffering that awaits those who will join Romulus and worship him in the future. They and the entire planet will soon feel the wrath of God in a way it has never been demonstrated before."

"Are you telling me that things will get worse?" Yusef Levison lifted his trembling head. "I cannot live through much more, Isaac Ben-David. If the Master of the Universe is compassionate, he would not do this to his people."

"God is compassionate, and he has been patient for generations." Isaac's voice broke with gentleness. "But we have been blinded by our laws and our own efforts to reach him. Don't you see? We wanted a triumphant king, not a suffering savior. We wanted a man who could work miracles for the nation, not a God in flesh who could work miracles in individual hearts. The prophets spoke clearly of him, but we confused his two appearings—the first, when he came to die, and the second, when he will come to reign."

"What about those who believe Romulus is the mashiach?" Ephraim Ben-David tossed the question to his son. "You have to admit, Isaac, he fits the profile almost perfectly."

"Too perfectly." Isaac tapped the open Bible in his hand. "But he will soon reveal his true colors. Jesus and Daniel both told us that he would set an abomination in the Holy Place— and I believe the abomination is a statue of himself. It's only a matter of time before he stops the daily sacrifices and demonstrates that while he pretends to love Israel, he truly hates us. He has been rounding up our people and imprisoning them without mercy—he is as ruthless as Hitler, and soon his evil will be even more evident. Soon all those who remain in Jerusalem will have to flee. We can't hide in these tunnels much longer."

"Where shall we go?" The question came from a young woman Sarah had never seen before. She sat next to Thomas Parker, and her brown eyes moved from Isaac's face to his. "Where will we be safe?"

"Petra." Isaac thumped the pages of his Bible. "I know this sounds a little bizarre, but there's a verse in Isaiah that seems to indicate that after the Lord returns and descends to the Mount of Olives, he will then go to Edom and Petra—and I can only assume he will come to gather his people who have gathered there for safety."

"It makes sense." Ephraim nodded, his eyes searching his son's face. "The only entrance to the city is by the Sik. That gorge is narrow, and the cliffs virtually inaccessible. And the homes carved by ancient Edomites are still usable for shelter."

"And defensible," Parker pointed out. "It would be the perfect place for us to wait and is easily defended if Romulus should try to drive us out."

"Romulus will have his hands full in Jerusalem for some time to come." Isaac looked around the circle, and his mouth softened when his gaze fell upon the little girl who had flip-flopped her way into the circle. "I suggest that we begin sending people to Petra as soon as possible."

He lifted his gaze and met the American's eyes. "Parker, you know the lay of the land, and you'll be able to help people find dwellings among the cliffs. We'll need your expertise about which caves are safe for habitation."

A spark of rebellion flashed in the archeologist's eyes, and Sarah suspected that he didn't want to leave the forthcoming adventure in Jerusalem. But after a moment, he nodded and folded one arm across his bent knee. "We should move people in small groups, no more than six at a time under the cover of darkness. We should be able to begin the transfer as soon as we've scouted the area."

"I was at Petra three months ago," Ephraim added. "The place will be perfect for our use. It's isolated, it's sheltered, and it has everything from private dwellings to a public amphitheater."

Isaac grinned. "Great. Parker, why don't you organize a scouting team to leave tomorrow night? We'll present the plan to the others here and begin transporting groups within the week."

"We'll need help." Sarah looked up at her husband. "This type of exfiltration will require careful planning. We'll need to know if and where there will be roadblocks."

"That's why I'm glad we have you." Isaac moved to stand behind her, then lowered his arms to her shoulders and squeezed gently. "This is the sort of operation you live for, right?"

Sarah could only smile in response.

†

Isaac sat up and blinked slowly, trying to bring himself back from the realm of sleep. He had caught a sorely needed nap in a quiet corner of one of the tunnels, and though he had posted guards at several major intersections and access points, he still found it hard to lose himself in sleep. Some part of his brain always seemed to stay awake, listening for the odd noise, waiting for the unexpected attack.

In the two weeks since the passing of Romulus's deadline,

Isaac had begun to hear the individual stories of Jews and Gentiles who had refused to accept the Universal Chip or the UFM code. Many resisters had been so wearied by the daily struggle to survive on the streets that they stood passively while a scanner searched for an ID chip in their hands. If one was not found, or if it lacked an authentic UFM code, wireless communications relayed the information to the massive databank at the new UF/IDF headquarters in Jerusalem. Within seconds, the arresting officers were instructed to take the resister to the appropriate prison camp. *No delay and no mercy*, went the new UF slogan, *or there will be no peace.*

Yet more than once Isaac heard eyewitnesses speak of Jews who had been arrested, scanned, and released after a UF patrol apparently failed to realize that he had encountered a resister. He had met one of the escapees, a ten-year-old boy, only a few hours before. "It was like he went blind or something," the boy told Isaac. "He stared right at the scanner in his hand—I saw the alert light flashing myself. And then he let me go."

Isaac folded his arms and looked down at the boy, trying to hide a smile. "Maybe the patrol took pity on you because you're young. After all, these are men, not monsters."

"I don't think so." An impish smile had played around the corners of the boy's mouth. "I think it was a miracle. The Holy One of Israel, blessed be his name, is protecting me."

Was God protecting them? Isaac's blood ran thick with guilt as his thoughts turned to Rachel Levison. Why would God spare Sarah and take Yusef's beloved Rachel? Why would he spare one ten-year-old and allow a thousand others to be arrested?

Isaac stood, coughed the dust from his lungs, then walked to an intersection where an air shaft poured a silvery stream of moonlight into the underground chamber. He knew far too little about the Bible and the prophets. As a yeshiva student, he should have applied himself more to the study of eschatology and less to the debate of kabala. As a mature man, he should have invested more energy in reaching for God than in turning away from him.

His mind skated away from the unchangeable past. What he needed now was help, guidance from God, because the people in this place had begun to look to Isaac for leadership . . .

"My son?"

Isaac's heart skipped a beat as he recognized his father's voice. Either his father had crept up without a sound, or Isaac had been too deeply lost in thought.

"Father? You should be sleeping."

"I slept today because I wanted to spend some time with Thomas before he leaves for Petra. And I am glad I have found you—there are things we should discuss . . . in case we are separated."

Isaac lifted a brow. "Are we to be separated? I was hoping you would remain with me and Sarah."

"I plan to, but who knows what tomorrow may bring?" As Ephraim stepped into the moonlight, Isaac saw the misery that darkened his face. "Can we talk, Son?"

"Let's sit here." Isaac gestured toward a cleared space near the air shaft. He had planned to go out on a foraging expedition, but such things could wait when a father had pressing matters on his heart.

He waited until his father settled himself with his back to the rough stone wall, then he sat next to him, facing the longest open tunnel. "What is on your mind, Father?"

"I want to confess my faults to you."

Isaac's voice went suddenly husky. "You have nothing to confess."

"Yes, I do. I was remiss in your education—I left your spiritual education to your mother, and when she died, I relegated such matters to the yeshiva school. Later, I left such things to chance. You were a Jew, an Israeli, and a man, and I thought that was all you needed to know." One corner of his mouth twisted upward. "As time has proven, I was wrong. I failed you, Son, and I would give anything to go back and change my life . . . in order to change yours."

Isaac rubbed his hand over his face, then swallowed the despair in his throat. "It's all right, Father. You did what you wanted to do, and so did I. A moment ago, I was thinking about the past, too, and I've realized we can't look back. We must press onward and do our best to ease the suffering around us. I am a soldier, and as a soldier I must defend the people of Israel—"

"That was the other thing I wanted to talk to you about." His father's face suddenly went grim. "I know you, Isaac, and I've watched you as you talk about Romulus. You used to admire him, then you wondered about him, later you seemed to be confused by him. But lately you say his name with iron in your voice and determination in your eyes. You have decided to do something—and I must know what you plan to do."

Isaac did not answer, but regarded his father with somber curiosity. If his father had seen through him, who else had realized that he planned to rid the world of Romulus? Did Sarah know?

"Father," he looked down at his hands, "I must do *something*. And since I helped pave the way for Romulus to influence Israel, I feel it is my responsibility to set things right. The situation will only grow worse until I act. Romulus is on a rampage, and the situation has escalated since I brought him that cursed spear—"

"Do you think you can resist what has been fore-ordained since the world began?" His father's voice, without rising in volume, took on a subtle urgency. "I've been reading the Scriptures, too, and I see now that these days were planned in advance. This Romulus is a pawn of Satan's, and he will deceive many. But the Lamb of God will vanquish him at the end of seven years. You must believe that, Isaac, for it is written!"

"I do believe that." Isaac answered with quiet firmness. "But how many more must die in the remaining time? Yes, much of the story has been written, but not all of it is foreordained. Perhaps I can do something to make Romulus leave Israel. Perhaps an attempt on his life will convince him to establish his religion's headquarters in Paris, or Brussels, or New York. I do not know if I will succeed in this plan, but I know I must do something for the sake of my suffering people. God does not command us to be passive."

A weight of sadness came to rest upon his father's dear face, but he did not argue. He and Isaac exchanged a long look that carried far more information than words could ever impart. Then he said, "So what will you do?"

Isaac took a deep breath. "The Scriptures foretell that Romulus will soon demand that the daily Temple sacrifices cease. Soon afterward, he will install an object that will desecrate the Holy Place—and I believe that object will be a life-size statue. At some point he will almost certainly institute some sort of religious ceremony to mark this occasion, and I believe I can get close to him during this ritual . . . if I can enlist the help of the Kohanim."

His father's face suddenly rippled with anguish. "You would try to—"

"Yes, Father. I'm going to attempt to kill him. Even if I don't succeed, the attempt may convince him that Israel will not ever accept his idolatry."

"But, Son—"

"Let him be, Father." Isaac looked up and saw Sarah standing in the darkness, her form dimly outlined by the silvery light. He had no idea how long she had been standing there, but lately she had regained her ability to read him like a book. She knew his heart and his temperament, and she had to know what he wanted to do.

She stepped forward and knelt by his side, then placed her hand on his shoulder. "I've been studying, too," she said, looking from the son to the father. "I wandered into an abandoned church the other day. The place was a shambles, but in an office I found a stack of books, one of them on eschatology. The author spent a great deal of time discussing 144,000 Jews who will be supernaturally sealed to endure a time of tribulation."

Isaac cracked a smile. "That's now—right? I'd hate to think this is just the warmup."

A melancholy frown flitted across Sarah's delicate features. "The time of tribulation began after the disappearance of the bride of Christ, the Church. And then the Holy Spirit will seal 12,000 Jews from each of the twelve tribes to serve as witnesses throughout the earth. These children of Israel will come through the tribulation safely, and they will be successful in their work. They will point all those who remain toward God and the Lamb. With the two witnesses, they will bear witness of Jesus Christ."

Isaac pondered this information in silence, but his father cracked a sardonic smile. "How do we know if we are sealed? Do I step out in front of a speeding car to see if I survive? Or perhaps I should allow Romulus's men to capture me and see if I can miraculously escape."

Sarah's voice softened. "I don't know how these things work. I don't know who is sealed and who isn't. But I know that God is in control, even now. We can trust our lives to him, whether we are sealed or not, because he reigns even in the darkest night, and the Lamb is coming soon to defeat Satan and his puppet. Each day we survive, beloveds, is one less day to endure."

She leaned closer, and Isaac felt the warmth of her soft lips against his stubbled cheek. "Do what you must do, Husband. And I will leave you in God's hands."

TWENTY-SIX

THOUGH ISAAC HAD EXPECTED THE NEWS, HE STILL FELT a profound sadness when the story circulated among the resisters: Adrian Romulus had issued a decree that all Temple sacrifices must cease as of April 22, the Sabbath before Pesach, or Passover. From their hiding places, the Orthodox rabbis, most of whom had scattered like chaff before the wind when the Universal Force patrols began checking for Universal Chips, called for a time of fasting, prayer, and repentance. The word spread like a grass fire.

Isaac read the text of Romulus's edict in the *Jerusalem Post:*

> Because all nations are one, and because the spark of divinity is to be found within us and not within an outmoded religious structure, all rituals, sacrifices, and other liturgical traditions must at once cease in every temple, church, synagogue, and mosque around the world. From this day forward, the universal center of worship is to be the golden Temple in Jerusalem, the Mount of Peace. Join Adrian Romulus, the world's leader, at sundown on April 24, for

the inauguration of global worship that transcends man and myth. In the absolute power of peace, the Universal Faith Movement will bring us together.

Angered by Romulus's arrogance, Isaac threw the paper to the ground. He had obviously selected Sunday, April 24, as the date for the investiture of his new religion to insult the Jews, for the festival of Passover would begin at sundown on that day. God had delivered the children of Israel from Egypt on the first Passover, but now, Romulus seemed to be saying, God would do nothing to deliver the Jews from the tyranny of the Universal Faith Movement.

Isaac's anger cooled as he realized another significant fact—Romulus was finally coming to Jerusalem. At long last, he would stop pulling strings from Brussels and Paris. Romulus would walk in the streets of the ancient city, over cobblestones that had recently been washed with the tears of innocent men, women, and children. In his arrogance and evil, he would climb the Temple Mount and face his destiny.

Eager to initiate his own plan, Isaac hurried to find Sarah and the others.

✝

Rabbi Baram Cohen walked north up Tiferet Yisrael to the Burnt House, then proceeded down the set of stairs that led to the security checkpoint. There he stopped and lifted his eyes to the empty plaza before the holiest shrine in all of Jewish civilization, the Western Wall. The crowds that had formerly filled this space had disappeared. The men who used to huddle here, shuckling as they prayed beneath fur-trimmed hats and kippot, were now in hiding, beating their breasts in sorrow as they prayed.

Baram could not think he would ever be able to walk upon the holy Temple Mount. Adrian Romulus, like Antiochus Epiphanes of old, was planning to defile the sanctuary. Just this afternoon a large truck had delivered a nine-foot golden statue to a storeroom inside the Temple. Rumor had it that godless Gentile workmen had mentioned that Romulus intended to place the statue on a pedestal beside the ark in the Holy of Holies.

Baram stopped walking, knowing he could not progress further. The Universal Force patrols at the checkpoint ahead would want to scan his Universal Chip, and Baram would never have one. And so he closed his eyes and stood in the windy street, the shock of defeat holding him immobile as a name kept slipping through his thoughts.

One hundred seventy years before the birth of the one called Jesus of Nazareth, Antiochus Epiphanes, a Syrian, had broken a peace treaty with Israel and marched on Palestine. Like Romulus, he wooed Jews who promised to serve him, and, like Romulus, Antiochus Epiphanes stopped the daily sacrifices. In a fit of murderous rage, he murdered over 40,000 Jews and sold at least that many into slavery. Finally, as an act of complete defiance of the Holy One of Israel, he offered the blood of a pig upon the sacred altar of Zerubbabel's Temple and set an image of Jupiter in the holy place.

If Baram did not know better, he would have said that history loved to repeat itself. But this was more than the overlapping of historical events. In his innermost heart, Baram knew that the Holy One intended the evil of Antiochus

Epiphanes to be a prophetic picture of the evil to come. That evil had appeared in Baram's lifetime, and even Hitler's monstrosity paled in comparison.

The wind moaned softly, lifting his beard, and a verse from the prophet Isaiah rose to the surface of his memory: "In that day Yahweh with his hard and great and strong sword will punish leviathan the swift serpent, and leviathan the crooked serpent; and he will kill the monster that is in the sea."

Where was HaShem's great and strong sword? The evil one had come out of the political sea and advanced to the holy mountain, and nothing stood in his way. The righteous Temple priests had been forbidden to serve on the holy mount because they would not cut their flesh for the ID chip, and only a handful of spineless priests remained to care for the sanctuary. These men had willingly taken the Universal Chip, and, in exchange, Romulus had given them the worthy positions reserved for generations for the sons of Aaron. Before the Temple dedication, Baram had sent a pleading message to one of Romulus's representatives, but the answer, when it came, was clear: Anyone who did not take the Universal Chip would forever be forbidden from entering the Temple. There would be no exceptions and no mercy, not even for the Kohanim.

Baram lifted his eyes to the ragged edge of the Wailing Wall as a suffocating sensation tightened his throat. As a leader of the Kohanim, he had failed his people. He had been blinded by Romulus's charm and dazzled by the prospects of seeing the Temple rise in his lifetime. He had been so distracted by the preparations and celebrations that he had failed to realize one thing—the Shekinah glory, which he had beheld on several occasions when the ark of the covenant rested in the underground shrine at the Air Force base, had not once appeared above the ark in this false Temple. The clouds that filled the Temple at the dedication ceremony had been man-made, as was the glow that surrounded Adrian Romulus every time he appeared on television.

Lowering his head, Baram slipped his hand into his pocket and felt the handle of the knife. It was a simple steak knife, someone's castoff kitchen utensil, but it would do the job if he asked it to. He could, of course, simply walk to the security checkpoint and ask to pass to the Wailing Wall, but he did not want to die at the hands of his enemy. After all, Saul had fallen on his sword rather than have the enemy make sport with him.

His children, Devorah and Asher, would understand. Like the Jews who died upon Masada, they possessed strong minds and the spirits of warriors. They would gladly take their own lives rather than surrender to Romulus's evil system.

The heaviness in Baram's chest felt like a millstone as he pulled the blade from his pocket. The serrated blade winked in the sunlight, and he turned to face a wall, in case the guard at the checkpoint below should happen to look up.

He pressed the tip of the blade to his coat and teased aside the heavy layer of wool. In a last gesture of humility, he lifted his eyes to the blue sky above and whispered a prayer: "You who know all things, the Holy One of Israel, surely you understand?"

No sound rumbled from the cloudless sky, but a clear voice whispered from the recesses of his heart: *A suicide is a sentinel who has deserted his post.*

Slowly, Baram lowered his gaze and the knife. He knew

the quotation; it came from Bahya ibn Pakuda, an ancient Jewish sage. He had not thought of that quote in years, but he knew why the Holy One had brought it to mind now.

He could not quit. For some reason, the Master of the Universe had assigned him a role to play in the coming days, and he could not neglect his duty.

He dropped the knife and heard the blade clatter on the stones. And then, like the still voice of an old friend, came another whisper: *Find Isaac Ben-David.*

Moving forward in the certainty of blind faith, Baram turned and walked back the way he had come.

†

Romulus closed his eyes as artic air brushed his cheeks and the exposed flesh of his neck. His body remained in his chair, recording impulses, feelings, and sights as his spirit soared over the rooftops of Paris, past the Eiffel Tower, up into the velvet blackness of the icy night. As he and Nadim floated on spirit wings through the second heaven, snatches of earthbound sounds came to him: the urgent whisper of a man plotting with his mistress, adenoidal wailing above a twanging stringed instrument, raucous laughter from an Italian restaurant.

Below him, like a slumbering dark giant, lay his future kingdom. He already controlled men's lives; soon he would control their hearts and spirits as well. Nadim had assured him that victory and glory awaited immediately after the test.

Nadim's strong arm tightened around Romulus's waist, then the ground rose up to meet them with a sudden sucking sound. Romulus tensed, then relaxed as his feet touched solid stone. He blinked, then focused on their surroundings. Beneath him, the silvery lights of a metropolitan city twinkled. Fragrant groves filled the spaces between hills and high-rise apartments, and behind him stood . . . the Temple.

"Ah." He slipped his hands into his pockets and returned Nadim's smile in full measure. "You didn't tell me we were going to Jerusalem."

"The Temple Mount, to be exact," Nadim answered, releasing Romulus's waist. "The pinnacle of the Temple, to be precise."

"Of course." Romulus looked to his right. The Al Aqsa Mosque stood within its enclosure, shimmering in the starlight. Behind it stood the Dome of the Rock, and behind it, the Temple rose in all its newfound glory. "It won't be long," he said, turning to face the Temple. "The preparations are complete. In two days I will enter the Holy of Holies and prove to Israel that the God of their fathers is a dead deity."

"Adrian," a note of rebuke filled Nadim's voice, "do not forget yourself. You are the mightiest man alive, true, but do not forget that your power comes from me."

Nadim's short warning sent a tremor scooting up the back of Romulus's neck. "Of course, you are right. Your power is great; I am only a channel."

"But you can soon be more than a mere channel." Nadim stretched out his hand, turning Romulus to face the expanse of the city. "Do you see this city? It and all other kingdoms will I give to you, if you will obey me, Adrian."

Romulus wavered, trying to comprehend the meaning behind the message. "Have I not always obeyed you without question?"

An inexplicable, lazy smile swept over Nadim's face as he

surveyed the sleeping city. "I once made that same offer to another, and he refused me. I offered him many things, and he threw my gifts back in my face."

Romulus smiled in the calm strength of knowledge. "That one was a fool, and he is dead. He died"—he stretched out his hand and pointed through the darkness toward the place of the skull—"somewhere over there, if the tour guides are correct."

Nadim's warm hand came to rest upon Romulus's shoulder. "I will not ask you to jump from this pinnacle, Adrian, but in the next two days I will ask you to do something equally as difficult. That one was willing to die for his beliefs—are you willing to die for yours?" His voice dropped to a low, sensuous growl. "Will you give your life for me, Adrian?"

The thought of death was like a rock dropped into the pool of Romulus's heart, sending ripples of fear in all directions. Death was the great equalizer of men, but Nadim had made Romulus more than a man. And just as a caterpillar had to die and rest in the cocoon before it could rise as a butterfly, so he would have to die and rest before he could fulfill his glorious destiny.

He did not flinch as he turned to face his master. "I will die for you," he said simply, falling to one knee. He grasped Nadim's hand and pressed it to his lips, then turned his head and rested his cheek on the leathery palm. "I will do anything you require because I believe you have the authority to imbue me with ultimate power. Yes, Nadim. I will willingly follow you into the grave."

Nadim pressed both hands to Romulus's face, then held his head for a long moment. Romulus remained very still, knowing that his master had the power to rip his head from his shoulders if he chose to, but Nadim only caressed Romulus's cheek with one hand, then lifted his head and split the night with a great peal of laughter.

TWENTY-SEVEN

BY SUNDAY MORNING, APRIL 24, ISAAC'S PLAN HAD come together. Two days before, he had met Rabbi Baram Cohen, who appeared at the mouth of the tunnels from out of nowhere and announced that he was searching for Isaac Ben-David. The sentry brought Cohen to Isaac immediately, and Isaac had listened in amazement as the rabbi explained that the Holy One of Israel had sent him to help Isaac defeat Romulus. "I have no idea what that means," he had said, lifting his hands and then letting them fall into his lap. "But I am here, and I am a willing vessel. Tell me what you need."

Grateful that God had provided, Isaac quickly outlined his plan, and the rabbi helped to fill in the missing pieces. Afterward, the rabbi placed his hands on Isaac's head and asked for God's blessing.

When he concluded his prayer, the aged rabbi stepped back and slowly stroked his beard as he stared at Isaac. "A month ago, if anyone had told me that I would allow a soldier to wear a replica of the high priest's breastplate, crown, and robe, I would have told them I would sooner be cursed," he had said, his eyes dark with gravity. "But such a sin is nothing compared to the abomination that now waits to be placed in the Most Holy Place. The Holy One of Israel, blessed be his name, cannot be compared to man-made images!"

Now Isaac stood in one of the small storage rooms of the Temple, waiting for the moment for which his entire life had been nothing but preparation. Getting onto the Temple Mount had been the hardest part, but Danny Melman, who bore the Universal Chip and was therefore trusted, took charge of Temple security and announced that a new man had been appointed to assume the position of chief priest for this all-important day. Dressed in copies of the authentic Temple garb and cloaked in the authority of the Shin Bet, Isaac had joined the other false priests and made the procession into the Temple through the underground gate of the Kohanim without having to pass through a security scanner.

Now he wiped his damp palms on the heavy robe as a tiny radio receiver buzzed in his ear. With help from Melman, Sarah and his father had procured a radio and earpieces, and from outside the Temple Mount they were monitoring Romulus and his entourage. Sarah had taken a position inside the outer courtyard; his father stood in a throng around the base of the Temple Mount. As Isaac suspected, the Universal Force had placed tight security all around the Temple complex, carefully scanning anyone who actually entered through the Temple gate, but the gathering outside the walls was so large that only troublemakers were being scanned for Universal Chips.

Isaac knew that video cameras monitored activities throughout the Temple, including the court outside the sanctuary. At the time of the Temple construction, not even

Romulus had dared to suggest that a camera be placed inside the Holy of Holies, but Isaac wouldn't have been surprised if he had installed one now. His arrogance knew no bounds.

Isaac's father's voice suddenly buzzed in his ear. "They're coming into the Temple area. Be ready, Isaac. ETA is ten minutes."

They had decided that it was too risky for Isaac to wear a microphone, so he could not answer. He pressed his hands together, however, and slowly paced in the open space of the storage room. He had no definite script to follow, nor did any of the other sycophantic priests scattered through the Temple enclave. A few strokes of Romulus's pen had wiped away five thousand years of history, and no one knew what he would do once he entered the Temple. He had demanded, however, that the Jewish high priest be present, and Isaac had been delighted by Romulus's overconfidence. The beast was planning to preen himself and flaunt his image before the Holy One's representative, but he would find his plans interrupted.

A trumpet blast broke the stillness of the vast chamber, the sound echoing across the high ceiling and setting Isaac's nerves on edge. He stepped out of the storage chamber and stood in the vast space of the courtyard, watching as Romulus strode forward, flanked by Elijah Reis on one side and General Archer on the other. Archer wore his military uniform; Reis wore a simple black cassock with a white collar. But Romulus was dressed in a spotless white robe that fell from his neck to the floor in a single piece. His dark hair gleamed in the light from the candlesticks, and in his hands he carried only one object: the Spear of Longinus.

Isaac felt a shiver of revulsion, a spasm of hatred and

disgust that rose from his core. He had known Romulus would carry his talisman of power, but the sight of that symbol wrenched at Isaac's gut. The blood of six million Jews and untold thousands of Christians had flowed because of ambitious men who had grasped at that spear and all it promised.

Wearing a superior smile, Romulus moved across the courtyard, barely acknowledging the priest who waited in the shadows. With the confidence of a man returning home, he flung open the double doors that led to the Holy Place and stepped through the portal.

Remaining a careful distance behind, Isaac followed with his gaze lowered and his hands tucked into the sleeves of his robe, as quiet as a nun. He did not want to be recognized yet, for there was still time for Romulus to sound an alarm.

Archer and Reis fell into step behind Isaac, though the rest of the entourage waited respectfully in the courtyard.

"Only the high priest shall accompany me now," Romulus called, his voice bouncing from wall to wall in the sanctuary. "When I have accomplished what I have come to do, he will open the curtain and show the world who I truly am."

A breath of cold wind seemed to blow through the closed room, shivering the curtain between the Holy Place and the Holy of Holies. Isaac steeled himself for what must come next, and a lifetime of obedience and holy awe fell away as he followed Romulus through the opening in the linen curtain. The wind blew again, lifting the hair at the back of his neck, and suddenly he stood in the Holy of Holies, before the golden ark of the covenant, beneath the sheltering cherubim that hung from the far walls.

Romulus stood before the ark, one hand gripping the

spear, the other extended toward the flat place beneath the two golden cherubim on the lid of the ark.

"They say that those who touch the ark of the covenant will be struck down," Romulus remarked, tossing the comment toward Isaac as casually as if he had been discussing the weather. "What do you say to that, priest?"

Isaac swallowed hard and took a step forward. He had not counted on having a conversation in this room; he only wanted to do what had to be done, and quickly. But Romulus turned slightly, and a small smile lifted his lips when he saw Isaac standing beside him.

"I shall never cease to be amazed at the enemy's bag of tricks." Romulus lowered his voice to a low hiss. "He has sent a Jew, one of my own officers, to kill me." Laughter floated up from his throat. "What a delicious sense of irony he has."

Isaac stopped dead, his heart beating hard enough to be heard a yard away.

"I know everything, friend." Romulus's voice wasn't much above a whisper, but the effect was as great as if he'd shouted in Isaac's ear. "Do you think I am a mere man? I am not. I am the son of the master of all—I am the one who will hold the keys to life and death. It is right that men worship me. And my worship shall begin today."

"You are not God." The words hurt Isaac's throat, as though he'd swallowed some jagged object. "You are not *worthy* of worship."

A feral light gleamed in the depths of Romulus's eyes as he turned toward the ark. "You are wrong, Isaac Ben-David. And before three days have passed, you will see how wrong you were."

The next events happened in a blur of motion so swift that later Isaac couldn't recall their exact order. Propping the spear against a wing of a suspended cherub, Romulus reached out with both hands to touch the holy ark. Turning, he sat upon it, and he didn't die. Instead, he seemed to glow in the light reflecting from the golden cherubim. And something in the sight of the beast sitting upon the ark of God drove Isaac to desperation. In a moment the curtain would open, and all of Israel would see this impostor posing as the Holy One himself . . .

As Reis drew the curtain, Isaac lunged for and grasped the spear. The air filled with gasps of awe and wonder and the metallic clink of golden rings sliding back upon one another. Romulus smiled out at the world, his hands upon the cherubim's heads, his body desecrating the holy ark, and Isaac knew he had to act or be killed. With a bellow of rage, he drew back the spear and let it fly. Romulus saw the movement and threw up his arm, but the spear flew straight and true, flashing through Romulus's arm and embedding itself in that arrogant eye . . .

Romulus's spotless white robe streaked and spattered crimson. General Archer gaped open-mouthed at his employer, while Reis turned to look at Isaac with eyes as expressionless as obsidian stone.

Pandemonium broke loose in the outer court, blood flowed freely in the Most Holy Place, and Isaac fled the sanctuary, running through the amazed and helpless priests. Entering the storeroom once again, he pushed aside the carved flagstone that led to the cisterns and the secret chambers. As the men above scrambled to save the evil one, Isaac dropped to the floor below, then ran for his life, gasping for air that burned his lungs even as the enormity of his deed seared his brain.

†

Hiding in a small apartment near the Jericho Road, Sarah and Thomas Parker sat in silence and watched the breaking news reports. Uri Shamir, the chief of detectives for the Universal Force Criminal Investigation Agency, spoke slowly to the horde of reporters assembled outside the Augusta Victoria Hospital in East Jerusalem.

"Ladies and gentlemen of the press," Shamir said, his expression a mask of stone, "I regret to inform you that Universal President Adrian Romulus was pronounced dead at 2:04 P.M. this afternoon."

A flutter of horror ran through the group, then faded to silent expectation as Shamir held up his notes and continued. "Doctors at the Augusta Victoria Hospital tried to revive him, but Adrian Romulus had lost too much blood at the scene. Though the doctors and emergency medical technicians made valiant efforts to save his life, nothing could be done."

"Who killed him?"

"Did he die in the Temple?"

"What was he doing in the Most Holy Place?"

"How'd the assailant get a weapon into the Temple?"

A host of questions filled the air, then were drowned out in a flood of reproachful shushing when the spokesman lifted his hand for silence.

"Apparently, President Romulus was attacked within the Holy of Holies by a man pretending to be the high priest,"

Shamir continued. "The assailant attacked Romulus with a personal possession the president often carried, an ancient spear that meant a great deal to him." Shamir paused and looked out over the rim of his glasses. "To my knowledge, no king or head of state has been assassinated by a sword or spear for several centuries. But since this assailant must have known Romulus would be carrying a spear, we can assume this attack was premeditated and carefully orchestrated by the resistance movement."

The spokesman lowered his notes and nodded grimly at the camera. "Eyewitnesses have confirmed that the assailant was a former major of the Israeli Defense Forces, Jerusalem resident Isaac Ben-David. Those who know Ben-David have stated that he once was an enthusiastic supporter of Romulus and the Universal Faith Movement but has been absent without leave from his military post since early March. He is considered armed, dangerous, and mentally unstable. Anyone who sees him must alert a Universal Force patrol immediately."

A reporter in the front of the mob waved his hand. "Where is this man now?"

If possible, Shamir's face took on an even harder look. "Unfortunately, Ben-David escaped into the tunnels beneath the Temple Mount. At the moment of crisis, all attentions were directed toward President Romulus, of course, and by the time security forces reached the sanctuary, the suspect had disappeared. The ancient tunnels, as you know, wind for miles beneath the Temple Mount and the Old City and have not been fully explored since the reopening of the area three years ago." Shamir narrowed his eyes at the reporter who had asked the question. "I guarantee you, we *will* find this man, and he will be executed. We have already executed Daniel

Melman, the Shin Bet director who was in charge of maintaining security upon the Temple Mount. Without a doubt, Melman helped Ben-David gain access to the president."

"Oh no." Grief struck Sarah like a blow in the stomach. She had to lean back and swallow several times to choke down the heavy bile that rose in her throat. Initially, Melman had been misguided, but he had lost his life in the effort to help them.

The questioning continued and the spokesman repeated himself, then someone shouted, "So who's running the world?"

The question came from someone outside the knot of reporters on the television screen, and from the look on Shamir's face, Sarah could tell he wasn't pleased with the questioner's jocular tone. "All matters of international security are firmly under control," he said, his brows drawing downward in a frown. "I assure you, all governments are fully operational. If any person or provincial government"— his gaze swept the crowd—"thinks they can override the president's authority during this moment of crisis, they are sorely mistaken."

Sarah looked at Thomas Parker, who squatted on the floor before the television, one hand pressed to his chin. "Do you think it's possible?" she asked, hearing a hopeful note in her voice. "Might some of the other governments rebel? Has Isaac given them the courage to act?"

Parker scratched gently at his bearded chin. "I don't know. The Bible indicates that several national leaders will rebel against the Antichrist during the latter years of his reign—"

"What is this, if not his latter year? He's dead, Parker."

The American only rocked back on his heels, his gaze fastened to the television. "We'll see."

†

The next day, in the twilight hour just before sunset, Sarah and Parker met again in the small apartment. The squatters who lived there, an Arab doctor and his wife, had several times provided medical care to the refugees hidden in and around the Temple Mount. Tonight Sarah and Parker were picking up a box of stolen antibiotics to take them to the refugee settlement at Petra.

After quickly pulling his guests into the safety of the apartment, the doctor pulled the precious box from a hiding place in the wall, then sent her and Parker on their way with a prayer for safety.

Their scouts had been watching the roads long enough to know when the guards changed shifts. As the sun balanced on the western horizon, the new shift approached from the city and the tired patrols lingered to exchange a smoke and a bit of gossip.

Crouching low, Sarah and Parker ran through the lengthening shadows, then reached the station where others had hidden a pair of motorbikes. By the time sunset stretched glowing fingers across the sky, they were on their way to the remote outpost known as Petra.

Sarah had good reason to feel happy about leaving Jerusalem. After the attack on Romulus yesterday, Ephraim and Rabbi Cohen had smuggled Isaac out of the city almost immediately. She had not had an opportunity to speak to him since the incident.

Her spirit lightened considerably once they reached the narrow passage that led to the stone city. An atmosphere of gaiety permeated the settlement; the mountains themselves echoed with the sound of a joyous chant as they arrived: "*Le Chaim!* To Life!" As Sarah moved among the refugees, accepting gratitude and congratulations for her small part in yesterday's drama, she found morale and enthusiasm high. Romulus had been dead two days, and many in the Petra settlement felt that no one in the Universal Movement could effectively take his place. Soon, an older man assured Sarah, the Universal Network would collapse, national governments would rise again, and they could all return to their homes.

Her heart nearly stopped when she finally found Isaac. He was leaning in a doorway of a cavern, watching her with eyes that bathed her in admiration. She flew into his arms, then wrapped her arms around his neck and covered him with relieved kisses.

Laughing, Isaac forcibly peeled her away. "Wife, you act as though you are surprised to see me."

"Maybe I am," she answered, reaching out to touch him again. "But I'm very glad you're here."

Knowing that time was short, Isaac led her into the small room hewn out of stone. The accommodations were rough— only an air mattress, a blanket, and a basin for water, but one of the refugees had managed to hook a laptop computer up to a portable generator. The computer sat on the air mattress, a screen saver floating idly across its silvered surface.

"We're planning to watch the state funeral tomorrow," Isaac told Sarah, smiling grimly as he slipped his hands into his pockets. "Only when Romulus is dead and buried will I rest safely."

"You don't really think—"

"I don't know. But I know it's not over. Only forty-two months have passed since the Disruption, and the prophets say we've another forty-two months to go before the Lord will return. So something will happen—I'd stake my life on it."

"That's why I'm going to the Temple Mount tomorrow." She lifted her chin as Isaac's jaw clenched. "I know what you're going to say, but I'm a big girl and a trained officer. I can handle myself in a crowd. Besides"—she looked down as her resolve wavered—"I have to do it for Director Melman. There are several Shabak agents who don't agree with Romulus. I think they'll agree to help us, if only for Danny's sake."

Isaac stared at her, the veins in his throat standing out like ropes, then he smoothed his disheveled hair and sat on the ground, radiating offended dignity. "You could at least let me protest. It's a husband's duty."

"A husband's duty," she said, sinking to his level, "is to love his wife. And you do a marvelous job of that, Isaac Ben-David."

His gaze caught and held hers as she wrapped her arms around his neck. "I wish I could go with you."

"Now *that* is too dangerous." She forced her lips to part in a curved, still smile. "You're the most wanted man in the world, Husband. So you will stay here among the rocks, hidden out of the way. You can watch the entire spectacle on the Net."

"I'd rather watch it with you."

Love, strong and sweet, wrapped around Sarah like a warm blanket. She bent and kissed her husband's forehead, then ran her fingers through his wavy hair. "I'm taking the point tomorrow. We're going to be spread throughout the outer court just in case the Universal Force patrols try to take out half of the crowd in retribution for Romulus's death. The UF patrols won't realize it, but every last one of them will be shadowed by a member of the resistance."

She tilted her head back and watched as guilt flickered across Isaac's face. He was struggling in the same way she had after Binyamin's death. She knew he didn't feel guilty for killing Romulus—that was an act of war, and Isaac had been trained to fight for the defense of his country. No, his guilt rose from the fact that he had worked for Romulus and participated in the process that bound Israel to the worst sort of evil.

"You couldn't have known what he was," she whispered as a tremor passed over Isaac's face. "How could you, a Jew, know what the Book of Revelation predicted?"

"There were other writings, Sarah." Reaching into the space between them, Isaac pulled the worn Bible from his coat and fumbled through the thin pages. "Listen—even the prophet Zechariah wrote about the false shepherd who would come to lead Israel. God told the prophet to write, 'I will give this nation a shepherd who will not care for the sheep that are threatened by death, nor look after the young, nor heal the injured, nor feed the healthy. Instead, this shepherd will eat of the meat of the fattest sheep and tear off their hooves. Doom is certain for this worthless shepherd who abandons the flock! The sword will cut his arm and pierce his right eye! His arm will become useless, and his right eye completely blind!'"

Sarah watched with acute and loving anxiety as her husband closed the Bible. "Israel did not accept the Good

Shepherd, the true Messiah, and so God has sent them a foolish, greedy, and corrupt shepherd," Isaac explained. "The Good Shepherd gave his life for the sheep, but the false shepherd will destroy the people because he cares nothing for them. But the sword will cut his arm and pierce his eye—it is written!"

A thrill of frightened anticipation touched Sarah's spine. "What are you saying?"

Isaac's expression darkened with unreadable emotions. "I didn't tell you, Sarah, and the news reports haven't given details, so I don't expect you to realize . . ."

"What, Husband?"

Isaac looked up at her, his mouth tight and grim. "I threw the spear at Romulus without thinking. I should have taken the time to aim for his heart, but he was moving, and I was horrified—"

"What are you saying?"

"The spear went through his arm and pierced his right eye."

Surprise siphoned the blood from her brain, leaving her lightheaded. "You think—"

"I think it may not be over."

Throwing up both hands, Sarah stood and stepped away. "I don't want to hear any more of this kind of talk. You killed him, Isaac, and I'm glad of it. You were trained as a soldier, and you have sworn to protect Israel. That's *all you did*—you killed an enemy of the state, a man who was killing your people, so you don't have to let yourself be tormented by guilt or—"

"I'm just saying," he interrupted, the tenderness in his expression amazing her, "that it might not be over. And you need to be ready for anything."

She pulled away, preparing to leave, but Isaac stood and caught her hand. "Promise me?"

"What?"

"You'll be careful tomorrow."

A knot rose in her chest as she stared at the man she loved. She had been relieved to hear of Romulus's death, grateful that their time of fear and insecurity might finally be at an end. Romulus had died, and that simple fact had proven that he was a man like anyone else. He was no god, but her husband seemed suddenly unsure . . .

"Do you trust me, Isaac?" she asked, struggling to speak over the lump in her throat.

"With my life."

"Then trust God. He led you to strike at Romulus, and he is still in control. And he is far more dependable than I am."

She pulled her hand free, and Isaac reluctantly let her go.

TWENTY-EIGHT

THE NEXT MORNING, SARAH AND A CIVILIAN ARAB resister who had volunteered for service three days earlier left the honeycomb of tunnels and flowed into the crowd of somber pedestrians making their way toward the Temple Court. In the manner of the Muslim women, Sarah wore a black robe and a matching veil that hid the headset and earpiece she wore. She and the Arab would work the lead position near a pair of guards stationed only twenty meters from the closed casket. Her co-conspirators at Shabak had assured her that due to the somber aspect of the ceremony UF patrols would not be scanning for Universal Chips on the Temple Mount.

Sarah had accepted this news with a lifted brow. The "no scanning" measure might be a trap to draw outlaws out of hiding, or it might be a simple public relations measure designed to insure the largest crowd possible at the event. In either case, she decided, this unusual freedom would work to their advantage.

Fog had seethed into the city overnight. It roiled along the street, softly nosing at the ankles of those who trod the steps leading to the Court of the Israelites. As she walked with her silent companion beneath an overcast sky, Sarah thought the Temple Mount had never looked lovelier . . . or more strange. Red roses covered every wall; their sickly sweet fragrance lacing each breath of wind that blew over the open area.

The casket itself, an ornate creation of white marble, sat on what used to be the altar in the inner court. A host of uniformed Universal Force guards stood around the casket, ostensibly to prevent any grief-stricken mourners from rushing toward the bier, but the faces around Sarah seemed more grim than grief-stricken. As she signed a false name to the book of remembrance in the outer court, she heard a few people weeping, but here, in the very presence of death, a certain resolute satisfaction seemed to fill the air.

The casket was not the only object in the Court of the Israelites. A large portrait of the late leader, depicting Romulus holding the Spear of Longinus, stood beside the casket. Someone had draped a garland of white roses over one corner of the gilded frame, and the flower petals moved gently in the breeze.

Just looking at Romulus's image gave Sarah a cold chill. He looked so confident, so defiant in that pose—and the spear in his hand was the very instrument her husband had used to send Romulus to his grave. What could Romulus's people have been thinking when they positioned the portrait so close to the casket?

A trumpet sounded, reminding her of the procession three days before, then a mournful drumbeat echoed over the hills as a mounted entourage moved toward the Temple. An elevated video screen high on the wall displayed the progress of the procession as it wound through the streets of old Jerusalem, through the Beautiful Gate, toward the outer court. A chorus of weeping and wailing followed the funereal parade, and Sarah watched in fascination as men and women along the route tore their clothes and collapsed in a frenzy of grief.

What was wrong with those people? Could they not see that Adrian Romulus had been another Hitler?

As the procession grew closer, she studied the screen. Three horses led the ceremonial parade, followed by a detachment of mounted Universal Force patrols and a band of funeral musicians. Sarah recognized the two men riding at the front almost immediately: Gen. Adam Archer, wearing a dress uniform with a black band at his upper arm, rode a splendid bay stallion, and Elijah Reis, garbed in his black robe, rode an ebony horse. Between the two men pranced a restless white stallion, a spirited creature that pulled at the reins in Reis's hand and tossed his head as if he did not care for the pounding drummers in the distance.

When they reached the Court of the Gentiles, Archer and Reis dismounted and entered the Court of the Israelites, where Sarah and a host of others waited and watched behind dark veils and hats and cloaks. Despite her training and her resolve, Sarah began to tremble as fearful images built in her mind. What if Archer ordered the guards to fire into the crowd? Romulus was nothing if not a megalomaniac, and it would be like him to want to go out in a frenzy of mourning. He was cast from the same mold as Herod the Great, who, on his deathbed, had confined all the Jewish rabbis of Israel in the hippodrome and ordered that they be executed at the moment of his death so "there would be grief throughout the country at his death rather than joy"!

Adam Archer fell back, stopping to hold the horses' reins

as Elijah Reis stepped to the side of the great white casket. Lifting his arms, he murmured something over the casket, then turned to face the television camera discreetly mounted on a platform in a corner of the courtyard.

"Citizens of the world," Reis said, his voice commanding the court, "today we have gathered to witness a miracle. The man you know as Adrian Romulus was no mere man. He was an elevated human, one who had burned away the dross of flaws and human imperfections through meditation and struggle. He had put human weakness and frailty behind him, and his spirit routinely ascended to levels far above this earthly plane. And though his body lies here, lifeless and slumbering, his spirit still moves among us."

The television camera zoomed in upon Reis's face so that his countenance filled the video screen on the wall. "Call to him," he said, his voice little more than a whisper in the silence. "Call to him from beyond the grave, and he will hear your prayer. Call, and he will come!"

Sarah felt an icy finger touch the base of her spine as the whisper began from the edges of the gathering. *"Rom-u-lus! Rom-u-lus!"*

She glanced at the Arab next to her. With wide eyes, he shook his head slightly, then together they wheeled to look around the room. Not a single person was speaking in the area where she stood, yet the sound grew like the crashing of a wave, growing stronger and more powerful with each repetition.

"Rom-u-lus! Rom-u-lus!"

Sarah drew her veil closer to her face as a shiver of panic swept through her. The rose-scented air around her suddenly felt heavy and threatening.

The sound continued to intensify. *"Rom-u-lus!"*

She closed her eyes and pressed her hand to her temple. Something was happening inside her head. The sound was all wrong, the voices distant, fuzzy, and unfocused. The people around her stirred with agitation, yet the refrain grew louder, as if every voice in the room had lifted to call Romulus from beyond the grave . . .

"Behold!" Reis shouted, lifting his arms. "I show you our leader!"

With a dramatic flourish, Elijah Reis turned toward the casket. A spotlight fell upon the gleaming portrait, highlighting each trembling petal on the floral garland. A fresh wail arose from the Romulus admirers in the outer courtyard, and Sarah froze, her eyes narrowing as she wondered what sort of tricks Elijah Reis had up his sleeve. Would he claim to "channel" Romulus's spirit through the portrait? Would he declare that it embodied the spirit of a god and place the cursed picture in the Holy of Holies?

And then, while she waited and mused, Reis tensed his fingers and turned his hand slowly, as if he were turning an unseen dial. Before Sarah's eyes, the cascade of roses atop the casket trembled in the breeze.

"Citizens of the world!" It was Romulus's voice; Sarah would have recognized it anywhere. The sound seemed to come from the casket, but Sarah could see no sign of audio speakers on the casket or its base. Still, a prerecorded digitized tape could be played and broadcast from almost anywhere.

"Citizens," the voice continued, "stand and prepare to worship the Man of Men." Sarah felt her stomach drop, and the empty place fill with a frightening hollowness. What did Reis have planned?

An unnatural silence prevailed as the crowd waited. The voice did not speak again, but every head within the court turned to look at the closed casket.

As Sarah stared in horror, the still air in the Temple shivered suddenly into bits, the echoes of a harsh grating sound repelling the guards who stood near the casket. *The lid moved!* Before Sarah's wide gaze, the heavy lid shifted . . .

"Don't just stand there," Reis said, calmly folding his hands as he stared at the startled guards. "Open the coffin of death and release your master. He is not dead, but lives!"

For an instant no one moved, then all six guards sprang into action. Sarah found herself pushed forward by a perversely curious crowd as the guards grunted and lifted the lid, then allowed it to topple to the marble floor.

As Sarah watched in horror, Adrian Romulus sat up in his coffin. He wore a white robe, a pale linen that nearly matched the drained color of his skin. His dark hair had been smoothed back from his pale face, and when he turned to survey the crowd, Sarah saw that only one black eye looked out upon them. The other eyelid had been sewn shut with long, black stitches—the marks of a practical physician who would not waste time on a body destined for a closed coffin.

A dozen arms reached toward Romulus, and in a silence that was the holding of a thousand breaths the guards released him from the confines of the coffin and set him on his feet. For the barest moment Sarah thought she saw him sway, but Romulus braced himself upon the cold white marble box and seemed to take strength from it. Looking out with one dark eye, he saw Elijah Reis . . . and smiled.

"Today"—his voice rang like chilled steel—"I have been granted the keys to life and death. Life and death, and heaven and hell, are mine to command!"

A wave of murmuring met this proclamation, a rising crest of sound that rose and fell only when Romulus lifted his hand for silence. His single eye sought the television camera and honed in upon it.

"Citizens of the world," he said, his voice filled with a quiet menace all the more frightening for its control, "no longer will the dead God of the Hebrews be worshiped in this Temple. This shall be *my* Temple, and I shall be God in Israel. I have felt the icy touch of death, and I have conquered it. I have wandered into the abyss of darkness, and with power I have fought my way back. I have felt the sharp bite of pain and suffering, and I have overcome."

Horror snaked down Sarah's backbone as the Beast stared out at the crowd, his pale skin and darkly closed eye more dreadful than any horror movie's zombie. He lifted his hand toward the spectators closest to him—instantly they shrank back.

"Yes," Romulus said, the word faintly underlined and spoken with a delicate ferocity. "You do well to respect my power. No longer will I share my glory with other gods, philosophies, or national loyalties. From this day forward, anyone who refuses to worship me as the one true God shall be instantly executed."

"You lie, Adrian Romulus!" The voice, coming from the outer court, rang with ridicule. Sarah craned her neck, overcome with fear and curiosity, until the crowd parted. There, in the gap, stood the two witnesses who called themselves Moses and Elijah. Moses strode forward with the unconscious confidence of an armed warrior, while Elijah glared at Romulus like an avenging angel.

"You are the worthless shepherd, the man of lawlessness doomed to destruction," Moses called. "Today you have fulfilled the Scripture and set yourself up in God's Temple, proclaiming yourself to be God. But you lie, Beast. You are the father of lies, and the truth is not in you."

Sarah saw a tiny flicker of shock widen Romulus' eyes. "I am God!" he snarled, taking a step forward. "And I have proven it!"

With long, purposeful strides Elijah came forward. Though he wore a serious expression, one corner of his mouth curled up in an inexplicable smile. "You have proven nothing, Romulus," he said. "The Lord Jesus will overthrow you with the breath of his mouth, with the sword of the Spirit, and the splendor of his coming. You may work counterfeit miracles, signs, and wonders, and you will deceive those who are perishing. But those who love the truth shall be saved."

Romulus's jaw clenched, his single eye narrowed, and across his pale face a flush raced like a fever. "You cannot save yourself, so how can you save others?" he asked, a smug expression settling onto his disfigured face. He lifted his head and turned to the camera. "So that all may know that I have power over these two and their *God*"—he spat the word— "watch and see how a prophet dies."

As Romulus lifted his hand, Sarah heard the metal-on-metal ratchet of a submachine gun's bolt sliding back. She lifted her gaze in time to see a Universal Force patrol step out from behind a portal, a black Uzi in his hand. Of course Reis would have agents hidden in the Temple; he would want to guard against a replay of that other tragic day, and yet—

A new thought skittered across her brain. Romulus had tried and failed to kill the witnesses before, but today he really believed he would succeed.

Why?

With no time for further thought, Sarah screamed. The people around her fell back, ducking for cover, and Reis flinched at the sound. But Romulus didn't move. His uplifted hand came down, pointing toward the witnesses, then Sarah heard the gentle puff-puff of two shots, the somewhat louder metallic sound of the cycling submachine gun's action, and the impact of both rounds on their targets.

The witnesses fell to the ground without a sound, bleeding through their rough garments. A liquid pool spread out from their bodies, staining the white marble floor like a crimson flower. Sarah stared in heartbroken horror as Romulus strolled forward and stood over the bodies, planting his feet in the river of blood.

"See"—he spread his arms wide—"how I have the power to give and take life. Know that I am alive today and forever more. Consider how easily I can destroy those who oppose me. And realize"—he swiveled, turning toward the very area where Sarah stood—"how easily I can identify those who are against me. You—the woman who screamed. Come here."

Instinctively, Sarah turned to flee, but a wall of bodies blocked her exit. With no other choice, she lifted her chin and walked forward to meet the false shepherd.

TWENTY-NINE

IN HIS TINY ROOM AT PETRA, ISAAC STARED DOWN AT the laptop screen and watched in hypnotized horror as Sarah walked toward Romulus as calmly as if he'd called her up to receive an award. The muscles of his throat moved in a convulsive swallow as he saw a pair of UF guards rush to her side. "Dear God, help her," he murmured. "What is happening?"

Thomas Parker rose and stared at the computer. His own terror was obvious, but he folded his trembling hands across his chest and jerked his head toward the screen. "She tried to warn the witnesses, Isaac. You know Sarah wouldn't have screamed for any other reason. She's not a hysterical woman; she's a well-trained operative."

"What is God doing?" Afraid to take his eyes from the flickering screen, Isaac dug his fingertips into his scalp as a sludge of nausea rolled back and forth in his belly. "I shouldn't have let her go. I should be there with her. Romulus wants to hurt *me*; he has nothing against Sarah."

"He has something against all of us who will not bow to him," Parker said, his voice seeming to come from far away. "Watch and see what God will do."

Holding Sarah's arms, the guards brought her to stand directly before Romulus, then they stepped back. One of them stooped as if asking for permission to move the prophets' bodies, and Romulus nodded grimly. "Take them to the plaza in front of the Western Wall and leave them there. They are not to be buried or anointed or mourned. Any man who touches them will die."

The guards obeyed, lifting the legs of the dead prophets and dragging them away, leaving a bloody smear over the gleaming floor. Isaac stared at the sole of a leather sandal as the camera focused on the departing bodies and remembered the day he had first heard the prophets speak about Jesus . . .

Romulus's voice caught his attention. The camera shifted, showing the Beast and Sarah, who seemed small and frail before him. "You." The suppressed hate in Romulus's voice echoed over the airwaves and struck Isaac low in the pit of his stomach. "You are Isaac Ben-David's wife."

Isaac winced, but Sarah met Romulus's accusing eyes without flinching. "I am."

"He is a murderer."

She lifted a brow, pretending not to understand his look. "How can that be? You are not dead."

"But you are, my dear."

Romulus held out his hand toward one of the guards, who unsnapped his holster and withdrew a pistol, then placed it in Romulus's hand. Sarah saw the exchange, of course, but she lifted her chin and boldly met the Beast's gaze. "I am not afraid of you," she said, her voice ringing like a bell in the spaciousness of the Temple. "I believe in Yeshua, my Lord and King. He will conquer you, Adrian Romulus, son of Satan, and he will use even you to bring glory to God."

In a silent fury that spoke louder than words, Romulus pressed the pistol to Sarah's heart and pulled the trigger.

Isaac felt the blow in his own chest, then black emptiness rushed up like the bottom of an elevator shaft in free fall.

†

As lightning sizzled and rainless thunder rattled the Temple Mount, Rabbi Baram Cohen stood in the darkness of the Western Wall Plaza where three bodies lay exposed to the whistling winds. In the dim glow of shifting moonlight he could see that the powerful blast of the gun had mangled the chests of the two witnesses, but the woman wore a look of peaceful resignation.

Baram folded his arms in an effort to resist the grip of terror that had seized him by the guts. He had known terrible things would happen before the coming of the Messiah, but never in all his days had he imagined that such atrocities would be committed in the holy Temple. He had held such high hopes for Israel as they labored to build this holy sanctuary. At one point he had even hoped that Adrian Romulus might prove to be the Messiah.

So many hopes . . . and now, so much blood.

Baram closed his eyes and swayed slightly on his feet, alarmed and horrified by the jovial carnival music that blared from speakers outside the Temple. After killing the woman, Romulus had announced that April 26 would henceforth be celebrated as an international holiday to commemorate his victory over death and the execution of certain "blemishes upon the name of the one true god, Adrian Romulus." Another celebratory chant had arisen from the gathering after this announcement, though Baram could not discern from where it had come. The people who stood around him wore expressions of shell-shocked disbelief.

The buzzing drone of flies brought Baram back to reality. A swarm of insects had settled over the bodies already, eager to feed upon the eviscerated flesh.

Baram felt his flesh prickle at the thought. This was an obscenity, and something that would never have been allowed in Israel before Romulus's coming. Did they not work for months to clean up the dead after Gogol's Invasion? Though Romulus had expressly forbidden anyone to touch the bodies of the witnesses, should such a law be obeyed? Surely these men of God deserved a dignified burial. And the woman—Baram knew she had a husband and a father who cherished her.

Baram knelt by the woman's side, ignoring every legalist prohibition about touching a dead body. What did the old rules matter anymore? Gently he ran his hand over her lovely face, smoothing the eyelids until she looked as if she slept. Standing, he moved to cover the mangled bodies of the prophets, then felt the unique inner voice he had heard only twice before in his lifetime: *Touch them not.*

Baram stepped back, rebuffed. Why would the Holy One allow him to touch the woman and not these two? They died for the same cause; they obviously believed the same things . . .

Touch them not.

Baram lifted his head and stared up into the swirling gray sky. "The Master of the Universe knows what is best."

Slowly, Baram walked toward a shadowy huddle of refugees from his synagogue. They waited in the recesses of Wilson's Arch with downcast eyes, wanting to know what he would have them do. "Take only the woman," he whispered, drawing his coat tighter around his shoulders. "Leave the prophets. But the woman should be taken to her husband, if you can find him."

One of the young men nodded, his eyes dark and deep beneath the wide brim of his hat. "I know where Isaac Ben-David is."

Baram nodded. "Then see that they are reunited. He will want to give her a proper burial."

THIRTY

THREE DAYS LATER, ISAAC STOOD IN THE CENTER OF A hollowed chamber beneath the Temple Mount. The crowd before him contained many new faces and included Jews and Arabs and Europeans who had decided to reject Romulus in favor of the living God.

He wiped damp dust from his face with the back of his hand. He had just come from a secret tunnel where they had discovered alcoves suitable for burying their dead. Sarah now lay there, wrapped in a silk garment someone had scavenged from an empty apartment and covered by the sandy soil of the Temple Mount. For three days Isaac had battled grief and depression, but a stern rebuke from Sarah's father brought him out of his stupor.

"These people look to you for leadership," Rabbi Lerner had said just before they prayed over Sarah's makeshift grave. "I know you miss her, but Sarah would not want you to quit. There is a time limit to all this, Isaac, and every day that passes is one less we will have to endure. Finish the race. Stay the course. And then you will be reunited with your wife."

Now, as Isaac looked out across the sea of faces, he took comfort in his father-in-law's words.

"Friends," he began, trying to be strong but torn by conflicting emotions, "the Lord is full of compassion and mercy. As an example of patience in the face of suffering, consider the prophets who spoke in the name of the Lord. As you know, those who have persevered are considered blessed. You have heard of Job's perseverance, and you have seen what the Lord finally brought about in his life. You have heard of Sarah's courage, and the two witnesses' boldness. We, my friends, must be patient until the Lord's coming. We see how the farmer waits for the land to yield its crop and how patiently he waits for the autumn and spring rains. We, too, must be long-suffering and stand firm because the Lord's coming is near."

He shifted his stance to look at those behind him and saw that he was looking through a ribbon of sunlight that angled down from another ventilation shaft. "Dear friends," he said, "do not be surprised at the painful trial you are suffering, as though something strange was happening to you. But rejoice that you participate in the sufferings of Christ, so that you may be overjoyed when his glory is revealed. When the Chief Shepherd appears, we will receive the crown of glory that will never fade away. The God of all grace, who called us to his eternal glory in Christ, after we have suffered yet a little while more, will himself restore us and make us strong, firm, and steadfast."

Several members of the group wept, the tracks of their tears shining in the light. Isaac paused, as touched by the sight of such emotion as he was by the burning wound that had recently seared his own soul. Struggling to find his voice, he was almost relieved when a little boy ran into the chamber and interrupted. "Come, quickly!" he said, his eyes as wide as saucers. "They're walking around!"

Isaac tilted his head, wondering where the boy had come from, but then another figure burst into the chamber. "The prophets!" A young woman leaned against the wall, her hand pressed to her ribs as she struggled to catch her breath. "They are *alive* and walking in the Temple courtyard! Romulus could not kill them!"

Without another word, the crowd jostled out of the chamber and snaked through the tunnels, then stumbled out into the bright light of morning. Isaac followed, walking with long strides even as his brain hummed with troubling questions. Had he been wrong to bury Sarah? Would she resurrect, too? Had all the natural laws of life and death been suspended in this supernatural war?

He passed through the Beautiful Gate, then stopped and gaped at the sight that met his eyes. Moses and Elijah were standing in the center of the Court of the Gentiles, their faces shining, their wounds gone. Their dark and dusty robes still bore the crusty stains of blood, however, and Elijah's hair had gone as white as his companion's. But the same fire burned in their eyes, and the same undeniable power filled their voices.

"Rejoice, children of God," Moses was saying as Isaac strode into the Temple courtyard. "I looked, and there before me stood a great multitude that no one could count, from every nation, tribe, people and language, standing before the throne and in front of the Lamb. They were wearing white robes and holding palm branches in their hands. And they cried out in a loud voice, 'Salvation belongs to our God, who sits on the throne, and to the Lamb.'"

With an effort, Isaac found his voice. "Who were they? Did you see my wife?"

Moses' eyes seemed to soften as his gaze met Isaac's. "They are the ones who have come out of the great tribulation; they have washed their robes and made them white in the blood of the Lamb. Never again will they hunger; never again will they thirst. For the Lamb at the center of the throne will be their shepherd; he will lead them to springs of living water. And God will wipe away every tear from their eyes."

A tumble of confused thoughts and feelings assailed Isaac as he stared at the two witnesses. And while he stood there, the clouds overhead rumbled as if with rain, and the sky moved. While every eye lifted toward the promise of much-needed moisture, a voice, deep and powerful, echoed over the Mount of Zion. And while Isaac watched, his heart in his throat, a dense cloud descended and wrapped itself around the two prophets. The mist seeped around their ankles and rose to their knees, their waists, and then their heads, and when it finally lifted, the witnesses had vanished.

For the next thirty minutes, pandemonium reigned upon the Temple Mount. Some searched for the prophets, certain that they had merely gone into hiding; others swore that a voice from heaven had called "Come up here!" and the witnesses had risen visibly through the air. Others declared that Romulus must have invented some new technology that could transport prisoners through the dimensions of time and space.

Isaac knew exactly what had happened: He had read it all in the Book of Revelation. He also knew that within the hour a severe earthquake would strike Jerusalem and a tenth of the city would collapse. Seven thousand people would die.

This was the beginning of great tribulation. Romulus would install his image in the Holy of Holies, the false prophet—probably Elijah Reis—would cause it to speak through the power of evil, and men would be required to take a visible mark to demonstrate their allegiance to the Beast . . . or they would die.

Isaac's eyes moved toward the horizon, where the rooftops of Jerusalem gleamed in the surreal light. Soon these streets would run red with blood again, but only for forty-two months. Then the reign of evil would end.

He moved toward one of the new, shining walls and pressed his hand to it, marveling at the care the builders had exercised in its construction. Those who built this Temple had considered everything but the Messiah. They had invited a shepherd to give them peace and prosperity, and that shepherd had turned out to be a wolf in sheep's clothing.

He was still standing there, lost in thought, when Thomas Parker approached. "It's like a war," Thomas said, running his hands over his arms as if he'd taken a chill. "We know we will suffer and give our lives. It is all written down."

"It's more than that." Isaac gave his friend a smile. "Revelation says that the people who are destined for prison will be arrested and taken away. Those who are destined for death will be killed. But we are not to be dismayed, for this is our opportunity to endure and have faith." Isaac paused, letting the silence stretch, then he added, "This war is already won. God is the victor, and we are his children. So let us fight the fight and finish the course. I know that at least 144,000 of us will come out as survivors."

Parker looked at Isaac with a wry smile hidden in his eyes. "Well, that's fine for you to say, you're Jewish and you've made it this far, so the odds are pretty good that you're one of the sealed ones. But what's a believing Gentile like me supposed to do?"

Isaac hooked an arm over his friend's shoulder and looked up at the shining Temple. "We can overcome Romulus by the blood of the Lamb and by the word of our testimony. We will not love our lives so much as to shrink from death. Romulus knows his time is short, but we who follow the Lamb will overcome with the King of kings and Lord of lords."

He looked out to the horizon where the Judean hills blended into the crimson-tinted sky. "Soon the Lamb will come from heaven on a white horse. He will wear a robe dipped in blood, and the armies of heaven will follow him, riding on white horses and dressed in fine linen, white and clean. Sarah will be with him. And if either of us dies before the end, we'll be with him, too. All those who trust in Jesus will ride in the army of heaven."

"I'll admit that I'm looking forward to that battle," Parker said, his eyes alight as he looked toward the heavens. "Gives me something to work for."

Isaac nodded as his own heart filled with bottomless peace. "Out of the Lamb's mouth will come a sharp sword with which to strike down Romulus and his father, the devil. The Spear of Longinus will not be able to stand against the sword of the Spirit of God."

ABOUT THE AUTHORS

GRANT R. JEFFREY IS THE AUTHOR OF THE #1 BESTSELLER *The Millennium Meltdown,* as well as *The Signature of God, The Mysterious Bible Codes, Armageddon, Flee the Darkness* (with Angela Hunt), and numerous other books. He has done extensive research in prophecy, history, and archaeology. With his wife, Kaye, he founded Frontier Research, a ministry that proclaims a warning of judgment to the world and a message of hope to the church.

AWARD-WINNING NOVELIST ANGELA ELWELL HUNT IS author of the popular series *The Keepers of the Ring, Legacies of the Ancient River, The Heirs of Cahira O'Connor,* and the co-author of *Flee the Darkness.* Angela is also the author of the best-selling *The Tale of Three Trees* and *The Rise of Babylon* (with Charles Dyer). Her second novel with Grant Jeffrey, *By Dawn's Early Light,* won the Christy Award for futuristic fiction.

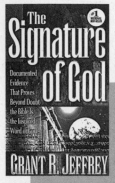

With compelling scientific and rational evidence, Grant Jeffrey offers proof that the Bible is accurate both as history and prophecy. *The Signature of God* verifies beyond a doubt God's authorship—not only of Scripture, but of all creation.

from
Grant Jeffrey

Best-selling author and noted prophetic scholar Grant Jeffrey explores the phenomenon of significant prophetic words found in codes throughout the New and Old Testaments, offering a Christain response to the *New York Times* bestseller, *The Bible Codes*.

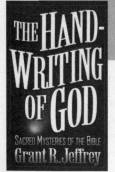

In *The Handwriting of God,* prophecy expert Grant Jeffrey shows how the codes encrypted in the Bible text demonstrate beyond doubt that the Bible is miraculous, prophetic, and divinely inspired. A best-selling follow-up to *The Signature of God.*

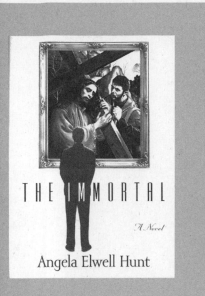
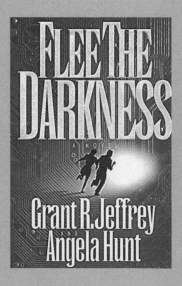

ISRAEL MUST CHOOSE— SURRENDER OR BE OBLITERATED.

BY DAWN'S EARLY LIGHT

A PROPHETIC NOVEL

Winner of the 2000
Christy Award
for Excellence in
Futuristic Fiction

GRANT JEFFREY & ANGELA HUNT

The fates of nations and individuals hang in the balance as Israel faces the threat of nuclear war and invasion of all four borders. Never have the forces of evil been stronger, the stakes higher, or the world's possible destruction nearer.

 WORD PUBLISHING